Mr Combes surreptitiously looked at his watch. He had, after all, broken into his Sunday afternoon and undertakers, like everyone else, need to have a day of rest sometimes.

'I'm keeping you,' I said. 'Thanks so much for letting me see her.' He looked relieved and all at once more human.

'The thing is, we've got the wife's mother coming over to Sunday tea,' he said.

'I understand,' I said. Then remembered the silver candlesticks.

'By the way, the Major wanted these put round the coffin. Will that be alright? Something of hers, he thought ...' I held up a plastic carrier bag from Tesco's. 'They're in here.'

He looked doubtful. 'We provide our own furnishings,' he said austerely, 'and of course there's always the risk of theft ...' In the end, however, he relented, albeit reluctantly, and took the bag I was holding out as a sort of limp offering.

'I'll see what I can do,' he said.

'Thank you again,' I said and shook him by the hand.

'Not at all, Mr ... er, er ... at your service any time. Always remember, life must go on.'

The door slammed behind me in the empty street. It had started to rain again.

Also by Virginia Budd

Summer's Spring
Fathers

RUNNING TO PARADISE

Virginia Budd

CORONET BOOKS
Hodder and Stoughton

The extract from 'Running to Paradise', taken from *The Collected Poems of
W. B. Yeats*, is reproduced by courtesy of A. P. Watt Ltd on behalf of Michael
B. Yeats and Macmillan London Ltd.

First published in 1988 by
Hodder and Stoughton Ltd

First published in paperback in 1994
by Hodder and Stoughton
A division of Hodder Headline PLC

A Coronet paperback

10 9 8 7 6 5 4 3 2 1

British Library Cataloguing in Publication Data

Budd, Virginia
Running to Paradise. - New ed
I. Title
823.914 [F]

ISBN 0 340 60388 7

Typeset by Avon Dataset Ltd, Bidford-on-Avon

Printed and bound in Great Britain by
Cox & Wyman Ltd

Hodder and Stoughton Ltd
A division of Hodder Headline PLC
338 Euston Road
London NW1 3BH

To Nink, with much thanks for
all her help and encouragement

The wind is old and still at play
While I must hurry upon my way,
For I am running to Paradise;
Yet never have I lit on a friend
To take my fancy like the wind
That nobody can buy or bind:
And there the king *is* but as the beggar.

WILLIAM BUTLER YEATS 'Running to Paradise'

Prologue

Evening. Summer lightning intermittently flashed across the grey-green sky, as though some inter-galactic signaller were trying to get a message through to the misguided denizens of planet earth. Thunder rolled far away and storm clouds spiralled. It was very hot. The people in the grey village houses shut their casement windows, left open to catch the least vestige of the sultry air, anticipating the coming storm. The people on the executive housing estate at the northern end of the village reached for their digital telephones to warn their friends that evening's barbecue was cancelled and what about a blue video session instead. The people in the council estate ignored the coming storm. They were most of them out anyway; there was nothing to do in the village on a Saturday night.

At the southern end of the village, in a small, bright, antiseptic room in St Hilda's Home for the Elderly, Charlotte Seymour lay dying. She lay on her back in the neat bed, covered by a pale blue eiderdown, her head propped up by pillows. She no longer smelt the scent from the stocks that grew beneath her bedroom window, nor saw the spruce fir silhouetted against the flashing sky, nor indeed heard the rumble of thunder: she felt neither heat nor cold, she had already entered the anteroom to death. An elderly man sat beside the bed, his large, baggy frame fitting with difficulty into the plastic-seated chair. He snored from time to time.

Death was long in coming and he had drunk heavily as was his wont, that evening.

Charlotte Seymour's breath rattled and scraped; her eyes were closed and her hands, each finger ring-encrusted, each fingernail a vivid scarlet, were still. But her mind, the mind she had lived with for over eighty years, that mind which had so frequently served her so ill, was awake alright, wide awake, as though at last, too late, prepared to use and employ the latent power within.

A few heavy drops of rain splashed on the window sill and the man in the chair awoke, gazed owlishly round the room, as though wondering where he was, then struggled to his feet and closed the window. He yawned, scratched his chest and looked down at the woman in the bed. It would have been hard to tell by his expression whether the look was one of indifference, anticipation or dislike; it was not a look of love. Charlotte opened her eyes suddenly.

'Go home,' she whispered, 'I can die without your help.' The man, however, did not seem to hear her. He reached in his pocket for a cigarette, then saw the notice above the bed. 'Visitors are respectfully requested not to smoke.' He sat down again in the chair, which wobbled dangerously under his weight, and closed his eyes.

Charlotte's eyes, too, closed: they would not open again.

Let go, Char Osborn, let go. There's nothing left – no point in hanging on – the party's over now. But had it been such a party? Had it . . . ?

1

The Sunday Char died I wondered if things would ever be the same again. To feel so bereft, so disorientated for the loss of one's ex-wife's mother verges on the eccentric, I suppose, but I loved her; for all her manifold faults, I loved her.

The day before she died I felt both oppressed and depressed and London sweltered in a grey, sticky heat. I did a bit of shopping in the Kings Road in the morning, then squash with Jack Pemberton, from the office, in the afternoon. He asked me back to dinner afterwards, but I refused. I wanted, suddenly, to be on my own.

The storm started around seven o'clock. I sat by the sitting-room window and watched the lightning crackling over Chelsea Reach and great globules of rain slowly turn the river from slate grey to muddy yellow. I was on my third Martini when George rang.

'Guy? I've been trying to get you all day. George here.'

'Sorry, I was playing squash, but I've been in since six thirty.' Somehow George always manages to put one on the defensive; it was none of his damned business where I'd been.

'Char's not too good.' Was this one of his euphemisms? Was Char, in fact, dying? Why else, God help him, would he be ringing?

'How bad?' I asked.

'Well, you know what these doctors are; she's got bronchial

3

pneumonia, her breathing's terrible. They say there's nothing more they can do.'

'What about hospital? Last time—'

'Too ill to be moved.' Was there a note of triumph; hard to say.

'They've given her the Last Rites and all that sort of thing, but of course she's had them before, when she had that stroke two years ago – you remember.' Yes, I remembered, and what a party that had been. Dr Weil insisted on ordering up a bottle of wine, and there we all were, George, Beth, myself and a nurse or two, sipping away like mad, allegedly helping Char into the next world and by the following morning she was sitting up in bed laughing her guts out.

'I've been with her all day.' George assumed his pathetic 'ill-done-by' voice, 'but Mrs McTavish, that's the new warden, said to go home for a kip and come back later.'

'D'you want me to come down?'

'Not yet. I'll let you know.' He sounded evasive.

'What about Beth and the others?' I said. 'Have you told them?'

'Look, could you ring Beth, then she can ring the others. I seem to have lost her phone number. Everything's so chaotic here.'

'I'd rather not speak to Beth, if you don't mind. I can give you her number, if you've really lost it.'

'Oh, alright, but I thought you two were back on speaking terms.' Now he sounded huffy and put upon. Why the hell shouldn't he tell his step-daughter her mother was dying?

'You'll let me know, won't you, if . . .'

'Yes,' he said, 'I'll let you know.' Odd how neither of us could mention the word death.

The storm stayed around until gone eleven. I made a bit of

supper and watched some nonsense on TV, but all the time thought of Char: as I last saw her, as I first saw her, and all the time in between. I went to bed, but couldn't get to sleep, not until the small hours, anyway, and woke to the bells of Battersea Church ringing for Holy Communion. I lay in bed listening and then the phone rang.

'George again. Sorry to wake you, but Char died between two and three this morning. I thought you'd like to know.'

For the life of me I couldn't think of a damned thing to say. Then at last: 'Did she speak? Were you with her when—'

'I was with her, but she never spoke again, not after the priest left her.'

'I should like to see her,' I said, 'just once more.'

'Well . . .' He sounded doubtful. 'They want to get the body out of the Home as soon as possible. They need the bed, you see.' Char was just a body now.

'What about at the undertakers, couldn't I see her there?'

'I suppose so,' he sounded grudging. 'Are you coming down? There's a hell of a lot to be done and I don't feel too well this morning. It's been a bit of a shock.'

'I'll be down soon after ten a.m. Give me time for a cup of coffee and a shave and I'll be on the M4 by eight o'clock. OK?'

'OK,' he said.

Char had three husbands and five children, but it's me, her ex-son-in-law, who always takes responsibility for her. Is it because I loved her and they didn't? No, that's far too simple an explanation. Perhaps I wanted to have the responsibility and they were only too glad to relinquish it. I just don't know. 'I'm leaving you to sort things out after I'm dead, Guy,' she had said, looking at me witchily over the top of her frightful 'butterfly' glasses. 'You can be a sort of literary executor. My children just don't care, you see.'

'And you know I do?' I held out an ash tray to catch the dripping ash from her cigarette.

'Yes, darling, I know you do,' she said. 'Anyway, you are a sort of historian after all, so going through a few papers wouldn't be too arduous, would it?'

'It'll need more than a historian to sort out your affairs, love.'

Char only smiled. 'But you will, won't you, my warrior?' she said.

'I suppose so . . .'

I had an absurd thought while I was stirring my instant coffee in the kitchen, later, after George rang. Should I wear a black tie? Death, after all, was a fairly formal occasion. In the end I compromised and wore my better weekend trousers and the corduroy jacket Char used to like. She said it reminded her of 'nice young poets in the thirties'.

There wasn't much traffic on the M4. Thunder was still about and those foul little thunder flies were creeping everywhere inside the car. Black clouds billowed over the Downs and the grass looked parched from the long, hot summer. Where, I wondered, was Char now?

'D'you want coffee, or something stronger?' George at the door of the grey stone house in the grey stone street. The house he'd bought for Char when everything was breaking up.

'Coffee would be great, thanks George.' The kitchen smelt of cat and something else, hard to define. George looked ghastly, his face, sagging, putty coloured, unshaven.

'Can't do a bloody thing,' he burst out suddenly. 'It's Sunday, you see.' He led me into the long, dark sitting-room. Char's stuff all over the place: the photo on the mantelpiece of her and George's wedding just after the War, Char in pre-

War shoes and a tiny hat like a muffin perched on her forehead, George in uniform, looking handsome and happy. We sat down.

'Shall I,' I asked, 'make a list of what we've got to do?'

'If you like,' he said morosely. 'We have to make a start somewhere, I suppose.'

Later, I walked down the village street to the St Hilda's Home for the Elderly: fear rolled around in my stomach. Char's body, by this time, had been removed to the Chapel of Rest. 'In this weather, Mr Horton, it has to be done quickly,' Mrs McTavish, the new warden, had said over the phone. The flowers were bright in the cottage gardens; red salvias in tidy regimentation round the car park.

'Ah, Mr Horton. We haven't met, but Mrs Seymour spoke of you often.' Mrs McTavish, jolly, ginger haired, red faced. A smell of cooking Sunday lunch.

'Wasn't Mrs Seymour's death rather sudden? I mean she'd had pneumonia before—'

'Mercifully quick, Mr Horton, mercifully quick. Your mother-in-law was lucky, believe me. She retained her faculties up to the end. Over eighty and with all the problems she'd had . . .'

The blue eiderdown on Char's bed was neatly folded back, the window open. A couple of cardboard boxes filled with books, letters and mangled bits of knitting and those frightful scarlet bedroom slippers she would wear were all that remained of her in the little room. I felt sick.

'I'll leave you alone for a few minutes, Mr Horton.' Mrs McTavish, the soul of tact; no doubt well versed in situations like this. 'If you wouldn't mind just going through her things and putting to one side those you want kept, we'll dispose of the rest. How is the Major coping?'

'Bearing up,' I said. 'What about her clothes?' I realised suddenly they were still hanging neatly in the deal wardrobe.

'If you could go through them as well, Mr Horton, it would be a great help. Perhaps the daughters might want something. Are they coming down?'

'For the funeral,' I said. She went then, shutting the door very gently behind her. I sat on the bed, so pristine and virginal, the bed Char had died in, and cried as I hadn't done since I was a child.

When I got back to the house, George was on the phone. He sounded conspiratorial: ' . . . must go now, ducky. Guy's back and I'll have to take him out to lunch, I suppose. I'll ring later.' The phone went click and he appeared. By this time he'd shaved and looked marginally better; I felt worse.

'How about lunch?' he said. 'They do quite a good pie and salad at the White Hart.'

'It's Sunday,' I said. 'I don't suppose they'll run to a pie.'

'Well, I'm sure they can knock up a couple of ham sandwiches. There's damn all to eat in the house. I was going out, you see . . .'

In the end, I paid my last respects to Char on my own. Halfway through his ham sandwich and into his fourth whisky, George announced he didn't feel too good. He thought he'd go home and have another kip.

'So you won't be coming to the undertakers, then?' George looked at a point somewhere over my left shoulder.

'I don't think I will, if you don't mind,' he said. 'I'm whacked. I was up most of the night.'

'OK then,' I said, 'I'll go on my own. The man will be at the Chapel of Rest at two thirty to "open up" as he so delicately put it.' I was on my third whisky by this time and I have a feeling it was beginning to show. George was silent for a minute or two. Muzak played selections from *South Pacific* and behind me soft West Country voices discussed Somerset's chances at cricket. Then he said, 'You can take those silver candlesticks to put round the coffin. I cleaned them up while you were out.'

'Alright,' I said. Suddenly I remembered, years ago when we were all young, sitting round the kitchen table at Maple, Char at the head. 'When I die, I want six candles round my bier and my children to watch over me all night. *All* night, d'you see?' I wondered if the old devil had remembered.

'Mr Horton? The Major's not coming then?' Mr Combes, the undertaker, immaculate in dark suit, gleaming white shirt and black tie: you could see your face in his polished shoes.

'Er, no, he didn't feel too well.'

'Only to be expected, I suppose. Do come this way Mr Horton. I'll just pop the fan on, you can't be too careful in this humid weather.' He opened the door of the Chapel of Rest with a flourish; he was obviously very proud of it. I must say it was very 'tasteful'. Only the noise of the whirring fan brought a slightly venal note to the proceedings. Char appeared to be made of wax. I'd never seen anyone look so dead: only her tobacco-stained fingers resting tidily on the coverlet gave any indication the effigy in the satin-lined box had once been human.

'Would you like a little music?' Mr Combes whispered in my ear. 'It helps, sometimes, when saying goodbye to the departed.'

'No . . . no, thank you.' I bent quickly over and kissed the 'thing' that had been Char on the lips. 'Goodbye, my love. God speed.' After all, she just might have been around somewhere. The lips were surprisingly soft: somehow I had

9

thought it would be more like kissing a statue. Char, however, was not there.

'The departed, she retained her faculties to the end?'

'You could say that, more or less.'

Mr Combes surreptitiously looked at his watch. He had, after all, broken into his Sunday afternoon and undertakers, like everyone else, need to have a day of rest sometimes.

'I'm keeping you,' I said. 'Thanks so much for letting me see her.' He looked relieved and all at once more human.

'The thing is, we've got the wife's mother coming over to Sunday tea,' he said.

'I understand,' I said. Then remembered the silver candlesticks.

'By the way, the Major wanted these put round the coffin. Will that be alright? Something of hers, he thought . . .' I held up a plastic carrier bag from Tesco's. 'They're in here.'

He looked doubtful. 'We provide our own furnishings,' he said austerely, 'and of course there's always the risk of theft . . .' In the end, however, he relented, albeit reluctantly, and took the bag I was holding out as a sort of limp offering.

'I'll see what I can do,' he said.

'Thank you again,' I said and shook him by the hand.

'Not at all, Mr . . . er, er . . . at your service any time. Always remember, life must go on.'

The door slammed behind me in the empty street. It had started to rain again.

2

St Hilda's Home for the Elderly   4th April
Belton   Hell – Friday, after coffee
                                    and before horrible lunch.

Dear Guy,

Can you go through my papers, darling, after I'm dead? I
know it's a bore, but I should like you to. You have such an
orderly mind! If I ask any of the children, they won't, you
know what they are. There's an awful lot, I'm afraid, but some
of it's quite funny. You never know, you might make
something of it. Do you remember that old green cabin trunk?
We had it in the back kitchen at Maple as a table for the cats to
eat off? Well, it's entirely full of my 'past'. Letters, newspaper
cuttings, old diaries and God knows what. I haven't gone
through it for years. You've kept (I hope) those stories of my
childhood at Renton I wrote some years ago, and the piece
about my meeting with H. A. Elliott for his centenary. My
copies have completely disappeared, pinched by one of the
girls no doubt. Apropos of the piece on H. A. Elliott: Dr Weil
was quite fascinated. 'My dear Mrs S,' he said, 'you'll be
telling me next that Wordsworth dandled you on his knee, or
you'd walked in the garden with Tennyson.' Damned cheek!
Of course, none of the freaks here have ever heard of Elliott,
but then the only public figures who evoke even the faintest

11

interest in this benighted place are the Royal Family and, possibly, Hughie Green. Where was I?

I *think* Georgy put the trunk up in the attic when we moved; he said it was much too big to have in my bedroom, moaning away as usual about all my belongings.

I've left my jewellery and furniture to the bloody children. I *had* to really, darling, didn't I? They were always so jealous of you – did you know? But I do want you to have my dear little red lacquer cabinet. It's eighteenth century, and I know you always loved it. It's been knocked off its stand a few times and I've always kept my medicines in it, but never mind, you'll be able to mend it. You're so good with your hands. Don't let Georgy have *anything*. I don't want my lovely things going to that Welsh tart.

I'm sending this letter sealed, to my Solicitor, to be opened by my dear Warrior after my death. Something to look forward to, darling, after I've gone!

Your loving, as always,
Char

I replaced the letter carefully back in its envelope and wandered over to the window. A batch of scavenging gulls suddenly took flight across the river, disturbed by something I couldn't see. It was early evening and a month since Char's death. Summer was still around, but there were signs of autumn. The trees along the Embankment already held a touch of yellow in their depths: soon it would be real autumn, the Chelsea streets would smell of dank leaves and in the mornings the river would have disappeared behind a cottonwool blanket of mist. I shut my eyes and heard the distant roar of traffic and the cry of gulls, suddenly feeling very alone. It was still hard to believe Char wasn't there any more.

The funeral was an oddly jolly affair. All Char's surviving children turned up. Ann and Sophia, the fruits of her first marriage to Algy Charterhouse – 'my first litter' as she always referred to them – looking rather distinguished, and in the case of Ann and her husband, Andrew McFee, rather aloof. There had been a third child of this marriage – Evelyn. I never met the latter: she and her husband, David Holloway, had gone to Australia in the early 1950s soon after they were married, where some years later she had died of a breast cancer too long untreated. Then there was Beth, my Beth, the child of Char's second marriage to Dave Brent, pale and tense, with her new husband in tow. We kissed; it somehow seemed the right thing to do. 'Poor Guy,' she said, 'you'll miss her.'

The church was full of flowers and elderly gentlemen, most of the latter in tears. George, very much the bereaved widower, handkerchief in hand, shambled about doing his duty. 'Damned good value,' he hissed at me in the hotel foyer afterwards, waving an arm in the direction of the funeral tea. 'Twenty quid cheaper than any other caterers.' He looked triumphant.

Ann McFee smiled vaguely at me as if she wasn't quite sure who I was – we hadn't met, I don't think, since Beth's and my wedding – and said it must be years, mustn't it, but living in the wilds of Scotland she seldom came south, and one did tend to lose touch. I believe Andrew actually owns a castle; I'm not certain. That may have been one of Char's exaggerations. I mumbled something suitable and she drifted away.

Her husband, however, took me to one side. 'I gather my ma-in-law made you her "literary" executor.' He smiled and suddenly looked almost human. 'You're not going to write her up, are you? Some of her life would make pretty lurid reading.'

'I think,' I said carefully, 'that she wanted me to, but at the moment I have no plans in that direction. There's an awful lot of stuff to be gone through.'

'You'd let us all know before you, er, did anything?'

'Of course,' I said.

Sophia I found distinctly intriguing. She'd kept her looks; indeed, in her late forties seemed much more attractive than I remembered her. She'd never married, perhaps that was the reason. She came over and stood beside me in the churchyard. The burial over, everyone was standing about in the long grass, loth, it seemed, to leave Char's body in its final resting place. Old ladies teetered on spindly legs over the rough, uneven ground and clutched their funeral hats, grandchildren and great-grandchildren chased one another in and out of the worn headstones and the undertaker's man looked at his watch.

'Hullo Guy,' she said. 'I think we'd better lead the way. At this rate we'll never reach the cold collation. I understand there's a room booked at the local pub.' She put her arm through mine and we set off at a brisk pace down the rutted path leading to the lychgate. Char had insisted on being buried in the graveyard of a forgotten parish church somewhere in the wilds of Dorset. She claimed it was the home of medieval Osborns. When pressed for supporting evidence, she became rather cross and said it was a lovely place anyway and that's where she wished to be buried. Surely to God Georgy could manage to siphon a few measly pence away from the Welsh woman for his unfortunate wife's earthly remains to be buried where she wished them to be buried; he was rolling now, wasn't he, now his dreary old parents were dead.

It was indeed a lovely place. Sophia and I stood together

on the crumbling, grey stone steps that led down into the steep, narrow lane off which the graveyard lay and looked out towards the Downs. Shadows were playing on the lower slopes and you could see the marks in the grass where once the Celtic fields had been. The hedge bordering the lane was scattered in sloes and soft, pink, blackberry flowers; somewhere a blackbird was calling. Suddenly there was a whirr of wings, a flash of black and white, and a magpie flew over our heads.

'Good morning, My Lord,' we said simultaneously, then looked at one another and laughed. 'No prizes for where you learned that one,' Sophia said. 'For someone so small, so frequently silly and always so maddening, Mum managed to spread her influence over a hell of a wide area. When did we last meet, Guy?'

'Wasn't it about ten years ago – that horrendous weekend at Maple when the pipes burst? It thawed in the night, or something, and the water came pouring down through the sitting-room ceiling.'

'Crumbs, not since then! D'you remember, you and I were laughing so much we were completely useless. There was poor old George in his dressing gown battling with buckets, Mum yelling instructions, and no one could find the stopcock.'

'Yes,' I said, 'who couldn't?' We both laughed again and it felt surprisingly good. By now the chattering mourners, led by a phalanx of Osborn cousins, had almost reached us.

'I'd better pull myself together and retrieve Aunty Phyllis,' Sophia said. 'I'm chauffeur for today, and although she's a pretty sprightly ninety-year-old, she does tend to tire quickly.' She put her hand on my arm. 'Look, Guy, I'm back in London now: five years in the States was enough. Come to dinner one evening. I've taken over the lease of a friend's flat in Hampstead. I'll give you a ring when I've settled in – that is if you would like me to.' It was then I noticed her eyes, surprised I never had before. They were large, green, like a cat's, with little flecks of brown in them, the brows above, thick and slanting; they held no devils in them, but a hint of something, I wasn't quite sure what.

'I'd like to very much,' I said.

I had not heard from her since and wondered whether I would. I looked helplessly across my sitting room at the battered green trunk as it reposed up-ended by the door. It had arrived that day, transported by Pickfords. I hadn't fancied the idea of going through it with George peering over my shoulder. I decided to drag it into the spare room and open it there. The thing was covered in labels dating back to God knows when: one showed the Rock Hotel, Gibraltar against a background of improbably green trees, and there was a splendid view of Raffles Hotel, Singapore. The keys were rusty and battered, like most of Char's belongings, but I got the wretched thing open in the end, after a struggle, then rather wished I hadn't. Had she ever thrown anything away? I picked up a large, faded pink drawing book, on which was inscribed in a bold, childish hand: 'Charlotte Mary Osborn, her book. Cursed be he who touches it. 20th June 1909. Renton House, Bedfordshire, England, The World, The Universe.' The drawings inside were striking, but I don't think Char would ever have made it as an artist. I threw the book back in the trunk and pulled out a wedding group: obviously Char's first marriage in the twenties. She looked unbelievably young and rather aggressive, peering through a luxuriant wreath of orange blossom, a diminutive figure in her waistless, satin wedding dress, flanked by a beaming Algy, looking like the juvenile lead from a production of *No No Nanette* and a posse of bridesmaids in dresses of surpassing hideosity. That too I tossed back into the trunk: I felt oppressed by the sheer weight of Char's past. Wouldn't it be easier to throw the stuff away? It would take me years to work through this lot. 'You are a historian, darling,' she said. 'People like that sort of thing nowadays.'

'What sort of thing? Anyway, it's not my period,' I'd said, feeling put upon.

'Well, how the servants used to live,' she'd said vaguely, 'and things like that. And I've met quite a few of the famous in my time—'

'Who?' I'd said sarcastically. 'Just tell me who.' We used to have these silly arguments from time to time, one somehow did with Char. 'Who else, apart from H. A. Elliott, and you were only five.'

'Aneurin Bevan,' she said defiantly, 'and I once trod on Evelyn Waugh's toe.'

The sounds of Battersea drifted through the open window; a jet roared overhead, and from somewhere came the whine of a police siren. I poured myself a drink and put on some Mozart, then wandered back to the spare room and sat down on the bed.

I'd have to have a go, wouldn't I? I owed her that at least. Perhaps, after all, there was something, somewhere, buried in all that mass of paper she'd wanted me to know; something she couldn't explain, something important. Yes, I'd have a go, and I'd do it in the way she'd wanted, as a totally objective exercise in historical research. 'Changing Social Patterns in the First Three Quarters of the Twentieth Century'. How about that? It might even merit an article in *History Today*. Char would love that. There I was again thinking of her in the present. But you couldn't really make a woman you'd loved a footnote to history, could you, it just wasn't possible.

17

Perhaps I should have mentioned, I'm not really a historian, I simply dabble in it as a hobby. Actually, I'm in the business of insurance. I've done quite well in it too: people call me Mr Horton, and I have my own secretary. I've worked hard, I suppose, and I've got the right sort of face. It's not a bad job, actually, a lot more interesting than most people think.

'Isn't insurance a bit of a bore, darling? I mean just paying money to people who've lost things,' Char said.

'It's much more than that,' I said. 'Have you ever heard of invisible assets?'

'No,' she said, 'and I don't wish to. They sound rather rude to me.'

In the end, having made my decision to go through the contents of the green trunk, I didn't actually get down to it until the leaves on the trees along Chelsea Embankment had fallen and already there were ominous signs the Christmas bonanza was about to erupt. Work had been hectic and anyway, I somehow wasn't ready. Then one Sunday evening in early December, I started. I decided initially I'd sort everything with a date on it chronologically into bundles, each individual bundle representing a year in Char's life: a mammoth task in itself, but by the time it was completed about a fortnight later, I was well and truly hooked. Nothing could have stopped me now. I even found myself leaving the office at the same time as everyone else. I usually stayed on until six thirty p.m., when the traffic was better and I could work in peace. Now, however, all I wanted to do was to get home, make myself a quick snack, pour myself a drink and dive head first once again into that other world, Char's world, a world so alien to mine it might have been another planet.

Sophia rang me at last shortly after the Christmas break. She'd had to return to the States, she said, for a few more

weeks to sort things out and stayed on to spend Christmas
with friends in New York.

Over dinner at her flat in Keats Grove in Hampstead, very
posh with a huge walnut tree in the garden, I told her about
my work on her mother's papers.

'What fun,' she said, rather to my surprise. 'Would you
like me to help? As one of my lovers once told me, I've got
practically total recall, so I could supply the background: we
might even make notes. But . . . perhaps you'd rather not. I
know how you felt about Mum.' Suddenly she looked young
and vulnerable, doubtful of my reaction to her offer.

'There's absolutely nothing I'd like more,' I said, meaning
every word of it and this time surprising myself.

'That's great,' she said. 'When do we start . . . ?'

3

I have to admit that although somewhat distracting, Sophia was a great help, and it was from her (over pleasant suppers at my place or hers, or Sunday walks in the park) that I gained what knowledge I have of Char's parents and general family background. I had heard snippets, of course, from Char herself, but never took too much note of these: Char, despite being spot on in, say, the subject of Wellington's deployment of troops at Waterloo, tended to be considerably less so on the subject of her own family history, inclining towards such generalities as 'Of course all Ma's family were thieves and horse-copers', or 'Whatever else the Osborns may have been, they were at least gentlemen'. Both these assertions, according to her more prosaic daughter, being some considerable distance from the truth. Be that as it may, the known facts, as given me by Sophia, are as follows.

Charlotte Mary Osborn was born the year the Boer War ended, two years into the twentieth century. Her parents, Constance – always known as Con – and Dick Osborn, an ill-matched couple of modest affluence, had married in 1900. Con was the youngest daughter of one Joseph Pratt, a shipping magnate, and he was the eldest son of Bertram Osborn, a tea merchant in the City of London. The marriage was a love match, in spite of the marked disparity of the two participants, who had apparently scarcely a taste in common. After their marriage, the pair set up a comfortable establishment in a large, rambling, early Victorian mansion in Bedfordshire, the Renton House of Char's drawing book, where both Char and her younger sister Rosie (the latter died of pneumonia in 1911) were born.

According to Sophia, her mother remembered little of her maternal grandfather, Joseph Pratt, apart from his funeral: apparently a spectacular affair only rivalled in her mother's memory by that of King Edward VII's some three years later. In his youth Joseph Pratt had been a Victorian merchant adventurer in the true swashbuckling tradition. Coming from yeoman farming stock in the Midlands, he managed in a comparatively short space of time to amass a considerable fortune. His descendants were never too sure how he accomplished this, but took the sensible view that the less they knew about his early business activities the better. One of his many youthful escapades had been to elope over the roofs of Seville with a sixteen-year-old Spanish heiress, whom he had snatched, quite literally, from the very jaws of the convent in which an irate father had been about to incarcerate her. She became Joseph's first wife, but the poor girl did not, however, manage to survive long: she died, probably from cold, her first winter in England. His second wife, Char's grandmother, was a shadowy figure, remembered by no one apart from the fact she brought some much needed capital into the flagging Pratt enterprises following the cessation of hostilities in the Crimea. This, one cannot but feel, rather unfortunate lady, after presenting her husband with eight sons and two daughters, died giving birth to Char's mother, Con. Sophia has an anaemic portrait of her great-grandmother: pale skinned, pale haired, wearing a pale blue taffeta dress, her hands folded patiently in her lap, her pale blue eyes sad.

On Joseph Pratt's demise from, so it was alleged, eating a bad oyster – on the face of it an unlikely way for so robust and powerful a figure to die – the Pratt fortune seems to have simply melted away. 'Gran had eight brothers and not one of them ever did a day's work,' Sophia said. 'She used to get quite steamed up about it.' It seems, instead, they lived in considerable style off the Pratt money which, luckily for them, appears to have lasted them out. By the time they were dead little remained of Joseph Pratt's fortune apart from a few useless shares in a now defunct South American railway.

I, myself, never really knew Char's mother. I only met her two or three times before she died. However, I do remember our first meeting. It was a bitterly cold day in January: Beth and I, chaperoned by Char, had been summoned to tea. I was to be given the once-over as a prospective grandson-in-law. Old Mrs Osborn's last years were spent at Cowleaze Farm, a disintegrating farmhouse about eight miles from Maple, crammed with good, but decrepit and extremely dusty furniture where she was looked after by a series of indigent relatives and an assortment of women who came in from the village. We were received on the verandah, our hostess reposing in an ancient basket chaise longue, enveloped in piles of equally ancient horse blankets. She wore a brown felt hat shaped like a pudding basin and was wrapped in a purple shawl of excruciating design. To an innocent young history graduate from Epping she appeared quite terrifying. She waved a gracious arm: 'Come in, dears, and sit down. Such a lovely, clear day, d'you see, no point in being cooped up in a fusty old drawing room.'

Of the ensuing tea party I remember little. I was probably too numb with cold to take much in. There was, however, one thing that struck me – later borne out by subsequent meetings

23

– and that was that Char was frightened of her mother, albeit concealing her fear behind a mask of what I can only describe as adolescent sulkiness. This attitude on the part of her daughter appeared to give Mrs Osborn considerable malicious pleasure, and I remember how she would turn to Beth and myself in mock surprise whenever she had goaded Char into behaving in this way. I found their relationship strange and rather disturbing. An only child from a comfortable, suburban home, this was the first time I had glimpsed that twilight world of locked human relationships, where two people, seemingly under a spell of their own making, find themselves repeating the same pattern of behaviour towards each other over and over again for reasons they have both long since forgotten.

Dick Osborn, Char's father, I never knew. He died in 1955, three years before I met Beth. He was, according to his granddaughter, quite irresistible to women. This, in spite of the fact he was bald at the age of twenty-five and only five feet tall.

'You've no idea,' Sophia said. 'Grandpa at eighty, incontinent and heaven knows what else, could still look you up and down in that special way some men have and make you feel a million dollars.'

'If he was like that at eighty, what can he have been like at twenty?' I asked, feeling for a moment a twinge of jealousy.

'The mind simply boggles,' she said.

Like his daughter, he married three times. His marriage to Con broke up some time during the First World War, entailing a lengthy and messy divorce. However, they appeared to have continued to see a great deal of one another and indeed, as soon as the Decree Absolute had been granted, they rushed off to France together on a second honeymoon.

'Gran only divorced him to tie up the money, you see. She

24

felt he was getting through it much too fast, but they still loved one another.'

'I see,' I said, but didn't really.

Love one another or not, several years after the divorce, Dick suddenly announced he was marrying again, this time a White Russian countess, thirty years his junior. Natasha Osborn was beautiful, funny and given to emotional outbursts of a quite horrendous nature. Sophia remembers a Christmas at Amberley, Dick's palatial home in Hampshire: he had apparently made a great deal of money between the wars and lived in some state. Sophia, herself, was only five years old at the time, but says the sight of her step-grandmother, her gorgeous red hair falling about her shoulders, bosom heaving, eyes wild, hurling the leg of a twenty-pound turkey at her grandpa, will be etched for ever on her memory.

'We simply watched in awe,' she said, 'while globules of bread sauce and gravy and little pieces of turkey ran down Grandpa's face and on to the front of his beautiful, red velvet smoking jacket.' And she was silent for a moment, remembering.

'What happened then?' I asked crossly. Sophia has this habit of starting stories and then forgetting to finish them.

'I can't remember,' she said maddeningly. 'I was only five. I expect Grandpa laughed, he was that sort of person.'

'I wouldn't have laughed if some bitch had thrown a leg of turkey at me in front of all my grandchildren,' I said.

'Ah, but you aren't Grandpa,' she said and I don't think she meant it as a compliment. However, I digress. Evenings with Sophia seem to have an odd effect on me.

To return, then, to Dick, or Pa as his daughters always called him. Natasha, it seems, eventually ran off with the gardener.

'You're sure it was the gardener?' I asked. 'A gardener

seems somehow an unlikely sort of person for a White Russian countess to run off with.'

'He was an Italian prisoner of war, actually. Grandpa had somehow managed to get hold of him towards the end of the War to help in the garden. He was frightfully handsome and Nat always had this earthy quality about her. He became naturalised later on and they went into the market garden business and did pretty well I believe.'

Pa, bereft, returned to Con, who welcomed him back with open arms. She, herself, hadn't re-married, but spent the years arranging her daughter's life, buying and selling horses and antique furniture and having what her granddaughter described as 'menopausal turns'. She must, however, have continued to hold a torch for Pa. Inevitably the idyll didn't last.

'You wouldn't believe it,' Sophia said. 'Their attraction for each other was still there. I saw it with my own eyes, but of course it was thirty years since they had lived together: Gran had got used to living in ramshackle houses with no servants, eating meals when she fancied and spending most of the day in her garden. Grandpa couldn't live like that and didn't want to try. Mum found the whole business upsetting: she was terribly steamed up about her parents, you know. She had this idea they behaved the way they did just to make her look silly.'

'And did they?'

'No, of course not. Quite honestly, I don't think she was that important to them.' Poor Char.

Pa's third and last marriage was to his secretary, Mildred, in 1947. Mildred, it seems, was a lady of surpassing dullness, but with a kind heart and considerable organising ability. She always referred to Pa as 'Mr Dick', a hangover from their office days together. 'Mum loathed Mildred,' Sophia said. 'I could never understand why. She was the most harmless creature and terribly kind. She and Grandpa had a little house in Hove. It always smelled of Crosse and Blackwell soup, I remember, and was so crammed with furniture you couldn't move. Mildred was a big woman, too. I used to stay there sometimes when I was a teenager.'

'Didn't Pa find it rather dull? It seems a far cry from Amberley and the Russian countess.'

'No, I don't think so. He spent most of the day watching TV. It had just come in then and they had one of those enormous sets that looked like a piece of antique furniture: you opened little doors in the front and everything on the screen seemed to be taking place in a snow storm. Mildred spent hours twiddling knobs while Grandpa shouted instructions.'

'Sounds fun,' I said. 'How did he die?'

Sophia lit another cigarette. She smokes twenty a day. It is her only vice.

'He picked up a tart on Brighton Pier one Sunday afternoon while Mildred was at Chapel and died in the act.'

'That must have been very embarrassing for Mildred.'

'She didn't mind that part of it too much. It was losing Pa she minded: she loved him, you see. But Mum did. She flatly refused to believe that was how he died and hinted Mildred had murdered Grandpa for his money. He left it all to her, you see, apart from a trust made at the time of his and Gran's divorce, and the tart story was just a cover up.'

'But the evidence, surely . . . ?'

Sophia shrugged. 'You must have known my mother long enough to realise she only believed what she chose to believe,' she said.

There was silence for a bit, then: 'Sophia,' I said, 'did you love your mum? You always speak of her so objectively, as though you had deliberately distanced yourself from her. Look, if that's prying, just don't answer, give me a kick on the shins instead. It's the researcher in me, or perhaps I'm a novelist *manqué*. I like to nose things out.'

Sophia shivered and thrust her gloved hands deep in the pockets of her fur coat. We were in Kensington Gardens; the winter trees stark against a grey-pink sky, a thin wind blew brown crunchy leaves across the grass, and you could hear the distant shouts of children sailing their boats on the Round Pond. We walked slowly towards the Albert Memorial. When she spoke, it was so softly I had to bend my head to hear the words.

'I had to distance myself from her,' she said, 'we all did.' She was silent again. High above us a skein of geese flew towards the setting sun, the lights were coming on in Kensington Gore. Then: 'It's sad how families come to an end; ours has, I think. Mum was the only reason we kept in touch: now she's dead there's nothing to bring us together any more, no common link. The thing about Mum was she had this massive capacity for love, but it was always destructive and in the end became sterile and destroyed itself. Can you understand what I mean?'

'I think,' I said, 'you judge her a little harshly.'

'I don't judge her, I'm simply stating a fact; it was how she was.'

Tentatively I took her arm, she seemed, all of a sudden, so sad. 'Come back and have tea. I bought crumpets this morning.'

She looked up at me and smiled. A strand of dark hair blew across her face in a sudden gust of wind and she pushed it back under her fur hat. 'Tempter! But no, I must get home and do some work.' We walked in silence under the bare trees.

'How does it go?' she said. 'I've had the damn thing on the brain for days, but I can't seem to get it right: that thing about golden girls and lads coming to dust?'

> 'Fear no more the heat o' the sun,
> Nor the furious winter's rages;
> Thou thy worldly task hast done,
> Home art gone, and ta'en thy wages:
> Golden lads and girls all must
> As chimney-sweepers, come to dust.'

'That's it,' she said. 'How sad, how very, very sad.' Suddenly she leaned forward and kissed me on the cheek, her lips were icy cold and she smelt of roses.

'Goodbye, get on with your digging, dear old Guy. Who knows what you'll find.'

'I'll see you again soon? I need your help . . .' But she'd gone, lost in the crowded pavements of early evening. It would be dark in a few minutes. I turned up my coat collar and decided to walk back to the flat: I'd leave the crumpets for another day. 'Golden girls and lads all must – as chimney-sweepers, come to dust . . .'

4

' "Miss Char, come back at once! At once, do you hear, it's long past tea time." '

So begins Char's piece on her meeting with H. A. Elliott, the poet. She wrote it at my suggestion on the occasion of Elliott's centenary, and we sent it in to the local newspaper. I well remember the excitement when we had their letter of acceptance – they even sent round a reporter for an interview – and the blood, sweat and tears entailed in its composition. Char persuaded me to write the biographical note on Elliott at the end, maintaining my literary style was more suited to such things than hers (her way of saying she couldn't be bothered). Her account of her early childhood at Renton and the events leading up to the birth of her sister, Rosie, came much later, when Char was already in St Hilda's. The former was also written at my suggestion and was intended originally to be much longer. I'd got both pieces out to lend to Sophia, then decided to re-read them myself first. Until Sophia asked about them, I'd forgotten their existence.

My First Great Adventure by C. Seymour

'Miss Char, come back at once! At once, do you hear, it's long past tea time.' The starched nurse seethed on the verandah steps. She was a jobbing nanny brought in while my Nanny was on holiday and she didn't much like the place. A light, summer rain was falling and she wasn't going to get her clean uniform skirt dirty for the likes of that one. Mr Osborn would be home from the City soon; let him give the child a walloping. That's what she needed. But with Mrs Osborn's potty ideas, she very much doubted if that's what she'd get. Probably some daft stuff about God not liking her to be disobedient, and what had he got to do with it, she'd like to know. The nurse retreated into the shelter of the verandah which ran along the length of the house and was littered with potted palms, lemon verbena, basket chairs, dogs' hairs and newspapers. She peered angrily through the glass at the tiny figure in the garden: it was raining quite heavily now. No good, she'd have to fetch the minx, but she'd be bothered if she wouldn't go and fetch a mac first from the cloakroom to put round her shoulders. She hurried huffily through the drawing room, the little watch she wore pinned to her chest bouncing angrily up and down on her bosom. The room was empty this afternoon: Mrs O was sitting on some committee somewhere. Crossing the hall, its parquet floor alive with growling tiger skins, she eventually reached the cloakroom at the end of a long passage that smelt slightly of cat. A few minutes later, arriving back at the garden door, now suitably enveloped in one of Mr O's voluminous mackintosh capes, she became aware of two things, both of them infuriating. One, it had stopped raining, and two, Miss Char had totally disappeared.

It was the summer of 1907. I was five years old and had just made the enchanting discovery that I could run really fast, and the faster I ran the more fun it was. I didn't care a hoot about the rain trickling down my neck through my liberty bodice or even that my knickers felt damp. I was, in fact, quite scantily clad in comparison with most Edwardian children; another of my mother's fads was that she strongly disapproved of flannel petticoats, button boots and the like, believing them to be restrictive to young children. I had seen with delight the angry Nurse Jump gesticulating from the verandah steps. I must have been a quite awful child, I adored enraging people.

'I'm Char Osborn, I'm Queen of the May,' I sang, jumping up and down, and stuck out my tongue at the luckless nurse. I'd been taken by Nanny to watch the May Day revels in the village and to be crowned Queen of the May, surrounded by suitably adoring attendants, was my current ambition. 'Naughty little girls are never asked to be Queen,' Nanny had said dampingly, 'and it's only for the village children. You're a little lady, dear, and don't you forget it.' But I didn't care. I should be Queen of the May if I wanted to and that was all there was to it.

Suddenly, ahead of me on the path, I noticed something that looked like a tiny pile of autumn leaves, only excitingly, it was gently pulsating. I knew at once what it was. It was one of my friends. 'Hullo, old Toad, and how are you?' I stroked him gently with one finger. He pulsated even more, glugged and tantalisingly hopped away, his long legs flying out behind him. By this time, need I say, my black stockinged knees were damp and muddy and there was green slime down the front of my pinafore. I looked back at the house to find that Nurse Jump had disappeared. Had she gone to fetch Ma? I felt a shiver of apprehension: Ma was someone to be reckoned with. Then I remembered the latter had driven away in the dog cart after nursery lunch, her red leather despatch case on the seat beside her. She wouldn't be home for ages. And Pa? He never got home until bedtime: he went away in a train each day to somewhere called the City, where people made money, so Nanny said. 'Look, Miss Char,' she would call, 'there's your Pa's train. He won't be long now.' And I would run to the nursery window and watch the smoke from the engine trail along the valley below and hear it whistle as it passed the signal box.

I licked the sweet raindrops trickling down from my nose and surveyed the empty rose garden: I was safe! It was then I decided to have an adventure. I started to run: through the wisteria arch, past the potting shed that stood the other side of the high, red brick wall enclosing the rose garden. A magic place the potting shed, and normally one I would love to spend a little time in: dipping my fingers in the sacks of compost, peat and fine sand, pulling at the seed heads hanging up to dry from the roof, peering into the dark recesses of the shed, lifting the lids of the huge crocks set on the earth floor and breathing in the fusty, musty, damp, earthy smell – but not today. Today I wanted adventure, real adventure, such as Tom Kitten experienced when he set off up the chimney, or Alice when she pursued the White Rabbit down the rabbit hole. After all, it wasn't every day you discovered you could run. Run really fast, that is: as fast as the foxes pursued so relentlessly by hounds when Pa and Ma went hunting. Past the potting shed came the greenhouses, and after these you could either go through a door in the wall that took you into the kitchen garden, or turn to the right outside the wall, where the path straggled through a small plantation to emerge three or four hundred yards further on at a kissing gate leading on to the road. This latter path was strictly out of bounds. Ragged boys from the town, so Nanny said, came and played on the Common opposite and sometimes tramps or gypsies camped there.

'Gypsies steal little girls, Miss Char, so you just watch out,' Polly the housemaid said. I had asked about the bright, painted caravans we'd seen that morning on the Common as we passed by in the governess cart on our way to the village to see old Mrs Simms.

'Why?' I asked, filled with excited curiosity.

'To train them for the circus, of course; make them swing about on them trapeze things, and if they ain't no good at that, then they eat 'em for their dinner.'

'I should be good, I know,' I said, and for a moment longed to be stolen by gypsies.

When I reached the door in the wall that led to the kitchen garden, I paused, trying to decide which path to take. The kitchen garden was a temptation, but Smith, the gardener, normally an ally, would be bound to be there and could I trust him not to take me back to Nurse Jump? I took a deep breath and decided to follow the forbidden path that led to the road. If the village boys were at the gate, I could always hide in the bushes, and if there were gypsies on the Common they'd never be able to catch me now I could run so fast.

I started down the path. Nettles on either side, heavy with rain, leaned forward and brushed my skirt, their brown seeds dribbling on to the muddy ground: everything steamed in the sudden warmth of the sun. It was farther than I had imagined to the road, and I had just begun to wonder if I would ever get there when the path began to diverge from the wall it had been following. One more bend and there in front of me was the kissing gate, set in the thick, hawthorn hedge that bordered the road.

Shivering with excitement, I crept up to the gate and peered through the slats. Before me lay the road, its normally dusty surface running in muddy rivulets. To the right lay the village, where we went to church and to see Mrs Simms and for lots of things; to the left lay the town, where we hardly ever went. A smelly, noisy place, Ma said, and riddled with disease. But it wasn't the road – in any case deserted – that caused the thrill of excitement that shot through me (a thrill so sharp I can feel it to this day), it was the sight of the strange man seated on the grass on the other side of the road.

He sat beside a small fire, his back to me, his long legs stretched out in front of him; there was string tied round the bottom of his trouser legs and his feet were bare. He wore a funny, broad-brimmed hat and his black, curly hair straggled on to his shoulders. I could not see his face, but I could see the smoke coming up from his pipe. Beside him on the ground was a large, untidy pack, things tumbling out of it on to the flattened grass. Then, most excitingly of all, I became aware that what I had first thought to be merely a branch or twig seen through the smoke haze of the fire in reality was a live monkey! Scarcely daring to believe my eyes, I watched, fascinated, while the monkey ran round the fire, jumped over the man's legs and climbing on to the pack on the ground began to fling things about in a seemingly frenzied search. At last he appeared to have found what he was looking for, a small paper packet, which he seized excitedly with both hands.

'Oscar,' the man shouted, roused from his apparent lethargy by the monkey's antics, 'leave my bloody humbugs alone, will you? A fellow must have a few rudiments of civilisation, you know. God knows, a bag of humbugs don't amount to much in the scheme of things, but it represents a certain humble pleasure.' My excitement turned to astonishment; the strange man sounded like Pa! Somehow I had imagined that when he spoke he would sound like Smith, or old Bramble, who swept the chimneys, or even Ben the garden boy, but not Pa. Then came a thought. Surely there could be nothing to fear from such a person: someone who talked like Pa wouldn't steal me or indeed force me to work in a circus, even though he did

36

happen to be the fortunate owner of a monkey. I doubted too if he would eat me. At least, I was pretty sure he wouldn't. And anyway, come what may, I had to get a closer view of that monkey. So up I got from my crouching position, and after dusting somewhat ineffectually the grass and mud from my knees, pushed my way through the kissing gate.

The man never turned round; he had resumed his smoking, having given the monkey a sharp slap that sent him gibbering with annoyance a few yards away on the other side of the fire. I trotted across the road, my boots making footprints in the fast caking mud, and creeping over the few yards of tussocky grass that separated me from the man, tapped him smartly on the shoulder.

'What the deuce—?' He spun round angrily alert and the monkey chattered in fright.

'Hullo,' I said, my voice squeaking with nerves. 'May I please talk to your monkey?' The man, by this time on his feet, looked down at me, the fear in his eyes receding to be replaced by wariness mixed with amusement.

'He doesn't like little girls, I'm afraid. Where's your nurse?'

'My nurse is an idjut and I know your monkey will like me. Please.' I smiled winningly and put on my 'wheedling' voice. The man, in spite of his strange clothes, was the most beautiful person I had ever seen. He was old, of course, but not as old as Pa. His face was golden brown from the sun. His eyebrows, thick and black as his hair, slanted in a funny way that reminded me of those pictures of the devil in Nanny's 'Jesus' book, the eyes beneath them green like Augustus the nursery cat's, but flecked with tiny spots of brown. The bottom part of his face was obscured by a black, silky beard and moustaches and from one ear dangled, fascinatingly, a single gold ear ring. He was tall and very thin.

The man glanced up and down the road and then at the peaceful, empty landscape behind him, as if to see if there was anyone watching, then satisfied, looked down again at me. He laughed, but it was not a happy sound, and suddenly pulled the ancient 'wideawake' hat from his head (it was then I saw his poor, mangled hand, the fingers claw-like, a deep gash encircling the wrist like some obscene bracelet) and spun the hat high into the air: it finally came to rest on one of the scrubby thorn bushes that dotted this part of the Common.

'Go bring me my *chapeau*, you son of Satan,' he yelled at the monkey. I watched, enchanted, while the little creature ran rapidly over to the thorn bush and seized the hat, which he proceeded to place upon his own head, then after executing a kind of jig, he slowly and with a wary eye on me, came towards the man.

'The lady won't hurt you, Oscar, or at least one hopes she won't,' he said very softly. And I held my breath as the monkey crept closer and closer, finally coming to a halt directly in front of us, chattering and nervously picking fleas out of his fur. He looked rather like a bedraggled mushroom.

'Thank you, Oscar, and now the lady will reward you.' The man, with one hand, relieved the monkey of his hat, which he replaced on the back of his head, and with the other patted the pocket of his tattered jacket, from which bulged the packet of humbugs. 'Offer him a humbug,' he hissed. The bag was sticky and the humbugs had all stuck together, but somehow I managed to dislodge one, and placing it on the palm of my hand (held flat with the thumb tucked neatly in, as I had been taught to do when offering a horse a lump of sugar) I thrust it, trembling only slightly, towards the monkey. Please God, don't let him bite me. I shut my eyes and waited. Suddenly a movement, a slight scratching on my outstretched hand;

I opened my eyes and the sweet had gone. A few feet away Oscar sat examining it with every appearance of delight.

'You know about animals, then,' the man said casually. 'There aren't many people he'll take food from. He and I are both on the run, you see: he from a circus, and me from . . . oh, many things.'

'His hand felt so funny on mine,' I said. 'Why did he run away from a circus?'

'It didn't suit him, I suppose,' the man said in a noncommittal sort of voice, and looked about him once again.

'Look here, I must sit down, there isn't much time and my foot hurts me like Hades. Stay and talk to me while I rest it, then home to Papa and Mama with you; I don't often nowadays get the chance to talk to a Christian. You are a Christian, I suppose?' He held out his hand: in a state of ecstasy I took it, my mouth too full of humbug to reply to his quite incomprehensible question.

I have never forgotten the ensuing half hour: the man, his looks, his voice and the magic of his charm will remain with me until the day I die. He sat me down between his long legs, on the damp grass beside the dying fire, the monkey now quite unafraid, chattering round us. What we talked of I was never afterwards able to remember. It was the timbre of his voice, his gentle self-mockery and above all, the way he treated me as an adult on his own level that was so unforgettably enchanting. At last, the sun that had shone so brightly it drew steam from the wet, glistening grass, went behind a cloud and the man looked up suddenly, raising his face to the sky in the manner of a hunted fox.

'I must be on my way,' he said in a different, harsher voice. 'I've a long way to go and little time.' I had just opened my

39

mouth to beg him not to go, not yet, when there was a sudden shout behind us.

' 'Enery Arthur Elliott, we are His Majesty's Law Officers. There's no escape, we've got you surrounded; just let go of the child and come quietly, there's a good chap.' The hoarse, Cockney voice rang out over the silent Common. A pheasant, disturbed, squawking wildly in sudden fright, rose from the grass in a whirr of wings and flew jerkily over the heads of the cordon of policemen that, as though by magic, had risen up out of the ground itself to encircle the man, his monkey and me. At the sound of the voice, the man turned to stone: he gripped me so tightly to him it hurt and I began to whimper.

'Come on now, son, let the little girl go. She won't do you no good.' The policeman's voice was soft, wheedling, but still the man hung on. I remember burying my face in his chest and feeling his heart banging through the torn, flannel shirt that smelt of stale sweat and fear. Above me crouched the monkey, who had jumped in terror on to the man's shoulder. The three of us clung together, utterly alone, against the world.

'No good, no good, I can't go back. I won't. Better to be dead.' Now the man was muttering to himself.

'Rush 'im, Sarge, 'e ain't armed.' This time a voice from behind, a younger voice. I opened my eyes and saw through a haze of sticky tears that we were completely surrounded by the ring of policemen, all carrying truncheons, except for one who carried a rifle. The big one, who had first called out, had a whistle on a string round his neck: he seemed uncertain what to do next.

The man whispered in my ear: 'I'm going to make a run for it; I haven't a cat's chance, but it's the only way. Sit still and you'll be alright.'

'Don't leave me, please don't leave me.' I was sobbing

now and quite beyond coherent thought.

'Shut up, you stupid little ass and sit still. There's nothing for you to be afraid of,' the man whispered furiously, then very gently relaxed his grip on me. There was silence, only the soft noises of the countryside and far away the clopping of a horse along the road from the town.

Suddenly, with one movement, the man was on his feet, hurling the terrified monkey straight at the momentarily off balance sergeant, now only a few feet away. With one bound he had jumped over the embers of the fire and, like a rabbit that, trapped in the last, small, square of uncut corn at harvest time, somehow manages to escape the ring of jeering men and boys armed with sticks, shot through the cordon of policemen and stumbled away over the Common. Knocked to the ground by the man's sudden bolt, I was by this time screaming blue murder; then there were other arms around me, another man's voice, friendly, cajoling. 'It's alright, Miss Char, nothing to be afeared of. It's PC Willis. You remember, I brought you back your kitty t'other day after you'd lost him.' Refusing to be comforted, I continued to sob and wriggle in a futile attempt to escape, when suddenly a shot rang out. Then yet another voice, this one full of excitement: 'We've got 'im, Sarge. Bullet went straight through the back of 'is 'ead; good, clean shot it wure.'

'Best thing all round, really.' The sergeant's voice: 'He were a bad un, but all the same I'll have to make a report—'

'What on earth is going on? Has Bagland Common suddenly become part of the Wild West of America?'

'Ma! Oh Ma! It's me. They've shot the nice man. Oh *Ma*!' For once in my life the presence on the scene of my mother was what I wanted most in the world and there, miraculously, she was. I was placed (no doubt with considerable relief) gently

41

in her arms by a deferential PC Willis.

'There, there, my pet, Ma is here now. There's nothing more to be afraid of.' And I, lying limp across my mother's shoulder, too tired to think any more, thrust my still sticky thumb in my mouth and let her take over.

It was as I was being lifted into the waiting dog cart – Ma had been driving home from her committee when she had heard the shot and seen the police on the Common – that I saw the man for the last time. He lay on his back on a rough stretcher covered by a red horse blanket. His face was white and his beautiful eyes closed. His poor, mangled hand seemed to be clutching at his throat and there was a little smear of blood on his forehead. Suddenly, I remembered: 'Ma, where's the dear little monkey? He was so funny, he—'

'He's gone to the animals' heaven, dear. He'll be quite happy there and he will be able to play all day long and never be hungry; you musn't be sad about him.' Ma's voice was unusually gentle as she turned my face away from the grisly scene at the roadside. Over her shoulder she crisply addressed the police sergeant: 'You'll be up to make your report shortly, no doubt, Sergeant. Meanwhile, I will telephone the Chief Constable.' With a flick of her whip, she brought Snowball, the grey mare, to life and the dog cart slowly trundled down the road and turned into the drive gates of Renton House.

And that was the end of my first great adventure. Or rather, the end of the adventure itself. There were to be many repercussions, not the least of which being that for a few, brief, exciting days I became quite famous.

The case of the man, 'my' man, had, it seemed, become quite a cause célèbre. I did not, of course, learn the full story until many years later: it was, for diverse reasons, not considered suitable for children's ears at the time. Annoyingly,

I can remember little of the immediate aftermath of that incredible afternoon apart from being lifted down from the dog cart by a grey-faced Pa still in his City clothes and being carried up the front steps into the hall to be greeted by an assortment of people all talking at once, in the centre of which was Nurse Jump having hysterics. I remember little, too, of subsequent interviews with the gentlemen of the press, except for one nice man with a ginger moustache and a brown bowler hat, who referred to me as 'the brave little Madam' and gave me a lollipop. Sadly, the latter was immediately confiscated by my mother, who was present at the interview and strongly disapproved of all forms of bribery.

But it wasn't all excitement: nightmares became frequent. One in particular plagued me for many years. I would find myself clinging with all my strength to someone or something, I was never sure which, but it would feel warm, lovely and secure. Then, without warning, there would be a crash as of shattering glass and I would be alone, suspended in mid-air, high above a sort of vast emptiness. My hands would scrabble desperately for something to catch on to, but there would be nothing: from this dream I would awake screaming, no matter how familiar it became.

Now for my piece. A little on the pompous side, but not bad really, I suppose.

Biographical Note

Henry Arthur Elliott was born in 1872, the son of a country parson who had married a rich wife. He was educated at Eton and Oxford, arriving at the latter in the early 1890s, when he at once became a member of the Aesthete Set that flourished at Oxford during the period. His first poems were published at the age of twenty and for the next few years he was very much part of the London *fin de siècle* literary scene. However, as the century drew to its close, Elliott's poetry began to change: it became harsh, brutal even, and its metre and vibrant rhythms incomprehensible to many. With the change in his work, there also came a change in his personality. From being gregarious and fun-loving, he became reclusive and would disappear for weeks at a time, no one knew where. Then suddenly, he who had never appeared to be interested in women, announced his engagement to a young woman whom, it was rumoured, he had picked up off the streets. The couple were married shortly afterwards amid more or less universal condemnation and from then on Elliott appears to have dropped out of London literary circles. His publishers turned down his next batch of poems: 'My dear fellow,' they said, 'we can't, we simply can't – such coarseness . . .' and that was that.

Several years elapsed during which little was heard of Elliott and no work published: there was talk of a child, but no one knew for certain. Then suddenly the amazing news broke; Elliott had killed his wife! The couple had apparently gone to live in a remote cottage somewhere in Gloucestershire and late one night Elliott had turned up at the local police station 'looking wild and dishevelled', or so the newspapers reported, and informed the police he had killed his wife. It later transpired he had, in fact, killed her in self-defence; she'd attacked him with a knife and there was a witness. The murder charge was changed to one of manslaughter and Elliott was sentenced to ten years' hard labour. After doing only six months in Wandsworth Gaol, however, he managed to escape in the course of being moved to another prison, half killing a warder in the process. Thereafter, he was on the run for three months before the law finally caught up with him on Bagland

Common, where, as a little girl of five, Mrs Seymour met him and where, tragically, he was shot in the back whilst trying to escape his pursuers.

It was while he was in prison awaiting trial that Elliott's notebooks were first discovered and the shocking truth revealed: the man was a sodomite! Luckily for posterity, however, there were a few who read the notebooks at the time who realised that their contents, although unpublishable in the then literary climate were, nevertheless, the work of genius. Now, of course, they form part of what is grandly known as our literary heritage and every girl or boy in the throes of A-level Eng Lit knows at least one of Elliott's poems by heart.

(Char's *Fragment of Autobiography* appeared to be missing a couple of pages at the beginning. It was originally written in her own big, scrawling handwriting on torn-off sheets from an old exercise book, but I somehow managed to inveigle a kindly secretary at work to type out a fair copy. I remember having to take the latter, at her request, out to dinner at The White Tower in Percy Street as recompense for her labours.)

... but there's no doubt that my parents, Con and Dick Osborn ('Ma' and 'Pa'), were an ill-assorted couple. They only had two things in common really. The first was their background: both children of the emergent, monied middle class, and the second an overpowering, mutual, physical attraction. The latter leading them to become engaged and married in a matter of weeks rather than the customary months after their first meeting at a dance given for Ma's best friend, Gwendoline Philbert's twenty-first birthday.

Their friends and relations watched in astonishment the couple's whirlwind courtship. She tall, angular, sandy haired, with nice eyes, good teeth and a magnificent seat on a horse:

not much else, apart from a mind like an adding machine. He small, emotional, attractive to women, full of charm and style and fun. Not a lot on top, but enough to get by in the family business of tea merchants. She, one of 'that damned fella Shaw's' New Women, an admirer of Ibsen, a believer in women's suffrage and all that sort of rot. He a believer in not much, really, except having a good time and keeping more or less within the guidelines laid down by his class and the era in which he lived. In other words, he believed in the Empire, the Class System, the Army, Navy and Public Schools, and the fact that sex should only be fun when practised with 'women of a certain order', i.e. tarts. Ladies, one's wife in particular, were merely serviced, as a stallion a mare, in order to continue the family line. Bearing all this in mind, it seems even odder that he and Ma ever got together, but the fact remains, they did.

'It's the attraction of opposites,' people said, as they sipped their champagne at the couple's wedding in May 1900. 'It couldn't be money.' (Ma's father was director of at least a dozen City companies and Pa made no mean living, himself, in the tea business.)

'It's passion,' said Gwendoline Philbert, greatly daring. 'They're mad for each other, can't you see?'

And passion, initially anyway, it was. Unfortunately, passion proved not to be enough, for despite the fact it not infrequently overpowered them both, it was unable, paradoxically, to overcome their mutual inhibitions about each other: namely, they continued to see in one another traits of which, in the ordinary course of events, they would strongly disapprove.

However, they settled down conventionally enough in a large, comfortable house in Bedfordshire, where two years later I was born. The birth was long and painful and the arrival of a daughter instead of the hoped-for son a disappointment shattering to them both.

'Never, never, never, will I go through that again,' Ma vowed and meant it, but Pa had other ideas: he wanted a son. He needed one, after all, to carry on the family business.

'Treat her gently,' chaps at his club advised. 'She'll get over it, they all do. Don't force the filly, it could lead to trouble in the long run.' But somehow or other as the months went by, Ma didn't seem to be getting over it. She still insisted on locking Pa's dressing-room door each night, whence he had been banished since before my birth, and filled the house at weekends with arty young men, female battle-axes and damned revolutionaries who couldn't even speak the King's English. So, after a year of enforced abstinence, with little regret, perhaps even a sense of relief, Pa returned to his old stamping grounds: in particular, a charmer by the name of Stella, who had a topping little hideaway in Pimlico and provided with considerable panache – she was very expensive – all the delights of the flesh he had for so long been deprived.

And so their life continued, a rough compromise, as are so many marriages. They even became reconciled to the fact of my not being a boy. Ma, I think, saw me as a sort of human guinea pig sent from heaven in order that she might put into practice her 'advanced' ideas on the bringing-up of children. And I made Pa laugh, albeit from the very beginning he always considered me 'too sharp by half'. In other words, he would have preferred a more amenable and fluffy-headed daughter of the 'Cuddles' variety so popular then. I think he feared too that I might grow up to be like Ma – God save the mark!

It was the Eton and Harrow match in the summer of 1908 that brought my parents together again in the bed department.

Pa, as was his custom, took a large party. Harrow was his old school and despite the fact a good deal of his time there had been spent in more or less total misery, he nevertheless, from the safe platform of adulthood, viewed it through a haze of nostalgic sentimentality, and would have died rather than miss the famous, annual cricket match at Lords.

They dined afterwards at the Savoy. Ma, for once, had sparkled and refrained from lecturing, and whether it was the heat, the champagne, or the fact Harrow had won, they never afterwards knew, but Ma left the door unlocked between their adjoining rooms at Brown's Hotel, and Pa at long last had his way.

For a few short weeks passion returned; the heady days of their honeymoon were lived all over again. Until, that is, just as cubbing was about to begin, the apples in the orchard were ripening and the cottage gardens ablaze with Michaelmas daisies, Ma discovered, to her considerable annoyance, she was once again pregnant. She took to lying about on sofas (a habit she continued to the end of her life), gave up hunting, and a governess was engaged for me. I was a precocious child anyway, and Ma was very hot on education for girls as well as boys.

The task of telling me of an addition to the family and of my own impending incarceration in the school room was given to my Nanny. Ma was feeling too unwell to cope with such trivialities as her daughter's possibly tiresome reaction to the news and Pa, naturally, would be useless at such a task.

So it was that one evening early in the year 1909 Nanny, seated in her special chair by the nursery fire, took me on her knee and cuddled me in the way she used to do, but had not done for a long time. I was feeling comfortable and sleepy after my bath, my skin tingling from the brisk towelling, with the delicious taste of toothpaste in my mouth. The high, nursery fender shone with polishing and through its mesh I could see the fire castles flickering in the blackleaded grate. Outside, the wind blew and rain pattered on the roof of the verandah, but inside all was peace. Old Nanny, as she always did, smelt of camphor, a not unpleasant smell, and I burrowed my head into the cleft between her enormous bosoms and listened to the fast tick of the tiny gold watch that hung on a black ribbon round her neck. It had once belonged to Nanny's mother, hard though it was to imagine Nanny having a mother, and was very old and fragile, so she said.

'Tell me a story, Nan, come on.' I knew all Nanny's stories by heart, but that wasn't important, it was the telling of the story that was important. Silence. 'Come on, Nan. Tell me the one about Queen Victoria bathing her dear little dog when the men came to fetch her for her coronation.'

'Not tonight, dear, I've things to say that must be said.' Nan's voice sounded a bit queer. I began to have that familiar feeling in my tummy. Nanny cleared her throat: 'Now then, dear, how would you like to have a lovely little baby brother?' (The entire Osborn household had by this time already made up their collective mind the baby would be a boy.)

I thought for a bit; this was unexpected news. Then I remembered Jane and Amelia had a baby brother. Jane and Amelia were the vicarage children and sometimes came to tea. They had recently acquired their baby brother, a small, wizened creature, enveloped in white shawls, who managed to produce a noise far out of proportion to his size, and what's more, smelt of pooh. 'They're noisy and smelly things,' I announced, 'and I don't want one.'

'Now, that's no way to talk and well you know it. God

sends little girls baby brothers and they should be happy and grateful.'

'Jane and Amelia don't like Geoffrey at all. They say he spoils simply everything, they—'

'Now, that's enough, Miss Char. It's wrong to think such things; what ever would your Ma say?'

'She doesn't like babies, she said so. She said there were far too many born into the world and the working class must be taught to exercise restraint.' I hadn't the slightest idea what all this meant, but could 'do' Ma to a T – it was one of my ways of getting round Pa. It always had him in convulsions. I could see by the look on Nan's face my random shot had found its mark.

'I said that's enough and when Nanny says that's enough, Nanny means it. Now, listen quietly to what I have to say. Whether you like it or not,' Nanny sounded quite cross, for the life of me I couldn't see why, 'you're going to have a dear little baby brother.' I sucked my thumb in silence. 'And, when the spring comes,' Nanny continued, using her storytelling voice, 'and the birds are building their nests, one fine day you will go upstairs to see your Ma in her bedroom and there, in a cradle by her bed, just like you were when you were little, you will find a lovely little baby, and you will kiss him and love him ever so much and . . . and when he gets bigger, you will be able to play with him and have such fun together.'

'I don't want to play with babies, and how could he get into Ma's bedroom, he—'

'God will send him, dear, you know that.'

'Well, I don't want God to send him. Why can't he be given to somebody else?' But at this point Nanny, without further ado, plunged into her second piece of news.

'Another nice thing is going to happen. My, aren't you a

lucky little girl?' But I seized one of the grey whiskers that sprouted from Nanny's chin and gave it a sharp tug. It was one of those things I never could resist doing.

'Don't do that, dear, or Nanny will get cross—'

'Why do you have a beard, Nan, why?'

'You're going to have lessons every day with a very nice lady who is coming to live here. Your Ma will be too busy now to give them you herself. The lady is ever so clever and pretty and will be able to answer all your questions. Smith is going to turn out the big attic upstairs and paint it and make it into such a nice school-room, and you will have your own little desk and pen and pencils. And Bobby Prescott from the Grange will be coming in every morning to do his lessons with you – now, won't that be nice?'

'No, it won't, and I don't want a baby brother either,' I said.

Miss Babs Bellingham, wearing a smartly tailored tweed coat and skirt and a straw boater perched on a mass of red-gold hair, arrived a fortnight later, bringing with her a bicycle and a Gladstone bag full of Fabian Society tracts. Miss Bellingham was the 'clever' but impecunious niece of one of Ma's fellow committee members: pretty, but the possessor of a rather strident voice. I took an instant dislike to her. Ma, enclosed now in her hypochondriac world of impending motherhood, paid little attention to the new governess, apart from briskly interviewing her on the day of her arrival. Summoned to a freezing morning room, she found Ma reclining on a mauve velvet chaise longue, placed strategically under an open window, through which blew a chill north-easter.

'My daughter needs a strong hand, Miss Bellingham,' she informed the shivering governess, herself warmly enwrapped in an assortment of woollen shawls. 'But above all, she must have stimulation for her over-active mind. I am, as I told your aunt, *hors de combat* for the time being and must therefore rely on you to provide that stimulation, within, naturally, a solid framework of discipline. The means by which you choose to enforce that discipline are your own affair, but let me make it clear, no child of mine will ever be the recipient of corporal punishment. Now, my dear . . . if you will excuse me . . .'

Miss Bellingham was a good teacher, no doubt of that, but I hated the routine of the school room and Bobby Prescott was such a little ass. He used to cry when I kicked him under the table and when I borrowed his pen one day (the nib to mine had gone funny and spluttered ink all over my writing book) he went straight home and told his mother I was a thief.

'Mama says God punishes little girls who steal,' he informed me smugly the following morning. 'He'll send a thunderbolt to kill you.'

'No, he won't, he doesn't do things like that, and you're a nasty little tell-tale-tit.'

'Children,' shouted Miss Bellingham, getting rather red in the face. Doubtless her fingers itched to bang our heads together. She refrained, wisely, perhaps remembering Ma's embargo on corporal punishment. 'Get on with your lessons. Charlotte, you're the eldest and must learn to set a good example. Any more nonsense and you will stand in the corner.'

'I don't mind standing in the corner in the least, it's better than stupid old arithmetic . . .'

Pa, on a walking tour in France at the time of Miss Bellingham's arrival, returned a few days later. He encountered her on her way back from the village. A tendril of hair had escaped from under her hat, her cheeks were rosy from the wind and her tight-waisted jacket accentuated the slimness of her figure. Pa, his blue eyes alight, looked her up and down in that special way he had, then held out his hand smiling. 'I'm Charlotte's father; you must be Miss Bellingham. And how are you managing with that little monkey of mine?'

'She's a lovely child, Mr Osborn, just a bit mischievous at times, but a ripping little learner.' At that precise moment a sudden gust of wind blew Miss Bellingham's hat off.

Pa laughingly retrieved it. 'Always remember to hang on to your hat, Miss Bellingham,' he said and looked straight into her eyes. And how do I know all this? Because I saw and heard it, from my secret look-out post at the nursery window. How ridiculous grown-ups were, especially Pa and Ma.

To be fair, however, despite the hours spent standing in the corner – imagination was not one of Miss Bellingham's many attributes – there was no doubt I did benefit greatly from her tuition. Anyway, one can get used to almost anything if one tries hard enough.

Week followed week and spring slowly turned to summer. The grass in the paddock grew green and lush, the first cuckoo was heard, Ma grew steadily bigger and everyone in the household, apart that is from Ma, became aware of a change in Miss Bellingham. She was softer, more lax in discipline and frequently inattentive. She even giggled at one of my rude drawings (I was a great one for rude drawings) and never even noticed when I stuffed the unfortunate Bobby's inkwell full of little bits of blotting paper. The school-room party took to having nature rambles instead of lessons. Miss Bellingham, her long skirts trailing over the dewy grass, her eyes dreaming, would lead us shouting and laughing over the fields and along the leafy lanes of early summer. Once we saw a pair of kingfishers darting through the willows that overhung the stream at the bottom of the paddock where the horses had already been put out to grass for their summer rest. And once I found a robin's nest in the high, stony bank bordering the lane that led to the village.

Sometimes, on a Saturday morning, Pa would join us, helping Miss Bellingham over stiles and pointing out the different species of butterflies. He had collected butterflies as a boy and indeed possessed quite an impressive collection, carefully preserved in a mahogany specimen chest in his dressing room.

As for me, I adored these expeditions, and it was through them that my love for wild flowers and the English countryside was born, remaining with me (despite the latter being, alas, no longer the unspoiled wonderland it was when I was a child) to this day, and has many, many times, when all else seems to have failed, continued to give me pleasure.

The affair of Pa and Miss Bellingham (for, of course, that is what it was) came to a head on the great river picnic. Pa, in his goodness, decided to give me and my governess a treat: he would hire a boat and the three of us would spend the day on the river; Ma, *hors de combat* as usual, would stay behind on the sofa.

We set off one glorious Saturday morning, taking the footpath that led from the paddock to the river, the latter only a mile if you went across the fields. Pa, wearing knickerbockers and Norfolk jacket, carrying the food hamper, led the way, laughing and joking like a schoolboy. Then came Miss Bellingham in a pink summer dress with tiny pearl buttons all the way down the front and a wide, shady straw hat, holding her skirts away from the brambles that wound across the path. And me in the rear, singing one of my made-up songs, carrying a long frond of lacy cow parsley as a wand. The boat was ready and waiting at the tiny landing stage, and once everyone, plus the food hamper and Miss Bellingham's parasol, were safely on board, Pa cast off.

We punted lazily between the river banks now alight with kingcups and yellow flag irises: me on my tummy in the stern peering into the brown depths of the water for trout, Pa, a small, sunburned, athletic figure, wielding the punt pole with considerable efficiency – by now he had discarded his Norfolk jacket – and Miss Bellingham, lying back on the punt cushions looking decorative.

When it was time for lunch, we tied the punt to an overhanging branch and unloaded the hamper and the punt cushions. There was much laughter when Pa nearly fell in and Miss Bellingham's hat caught in a tree. Everything seemed to be going right; even lunch was good. I disliked food and regarded eating as a waste of valuable time (I still do), but today there were my favourite chicken sandwiches, the chocolate cake cook always made for special occasions and even my own private bottle of lemonade. Pa opened a bottle of champagne for himself and Miss Bellingham with a flourish.

'Oh, but I shouldn't, Mr Osborn. It makes me so silly,' said Miss Bellingham, her eyes all big and soft like a rabbit's, one hand playing with the little pearl buttons at her throat.

'Fizz never did anyone any harm,' Pa said, 'and today is a special holiday, isn't it, Scamp?' I loved Pa calling me Scamp, it made me feel wicked.

'Why is it a special day, Pa, why?'

'Because, because, because . . . it just is,' he said, smiling, annoyingly, at Miss Bellingham. Suddenly, there was a splash of water, and out from under the bulrushes swam a mother moorhen and her chicks.

'Look, look.' I ran to the water's edge to watch the small flotilla swim by, agitated now by all the noise. 'Oh, aren't they sweet, Pa, look . . .' But Pa wasn't there. He and Miss Bellingham were kneeling on the punt cushions looking at one another in a silly way and they hadn't even seen the moorhens. The day, somehow, didn't seem so bright now. 'You missed the moorhens, you stupid things.'

'Don't speak to your father like that, dear.' Miss Bellingham dabbed her forehead with a minute, white, lace handkerchief. I promptly stuck out my tongue. A scene was imminent. Pa, pushing his panama hat to the back of his head held out his arms. 'Come on, you scallywag, we don't want any tantrums today, it's too hot. Let's start lunch. I'm ravenous.'

Lunch was fun and Pa in such a good mood he even gave me a sip of champagne. By the end of the meal Miss Bellingham's hair was getting all wispy and untidy; there were beads of sweat on her forehead and a few crumbs adhered to her chin, and I was feeling sleepy. I licked my fingers and yawned, then rolled back on the warm cushions and lay looking up at the sun flickering through the branches above me.

'That's right, dear, have a nap.' Miss Bellingham bent over me, solicitously adjusting the cushions. For a while I sought to fight the drowsiness, then couldn't be bothered, and fell asleep.

I was woken some time later by the sound of a bumble bee, and sat up instantly, ready for action.

'Pa, Pa, what shall we do now?' But there was no answer: Pa and Miss Bellingham had completely disappeared. Just for a minute I was a little frightened; surely they hadn't run away and left me? Then I saw Pa's hat and the food hamper: it was alright, they couldn't be far. I decided to go and look for them.

I was just wondering which way to go first, when I saw them. They had, for some reason, climbed back into the punt. But what on earth were they doing? Pa appeared to be bouncing up and down on top of Miss Bellingham, who was squeaking like one of the moorhens, and the boat was rocking like anything. What fun! Surely they'd like me to join in the game? I'd give them a surprise. What a joke!

I crept down the bank and waded into the muddy water, which rose nearly to my waist. In a few short steps I had reached the side of the punt and shouting, 'Let me have a go,' tried unsuccessfully to haul myself in. In the ensuing scuffle, amidst screams from Miss Bellingham and oaths from Pa, the punt capsized, tipping its occupants into the river.

'You little fool,' yelled Pa, frantically trying to pull up his trousers, his face red with rage. 'What in Hades did you do that for?'

'I wanted to play, I wanted to play,' I shrieked, jumping up and down in the water. 'You're stupid babies; grown-ups don't play games, it's silly.'

'Don't you dare speak to me like that . . .' Pa had his trousers up by this time, but Miss Bellingham had caught her dress on a branch when she was tipped out of the punt, and as she frantically tried to free herself, it became horribly apparent that all her little pearl buttons were undone and quite a bit of her bosom could be seen, rising creamy white above her camisole . . .

Miss Bellingham left the following day, watched (I have to admit with some satisfaction) by me from my post at the nursery window. She was driven to the station in the dog cart by Smith, her back straight, her head high and the Gladstone bag full of Fabian tracts (unread) at her feet. She had learned her lesson the hard way and would later become one of the leading lights of the Women's Suffrage Movement and a passionate disciple of Marie Stopes. As for Pa, he took a small flat in town, where he stayed during the week, and Ma took to her bed.

Shortly after the disastrous boating picnic, on a wild, stormy night in June, my sister, Rosie, was born. Thunder crashed deafeningly around the house and Dr Jervis was delayed for an hour because of an elm struck by lightning blocking the road from the village. Ma's labour went on for hours and Pa was summoned from London. You could hear Ma's cries right down the passage that led to the night nursery and there was a funny hospital smell everywhere.

'Well, lovey, you have a dear little sister to play with,' Nanny informed me next morning. 'When you've finished your breakfast you may see her, but you must be very good and quiet, because it's been a terrible ordeal for your poor mother and she's very weak and tired.'

'I don't want to see a stupid little sister and what's an ordeal, Nan?' I smashed in the top of my boiled egg with a teaspoon: it was all runny inside and I hated boiled eggs anyway.

'Of course you want to see your little sister. You must love her, because Jesus sent her. Now, eat up your egg, dear, and stop asking questions.'

'What's an ordeal, Ma?' I stood beside my mother's big bed. Ma lay on her back, her sandy hair, usually so neatly coiled, tumbling on her shoulders, her face grey with fatigue and her big, green, slightly myopic eyes sad. The curtains were drawn across the windows shutting out the bright sunlight that had followed last night's storm. A subdued Pa sat on a red velvet chair by the window smoking a cigarette.

'An ordeal is a bad time, darling,' Ma said and her voice lacked its usual authority.

'Like when Pa and Miss Bellingham fell in the river—?'

'Ach!' Pa made a noise that sounded like a cross between a laugh and a groan.

'No, not like that; that was what is known as farce.' Ma's voice was acid. 'An ordeal is a bad time you go through to test how strong you are. Like Christian in the *Pilgrim's Progress*, when he journeys through the Vale of Tears. Why do you want to know?'

'Nanny said you'd had one.'

'It was not pleasant, not pleasant . . .' Ma closed her eyes. The darkened room smelled of hospitals and Pa's cigarettes. Outside on the lawn, Rags, the fox terrier, barked raucously at the stable cat as it picked its supercilious way across the neatly swept gravel.

'Come and see your sister. Ma must rest now.' Pa took my hand and led me into the little room next door. The monthly nurse, a gaunt lady in starched blue and white, sat sewing beside a cradle; she rose to her feet.

'Ah, you've come to see Baby, dear. She's such a pretty little soul.' I ran to the cradle and peered inside. A red, pointed head topped by a fuzz of dark hair lay on the snow-white pillow. The eyes were fast shut and one tiny, clenched hand, like a pink sea anemone, rested on the blue satin coverlet.

'She's not pretty; she looks like a lobster.'

Pa snorted again. 'That's no way to talk of your new sister, Scamp. One day she will be as pretty as you and what will you do then?'

'Push her under a railway engine so she gets squashed like strawberry jam, then—'

'Be quiet, dear, we don't want to wake Baby, now do we?' said the monthly nurse, and I was led away.

The looked-for boy had turned out to be a girl after all. The

59

doctor said there could never be another child. Ma and Pa hid their disappointment, but the rift between them widened.

There was a grand christening, of course, and the new baby was named Mary Rose, although throughout her short life she was always known as Rosie. She was a lovely child, who rarely cried and Pa, after his initial disappointment at her being the wrong sex, doted on her. Ma, however, had reservations: somehow she could not forget the ordeal of the child's birth, or the events that had led up to it.

And me? I had a new governess to contend with, or to be more accurate, a succession of governesses, for none of them stayed long. Some were French, some English, some old, some young, but they all had two things in common: they were extremely plain and none of them seemed to be able to cope with me.

5

'Tell me about Aunt Beth; some of her diaries are in my pile for pre-1914.'

'Guy, you're so organised.' Sophia gazed in mock amazement at the neatly labelled bundles ranged about us. 'What happens if someone wants to stay? I mean where will they sleep?' We were standing in my spare bedroom: my task of sorting Char's papers done, I was about to embark on the reading of them.

'No one ever does want to stay,' I said huffily. 'And the first rule for any researcher is to catalogue his primary sources: it's no use just diving in at random, you'd never get anywhere.'

'Are you trying to get somewhere then, dear old Guy? You do seem to be taking all this rather seriously.'

'Don't call me "dear old Guy", it makes me sound like the family dog.' I felt tired and irritable. It had been a hell of a day at the office and the last thing I needed was Sophia in one of her patronising moods. 'Now, are you going to tell me about Aunt Beth?' Sophia sat down on the bed, having carefully removed the years 1924 and 1925 and placed them on the floor beside a large, enigmatic photograph of a group of people in pudding-basin hats standing glumly in front of what looked like a gasometer.

'Aunt Beth was Grandpa's sister. She died before I was born, but she was one of Mum's favourite people. She never

married and lived with Aunty Roo – I do just remember her –
who was a sort of Osborn cousin, in a large flat in Garden
Court, Kensington. They lived there for years and years and it
became a family meeting place. Mum stayed there a lot when
she was a child. When Aunt Beth died she left some of her
things to Mum, hence, I suppose, the existence of her diaries.
But what are all these bits and pieces with them?' She pulled
out a brilliantly coloured picture postcard of St Peter's, Rome.

'Sophia, don't mix everything up, *please*. They're all in
chronological order; you see the letters and postcards fit in
with the diaries—'

'Am I being a bore, Guy? You will tell me, won't you, if I
am?'

'You're being a bore,' I said, 'but rather a beautiful one,'
and was instantly amazed at my temerity.

Sophia was silent for a moment while she lit a cigarette.
Then: 'That's better,' she said. 'That's what I like to hear.'

'Let's eat,' I said. 'Everything's ready.' She got up from
the bed and took my arm. 'And afterwards can we look at the
diaries together?' she said. 'We could read them out loud to
each other, take it in turns; make them come alive . . .'

The Grand Hotel, St, Moritz   10th, March, 1910

My dearest Scamp,

We arrived here yesterday from Paris. The weather good
and the snow just right for skiing. I do wish you and Baby
were here – what fun we all would have! Did you get our
postcards from Paris? Don't forget to keep the stamps for your
album that Aunt Beth gave you.

Ma was a little unwell on the train journey out, but is much better now and sends her fondest love to you and Baby. I hope you are looking after Rags and Augustus and remembering to give the horses their Sunday lumps of sugar.

We will be home for Easter. They have some fine chocolate eggs in the shops here and if you are a good girl while we are away and work hard at your lessons with Miss Lamont, I'll bring one back for you. We leave here next Tuesday and take the night express to Rome.

All love, dear child, to you and Baby

Yr loving Pa

PS I fell over in the snow today, right on my behind. How you would have laughed!

Hotel Trevi, Roma   25th March 1910

My Char –

Rome is so lovely and here I am confined to bed – isn't it absurd! Pa has to go sight-seeing on his own. Never mind, our hotel is on one of the seven hills of Rome and from my bed I can see through the open window right over this beautiful city. The church bells ring all day long, such a lovely sound, I think, and not in the least like English bells. Some kind friends have just been in to sit with me while Pa is out. A Miss Peacock and Miss Lovridge, do you remember them? They stayed with us last year. Miss Peacock is a first-class croquet player and they are both such clever artists. They are staying in a pension quite close to our hotel and call daily. Doctor Piozzi is to visit today and give his verdict on whether I am allowed up. He's such a killing little man, rather like an organ-grinder's monkey!

Now, dear, I hope you are being a good girl and working your hardest at your lessons. Miss Lamont came to us very highly recommended, and if you concentrate, especially in your arithmetic, and behave to her as you would to a friend of your father's and mine, I am sure you will get along splendidly together. Remember the poor lady is on her own in a foreign land and needs some kindness shown her; even from naughty little girls! A week today and we shall be on our way home, if I have recovered from this stupid illness. Pa has gone to see the Catacombs, but sends his love. All my love, dear, too –

Your loving Ma

Hotel Trevi, Roma   27th March 1910

Dear Char –

Both Pa and I were *most* upset to hear from Nanny that Miss Lamont has already left. How can this be? I was feeling so much better and Dr Piozzi so pleased with my progress I was to be allowed down to dinner this evening. Then the English mail arrives and we have this shocking news from home.

Now Char, your father and I want the truth. As I have so often told you, it is *always* better to 'Tell the truth and shame the devil' as God would have us do. Why did Miss Lamont leave so suddenly? I should like the whole story, no leaving any little bits out, and so would your father.

I will write no more now. I feel most unwell and upset. Your father talks of curtailing our holiday: see what trouble naughty, selfish, little girls can cause. Pa and I are *most* displeased.

Your loving Ma

Garden Court, Kensington – 28th March 1910
Such a tiresome day. First we find the new cover for the
drawing-room sofa does not match the chairs: the colour is
quite, quite wrong. Roo must have had one of her 'blind' fits
when she chose it. Then Cook was taken ill with one of her
'turns' and had to be carted off to bed by Mabel and Dr S
called in. Roo and I had just sat down to a cold luncheon
prepared by Mabel – v. odd potatoes, Roo's were quite hard
in the middle and tasted of soap – when a telegram arrived
from Con and Dick in Rome. I felt for a minute quite sick
with fright! Can I go down to Renton at once, the latest gov
has left in high dudgeon and pandemonium rages! So
inconvenient. I wired back: 'What am I to do when I get
there?'

Con replied: 'Show the flag and calm things down.' So
there we are. I am to catch the 8.10 train from King's Cross
tomorrow morn. Rehearsal tonight and I simply can't miss it;
we're behind enough as it is, what with no one bothering to
learn their parts, and the chorus so ragged and off key. Oh
dear . . .

Renton House, Beds – 31st March 1910
Char and I to the village today to see dear old Mrs Simms,
then on to tea at the Vicarage. The Vicarage children such fun
and little Geoffrey a perfect darling. Char has been so good
and sweet, I cannot understand what all the furore has been
about! She says Miss Lamont left because she didn't like
England and the house was too cold. I feel there must be a
little more to it than that, but Vera the new parlour-maid – a v.
quiet, sensible girl – says that Miss Lamont did complain a
great deal and positively *tyrannised* the staff. Vera said, 'Miss
Char was only sticking up for us Ma'am.' Can this be true?

Of course, old Nanny tells a different story, but then she's so busy now with dear Baby, I doubt whether she has much time to know what is going on in the rest of the house. *Nous verrons . . .*

Dear Char is such a funny, clever, little thing. She said to me today as we were driving to the village, 'Oh, how I *hate* Oliver Cromwell, Aunt Beth. I've covered his picture in my history book with ink blots.' Did Miss Lamont approve, I wonder? Roo writes all is well at home and Cook recovered from her fit. Con and Dick return next week. Such lovely primroses in Bagland Wood. Char and I to pick them tomorrow to decorate the church.

Renton House, Beds – 2nd April 1910
Such a happy day yesterday with Char. Perfect spring sunshine. We took a picnic to the woods, I driving old Snowball in the dog cart. The wild flowers quite lovely. I did some sketching and Char played in and out of the trees. We saw a red squirrel and Char shouted: 'Look, look, Aunt Beth, there's Squirrel Nutkin.' She's such an original child: no beauty, but there's something there.

Long letter from Con. The doctors don't seem to know what is wrong with her. A return to England and good, plain food should do the trick! Gallivanting about the continent won't help to patch up her and Dick's differences. Tried to talk to Char about her behaviour with the govs, but all she would say was, 'Aunt Beth, they were all so stupid.' Can she be right? Con does sometimes choose some rather odd people. This evening I set the child a little essay, 'A Day in the Woods'. She ran straight upstairs to the school room to write it and stayed there until bedtime.

Dear Baby – I must remember now to call her Rosie – is

walking everywhere, such a lovely child, always so happy.

Renton House, Beds – 4th April 1910
A wire last night – Con and Dick home tomorrow. The boat
train arrives at Victoria four o'clock, then straight down here
in time for a late dinner. I must remember to tell Cook.
Everyone frantically busy getting ready – Char rather quiet.
'Ma will be so angry,' she keeps saying, 'and it wasn't all my
fault, not this time.' I told her not to be absurd: if she gave her
mother the truth and apologised properly for any worry she'd
caused, I know she would understand. The trouble is, I'm not
sure if I'm right to say this to her. Con can be so difficult and
after being ill and Dick leaving her in the hotel in Rome while
he went cavorting off to Sienna . . . I shall just have to plead
the child's case I suppose. No one else will. Such a beautiful
little essay she wrote – really quite poetic. I wonder if school
would be the answer?

Garden Court, Kensington – 6th April 1910
Home again – such a relief – despite the troubles that beset us
here. Roo has a bad cold and feels quite wretched with it. Mr
Flinders escaped and simply vanished into thin air for three
hours. He was returned to us by old Lady Manver's footman.
Apparently, the footman told Mabel, their Susy is in a 'certain
condition' and every dog in the Borough is after her, including,
it seems, our Mr Flinders!

    I departed from Renton under a cloud! Con looked very
seedy. The trip seems to have done her no good at all. Dick
just goes his own sweet way, as usual. Dick and I dined alone
the night of their return; Con straight to bed. No present for
poor little Char, such a disappointment for her: such a pretty
embroidered dress for Rosie and a dear little music box.

At breakfast I told Con I didn't think the gov's departure was entirely Char's naughtiness; I had it from the servants the woman was difficult, but she wouldn't allow it and said Char must be punished, so that was that. I'm afraid I became a little angry; it did no good, of course, it never does. Con simply informed me I was unmarried (an unnecessary piece of information under the circumstances!) and therefore knew nothing of how to bring up children. Dick just said: 'Con's right, Beth old thing, the child must be punished,' and drifted off before I could reply. Typical! Char v. tight and angry when I left; said she didn't care what anyone said, and if she had another governess who was 'stoopid and bossy', she'd 'get rid of her too', so there we stand. I plucked up courage to ask Con why she'd insisted on my dashing down to Renton to hold the fort and then refused to listen to anything I had to say on the situation I found there, but she simply looked wan and said she felt too seedy to discuss the matter further!

Garden Court, Kensington – 10th November 1912
Dick to see me. He arrived unexpectedly, straight from the office. Nothing suitable to eat, of course. Roo at her people's and I had told Cook just a tray for me would do. So he took me out to dine – quite like old times! We laughed a lot during dinner (at that new Hungarian place, violins sawing away like billy-o and everybody there, *such* fun. I felt quite gay and giggly). It was splendid to hear dear Dick laugh again. Poor old boy, I've not heard him do so since darling Rosie's death and that is over a year ago now. Although I never cease to think of our poor little one and her happy ways, it is good to forget sometimes – life must go on.

After dinner, we walked along the Embankment, arm in arm: brilliant stars and moonlight. The river looked so beautiful, but the air so cold the pavement was white with frost.

'I'm in trouble, Beth dear,' Dick said. 'Things are so damned difficult I don't seem able to see a way out.' I asked him what he meant. I had thought matters between him and Con were better again after the trouble last April. 'It's not just that,' he burst out, 'though God knows that's bad enough. It's the business. I made a few unwise speculations – a chap I met at the club, seemed to know what's what, old Etonian, member of the MCC, said it was a cert, couldn't lose. He went down for thousands, but I lost enough.' What to say? I was flummoxed. Dick was never good over money, but Con took over the purse strings when they married. As Papa said: 'Filly's got a damned good head for business on her shoulders. Should have been a man. She's a damned sight more of one than all those brothers of hers.'

'You must tell Con,' I said. 'She will know what to do for the best.'

'You too?' he said, oh so bitterly. 'You agree with everyone else: I'm incapable of providing properly for my own family, my wife must do it for me.' I tried to calm him down and made him tell me everything. Renton won't have to go – yet – but they must cut down, because the business has to come first. I offered to help. My portion from Mama is untouched: Roo and I are quite able to live as we wish on our incomes.

'You're a Trojan, Beth,' he said and hugged me, 'you always were.' He promised he would tell Con the whole, but will he stick to his promise? He's such a dear, but has he told me all? Only the other day Polly Bigland saw him outside the Ritz in Paris with a woman of a certain class 'simply covered in fox and smelling of cheap scent,' Polly said. Con thought he was shooting with the Ainsleys in Gloucestershire. What can one say at such times? We walked as far as Chelsea Old Church, where he put me in a hansom for home. He would walk to his rooms, he said. So strange, he hasn't bared his soul in that way for years; not since his last half at Harrow when there was all that trouble.

Roo returns tomorrow. I'm glad. Tiresome though she is at times, the flat is empty without her.

Garden Court, Kensington – 10th December 1912
Con to stay for shopping. Such fun! The flat is full of parcels and pretty Christmas paper. Con told me about the money. I'd promised Dick to pretend I knew nothing of it so showed (I hope) surprise when she broached the matter.

'He's such a fool,' she said, 'to take such people seriously just because they were at school at Eton and a member of the MCC! If Father had used such criteria for doing business, we would still be selling clothes pegs in Shropshire.' Dear Con, she does exaggerate, but, of course (as usual), she's right. It was foolish of Dick to take the advice of such a man. They've been forced to cut down at Renton. Con has sold one of her hunters. 'I'm rarely fit to ride now,' she said. No great sacrifice, then, I thought. Dick to give up his rooms in town for the time being; Con wants him under her eye!

'I have been down to the office,' she announced, while we took tea at Gunters – such delicious ices. 'The waste there, you cannot believe.' Poor old Dick, I do feel sorry for him, although he has brought the trouble on himself, silly boy.

We dine out tonight, Con back to Renton tomorrow. Char to come next week to see Mr Boyce. I'm afraid she will have to have a brace for her teeth. Such a shame, poor child. The latest gov has lasted three months – a record! Perhaps it's because she lives out; not so much opportunity for discord!

Renton House   12th May 1913

Dearest Beth,

So nice to get your postcards from Brittany. I am glad you and Roo had such a splendid holiday, with plenty of opportunities for sketching. I am afraid I have been a little seedy lately with these wretched heads – so absurd. Have managed to carry on with my hospital work, but the Lord knows how sometimes. All well here otherwise and all send their love.

Now, Beth dear: Dick and I have a proposal to make. We are wondering whether you would consider having Char to live with you in London during term time and attend one of the Kensington day schools; I have it on good authority that there are several good ones. We feel school would be the best thing for Char now. I cannot approve of her going as a boarder and there are no suitable day schools close to Renton. Miss Izzard, the latest gov, is leaving the area at the end of June to be married. Such a nuisance. One would have thought her past all that sort of nonsense. However, the woman has her life to lead, I suppose, but quite frankly I cannot face the thought of finding a new gov to replace her. Now, dear, say right out if you would rather not. You know I prefer people to speak their minds, but I do know how fond you are of the child and she of you, and Dick and I both feel it would be splendid if you agreed. Char is racing ahead at her lessons, but has not enough to occupy her mind. She has become the leader of the little group of children who do their lessons with her now and encourages them into every kind of mischief: for this reason alone, we feel it would be better for the child to be away from home for a time. Please write me your thoughts on the plan, dear.

Your loving Con

Virginia Budd

Garden Court, Kensington – 15th September 1913
Dear Char arrives tomorrow – so thrilling! I hope all will go
well. The box room looks quite charming and Roo, at the last
minute, has bought such a nice little desk; there's just enough
space for it under the window: as my contribution, I have fitted
it out with pens and pencils.

I'm to take the child to school each morning to start with,
until she feels she can do it herself. Only ten minutes' walk
and one road to cross. Cook has made her a special cake – a
great honour! The train arrives 3.10 at King's Cross; Dick to
meet her and bring her here. Will she be homesick, I wonder?
When I asked her she said: 'Of course not, it's home I'm sick
of.' She doesn't mean that, of course. If nothing else, she will
surely miss the animals.

Garden Court, Kensington – 17th September 1913
Char has settled in *so* well. Not a whiff of homesickness, not
even on her first night.

Dick brought her from the station, but couldn't stay. So
there she stood in the middle of the drawing-room, hat on the
back of her head grinning at me so wickedly!

'We'll have lots of larks, Aunt Beth,' she said, 'now we've
got rid of cross old Ma and Pa.' I was hard put to it not to
giggle, but Roo was a little shocked and looked at me to correct
the child for speaking of her parents in that way. But what to
say? I funked it, of course, and Roo put on her emu face and
rummaged about in her work box: I can always tell when she's
annoyed.

However, all was well. Char thanked her so prettily for the
desk: 'Oh, Cousin Roo, the very best present I've ever had,'
and Roo was all smiles again and even offered to take the
child to the Natural History Museum! Wicked little puss, she

has her father's charm. Only once did I detect a sign of missing Renton. When I kissed her goodnight she asked if I thought that Augustus, her cat, would be alright without her. 'You see,' she said, 'I'm the only person he can talk to, no one else understands him.'

Dick still down in the dumps. Things no better between him and Con. 'She fills the house with poets and anarchists,' he told me. 'Rum people who sit about all day in the drawing room talking nonsense.' Apparently the other evening Con, in front of everyone, ordered him upstairs to bed: he wasn't contributing anything useful to their conversation, she said!

Life so busy now I scarcely have time to write this journal. Four o'clock already. I must put on my hat and coat and fetch Char from school . . .

Garden Court, Kensington – 4th October 1913
Miss Ryder, Char's form mistress, says she is settling in *so* well, such good news. Roo is beginning to dote on her, as I do, and indeed is halfway to spoiling the child!

Milly Fenton-Wright tells me people are beginning to talk – Con and some young man called Hubert Stokes, who writes avant garde plays. He has apparently stayed alone at Renton with her and is telling people they are going to Paris together! To cap that, Dick was seen at Cheltenham Races with Bunny Burgoyne's wife!

Where, I wonder, will it all end?

Char to tea on Sunday with a little school friend, Polly Everett. Such nice people. He's something in the City and she's a friend of Barbara Dundas and does such charming watercolours.

Garden Court, Kensington – 18th December 1913
Char to Renton tomorrow, how sad and how we shall miss her. No Renton for me this Christmas: Con (apparently) too seedy to entertain or so she says. Roo and I go North to her people instead.

Char made such an enchanting little fairy in the school Christmas play. She had one line to speak and did a little dance as well. Roo says she thinks the dance must have been extempore and not in her part. She says she heard someone whispering from the wings, 'Osborn, come off at once!' Never mind, the audience was charmed, especially the papas!

Nearly 1914 – how old I am getting. I wonder what the New Year will bring for us all . . . ?

This is the secret diary of Charlotte Mary Osborn. Anyone who reads it without asking her first will have a curse laid on them and they will surely die.

Renton House, Beds – 2nd January 1914
No hunting because of frost. Horrible boiled eggs for breakfast and liver for lunch. Helped Smith in the potting shed. Went with Ma and Uncle Hubert to a concert in the village. Sat on Uncle Hubert's knee and he laughed when a fat lady sang a song about fairies. I love Uncle H. He is not like a grown-up. He calls me his mermaid because I have green eyes.

Renton House, Beds – 3rd January 1914
I will write this diary every day. Uncle H went away today. We saw him off at the station. Ma was cross. A smut went in her eye and Uncle H got it out. He gave me a lovely little lucky charm on a ring all the way from Egypt. I had fun in the bath tonite.

Renton House, Beds – 6th January 1914
Nothing happened today.

Renton House, Beds – 10th January 1914
Pa came home today. He was cross because I had been in Warrior's stable. He says it is dangerous as Warrior kicks and anyway he told me not to. Warrior is *not* dangerous. He is lovely and would never kick me. The new groom who is called Gilles said I must not do it again or he will get into trouble. Gilles is ever so nice. He showed me his cigarette cards. He has some good ones.

We saw the soldiers marching through the village again today. All the village children were shouting and waving flags. A soldier winked at me as he marched by. Ma is ill. She read Bevis to me at rest. It is a luvly book.

Renton House, Beds – 12th January 1914
Gilles showed me how to clean the tack. He says spit is best. He says he was going to be a jockey but he did not smoke enuff so he grew too tall for one. He says he likes Renton and Pa is a good master. He says he gets a good wage, much better than where he was. He says he will save up his money so one day he can buy a farm and breed horses. I do like Gilles.

Ma is still in bed. Two more days and I will be back at horrid old school. Ma says I am to travel to London on the train by myself but I will be in charge of the gard. Uncle H is meeting me. Hooray.

Garden Court, Kensington – 14th January 1914
I am writing this diary in my bed at Garden Court. Gilles gave me a set of cigarette cards when I said goodbye to him this morning. They are splendid ones. I shall keep them always.

He squeezed my hand and said I was an A1 kid. Ma says I spend too much time in the stables talking to Gilles. I don't care. He is much nicer than all the silly stuffy people she makes me meet. It was fun on the train. The gard gave me a bag of sweets and showed me his little office in the gardsvan. There was a lovely little puppy in a box in the van and I gave it one of my sweets. Uncle H met me at King's Cross. He let me ride on top of a horse bus instead of going in a boring old cab and we sent my trunk on to Aunt Beth by carrier. It was a lovely ride and we sang songs all the way to Kensington. Aunt Beth thought we had got lost and where was my trunk. Uncle H said, 'Oh pooh, don't fuss woman.' Aunt Beth went red.

Garden Court, Kensington – 15th January 1914
Today I went for a bicycle ride with Uncle H in Battersea Park. When we got home Aunt Beth was cross. She said Uncle H should have asked her first. Uncle H got cross too and went red. He said, just because I write plays you don't approve of does not mean I kidnap little girls. I did not hear any more cos I was sent out of the room. Uncle H is so funny. He rode his bicycle with no hands and nearly fell off into some horse mush. An old lady sitting on a seat shouted, 'Mind how you go, young man, or we'll all be in the soup.'

Horrid old school in the morning. I hope . . .

Garden Court, Kensington – 16th January 1914
Two new girls in our form. Aunt Beth says I can walk to school by myself this term. Polly and her brother, who is called Tom, are coming to tea on Sunday. Mr Flinders was sick on the drawing-room carpet. Cook says it is cos the people next door give him rubbish to eat. She says it is a shocking waist: they throw out joints of meat and cream buns even.

Garden Court, Kensington – 18th January 1914
Uncle H has sent me such a funny postcard from Paris. It says
'Oh la la!' and it is of a big fat lady undressing. Cousin Roo
said it was not funny at all and Uncle H was an irresponsible
young man. Aunt Beth did not say anything, just looked. I
sent a letter to Gilles today and thanked him for the lovely
cigarette cards. When I asked Aunt Beth for a stamp she said
who was I writing to. I said it was to a very rich young man
who is staying with Ma for the hunting. Ha ha.

Garden Court, Kensington – 19th January 1914
I lost my collection money in church this morning. It rolled
right down the pew. When I crawled under to try and get it
back the lady behind banged me on my head with her prayer
book. I stuck out my tongue. I think it was her who stole my
money.

   Polly and Tom came to tea. Cook made flapjacks. We
played pelmanism. I won three times. Tom is a sissy and a cry
baby. He was afraid of Mr Flinders cos he jumped up at him.
He says dogs are smelly and spread disease. Polly and I hid
his cap and he blubbed. Aunt Beth said we are naughty and
unkind but I should not be a stupid cry baby if someone stole
my hat. I like Polly. She is my very best friend.

Garden Court, Kensington – 22nd January 1914
Went skating at Queens with Polly and her big brother. He is
called Edward and is on leave from his regiment. His regiment
is the Irish Guards. Uncle H, Gilles and Edward are my three
favourite men. Edward put his arm round me and guided me
round the ice rink. The band played 'Alexander's Ragtime
Band'. It was such fun. Polly fell down on the ice six times.

Garden Court, Kensington – 23rd January 1914
Nothing happened today.

No more from Char. She obviously lost interest in the diary. Some interesting stuff from Gilles, though, and a few more pages from Aunt Beth before 1914 runs out.

Renton House, Renton, Beds   24th January 1914

Dear Miss Char,

I am in receipt of yours of 18th Jan. Am glad you like the cards, they are a good set, I think. All well here, Miss Char. Old Warrior is missing his sugar lumps. The Guvnor came off him on Sat. jumping that gate out of Bagland Wood. No harm done but he let fly with some choice language I can tell you! No time for more now Miss Char. Hope this finds you as it leaves me, in the pink.

Yrs rspctfly
P. E. Gilles

Garden Court, Kensington – 6th March 1914
Hubert Stokes called today and took Char out for the afternoon; to a museum, he said. How could I say no? I cannot approve of the young man: he's clever, one has to admit, but has such modern views. Dick says he's a 'damned Socialist'. He's a gentleman, of course: his father, Colonel Stokes, fought at Omdurman and the boy went to Rugby. But why, oh why, does he have to interest himself in Char? The child is so impressionable and, of course, adores him. Isn't it enough, the trouble he's causing between Con and Dick?

I told him firmly they must be home by six o'clock: by

78

seven o'clock, I ready to ring the police and Roo in tears, in they burst as cool as you please. 'We've had such a ripping time, Aunt Beth. Uncle Hubert's taken me to Whitechapel to see how the poor people live, and we went to such a lovely market. Look what we've bought for you.' Out of her pocket the child produces a tiny, white kitten! We have called him 'Bow Bells'. Half starved, of course, and riddled with fleas. Mr Flinders is not pleased. He registered his protest this morning by lifting a leg against Roo's piano!

Tried to remonstrate with Hubert about taking Char to such places. 'Think of the risk of disease,' I said.

'She should know how some people have to live,' he said. 'It ought to be part of every pampered brat's education.' I cannot argue with him, I'm simply not clever enough. But if he is so sure he is right, why did he lie to me and say they were going to a museum? Oh, how I wish he would go away somewhere, he disrupts us all.

Garden Court, Kensington – 15th March 1914
Char has been corresponding with the groom at Renton! The child is so precocious, it's hard to know what to do for the best. When I taxed her on the subject, she merely said: 'Gilles is a great friend of mine, he sends me cigarette cards.' I know I should put an end to it – writing to servants in that way can only lead to trouble – but how? The exchanging of cigarette cards is, after all, a harmless pastime and Dick speaks well of the young man. Should I tell Con?

Bow, the kitten, is quite killing now. I found him (or her) asleep in Roo's best hat! A bunch of the reddest, biggest (rather vulgar) roses from Hubert. 'To dear, long-suffering Aunt Beth. Your devoted admirer – Hubert Stokes.'

What to think? Dick to dine tomorrow. I mustn't tell him

who sent the roses, or the feathers will certainly fly! Char tells me when she grows up she is going to help 'the poor people'. *Nous verrons.*

Renton House, Renton, Beds   6th June 1914

Dear Miss Char

    Am in receipt of yours of the 1st. All well here I am glad to report. We've a new stable lad. He's a lazy young devil, if you'll pardon my language, and not half as good at cleaning tack as you, Miss Char.

    Fancy playing tennis at school! All we learned in our playground was how to punch each other's heads in (ha ha). Yes, I expect it's hot in dirty old London this weather. You should get those school teachers of yours to take you out for a day at the seaside. We had Renton village Cricket Match last Sat. Phew, it was hot! Yours truly made forty runs before your Guvnor caught him out! Mr Mills at the Feathers says there's going to be a war. Think I'll enlist – might see a bit more of the world that way. Mr Mills says they'll need trained horsemen.

    Must dash now Miss Char. All the best.

Yrs resptfly – P. E. Gilles

Garden Court, Kensington – 24th June 1914
Dear Char's twelfth birthday yesterday. How fast she grows. She's started her periods – so difficult to explain.

    Phyllis Pratt is staying: Con's niece and daughter of Don. Such a jolly girl and so good with Char. We had a picnic in Richmond Park for the birthday tea – strawberries and cream and flies in the sandwiches and oh, so hot. But we were a merry party for all that, and the birthday girl enjoyed herself. Young Edward Everett, Polly's elder brother, came with Polly and Tom. He and Phyllis were so good organising games for the little ones. Such a nice boy. He's in the Irish Guards stationed at Wellington Barracks. I asked him what about all this war talk: he says no, but he wishes there would be! Char said suddenly: 'Uncle Hubert says war is wrong and is only waged for capitalist arms dealers to get fat on the profits.' That child! Edward looked quite stunned, indeed we all did, then dear, sensible Phyllis burst out laughing and all was well. Of course, the child has no idea what she is talking about; just copies everything her adored Uncle Hubert says like a parrot.

Dick to France for a short bicycling holiday. He needs one, poor old boy. He's looked quite wretched of late.

Renton House, Renton, Beds   1st July 1914

Dear Miss Char,

Yours arrived by yesterday's second post. Sounds as though you and your pal have been having a high old time – right pair of gadabouts you are!

All well down here. No rain – old Smith's proper worried over his Veg, says he's never seen the well so empty. They are rationing water down in the village, the brook's dried up, and yours truly can only take a bath once a week!

Managed to get the motor up to 30 m.p.h. (miles per hour to the green'uns!) yesterday. Your Ma wasn't half pleased. 'Gilles,' she says, 'we'll have you racing her yet.' Engine boiled again, though, going up Leather Bottle Hill. Mr Mills at the Feathers is telling everyone he were right about war coming. He says that old Arch Duke whatsisname being bumped off will be the start of it. I'm blessed if I see how. We need that Mr Stokes to come back from Germany and put us right.

Tata for now Miss Char, you'll be home now in two shakes.

Yrs rspectfly

P. E. Gilles

Garden Court, Kensington – 6th July 1914

How stifling it is. I long to get away from smoky old London. Only another fortnight and Char will be off home for the holidays and Roo and I depart for Lucerne, what a splendid thought.

I do believe dear Phyllis and young Edward Everett have 'clicked'. Such a vulgar way of describing falling in love, but so expressive. Before she left us she asked the young man to stay at her people's for some tennis. He showed every sign of delight – such a suitable match. Char a little put out, I thought. 'He's *my* friend, not Phyll's,' she said at tea. A short respite from Hubert S, such a relief! He, it seems, has gone to Hamburg to supervise rehearsals of one of his extraordinary plays. If I can't understand a word of them, I'm sure the Germans won't. Con writes he's a genius, but born before his time. I'm sure she's right (she always is), but I, for one, heartily wish he'd been born in his right time, whenever that may be. Char corresponds with him, what about one dares not think. She also writes regularly to that wretched groom – such a contrast one would have thought. The groom, she tells me with pride, is learning to drive the motor Dick and Con have bought – such an extravagance. Especially as one hears the wretched, smelly machine is continually breaking down. Dick says they spend more time underneath it than in it!

Must try to sleep. So difficult, there's no air.

* * *

And after that, maddeningly, Aunt Beth's diary simply peters out, apart from a scrawled entry in October on the subject of Belgian refugees. There are no more letters either from P. E. Gilles. The year 1914 draws to its close without further comment. I looked at my watch. Christ! It was nearly two a.m.; I'd got a finance meeting at nine thirty. Sophia had left around eleven p.m. 'It's such miles from you to Hampstead, Guy, and I want to be at the office by eight thirty. Promise you won't read any more till we meet again on Thursday.' I'd promised, but after she'd gone I couldn't sleep, so made myself a hot drink and went on reading. In a way I preferred to do it on my own. Somehow I was beginning to feel the contents of the green trunk were a sort of private message from Char to me: as though she were trying in some way to explain something about herself. Perhaps this was fanciful, I don't know, but it was what I believed. Under these circumstances anyone, even Sophia, would inevitably constitute an intrusion.

Next day Sophia rang postponing our date. A business dinner she couldn't get out of and after that she was away for a week. 'You'll have to carry on without me,' she said, 'but somehow I don't think you'll mind.'

I felt guilty then; a woman as perceptive as Sophia can be rather unnerving. 'Don't be silly,' I said, feeling my voice lacked conviction, 'but when you come back, can we go and see your Aunty Phyll? You said she's on the ball and she might be able to fill in some gaps.'

'Good thinking,' she said. 'I owe her a visit and she'd love to see a man for a change. I'll be in touch, then. And Guy . . .'

'Yes?'

'Take care . . .'

6

P. E. Gilles did turn up again; in quite another context: he had to, I suppose, he was one of those sorts of people.

The incident occurred a month or so after Sophia's and my visit to Aunty Phyll when we were staying with, of all people, George and his new wife, Bronwen. We had both been asked independently of each other and both, with a string of flimsy excuses, managed to postpone a visit which neither of us wished to make. Then George began to get miffed; to fob him off again might create a complete rift and I didn't wish for this, not yet at any rate. Sophia, even more loth to go than I was, suggested we brave it together and this proving acceptable to George, we did.

It was on the Saturday afternoon, rain cascading against the sitting-room windows, George sleeping the sleep of the just and overfed before his enormous television set and Bronwen doing something in the kitchen – she was always 'doing something' in the kitchen – that for want of anything better to do I picked up the local rag and glanced idly through it. I turned a page and a name jumped out at me. 'Mons Veteran's ninety-third Birthday. Mr Peter Edgar Gilles celebrates his birthday with his usual pint of bitter in the bar of the Crown and Anchor public house.' The accompanying photograph showed a small, gnome-like individual, pint mug in hand, smiling toothily into the camera, backed by a sea of smiling faces. 'Mr Gilles, a twinkling nonagenarian, seen here with his great-grandson Kevin and friends, says . . .'

'Sophia,' I whispered, 'Sophia, look.'

She looked. 'It couldn't be,' she said, 'could it?'

'The right age,' I said. 'And it says he ran a garage until he retired in 1960. P. E. Gilles was into cars.'

'Let's ring,' said Sophia. 'It gives his address.' George snored gustily as we crept away to the telephone. Somehow neither of us wished to involve him; Char's name had not been mentioned over the weekend.

'Pop in for a cup of tea tomorrow then. Grandad loves a bit of company,' said P. E. Gilles' granddaughter.

A smart bungalow, two cars in the garage, a boat on the lawn and a general air of prosperity. A stout, blonde lady in pink trousers opened the front door. 'Grandad's in the lounge,' she said. 'I'll get a cup of tea.' P. E. Gilles was seated in a smart, tweed-covered armchair, hands on knees, hair carefully brushed. A flight of china ducks pursued one another across the bamboo-patterned wallpaper behind his head; by his side a small table, on which was placed a cardboard box.

He grinned jauntily at us and waved a yellowing sheet of paper. 'This what you come to see, then?' It was an extremely bad drawing of a large, black horse; underneath in writing unmistakably that of the twelve-year-old Char, was the caption, 'Warrior, July 1914'.

'Mr Gilles, this is such a surprise.' Sophia sounded quite breathless with excitement. 'I, that is Mr Horton and I, thought you were killed in the First World War, you see—'

'Damn near was, my dear, several times over.' Mr Gilles' small frame shook with laughter. 'Lucky for me I copped a blighty one in '17 and was invalided out of the Army. No more fighting for me – spent the next lot in the Home Guard.'

'Now, don't get excited Grandad, or we'll have you up all night.' The blonde lady was back carrying a neatly laid tea tray. P. E. Gilles ignored her and patted a chair.

'Come and sit down here, Ma'am,' he said to Sophia. 'You're Miss Char's daughter or I'm much mistaken. You've got her look.'

Sophia obeyed. 'My mother died last year,' she said. 'We found your letters, you see.'

'I'm sorry to hear that,' he said. 'She was a fine one, your Ma. Never met anyone quite like her, even though she were only a nipper at the time I knew her.'

We talked for over an hour, the blonde lady appearing at intervals to replenish the tea pot. The old man's memory was remarkable. Reticent at first about the domestic dramas that appeared to have taken place during his time in service with the Osborns at Renton, he soon warmed to his subject.

'My Uncle George, he got me the job there as groom,' he told us. 'And I was that pleased to get it. Six hunters they had in the stables in those days, besides the pony for Miss Char. Then Mr Osborn, that would be your grandpa, Ma'am; he were still a young man then and what an eye for the girls – Oh my! Anyway, your grandpa came home early one day when Mrs O – your grandma – were in the stable with me looking at Warrior's near fore. It were a bit swollen like and your grandma were better than any veterinary. "Con," says Mr O putting his head round the door – he always called Mrs O Con. "I've bought a motor; had it made specially. Now what d'you think of that?" '

Sophia choked over her biscuit. Mr Gilles was obviously a first-rate mimic as well as everything else.

' "I think it's a damned stupid thing to have done," says Mrs O. "And whoever made it can take it back. We can't afford a motor, we don't want a motor, and if we had one, you'd be incapable of driving it. You know what you're like with anything mechanical."

' "But Gilles here," he says all crestfallen. "He can learn to drive it. You'd like that, Gilles, wouldn't you?"

' "Yes Sir," I said prompt and meant it.

' "Gilles has quite enough to do as it is and who, may one ask, is going to pay for it?"

' "*Pas devant les domestiques*," he says in French. The gentry used to talk like that in those days; they thought we wouldn't understand, but of course we did. I'd kept company at my last place with a Frog lady's maid and she taught me quite a lot of the lingo – helped me later in France, I can tell you. After that they went for each other hammer and tongs. I just busied myself with the horse, but they were like that, those two. Mr O won though: we had the motor. I learned to drive it down at the garage in the village – it were the first garage they ever had in those parts. Two of the hunters had to go and when the War came, Mr O gave two more to the army.'

'Do you remember someone called Hubert Stokes?' I asked.

'Bless me, I remember Mr Stokes alright, poor devil. He was always there; he and Mrs O they were, well they—'

'Were lovers,' Sophia prompted gently.

Mr Gilles shook once again with laughter. 'I don't know about lovers, Ma'am, but I well remember coming back one night; quite late it was. I'd had a few, I don't mind telling you, but not enough not to know what's what. Well, I took a short cut across the rose garden to the stables, where I had my room. Usually I'd never walk past the front of the house, I'd have lost my place if I'd have been seen, but it was late and I was a bit "how's your father". Well, I was halfway across the garden and suddenly, there they were.' He paused dramatically.

'Naked as the day they were born – Mrs O and Mr Stokes, playing leapfrog round the sundial! I just took to me heels and ran and lucky for me they were too busy to see me. The gentry didn't half get up to some larks in those days, you'd never believe. Talk about permissive society – my eye!

'He were a good bloke, Mr Stokes, all the same, though I don't hold with canoodling with someone else's missus, never have. Many's the time he'd climb the ladder to my room for a chat. "Gilles," he'd say, "I've come to hear some sense talked. Get the glasses, will you?" And he'd bring out a bottle of brandy and light up his old pipe and there we'd sit jawing away till gone midnight sometimes. He was all for the working man and a lot of what he said made sense to me then and still does now. It was him that put me on the right road.' He paused again.

'How was that?' I asked softly. I didn't want to break his train of thought. 'Well, he made me understand there was more to life than just being a servant, I suppose. And when I came out of the Army in 1918 I told myself I'd never be one again, no matter what, and I never was. Got a job in a garage, learned the trade, and in 1925, when the missus and I were married, I'd saved enough to buy a garage and have my own business. Had plenty of ups and downs mind you, but I never regretted it. Then in 1960 I sold out for a tidy sum and the missus never wanted for anything till the end of her days.' He was silent again, his blue eyes staring into space, then: 'Ay, it were your Ma, Ma'am and Mr Stokes, they started me on the right road . . .'

'My mother, Mr Gilles?'

P. E. Gilles' gaze focused on a rather vivid view of a Cornish fishing village hanging on the wall opposite, as though seeking inspiration. 'It were different then, you see. My dad had been a strapper in Lord Hanton's stables; my mum were in service and it were the natural thing like for me to go into service myself. I wanted to better myself, of course, but it were always them and us. You'd never speak to gentry – never think of it – they spoke to you; told you what to do. They might ask you how you were getting on, or how your family were, that kind of thing, but you'd never *talk* to them.

'Then along comes Miss Char, and she don't seem to understand all that. I remember as though it were yesterday, when I first saw her. I'd only been at the job a week or so. I was in my harness room, cleaning tack like and this head comes round the door. "Can you help me with Rags, Mr Gilles, he's got a thorn in his foot and he won't let me get it out." In she comes, carrying the dog in her arms. Tiny little thing she were, freckles all over her nose, mud on her cheek and a red knitted beret on her head. Well, I managed to get the thorn out and somehow we got chatting.'

He stopped, trying to put into words how he had felt. 'It was like talking to one of my own,' he said simply. 'No side, just interested in everything I had to say. After that, she'd come most days when she were at home. It was Miss Char who brought Mr Stokes round – introduced us all proper like. Of course, her Pa didn't like it. "Gilles," he'd say, "don't let that imp of mine waste your time."

' "Very good Sir," I'd say, but it wouldn't make no difference, she'd still come round. Cor, I'll never forget the day she told her Pa he didn't pay me high enough wages. Oh Lor!

' "Uncle Hubert says every man in England should earn enough to live in dignity," she says, bold as brass. She were standing on the mounting block in the stable yard. Her Pa were up on that big chestnut gelding he had then. I thought he were going to hit her. He were a kind man, but he'd got a temper alright.'

'Did he?' Sophia asked. 'Hit her, I mean.'

'No, he just kicked his heels vicious like into the horse and galloped out of the yard. Then they sent her away to London to school. She were too much of a handful, I reckon. She used to write to me, you know.'

'That's how we knew about you,' I said. 'You see, she kept your letters.'

'She never! She never did – all those years – just fancy keeping them all those years.' Suddenly P. E. Gilles looked his age; he lapsed into muttering, one hand stroking the drawing of Warrior. It was as though he were caressing it.

'Time for your pills, Grandad.' The blonde lady had returned; our time was up. 'He gets tired, you see,' she said.

'Don't fuss,' said P. E. Gilles, pulling himself together with a visible effort. 'I'll see a hundred, and it ain't every day I meet Miss Char's daughter.'

Sophia rose to her feet. 'We'll come again,' she said, 'if we may. Your granddaughter's quite right, we mustn't tire you.' The blonde lady saw us out: I had the impression she did not wholly approve of her grandfather's reminiscences of his days in service.

'Oh, wasn't he lovely?' Sophia said as we climbed back into the car. 'No wonder Mum liked him; we must see him again.'

But it was not to be. Only a few weeks after our visit a letter arrived from his granddaughter to say she thought we'd like to know that P. E. Gilles had died peacefully in his sleep. He had backed the winner of the Ascot Gold Cup the day before, and it was thought the excitement had proved too much for him.

7

'Guy? How quiet you've been.' Sophia's voice on the phone, ringing to say she'd arranged the visit to Aunty Phyll. 'You're not sulking, are you?'

'Of course not,' I said, feeling unreasonably irritated. 'I've been busy, that's all. Anyway, I thought you said you'd ring me. I'm sorry if I misunderstood you.'

'Ach!' A distinctly odd noise came down the wire. 'Don't be so pompous. Next Sunday four o'clock, Aunty Phyll said. We could meet for a pub lunch and then go on from there – OK?'

Aunty Phyll, once 'jolly Phyllis Pratt' and daughter of Con Osborn's brother, Don, lived in a house just off Kensington Church Street. 'She's been there for about fifty years,' Sophia said, lighting yet another cigarette. 'Uncle Ronnie, that was her husband, bought the freehold for a song and now I suppose it's worth a fortune.' It was Sunday and we were seated on top of a Number 9 bus on our way to Kensington.

'Her husband's name wasn't Edward, then?'

'No, why?'

'It doesn't matter,' I said, feeling superior. Already I knew more about her family than she did: about Hubert and Gilles, and Edward in the Irish Guards; about that fly-ridden birthday party in Richmond Park when Phyllis Pratt and Edward Everett organised games for the little ones. I looked down at the thronged pavements of Kensington High Street; the garish boutiques, the video shops, the nose-to-tail traffic and general air of tawdriness and thought of the twelve-year-old Char. These streets would have been her playground. The bus stopped at the lights at the bottom of Kensington Church Street: a girl, no more than twelve, wearing jeans and a blue anorak, crossed the road in front of it, pulled by a large, black, hairy dog on a red lead. The wind blew her bright, brown hair in a halo round her head. She was smiling; alight with life. Char would have looked like that, I thought, seventy years ago.

'Come in, dears. Isn't this jolly?' Aunty Phyllis, a small, wizened figure, shoulders hunched with age, wearing purple trousers and an orange knitted jacket, greeted us at the door of the rather run-down looking little house in Peel Street. We trailed behind her up the steep, narrow staircase to a small, cramped sitting room on the first floor. Reggae music wafted down from above; there was a smell of curry on the air. Aunty Phyll pointed a shaky finger skywards. 'My lodgers,' she whispered. 'Such a charming couple.'

Later, sunk in the massive depths of a sea-green sofa that had seen better days, a Crown Derby cup and saucer balanced precariously on my knee, I tried to explain to my hostess my reason for wanting to meet her. She looked at me quizzically, her eyes behind the thick spectacles, shrewd and rather mocking. 'Another of those researchers, are you, young man? Once one gets beyond eighty-five nowadays, one's anybody's property,' and she gave a macaw-like shriek of laughter.

'Mum made Guy her literary executor, Aunty Phyll,' Sophia came to my rescue. 'She left all these papers, you see. He thought you might remember some of the people mentioned: Aunty Beth, Cousin Roo and there's a playwright called Hubert Stokes.'

'I remember them all, dear, and especially Hubert; we all adored him, you know, including your grandmother, who was head over heels in love with him.'

'And Char?' I asked.

'Char simply worshipped him. She was a funny little thing in those days – so intense. I remember when I was staying at Beth's during the summer of '14 – Char lived with Beth, d'you see, during term time. Aunt Con was too busy setting the world to rights and canoodling with Hubert Stokes to have much time for her daughter. Where was I? Oh yes, Char said to me: "If I can't marry Uncle Hubert, I shan't marry anyone, ever." '

'It's odd,' said Sophia, her mouth full of chocolate cake, 'that I've never heard about Hubert Stokes before. What happened to him, Aunty Phyll; he's not still alive is he? Mum never—'

'Killed,' said Aunty Phyll laconically. 'They all were, don't you know, all our chums. The only reason they didn't get my old Ronnie was because he had such rotten eyesight. But Hubert didn't die in battle, he was a conchie. Just as brave as the other boys, I always thought. At·least they died together; if you were a conchie you were on your own. They were treated quite dreadfully, you know, in our War. Hubert refused to help in any way. He was what they called an "Absolutist", and of course he was sent to prison. He died of pneumonia in Wormwood Scrubs in the autumn of '16, I think it was.'

We were all of us silent for a moment. Then: 'There's an Edward Everett mentioned,' I said. 'I wondered if—'

'You have done your homework, young man.' The old lady looked at me coldly. I felt suddenly ashamed. 'And what, may I ask, do you know about him?'

'Only,' I said hastily, 'that he was the elder brother of Char's best friend at school, Polly Everett.'

'We were engaged: Polly and Char were to be bridesmaids – a grand affair at Holy Trinity, Brompton, with a reception at the Hyde Park Hotel. My wedding dress was so pretty; seed pearls round the neck and waist and my veil was Honiton lace.' Aunty Phyll lit a cigarette, her hands, mottled with the brown marks of the aged, trembling a little as she struck the match. The reggae music from upstairs had changed to rock. It was almost dark outside. 'Such a waste – Edward never made it d'you see. He was killed the day before he began his leave. Little Char was so disappointed.' The house shook as a train rumbled underneath; I placed my cup and saucer carefully on the table.

Suddenly Aunty Phyll leaned forward and took my hand. 'Don't be silly, dear. I don't mind any more. In time, you know, everything passes.' She shook herself. 'Now, Sophia dear, if you look in that drawer, you should find the snaps. They're in a big, red album; some of them are really rather killing and it might interest Mr Horton to have a look at them.'

And there they all were; much as I had imagined, strangely enough. Beth and Roo laughing under a window, clutching Mr Flinders. Hubert Stokes, boater tipped over his eyes, cigarette between his lips, looking darkly decadent. Phyll, herself, looking jolly, tennis racket at the ready. And Char, little Char, squinting into the camera, hair held back by a ribbon, the eyes as I had so often seen them, slanting with wickedness. Another one of Mr Flinders, this time on his own, all lolling tongue and whiskers. Cats, dogs, people, smiling away like mad, from punts, from the backs of horses, at the seat of monolithic cars – another time, another world – 'Golden lads and girls all must . . .'

'Come on Guy, that's enough now.' Sophia was tugging at my sleeve. 'Aunty Phyll's tired. Mrs Mills will be here any moment to see her to bed. We must go.'

I jumped up guiltily. 'I'm so sorry, how thoughtless of me.'

Aunty Phyll smiled vaguely, only half with us. 'So nice of you both to come,' she said. On an impulse I bent down and kissed her; the skin of her cheek felt like last year's leaves.

We were out in the street in the gathering darkness. 'Each time I see Aunty Phyll,' said Sophia taking my arm, 'I wonder if it will be the last.' There was no answer to this, so we walked in silence down the hill, the lights of Kensington High Street ahead of us.

That night we slept together for the first time. I woke early, Sophia curled up like a puppy beside me, wondering whether someone some day would try to piece together our past. On balance, I thought not, and began to worry about what Sophia had for breakfast.

A letter or two, a tobacco tin containing some regimental buttons and a postcard on the back of which was scrawled: 'All the best from Reckless Reg – Italy 1918,' was all the evidence the green trunk could offer for Char's War. No mementoes of poor Hubert Stokes, no cheery cards from P. E. Gilles, not even a newspaper cutting or a casualty list. Had Char, like so many of her generation, only wanted to forget those years when so many 'chums' had fallen and so much that had seem so safe, had changed irrevocably – I don't know.

Certainly, those four years of War must, by any standards, have had a profound effect on Char. The ages between twelve and sixteen are pretty formative years, but in her case would surely have been cataclysmic, for not only did her parents' marriage break up, but her adored 'Uncle H' was sent to prison for his beliefs, and subsequently died there. In so doing, and thereby showing her the brutal reality of how society dealt with all those high-flown ideals he had propounded to her so spell-bindingly as they rode their bicycles in Battersea Park in the heady days before the War, had he fallen from grace in her eyes? Or was his death to her just a re-enactment of that other death, the death of the vagrant poet, Henry Arthur Elliott on that summer afternoon on Bagland Common, years before? Again, I don't know, but the fact that no letters from Hubert Stokes exist out of what by all accounts seems to have been a voluminous correspondence, and even Sophia, with her total recall, claims never to have heard his name mentioned by her mother, seems to point to the former. It's strange that I who loved her never learned from her of those years, or of the desolation she must surely have felt at Hubert's death and the disruption and fragmentation of her own family.

'Were the two connected?' I asked Aunty Phyll, as we sat together in her over-crowded sitting-room. Outside the window an almond tree bloomed, its soft, pink flowers and brown branches making a lace pattern against the grey, windy sky. Above the noise of distant traffic, a blackbird sang. The house, for once was silent; the lodgers, it seemed, had gone to Lanzarote in search of sun.

Aunty Phyll sipped her cocktail then placed it carefully down on the little mat with a picture of the Leaning Tower of Pisa on it; mine had one of the Colosseum.

'You mean Hubert Stokes' death and Dick leaving Con? Perhaps. Of course, things had gone from bad to worse ever since the baby died of pneumonia in 1911. But certainly, Con made the most frightful hoo-hah over Hubert's death: didn't seem to care who knew what they'd been to each other; even went into a sort of purdah, d'you see. Well, by that time poor old Dick had had enough. He sent a wire: "Gone to Paris with Edna – do your damnedest," and Con did: to everyone's surprise she divorced him. I didn't see much of either of them at that time, I was out in France nursing. When I came home for good in Christmas '18, the whole thing was more or less a fait accompli. Con had Char in that frightful little villa in Surrey and Dick had a flat in Chelsea.'

I said I found it strange that although Char and I were close, she had never talked of these things with me. Her attitude towards her parents had always been that they were rather a bad joke. We'd often spoken of the First World War, but always its military aspect; she never mentioned she'd lost anyone close.

Aunty Phyll surprised me then. 'She was a hard woman, you know. Guts and brains when she chose to use 'em and could charm the men – as you well know, young man – but there was a callous streak in her. You came up against it quite unexpectedly, and when you did, it was rather like stubbing your toe on a block of ice when swimming in the Mediterranean. Give me another drink, dear, I know it's naughty, but I feel naughty tonight.'

I filled her glass in silence, waiting for her to continue.

'I don't know if you knew,' she said, 'that Char and I fell out in later years.' I didn't, and said so. 'We used to be such chums between the wars. Although I was six years older, my Adam was the same age as her Ann, and we spent several jolly summer holidays together when she was married to Algy. We used to take a large house on the Norfolk coast and let the kids run wild. But later – I don't know – she changed, or I changed, and I never could take George. He was good looking enough in his way as a young man, I suppose, but after Algy . . .'

'He's married again already – George.'

'I heard,' she said, and we left it at that.

'This callousness you mention,' I said. 'I never encountered it in her myself, but others have, I know. Do you think it may have developed in those years when she was growing up?'

'You're a romantic, Guy Horton. Life isn't as simple as that. Char was born callous, as a cat's born to catch mice. What happened during the Great War must have affected her, I suppose. No one who lived through it was the same afterwards, but I dread to think what she'd have been like with doting parents and a happy home. She'd have walked all over the parents and the happy home would have bored her to death.'

'What about Hubert Stokes?' I asked.

'Oh, there were always Huberts: those "heroes" of hers. "The thin bright faces" as she used to call them. She turned them into cardboard cut-out figures, no use to man nor beast.'

'I still think it's significant she kept so much evidence of her past, but nothing for those years,' I said, sticking to my guns.

'Come off it, dear,' she said. 'She probably lost the stuff, that's all.'

'I must be going,' I said huffily, rising to my feet.

'Don't sulk, dear,' she said, raising her face for a kiss. I bent down and she patted my arm. 'Silly boy to fall in love with a ghost.'

'It's not that,' I said and could hear my own voice rising in anger. 'It's not that at all. I just feel she had a raw deal out of life and no one seemed to care.' There was no answer; Aunty Phyll had fallen asleep.

8

The Vicarage, Durzebridge, Devon – 10th January 1918
I have decided to write my diary every day for an hour before
tea. I must not shirk this small duty and I must not waste time
merely cataloguing a series of routine trivia. I shall simply try
and put down my thoughts on all aspects of life as clearly and
concisely as I can. It will be difficult, surrounded as I am by
such IDIOTS, but I shall try. (Peewhit has just knocked over my
bottle of ink – see what I am up against).

Char had grown up a bit since the birthday picnic in Richmond
Park in the summer of 1914. Young Edward Everett and Hubert
Stokes were both dead, along with the greater part of their
generation: only a few more months to go and the War would
be over.

 'I suppose, when one comes to think of it, my own education
was rather unusual,' I remember Char herself telling me. We
were having one of our perennial arguments about public
school, and I had said her insistence on their paramount
importance for boys was absurd and what's more made a
nonsense of her Socialist views. 'Don't be a bore, darling' –
invariably her reaction when cornered in an argument 'Now,
do you want to hear about my education or not?'

 'Roedean?' I said. 'I'm sure you were the "terror of the
Fourth" and finished up as Head Girl.'

Char snorted. 'Not at all,' she said rather smugly. 'I went to a crammer's on Dartmoor.'

'Really? I thought dim young men wanting to go up to university or get into the Indian Civil Service went to crammers, not girls.'

'Ma knew the man who ran it, you see. So when the zeppelin raids on London got bad, she panicked, as usual; took me away from my lovely school and sent me to "Old Bats".'

'From what you've told me about your mother, it sounds as though she were running true to form.'

Char extracted a lipstick from her handbag and, squinting into a tiny, cracked mirror, proceeded to paint her mouth a deep scarlet. 'There was me,' she said, 'aged fifteen, Old Bats and half a dozen seventeen-year-old boys.' She smiled into the mirror while I digested this. 'But to give Ma her due, Old Bats was a superb teacher and I learned a great deal there.' She paused again. 'Not all of it academic.'

Sophia and Aunty Phyllis between them had been able to fill in most of the gaps. Char had stayed on at Garden Court and continued at St Winifred's, where apparently she did extremely well, until 1917. Then with the zeppelin raids becoming more and more frequent it was decided London was too dangerous and that autumn she was packed off to live and study at what was known in those days as a crammer. The crammer in this case was the Rev Bertrand Skinner, who held a living at a small village called Durzebridge, near Okehampton. Skinner, an aged bachelor, apparently specialised in coaching young men for the Oxbridge entrance exam and normally had around six pupils living in at any one time. Taking Char was a special concession to Con, for whom, rather improbably, it was said he once held a torch. Sophia said her mother's main comment on her life at the Vicarage had been that it had caused her (temporarily) to become an agnostic; this state of mind apparently triggered off by having to cut up the bread and pour out the Communion wine on Sunday mornings.

Doubly lucky, therefore, I had her 1918 journal. This is extremely revealing, although scrappy in places, and like so many enterprises of Char's, peters out altogether halfway through. It is written in a stout, shiny red exercise book – still bearing the name of the stationer in Okehampton where it was purchased at the price of 6d – in Char's bold, strong handwriting, which appears to have altered little over the years. I have letters of hers dating from the sixties in which the writing is instantly recognisable as that of the author of the journal.

Pushed into the back of the notebook is a packet of photographs: small, blurred and yellow with age. They're mostly incomprehensible views of what must presumably be Dartmoor, but there are also about half a dozen of people. All except one of the latter are of young men posing theatrically against some sort of painted backcloth, including one in a turban, holding what looks like a scimitar raised menacingly above his head. I assumed at first he must be wearing fancy dress, but from perusal of the journal I discovered one of the pupils was, in fact, the son of an Indian rajah. The exception to these was a photo of Char herself. She is standing in a garden, draped in what looks like a lace table cloth, a rose in her hand. By now her hair is short and curly with a fringe, the face plump and vulnerable, but the eyes under the thick, arched brows staring aggressively at the camera are recognisably Char's. The photographer was, I think, trying to get her to simper; inevitably he failed. Char was quite incapable of simpering.

And so, *nous verrons*, as Aunt Beth would say . . .

Virginia Budd

The Vicarage, Durzebridge, Devon – 10th January 1918
I have decided to write my diary every day . . .

Christmas at Holly Villas was hell. More and more I feel the whole religious business is rot. Twice to church on Christmas Day; everyone singing 'Peace and Goodwill to all Men' and look what's happening in France. There was a poor young man on leave from the Front in church. His face grey and twitching and his left eye all pulled to one side. It reminded me of when Aunt Beth used to tell me not to make a face in case 'the wind changed' and I was stuck with it. The young man's mother had to take him out before the end of the service because he'd wet himself. Ma is such a hypocrite: for ever talking about God and how he's watching us. Was he watching her when she sent poor old Pa away, I wonder? She said to me on Christmas morning: 'We must brave it out, dear, on our own, now your father no longer wishes to help us.' This is a downright lie: Pa was crying when he said goodbye to me at Waterloo: it was awful, and all the way in the taxi he held my hand. I've decided I will never marry. It only brings unhappiness. Old Bat says if I work really hard I could get into Oxford and become a historian – much more fun than being some ass's wife!

There's a new boy here this term, Tom Riley. Rather absurd really, but funny. He travelled in the train from London with me, but of course we didn't know we were both bound for Old Bat's until we reached Okehampton: it was raining and pitch dark when we arrived and no sign of Potkin or the dog cart. We waited and waited, sitting on my trunk under the only lamp left alight. We were just going to start walking, when Potkin and the dog cart galloped into the station yard. His excuse, Mollie had gone lame on the way in, but Tom said afterwards he was pretty sure the real reason was he'd managed to get drunk. If not, how had Mollie suddenly stopped being lame? We sang songs from *Chu Chin Chow* all the way to Durzebridge: Tom's people had taken him to see it too in the Christmas hols. Potkin said we 'Zounded loike they ould caa'ts howling.' He is a rude old man.

Rashi, Edward and little Bob are still here. Rashi said he spent Christmas with his aunt at the Ritz. He would. I said my Pa dines there practically every night, so Rashi, just to be clever, said, 'Isn't that rather boring for him?'

My little bedroom looks so pretty. Aunt Beth gave me a lovely drawing of a girl's head, by an artist she knows called Walter Sickert, for Christmas and I've hung it on the wall opposite my bed. Mrs Oates said, 'Better not let the Reverend see that. He don't like modern things.' Rashi and Bob are sharing this term and I've given them 'The Death of Nelson': Rashi loves awful pictures like that. He says they show the English at their best. What cheek! Old Bats's starting me on Horace this term – hooray!

The Vicarage, Durzebridge, Devon – 20th January 1918
I am not going to be confirmed. I decided finally in church on Sunday. I was cutting up the bread ready for early service, and all of a sudden I thought I would eat a piece, just to see . . . I chewed and chewed – it was pretty stale – but it was just plain, ordinary bread, nothing more. The idea of eating stale bread and pretending it's someone's body is totally abhorrent to me. Even worse, to drink wine and pretend it's someone's blood. Incidentally, Tom and I are now pretty sure it's Potkin who pinches the Communion wine and that's why he's so often squiffy. Mrs Oates says, no, but we're certain we're right. Someone is, and if not Potkin – who?

We're reading Shakespeare's sonnets in the evenings now

after supper. We all sit round the fire in Old Bats' study and take it in turns to read one out loud. It's rather splendid, really. Rashi has a marvellous voice, even though he is an Indian.

Letters from Ma and Pa yesterday. Pa's had to join the Army! He says they are taking old men now, having run out of young ones. He says he's no good at drill and cleaning a rifle is quite beyond him. Uncle Bobby at the War Office is going to try and get him out. Ma says she's taking a cottage at St Ives in Cornwall for the summer holidays, and Cousin Milly Phillips is to come with us. Aunt Agnes is having an operation, so we're stuck with Milly. Actually, she's not a bad kid, a bit weepy, that's all.

Yesterday, Tom and I rode for miles over the moors. It was such fun. It rained and rained, but we didn't mind a bit. I said let's pretend we're Cathy and Heathcliffe, but Tom said, no, he didn't like Heathcliffe, and Cathy was a pretty rotten sort of girl anyway, so we sang songs instead.

The Vicarage, Durzebridge, Devon – 1st March 1918
Ma writes I don't have to be confirmed if I don't want to – hooray! She says we'll 'talk it over together at Easter'. Oh dear! Oh Lor! Pa still in the Army. Uncle Bobby's been no help at all so far. Pa's letters are frightfully funny. He's stationed near Trowbridge with 'some infernal young pipsqueak of eighteen in charge of us'. He says it's nice country, though, and he's managed to get some hunting in.

I'm going to learn to drive a motor! A boy in the village has promised to teach me. I met him while I was having Mollie shod last week. His name's Peter Durrant and his father keeps the butcher's at Down Cross. He says soon there won't be any horses, they won't be needed, everyone will have motors.

'Learn to drive, Miss Osborn,' he said, 'then you'll be one jump ahead of the rest.'

'Alright,' I said, 'if you'll teach me,' and so he is. Tom and Rashi say I'm an idiot, and what does a butcher's son know about motors; they're such snobs. I think they're jealous really.

'Don't be such an ass, my child,' Rashi said. 'My father has six gold-plated Daimlers in his stables at Borepore, why on earth should I be jealous?' He is, though, all the same.

Lovely snowdrops out under the laurels along the drive; so frail and pretty. One day no sign of them and then suddenly there they are.

Horrid old Holly Villas for Easter. How I wish I didn't have to go home.

Holly Villas – Easter Day, 1918
Church, church and church again. Ma seems to be going through a religious phase. Is it guilt, I wonder? No room in this ghastly little house for anything. My bedroom is like a box, and the only staff we have is a Cook General called Mrs Churnside. She's the most hopeless cook. Yesterday, when Mr and Mrs McWhirter came to lunch (dreadful bores who live next door), she left most of the insides in the chicken. I was nearly sick. Ma didn't notice, of course, but Mr McW looked a bit odd and I saw him surreptitiously put something in his handkerchief. Ma says we'll be able to have a better house 'when the money comes through'. Will it ever, I wonder? Anyway, there'll never be another house like darling Renton. How I hate, hate to think of other people living there.

Uncle Bobby's managed to get Pa out of the Army – hurrah! Ma said all that drilling would have done him good – I can't see how. I wonder if the War will ever end, or will it just grind on and on until there are no more men left to fight? Next year I shall train to be an ambulance driver and go out to France. Better than being a VAD and spending all day emptying chamber pots. Ma says, certainly not, I'm much too young and the War will be over by next year – how does she know, pray? The poor young man we saw in church at Christmas is dead. Ma has made friends with his mother, and she told her.

How I long to be back at Durzebridge. Rashi is spending Easter in Paris with some uncle who he claims is a general – can Indians be generals?

The Vicarage, Durzebridge, Devon – 23rd April 1918
Shakespeare's birthday. I'm sitting on my bed in a patch of sun. Mrs Oates sent me up to rest with a hot water bottle on my tummy. I had such awful curse pains this morning. Why do women have to suffer like this? Just another proof that there's no God: if there was, why should he have made people so badly? Peewhit's lying beside me. He is truly a beautiful cat. He's looking straight at me, his great greenery yallery eyes unblinking and now and again he pats my face with a paw. I can't write anymore I feel so strange . . .

The Vicarage, Durzebridge, Devon – 2nd May 1918
Peter Durrant kissed me today. I'm not sure whether or not I liked it. I wanted him to, of course, but when he did? His breath smelt of Woodbine cigarettes and something else, rather nasty. He put his tongue right in my mouth and suddenly I felt cross and pushed him away. He went red and said it wasn't fair 'to tease'. Damned cheek. I can drive now anyway, so I don't need him any more. It's absolutely ripping driving a motor, such a feeling of power. Peter says I'm a born motorist.

Rashi and Tom are swatting like mad. They never come out of their books – so boring. Rashi has laid down a strict timetable for them to follow. 'Work now,' he says, 'and later we will play.' He's such a pompous ass, he drives me mad.

Was I foul to Peter? Yes. I know, I'll buy him a little present in Okehampton and take it round to the garage. He's joining up next month and I suppose will be killed like all the rest. I'd like us to stay friends. I just won't let him kiss me, that's all.

The Vicarage, Durzebridge, Devon – 23rd June 1918, 11.30 p.m.
Only another half hour and my birthday will be over. Do I feel different? Perhaps a little. Certainly, it would be true to say I'm learning fast about men. I'm not awfully pretty, really, but I seem able to make boys keen on me. Not, of course, the lordly Rashi: he treats me like a child, but the others . . .

Yesterday, I lost my temper with Rashi and called him a damned impertinent nigger (which he is). He immediately picked me up and sat me on top of the tallest bookcase in the study, then went away and left me. I shouted and screamed like anything and of course Old Bats came in. 'What are you doing up there, my dear? I would come down if I were you.' I was speechless by that time and just glowered at him. Tom got me down eventually, but he was laughing so much he nearly dropped me, the idiot.

Today was different. Today was my birthday and everyone was splendid: they all, even Old Bats, gave me a present. *A Shropshire Lad* by A. E. Housman. 'I know your predilection for the countryside, my dear, and thought this might appeal.' He is rather a dear.

Rashi gave me a 'kukri' knife that belonged, he says, to his great-great-grandfather. It's in a carved wooden sheath with two little knives to go with it. 'For cutting up the meat,' Rashi says. It's very beautiful and very murderous looking and I'm very pleased with it. Rashi also says each nick in the curved blade represents a killing – there are six! I had such a pile of presents at breakfast it took me ages to open them. Pearls from Pa and gold bangles from Ma, quite pretty actually.

In the morning we did lessons as usual, but after lunch the boys said they had a surprise for me. I was to sit in a special chair on the lawn as Mistress of the Revels and they did a series of the most absurd tableaux: 'in honour of Queen Charlotte on her Sixteenth Birthday'. They were so priceless I cried with laughing. Amongst other things, Rashi, wearing his robes and a turban, executed an Indian dance and little Bob played the banjo. Then I stood on the table and made a speech and after that we had a most stupendous tea.

In the evening Peter came round and pushed a little parcel, carefully wrapped, into my hand. He was blushing and wouldn't speak and just walked away. He had carved me a beautiful, tiny wooden stag – so pretty – I didn't realise he could do work like that.

Oh, I wish this term would never end; I dread the holidays in Cornwall. Pa is to come for a week while we're there. Old Bats says I must choose now: do I want to try for Oxford, or do I want to be 'just a lady of leisure'. How I wish I knew.

The Vicarage, Durzebridge, Devon – 20th July 1918
The end of term. Tomorrow I catch the train to St Ives. The others are already there. Ma writes, 'such an adorable cottage'. I wonder. I probably won't be coming back here next term now. Everyone is saying the War will be over soon and if it is, Pa wants me to go to finishing school in Paris. Ma says I can choose – be 'finished' or study for Oxford at a High School.

All the boys are leaving, so it wouldn't be the same here if I did come back.

How sad. Think, never again to open up the church in the early morning; to light the candles on the altar; to fight with Rashi and rag with the others; to sit at Old Bats' table with the red baize cloth on it and the inkwell made from a horse's hoof, construing Virgil; never to ride on the moors; hear Rashi's voice calling us from the garden: 'Come on, you slackers, you're late for prep and our aged mentor is becoming the tiniest bit waxy . . .' Oh misery!

We had a little party tonight. Mrs Oates roasted a chicken and there were raspberries and cream. The boys drank cider and Old Bats opened a bottle of his '89 claret. 'For you and me, my dear, and let us drink a toast together,' he said and raised his glass: '*Sic itur ad astra*, my pupils, and God speed.' We all drank and Rashi made a speech (naturally) but it was a good one, and then we joined hands and sang 'Auld Lang Syne'. I wanted to cry, really, but wouldn't let myself.

A postcard came from Peter Durrant. He's at a training camp in Yorkshire. He says it's not too bad there, except it rains all the time. Poor old Peter, perhaps he won't be killed after all; the War may be over before he gets out to France.

A sudden thought: I shall never see my darling Peewhit again.

Heather Cottage, St Ives, Cornwall – 12th August 1918
Pa left today. He's been here a week. He and Ma are quite mad, I think. Last night I came downstairs late – I'd left my book in the parlour – and there they were, kissing one another like anything: it made me feel sick and I ran back upstairs before they saw me. If they do things like that, why did they divorce? Why, oh why can't they be like other people's parents?

Heather Cottage, St Ives, Cornwall – 20th August 1918
I think I've fallen in love, but how can one know for certain? His name is Piers Gurney and he's an artist. Milly and I met him on the beach a week ago. He has black, curly hair and brown eyes and such a lovely, deep voice. He walked along the sands with us and showed us a starfish. He said he thought I must be eighteen, then Milly (the little ass) said, 'No, she's not. She's only just sixteen.'

He laughed and said, 'Eighteen or sixteen, what does it matter? She's beautiful, that's what matters.'

I've seen him every day since then and tomorrow he's asked me to tea in his studio. Ma doesn't know about him. She's been too busy oiling round Pa to take much notice of me and I don't want her to know about Piers. He's my secret. Milly has promised not to tell. I've warned her that if she does, I'll tell how she pinched that little china lighthouse from the shop in Penzance.

Oh Piers, Piers, I love you. I should like us to be married in a cathedral, I think, with twelve bridesmaids and pages dressed in sea-green velvet.

Heather Cottage, St Ives, Cornwall – 21st August 1918
I'm definitely, certainly, totally, completely in love! I can't eat, or sleep, or read, or do anything but think of – Piers! Imagine, Ma might not have taken Heather Cottage and I would never have met him.

The tea? Oh, the tea was heaven. I arrived at the studio at four o'clock, so breathless I couldn't speak, but he took my hand and led me in as though I were a princess. His pictures are bliss – all seaweedy things and brilliantly coloured fish. He says no one wants to buy them. They must be mad. We had China tea in blue and gold cups with peacocks in the bottom and seed cake he bought specially for me, and we just talked and talked. I told him the story of the man on Bagland Common when I was a little girl, who turned out to be a famous poet and, wonder of wonders, he knew all about him. I said why, if he was such a good poet, did no one ever mention his name? He said they weren't ready for his poetry yet, but his time had nearly come.

I was late back for supper – didn't want any, anyway. Ma in one of her moods, kept asking questions and Milly kept giggling. They just can't understand what it's like to be me and in love. Piers is going to paint me; perhaps the picture will hang one day in the National Gallery in London. Will he kiss me tomorrow, I wonder?

Heather Cottage, St Ives, Cornwall – 23rd August 1918
I love Piers more than ever. Yesterday we walked along the cliffs holding hands. It was so incredibly beautiful. In fact, everything about yesterday was incredibly beautiful. The sun, the sea, the brown-gold rocks, the green grass – just everything. And to make it extra special, Ma took Milly to Truro for the day: she wanted me to go, but I said I would rather stay. I didn't want to waste the sun (ha ha). Piers took me back to his studio again for tea and afterwards we played the piano and sang all sorts of funny songs. He did kiss me once, but not in the way Peter Durrant did; just gently on the lips, as though he loved me. He has a friend coming to stay tomorrow. He says I must meet him, he knows we'll like each other awfully.

Heather Cottage, St Ives, Cornwall – 24th August 1918
Met Piers' friend today. His name is Duncan Faulkner and he's *old* – years and years older than darling Piers. Milly and I met them as we were coming out of the Post Office this

morning. Piers introduced us. Mr Faulkner, who was wearing a panama and smoking a cheroot, has a belly that bulges over the top of his trousers; just looked us up and down as though we were a pair of village idiots and mumbled, 'Charmed.' I could feel myself blushing and said to Milly we must hurry home, Ma was waiting for us. But, 'No, she isn't,' said the brat, 'Don't you remember, she said she'd see us at lunchtime.'

Of course, Mr Faulkner thought this was frightfully funny and smirked all over his ugly face, and even Piers (traitor) smiled. He then (Mr F) took Piers' arm and started talking to him as though we weren't there. I was so angry and hurt, I just turned and ran, dragging Milly with me. Then Piers came after us and took my hand. He said he and Duncan were lunching with friends in Newlyn and wouldn't be back until late, but could I come to tea tomorrow? He looked so sad his friend had been rude, that I agreed to go.

Goodness, I hope the horrible Duncan isn't down for long.

Heather Cottage, St Ives, Cornwall – 25th August 1918
Ghastly, miserable day. I hate this place and long to leave; awful Holly Villas would be better than this.

The tea party was too frightful for words. Piers is quite different when Duncan's there. They laugh and talk and make jokes all the time as if I didn't exist. I just sat on the divan where only two days before we had been so wonderfully, exhilaratingly happy – and read the newspaper. They completely ignored me until the unspeakable Duncan suddenly said in his horrible, drawly voice: 'I suppose we'd better give the child its tea.' I shouted I didn't want any bloody tea, thank you and slammed out of the studio. As I went through the door, I saw Piers' face for a second; he looked so sad and hurt I wanted to run straight back into his arms, but didn't, of course.

Please God work a miracle, make the horrible Duncan go away.

Heather Cottage, St Ives, Cornwall – 26th August 1918, midnight
Can't sleep, I don't think I'll ever sleep again.

The most awful thing has happened; I still can't believe what I've seen, but suppose I must. I try shutting my eyes and thinking of something else – anything else – but all I can see are those two disgusting bodies and I become hot all over and want to be sick. I've decided to write down exactly what I saw this evening, then burn the paper. Perhaps the very act of writing will help a little to cleanse my mind.

I can hear the sea slapping against the rocks far below my bedroom window. A brown, velvet moth is fluttering round the lamp – I must catch him and put him outside before he burns his wings – and all the time I think of those two together and know that if I get out of bed, walk along the lane past the monkey puzzle tree and the house with the blue hydrangeas and the brass door knocker shaped like an owl, up the narrow path between the grey stone walls that are covered in pennywort, until I reach the studio, climb on the stone seat outside, so that I may peep through the big window with the blue curtains, that faces the sea, I should find . . .

This morning when I awoke, I felt so miserable and awful about being angry with Piers yesterday. I began to wonder if I had only imagined Duncan to be sarcastic and patronising; that it was really me who had been in the wrong for being so jealous. I remembered Piers' poor, hurt face and felt worse than ever. Milly and I walked on the beach in the morning, but no sign of Piers. After lunch Ma took us for a picnic. She'd hired a pony and trap and we found a wonderful, peaceful little cove to swim in, but it was no good, I couldn't enjoy it.

I could only think of Piers and wonder what he was doing. In the end I decided I would write him a note telling him how sorry I was I'd been rude yesterday and ask him to reply if he forgave me. As soon as we got back from the picnic, I ran up to my room and wrote the note. I couldn't deliver it until after supper, when they would most likely be down in the town drinking at one of the harbour pubs.

It was after nine o'clock when I finally left. Ma insisted on my helping with the washing up. There was no sign of life at the studio when I arrived and I decided to walk round to the back and slip my note through the window that looks on to the tiny garden; there's no letter box at the front and I didn't want Piers to miss seeing it. It was while I was in the narrow passage between the studio and the tumbledown fish store next door that I heard them laughing. I didn't know what to do; I couldn't leave the note now, they'd see me and make a joke of it. I just stood there in the dark passage listening to their laughter.

Then something made me go on. I had to see them and see what they were doing. There's a rickety old wooden lattice screen, with a white flowering summer jasmine entwined in it, bordering the garden at the rear of the studio, and by standing on tiptoe I could just see through the trellis. The scent of jasmine will always remind me of tonight. What I saw was quite horrible. How could they – two men? They were both naked: even in my misery I thought how beautiful Piers' body was; Duncan's was beastly, all fat, white and hairy. Duncan was sitting in a basket chair with his legs apart and Piers, my Piers, was kneeling in front of him licking him, as a dog does a bitch, while Duncan ruffled his hair. Then Duncan picked up his glass of wine from the table beside him and very slowly poured the contents over Piers. They began to laugh again.

Piers pulled Duncan down on to the ground and they started to fight, laughing all the time, whilst the red wine trickled over their naked bodies. I turned and ran; I'm sure they must have heard me, but I didn't care who heard me: I ran all the way home and locked myself in my room. Ma called out as I passed the parlour door, but I didn't answer, and I've been here ever since.

I think it may have helped a little writing down what I saw tonight, but I shall tear these pages out of my journal in the morning.

She didn't, but the entry for 26th August is the last in the notebook.

I remembered Char telling me how in her teens a young artist had fallen in love with her and wanted to paint her in the nude. Had the artist been Piers Gurney? If so, she'd left out the important part, but then that was typical of Char: that Gurney had been a practising homosexual and let her down pretty badly would have been erased from her conscious memory with the efficiency of a Communist propaganda machine.

Paradoxically, though, like the perfect murderer who always manages to leave behind him a clue as to his real identity, she, after giving you her version of an event, would somehow leave you with the impression she wanted you to know it had not been quite as she'd claimed, but it was up to you to test the veracity of her statement. It was as though she played a game with you, points being awarded, or taken away as the case may be, according to your capacity for belief. Perhaps the contents of the green trunk too were part of the game: the final clue, the absolute denouement. Or was I imbuing Char with complicated motives and feelings she simply didn't possess? Sophia and Aunty Phyll certainly thought so; I just didn't know, but I couldn't help wondering, and it was an interesting speculation.

To return to the record itself. There is little to show for Char's time at the finishing school in Paris which must have begun in the summer of 1919. Apart, that is, from a couple of very small, very blurred snaps of a group of girls in broad-brimmed hats and buttoned boots, standing in front of a fountain – a trip to Versailles perhaps? Sophia said all her mother had told her about that time was that they had cream cakes every morning at Rumplemayers and endlessly went to the opera. Did she dream, I wondered, of Piers and the infamous Duncan, as in the company of twenty young ladies from respectable middle-class English homes she trailed in and out of art galleries and learned how to arrange a menu, interview a cook and choose what wine to drink with what? Sadly, I shall never know.

The next hard news I had of her comes from Algy Charterhouse's diaries loaned to me by Sophia. Cheating in a way, I suppose – they didn't actually come from the green trunk but legitimate under the circumstances. Sophia, the only one of her family to show interest in such things, inherited them together with a number of letters at her father's death. With the help of these and assorted memorabilia from the same period, plus yet another of Char's diaries – this time covering the year 1933 – I was able to get at least some idea of the couple's courtship and subsequent marriage.

Algy Charterhouse, according to Sophia, was twenty-three years old at the time of his first meeting with Char in 1923. He had served in the army for the last few months of the War and then gone into the family merchant bank in the City. Before his marriage to Char, he lodged with an elderly Charterhouse aunt in Bryanston Square, preferring the comparative freedom this gave him to living with his family who resided in somewhat gloomy state, in Surrey.

9

Dined with the Cartwrights – some amusing people there, but somehow felt depressed and unable to join in. Maggy Cartwright is enchanting, I'll allow, but everyone shouted and laughed too much. That frightful ass Tommy Maddox comes up: 'What ho, Algy, old fruit – sickening for something, are we?' I told him to shut up and go away, but perhaps he's right, perhaps I am sickening for something.

1923 already seems an anticlimax. Is the brave new world fading so fast?

Bryanston Square, London WC – 30th January 1923
Home for the weekend. Father never spoke at all; except once at dinner on Saturday.

We were sitting together over the port; me absolutely racking my brains for something to say, but as usual, not being able to come up with a damned thing. Then, like a fool, I managed to get a piece of walnut stuck in my throat and started choking. This, at least, provoked some response. 'You eat too fast, my boy,' Father announced, as purple in the face, tears pouring down my cheeks, I groped for my glass, 'bad for the digestion.' Through paroxysms of coughing I waved my thanks for this helpful advice and that was the end of our conversation. It's really time Father snapped out of it. Of course, we were

121

all beastly cut up about Ted being killed, but it was five years ago and you can't mourn for ever.

Frightfully busy at the office. Smith and old Pultney down with flu. Dine with Podge and Bunny Anstey on Wed and then to Dorset for the weekend. The Bradleys have asked me for the hunting. Hope the good weather holds.

Bryanston Square, London WC – 31st January 1923
Aunt Min insists I drink a glass of hot milk each night before I turn in. It's quite revolting, but I can't persuade her I don't want the stuff. When I told Hilda to take the nauseous liquid back to where it came from, last night, she begged me with tears in her eyes not to make her. 'Oh please, sir, don't make me. Her Ladyship will never forgive me.'

'Alright,' I said. 'We can't have that happening,' and I took the damned glass and hurled the contents out of the window. Perhaps I should get rooms of my own; Aunt Min's a dear, but life at Bryanston Square too closely resembles a comfortable strait-jacket (if there is such a thing) for my liking.

Bryanston Square, London WC – Monday late, 23rd February 1923
I've met such a funny, quirky, rumbustious, *adorable* girl: by chance too, not at all official-like. The absurd thing is I simply cannot get her out of my mind. All the way back in the train from Sherborne I could think of nothing else, and yet I don't even know her full name: all I know is, her first name is Charlotte. It happened like this, Me Lud . . .

My weekend hosts, the Bradleys, run a pleasant enough ménage, but on the dull side. Caroline, daughter, fat, fair and flapperish, full of gush but not much else: in twenty years' time she'll be a replica of Mrs B. Father B a decent enough chap – served with Ted in the War – dabbles in farming.

Left the office early on Friday afternoon and caught the 4.30 train to Sherborne, accompanied by Major B. That evening after dinner, we played a rousing game of whist until ten thirty, then Major B, reaching for his candle, announced in tones that brooked no argument from other ranks: 'Bed, everybody, I think. Hunting tomorrow,' and up we all trooped, one behind the other like geese to market. God, how I'm waffling on – is it because I don't know how to describe my meeting with that funny girl? Oh, I've just remembered, she has the most enchanting turned-up nose; if it pointed to the sky one whit further it would be a caricature of a nose, but as it is it's simply the prettiest nose I've ever seen.

Well . . . next day Caroline, Major B and myself hacked to the meet in a tiny village – I've already forgotten its name – consisting of a small pub, an even smaller church and half a dozen cottages. My mount wasn't half bad; a big-boned bay with a passing hard mouth, but he could go like billy-o once his enthusiasm was roused. We found almost immediately, and though the going was hard, hounds ran like hell for about four miles. Well, somehow or other dauntless Algy C, always keen to be in the forefront of things, managed to mislay his two companions along the way (he didn't look back actually) and found himself, to his surprise, so far out in front that not only had he lost the Bs, but hounds, huntsman and the rest of the field as well.

Not as put out by this state of affairs as some might be, I decided to take a breather, find a gate, smoke a cigarette and generally drink in the ambience. Did I say the weather was perfect? It was. After proceeding gently across a couple of fields in a somewhat aimless fashion, I came to a gate that led into a narrow lane, with wide turf verges on either side. This seemed to me a likely spot for taking my breather in and I'd just dismounted and was loosening the bay's girths, when I espied a few yards up the lane, a small figure, bowler on the back of its head, legs outstretched, seated on a gravel heap. It appeared to be in hunting kit, but there was no sign of a horse. At first I thought the figure was a boy, but on closer inspection it turned out to be a girl. Naturally, I hurried to the rescue.

'Can I be of any assistance?' I asked, politely touching my hat.

'Not unless you know of a quick cure for indigestion,' replied the figure surprisingly.

'Only bicarbonate of soda,' I said. 'Not having any handy, would a cigarette do?'

'It might,' she said, 'and if you're wondering where my horse is, he's tied up just inside that gate. I get these pains, you see, and when I do, I find it helps to sit on a gravel heap.' It was then I noticed the figure's eyes – enormous, green, deep set, with long, dark curling lashes under arched brows.

'May I join you?' I said. 'Perhaps the company of a passing stranger might be beneficial, for want, that is, of any bicarb.'

'You never know,' she said and patted the heap beside her. Then she smiled – oh Lord! I was lost then and have been ever since. I don't know what on earth we talked about, because by that time I'd entered a sort of trance-like state. I do remember she said she lived with her mother at a place called Cuckoo Farm a mile or two from where we were sitting, and that her mother did a bit of horse breaking and dealing, and that her name was Charlotte, but she was always known as 'Char'. What else was said I simply can't remember, but we finished our cigarettes and realised the time (or she realised the time).

'I believe it's better,' she announced. 'What a funny thing.'

We remounted. 'Can I ride you home?' I offered hopefully.

'There isn't any need,' she said. 'I turn off here and it's only a mile. If you go straight on, you'll soon come to the village and someone will point you in the direction of the hunt.'

Helpless, I searched my pockets for one of my cards; she couldn't just ride away out of my life like that. She turned her horse and trotted away up the lane.

'My name's Algy, Algy Charterhouse,' I shouted after her, feeling a perfect ass. 'May I see you again?' She turned round and waved her whip: I thought I caught the words, 'if you like,' but I wasn't sure, then she was gone, round a bend in the lane and all I could hear was the diminishing sound of her horse's hooves.

2 Bryanston Square, London WC   14th February 1923

Dear Miss Osborn,

I do hope you won't think me a frightful cad writing to you out of the blue like this, but I remember you telling me your mother sometimes placed horses, and as my father happens to be looking for one, I wondered if she might know of something suitable. What he wants is a plodder: he hunts occasionally with the Surrey Union, but prefers it to be an 'armchair' ride. 'Must be at least 16.2 and nothing flashy,' (his words). I should be most awfully grateful if you could possibly let me know whether your mother knows of such a paragon and if she does, perhaps I could come down and look at it for him.

I trust you reached home safely on Saturday and there's been no recurrence of the indigestion. By the by, I seem to have stolen your box of matches! I am most frightfully sorry. I found them in my pocket on my return to the Bradleys.

Major Bradley (my weekend host) knows your mother slightly: they apparently serve on the same committee, and he was able to give me your address.

I do hope you don't think it awfully presumptuous of me to write.

Yours sincerely,
A. G. Charterhouse

PS The above address will always find me. I live with my aunt, Lady Rowland, during the week.

2 Bryanston Square, London WC   20th February 1923

Dear Miss Osborn,

It was most frightfully decent of you to reply so promptly to my letter. How splendid that your mother thinks she might have a suitable horse.

About arrangements for viewing the animal: as luck would have it, I'm staying next weekend with a cousin at Dorchester, and nothing could be easier than to arrange for him to drive me over to Cuckoo Farm on either the Saturday or Sunday afternoon. Would you mind awfully dropping me a line to let me know what time your mother would like us and we'll be there.

Yours sincerely,
A. G. Charterhouse

PS I shall be able to return your matches in person!

Cuckoo Farm, Upper Blatchford, Sherborne, Dorset
22nd February 1923

Dear Mr Charterhouse,

Thank you for your letter. My mother now says Starlight

might not be up to your father's weight and therefore not suitable, but by all means come and have a look at him. Can you manage three o'clock on Saturday and stay to tea?

Bring boots – it's beastly wet.
Yours sincerely,
C. Osborn

Red Lion Yard, London EC   27th February 1923

Dear Miss Osborn,

I have given my father full particulars of Starlight, but he now tells me he has a horse on trial and agrees with your mother that Starlight would probably not be up to his weight, so it now looks as if a deal is rather unlikely. I am most frightfully sorry to have put you to so much trouble. On the other hand, I wouldn't have missed that perfectly splendid tea for anything, or the chance to return your box of matches!

Are you really coming to town to stay with your aunt? If so, perhaps we could dine? Do write and let me know if and when and I'll arrange a party.

Please thank your mother for all her help and kindness.
Yours very sincerely,
Algy Charterhouse

And so it went on, all through the spring of 1923; by midsummer Char and Algy were engaged.

Char appeared to have kept most of Algy's letters for the period, and even a brief perusal of them shows how quite preposterously in love with her he was. From such dizzy emotional heights there was only one way out, surely, and that was down. He appears to have been totally blind to the 'dark side' of Char: to him then she was 'adorable', 'funny', 'absurd' and above all, wildly physically attractive. Of her own, possibly distorted view of sex, influenced as it was by the behaviour of her parents and by her experience of Hubert Stokes and Piers Gurney, he was presumably ignorant. It seems that at the time Char turned away from all that was difficult, unaccountable or uncertain in life – for her twenty-one years she appears to have experienced her fair share of this – and embraced wholeheartedly all that was safe, conventional and familiar. Algy Charterhouse in her eyes must have epitomised these virtues and was good-looking, rich and adored her to boot. To him she must have seemed a simple, country, middle-class girl of her period: fond of all the right things, knowing the right sort of people, a little daring perhaps superficially, but at heart a dear, sweet creature, who would make a perfect wife, hostess, mother and, in some undefined way, a perfect bedmate. Poor old Algy, he was, of course, entirely unaware that, as with the moon, this was but a temporary phase and could not possibly last.

It's difficult to assess Char's feelings towards Algy. There can be no doubt he influenced her, simply by being a man two years her senior and in love, whose inalienable right it was to take charge of her, both in mind and in body. Theoretically at least, she always claimed she preferred masterful men, though I had my doubts on that score. But even years later when I came to know her, and she'd long since forsaken the way of life that Algy represented – gentle affluence, City dinners, the Old School Tie, the correct regiment, the 'right' ideas – she would still produce anachronisms such as: 'But darling, he was wearing a Leander tie, he simply must be OK.' That she was in love with Algy is certain, but because of his later defection, she would never admit how much he had really meant to her. She would dwell at length and, it must be admitted, with relish, on his physical violence towards her, but dismiss their love as being something akin to an attack of the measles. His letters, however, passionate, silly and oddly moving, remain.

Algy's journal, which he kept fairly conscientiously until his marriage in April 1924, is mainly a record of dinners, parties, theatres and the like; his passion for Char is confined to his letters. However, there are a couple of entries which interested me as they show a fleeting glimpse of that other Char, the Char of whose existence then he was so blissfully ignorant.

Bryanston Square, London WC – 1st September 1923
Weekend at Cuckoo Farm. Each time I leave Char is worse than the last time. I feel more and more I simply cannot bear to part from her. An odd thing happened, though.

I caught the 1.30 train to Sherborne on Saturday, as usual. My darling met me in the Ford. I came out into the station yard and saw her, hatless, talking to a tall, dark-skinned, dark-haired fellow, who looked like some sort of workman. I stood there for a moment, watching them. Char was laughing up at the chap, her head back, her hair blowing about in the wind, oblivious of the arrival of the train and general exodus of passengers from London, including myself. Then as I watched, the fellow, still laughing, bent over and pressing her with some familiarity on the shoulder, turned away into the crowd. I felt as though someone had doused me with cold water, and stood there like an idiot, my bag at my feet, being bumped into by people rushing for cabs or taxis. Then she saw me and came running into my arms, lifting her face to be kissed. Of course, I couldn't think of a blessed thing to say, just buried my face in her hair. Only when we were out of the town, bowling along through the harvest fields, dust from the road blowing about us, did I venture to ask who the man was she'd been talking to in the station yard. 'Jeff Sparkes. He works on the Home Farm. He was a sergeant in the Dorset Regiment in the War and had his leg smashed by a shell. He helps Ma sometimes with the horses.'

'You seem on very friendly terms,' I said, idiot that I am, but I couldn't help it. For an answer she put her foot hard down on the accelerator making the car leap forward so suddenly I banged my face on the windscreen. 'Steady on, old thing,' I shouted above the roar of the engine. 'I only asked a simple question. It gave me a bit of a shock, you see, seeing you with . . .'

Just as suddenly as she had accelerated, she braked and pulled the car into the side of the road beside a small spinney. She switched off the engine, and for a moment there was silence, apart from the cawing of rooks in the trees behind us. Then she said so softly I could barely hear her: 'Why don't you make love to me now, here, Alge? It's such a lovely little wood and the grass is nice and dry. We'll be married soon – why wait?'

I just sat there paralysed. I wanted to make love to her more than anything in my whole life, but I knew if I laid a finger on her then, we'd both be lost. I tried to explain what a caddish thing it would be for me to take advantage of her innocence; that one simply did not do such things. But she just looked straight ahead of her and kept repeating, 'But it's such a lovely place; it would be right here, I know it would.' God, I was tempted, but she just didn't understand – the silly child. After a little while we drove on and talked of other things. The remainder of the weekend was so busy – cricket in the

130

afternoon, I took two wickets (!), the Petersons' dance in the evening, and we never had another minute to ourselves. God, how I long for next April to come, when she really will belong to me.

Bryanston Square, London WC – 20th March 1924
Feel a bit low tonight: silly really. All these wedding preparations are getting us both down, I think. We seemed to spend most of the weekend making lists and unpacking the most frightful presents. Mrs O didn't help: she's in bed with some back complaint or other.

I thought at first that with Mrs O *hors de combat* Char and I would have more time to ourselves, but not a bit of it. If she called my bird upstairs to her bedroom once, she called her twenty times and always on some trifling pretext or other. When she shouted down for the twenty-first time (or rather banged her stick on the floor) I told Char to stay downstairs and went up myself. Mrs O was sitting in bed draped in shawls looking exactly like a witch. 'Algy my dear, so kind of you,' she said, taking my hand and squeezing it. 'But you mustn't give in to my little Char, you know. If you do she'll trample all over you.'

Not bothering to keep the sarcasm out of my voice, I told her that I wasn't 'giving in' as she put it. It was simply that Char was tired, had one of her heads, and as she'd been up and downstairs quite a number of times already that evening, I thought it only fair to offer to go in her place. Of course, she ignored the sarcasm, and smiling in that maddening way of hers, patted the end of the bed and pronounced (she never just says things, she makes pronouncements): 'Fairness is totally irrelevant to human relationships, Algy dear. If you're entering marriage under

the impression it will be played according to the Queens-
berry Rules or some splendid set of public school
ethics, you are doomed to disappointment. Life is not like
that, neither is marriage, and least of all marriage to my
Char.'

Suddenly I felt furious; furious that she should denigrate
her own daughter to me; furious, for a moment, with
everything. I put my hands in the pockets of my reefer jacket,
for, Lord help me, I felt like hitting the woman. 'What can I
fetch you, Mrs Osborn? Our dinner's on the table and getting
cold,' was all I could think of to say.

She didn't answer for a minute, trying to think of something
for me to fetch, I suppose. Then she said in quite a different,
quavery sort of voice: 'My Bible dear, if you don't mind. It's
on the top shelf of the bookcase under the window. I always
find a browse through the Gospels helps to relieve pain – the
English – so beautiful.'

When I returned downstairs Char was already seated at
the dining-room table. She had a spoon in her hand and
was examining the pattern on its handle, a sulky, lowering
expression on her face. For an instant, as I stood watching
her through the doorway before she realised I was there, I
saw her completely objectively: not as the girl I loved and
was about to marry, but through the eyes of a stranger, criti-
cal, appraising and, quite inexplicably, found myself
shivering. Suddenly aware of my presence, she looked
across the room at me and her eyes appeared to glitter in
the candlelight. She put down the spoon and leaning forward, very deliberately, took an apple from the silver fruit
bowl in front of her, then, taking careful aim, hurled it with
all her strength straight at my face. Without thinking, I put
out my arm to protect myself and fielding the apple (quite

expertly I thought) threw it back into the bowl. Then we both burst out laughing, the tension between us gone. But for a moment I'd wanted her so much, I could have killed to have her.

Only three more weeks to go and this testing time will be over and my darling and I will be together always.

From *The Times,* 9th May 1927.
CHARTERHOUSE: on 6th May, to Charlotte Mary Charterhouse, wife of Algernon George Charterhouse of 3 Cheyne Square, Chelsea, London SW3 – a daughter.

Garden Court, Kensington   9th May 1927

Dearest Char,
    We are all so thrilled about the baby! When Algy rang with the news I couldn't help shedding a tear or two – absurd I know, but somehow the thought of my prickly little Char becoming a mother was too much. Roo, right as usual, accused me of being a silly, sentimental old woman and opened a bottle of champagne!
    Darling, I'm sorry to hear you had such a painful time; Algy says you were so brave and patient. Am longing to see you and the little one – I hear she is to be called Ann.
All my love, darling
Aunty Beth
PS Such a nuisance, this wretched hip. It means I'm confined to a chair and can't get out.

From *The Times,* 12th August 1930.
CHARTERHOUSE: On 10th August, to Charlotte Mary Charter-

house, wife of Algernon George Charterhouse of 3 Cheyne Square, Chelsea, London SW3 – a daughter.

From *The Times* of the same date.
OSBORN, Elizabeth Mary: on 10th August, peacefully at her home 8 Garden Court, Kensington, after a long illness bravely borne. No flowers please.

Garden Court   13th August 1930

My dear Char,
   Thank you for your sweet letter. It is indeed a sad time for all of us. Beth was the finest person I ever knew, or am ever likely to know, and although her death was expected, and indeed she was prepared for it, it still came as an immeasurable shock to those of us who loved her.
   Char, my dear, you musn't blame yourself for not visiting Beth enough these last months. She perfectly understood the demands made on your time, and loved to read of your doings in the society papers. How very strange that your daughter was born and Beth died on the very same day. I was able to tell her of the birth before she died and I am sure she heard me, for her last words were 'dear Char', and she was smiling so happily.
   Algy tells me you had another bad time and Dr Scott (such a dear man) advises complete rest. Do take his advice, dear, for all our sakes. Con writes she cannot attend the funeral, but Dick is coming up and staying for it.
                          All my love, dear,
                          Aunty Roo

Cuckoo Farm   21st June 1932

My dearest Char,

Your worrying letter arrived second post yesterday, since when I've thought of nothing else.

Darling, there's so little I can do to help; these matters simply must be sorted out between a husband and wife alone. If you really feel you cannot give yourself to Algy in that way, you must tell him so and not make excuses. However, if you do, you must accept that he will look elsewhere for solace; it's men's nature to do this and in the main they're selfish creatures. You have your dear girls to love, your household to manage, and your work at the Battersea Settlement – by the by, Roo writes a glowing account of all your help – and this, perforce, must be your life. I am sure Algy still loves and respects you, and perhaps in time you will be able to love him again in the way he needs. But you must try to explain to him how you feel and make him understand these things are different for a woman. You say in your letter he's 'insanely jealous'. Well, dear, he would be. No doubt he thinks you've fallen in love with another man. You see, it would be impossible for him to understand that you do not wish to be made love to by anyone. That's why it's so important that you make him understand how you feel.

You've had two difficult births in quick succession, followed by dear Beth dying: you and Algy have been married eight years (always a testing time) and all these things have come together to make you feel as you do. But to talk of leaving Algy is nonsense. You're made of sterner stuff than that surely? You must be brave, dear, stick it out and ride the storm; you have two little girls to think of now.

Your father writes he and the Russian woman are buying a

place in Hampshire, what with, I cannot imagine, as I gather she spends his money like water.

Had such a nice card from Milly and Harold honeymooning in Florence. They sound so happy.

Be brave and strong, my Char –
Your loving Ma

Hotel Majestic, Madrid   4th October 1932

Darling,

Arrived last night and have been hectically busy all day. Penny de Vere-Carson is staying here – isn't it a coincidence! We met in the bar last night when I arrived, and are dining together tonight. She sends her love and wishes you were here. She's got her divorce at last, but claims she leads the life of a nun!

My dear, I've been so busy these past few weeks organising the Spanish trip, I know I've been an absolute bear. I am sorry, really I am, and promise to be a good boy in future. When I get back perhaps we could arrange a little holiday together, just the two of us. We could go to that fishing pub on the Usk, Berty Townsend told me about; three or four days complete rest would do us both good.

Lisbon on Friday the 7th and home on Wed, 12th. By the bye, I don't think much of Vera's packing, she forgot to put my sponge bag in. Never mind, Penny has braved the local chemist and bought me another!

All my love, darling
Alge

10

It was time now for Char's 1933 diary. This was a large, expensive-looking notebook of green and gold tooled leather that testified quite clearly to her material affluence at that time. I remember a feeling of anticipation as I opened it. Other years were represented by tiny pocket diaries – all of which seem to have been supplied by the Gargoyle Club in Soho – simply cataloguing such mundane events as visits to the dentist, dinner guests and the dates of her period. What was so special, then, about 1933 that it merited a full-scale journal? Had she thrown all the others away, or was it just a one-off affair? I'd soon see.

Sophia was in Montreal on some conference or other, but by tacit consent she had left me to plough through her mother's papers on my own. 'You can show me the juicy bits afterwards,' she said, with typical flippancy. I picked up a large, glossy photograph by Lenare: Char looking soulfully beautiful, gazing down at a sleeping, shawl-wrapped baby, presumably Evelyn, who was born in 1930. Somehow the photographer had managed to squeeze all of Char from the likeness; what remained was a lovely, fashionable shell bearing a marked resemblance to all the other Lenare subjects. It was a nice picture to have around, all the same.

In the back of the notebook was a bundle of letters tied with a red ribbon. On the top envelope Char had written, B.E.'s letters – destroy. Was that an instruction for me, or had she written the note years ago for herself?

I began to read.

3 Cheyne Square, Chelsea – 2nd January 1933
Writing makes me feel self-conscious: as though someone sitting behind me were laughing at my feeble attempts at self-expression, but here goes . . .

I am sitting up in bed in my bright yellow room. It's nine o'clock in the morning; fog drifts outside the windows and the street lamps are still on. Cook has been for orders, I've rung the butcher and the fishmonger. Later, Aunty Roo, Milly, Harold and I will lunch – liver and bacon and apple fritters – and take Ann and Deirdre (Harold's whining niece) to *Peter Pan.* Ann has an upset tummy, Evie is teething, Nanny is in love with a man called Charlie who runs a greengrocer's shop in Pimlico, and me? I'm dead, I think. I look in the mirror and someone's there alright: 'popular hostess, Mrs Algy Charterhouse', with her marcelled hair, her Molyneux dresses, her sables and her Hispano Suiza, but where the hell is Char Osborn, that's what I'd like to know.

'Write a little every day and you'll find she'll come back,' was what that funny young man at the Chelsea Arts Ball on Saturday told me and, *voilà*, that's what I'm doing. God, I must have been tight though; we all were, I suppose. Algy a matador, me a Carmen, and frantic Diana M a bilious raspberry ice, masquerading as a Dresden shepherdess.

How did it happen, our meeting – the funny young man and mine? I know: I was alone in our box, Algy and Diana dancing, Bunny taking Perdita home in a cab as she'd been sick, Richard (or was it Tommy, they're all beginning to look alike) gone to fetch more drink. I was sitting dropping cigarette ash on the heads of the crowd below, the band was playing that thing from 'Cavalcade' and in he came and sat down beside me.

'That's a rather childish game you're playing, isn't it?' he said. 'Can anyone join in?' I said yes, and he promptly emptied the ashtray on to the head of a huge man dressed as a pierrot, who happened to be jigging about immediately below the box. The huge man looked up in fury, his face a purple half moon under his pointed pierrot's cap, and we quickly ducked down behind the parapet of the box. It was then I realised that the young man wasn't wearing fancy dress. He was tall and heavily built, about my age, with thick, black hair, a wide, sensuous mouth and looked as if he needed a shave. But it was his eyes I really noticed; they were green, cat's eyes, but with tiny flecks of brown in them, and I know I've seen those eyes before.

'Let's sit down here,' he said. 'It's more comfortable on the floor and the parapet helps deaden the sound of that ghastly rubbish of Coward's.'

'I like Coward,' I said, beginning to get a bit annoyed. 'And if you don't, why do you bother to come to a dance like this? You aren't even in fancy dress.'

'And how do you deduce that?' he said, pointing to the rather shiny tail coat he was wearing. 'For all you know this might well be my fancy dress.' Suddenly, and I can't imagine why, we both began to laugh; we just laughed and laughed and couldn't stop. There we sat on the floor of the box like a couple of zanies, holding on to one another in paroxysms of mirth.

After a bit we managed to pull ourselves together and wiped our eyes, or rather he wiped mine as well as his own, I hadn't got a handkerchief, and he said: 'I knew you'd be like that, I knew from the moment I saw you through the door of the box. That's why I came in.' He took a quick swig from a silver flask he pulled out of the pocket of his tailcoat and said, 'Tell me before all the ghastlies return and the clock strikes twelve, why are you so sad?' For a moment I felt so odd; he was looking straight into my eyes, his own bright, full of curiosity like those of a child. I felt as though he had opened a door into my soul and was briskly shining a torch round it to see what was wrong. Then I found myself trying to explain; to explain how I felt; how Algy and I were drifting further and further apart; how the only time we reached one another now at all was when we fought; how bored I was, how hopeless. And that was when he told me I must write a little about myself each day.

'It might help,' he said, 'you never know, and then we'll see . . .' He sounded like a doctor.

Then the band stopped playing, Algy dragging Diana behind him, barged through the box door, the others with more champagne, behind him. My young man leaped to his feet, towering over everyone. He clapped his hand to his head, and looking wildly round shouted: 'Christ, the witching hour's upon us, I must fly lest my coachman turns himself into a rat,' and dashed out of the box.

'And who in God's name is that frightful bounder?' Algy said, and of course we had another row. The absurd thing is, I don't even know my young man's name. Shall I, I wonder, find out?

Goodness, I do believe his advice has worked. I'm beginning to come alive just a little. I might be able to face my lunch party – even the liver and bacon – with a modicum of enthusiasm. By the time my dear husband returns from his holiday in Switzerland, who knows how I shall feel?

* * *

3 Cheyne Square, Chelsea – 6th January 1933
A card from Algy in St Moritz; he's having a lovely time (of course), but poor, dear Diana has sprained her ankle – a small comfort in a sea of gloom. Nothing from my young man and no one knows who he is – even Perdita who knows everyone. Did I imagine him? Nanny's greengrocer has proposed and she can't make up her mind whether to accept him. 'I shall miss the life here, Madam,' she says. 'Handling cold veg all day wouldn't be the same.' I advised her not; marriage is grossly over-rated, although a greengrocer's shop in Pimlico might be more fun than ghastly Cheyne Square.

I shall have my bedroom painted Bakst blue. This yellow is driving me mad.

3 Cheyne Square, Chelsea – 7th January 1933
I've heard from my mysterious young man! A letter arrived last night. Big, bold, black writing. Rather scruffy paper though, postmarked Chelsea.
Dear Mrs Charterhouse (he writes)

Sorry to leave you to your own devices for so long after my promise (rash no doubt) of help, but the party went on rather longer than expected. How is the writing, is there any sign of improvement yet?

May I come to tea on Sunday, or will your husband eat me? Got up as a matador (that was what he was supposed to be, wasn't it?) he looked a bit frightening and I'm feeling frail. Please let me come, I promise I'll behave; I can actually, if I try very hard. If you're absolutely adamant not, ring me on Flaxman 8077, otherwise I'll be there. I'm camping in Peter Steerforth's house in Flood Street while he's away in New York.

Yours, etc,
Barny Elliott

PS Get in a good supply of cig ash and we can have another game.

Thank God Algy's still away, but Sunday tea – how odd. I think I'll ask Perdita too; better still, get her to 'drop in' unexpected like. A tête-à-tête might be overwhelming. Will he like the children? Hard to imagine him listening to *Jeremy Fisher,* but one never knows.

A letter from Algy; Diana's ankle is improving and it's snowing again. To *Evergreen* tonight with Tommy and Co. Will wear my pink chiffon, I think.

3 Cheyne Square, Chelsea – Sunday late, 8th January 1933
I'm alone by the drawing-room fire with just the table lamp on. I can see the reflection of the flames flickering across the prim faces of the brass sphinxes on the fender. The curtains are drawn tight to keep out the fog, but it seeps in all the same and leaves a smoky haze across the room. The house is quite quiet and only muffled footsteps from the street outside break the silence.

And my young man? Well, we dine tomorrow night, that's all. Except I've never met anyone like him, yet I know I've seen those eyes before. He arrived late (of course). Perdita already ensconced. He carried a small bunch of freesias and was dressed most correctly, in a dark suit, but he still needed a shave. I was impressed by the suit, but felt the jacket to be a bit short in the arms. 'You've noticed,' he said (does he know *all* things about me?). 'This suit is of respectable lineage, but belongs to my host. All my clothes disappeared in a train on the way to Kathmandu.'

'Oh,' I said, rather inadequately I suppose, 'what a bore for you.'

But Per looked impressed. Peter Steerforth is, apparently, the son of a viscount. She smiled at him through her hair – someone the other night, I forget who, told her she had a look of Garbo and it's been on her mind ever since – and said: 'How frightful, my dear. Come and sit by me and have a muffin. Tell me, does Peter still have that perfectly adorable dog?' And it went on like that for most of the time. Then Nanny brought the children down and Per went – children, she always says, exhaust her – and things were much better. Ann had brought *Jeremy Fisher* with her, I knew she would, and Evie the singing top she had for Christmas.

'Do go, Mr Elliott, if you like,' I said. 'I'm afraid I've contracted to read to my daughters and don't think I can back out now.'

'Don't be absurd,' he said. 'I used to love those books. I'll read if you like. People say my imitation of a frog in labour is quite marvellous.' And he did, read, I mean. The children loved it – so did I, but kept wondering where I'd heard the voice before – and sat quite still all the way through; when he'd finished they shouted for more.

After Nanny came to take them to bed, he said a bit abruptly, 'I must go now. Will you dine tomorrow night?' I said yes before I'd thought whether I could or not, and that's how it will be; he calls for me at seven thirty.

This room is cold and I must go to bed.

3 Cheyne Square, Chelsea – 10th January 1933
Cook has been: 'Don't bother about tonight, Mrs Andrews. I'll be dining out after all. We can keep the lamb cutlets for tomorrow.'

Cook purses her lips: 'What about the scallops then, Madam?' she says.

But I don't care about the scallops, or about Ann's throat. 'I only hope it isn't thrush, Madam,' or about my fitting at the dress-maker. 'I've had to re-do that seam, Mrs Charterhouse, can I see you at say two thirty?' I can only think of walking through the silent City with Barny.

'Have you ever done it before?' he asked. 'It's rather fun. Everyone's gone home, you see, and there's only you and the cats and the rats. I do it quite often.' I said no, never, but I'd like to and so we went.

But first we were conventional. We dined at the Ritz. 'Why the Ritz?' I asked, surprised. 'I shouldn't have thought it was your sort of place.'

'Well, you see, I'm doing a piece on financiers and I have this little arrangement with the head waiter. Also, one won't meet anyone one knows.'

We sat under a palm too near the violins; the food was too rich and the head waiter not as friendly as I'd been led to believe. Somehow it didn't matter, though. We giggled a great deal and I told him about ghastly City dinners with ghastly City bores, and he told me about beastly newspaper editors, beastly deadlines and losing one's luggage on the train to Kathmandu. We smoked incessantly, drank champagne like water and hardly ate a thing. It was when the orchestra had played the 'Merry Widow' waltz for the umpteenth time that he said we'd better go as the head waiter wanted our table. Would I like to dance at the Gargoyle or walk? I said walk, please. 'Alright then,' he said, 'we will but first I've got to do some horse trading over the bill.'

So I went to the Ladies, and there was Rachel Cohen. 'Char, darling. I thought it was you hiding under the palms with that

frightfully interesting-looking young man. Won't you join us?
Lew's in one of his moods and being too boring for words.'

'No,' I said. 'We're going for a walk round the City,' and
left her with her mouth open.

We took a cab to St Paul's; it was icy cold when we got out
and we held hands and ran up Cannon Street trying to get
warm. It was in a tiny churchyard reached by a dark alley,
that he said: 'Beautiful, angry, sad little Char, d'you want to
be fucked? If you don't it doesn't matter, but if you did, it
would be nice.'

I felt shocked at first. Silly really, I'd heard the word before,
of course. Pa trying to get through a gate out hunting and
Gilles, the groom, once when he didn't know I was there, but
never as a verb. I stood with my hands in the pockets of my
fur coat, thinking, my ears stinging with the cold. Then the
church clock above us whirred and began to chime midnight
and all the other City churches joined in. The noise was so
terrific, we simply clung to one another waiting for it to stop.
When everything was quiet again, I said alright, but where.

He looked searchingly at me, with that bright, childish look
he has, then after a moment seemed to have found what he
was looking for in my face. 'Here,' he said, 'between the
tombstones. It's much more fun outside, you know, and
Ebenezer Wentworth and his dear wife Martha should make
good company if we felt we needed it.'

So we made love on the cold, frosty grass, between the
tombstones of Ebenezer and Martha who 'Departed this Vale
of Tears 14th September 1741'.

It was lovely, and funny, too. How could two men
performing the same act be so entirely different? Algy,
outwardly so polite, restrained, never going too near the edge,
always so cool, collected and correct; in bed an ape man, a

Viking raping his woman, a Crusader home from the wars. Barny, outwardly abrupt, uncouth, with no finesse, always saying the first thing that comes into his head, in bed becomes a gentle, understanding, imaginative purveyor of love, a 'parfit knight' indeed. I felt my cold body slowly coming to life under his touch, all the pains and stupid discomforts forgotten. I cried a little after we had 'come'. Now I know what that means: Per's talked of it in women, but I never really believed her. I wonder if she's ever come with Bunny. Surely not?

Later, we walked along the Embankment and he put me in a cab at the river entrance to the Savoy, 'Tomorrow, or tonight, it's nearly four a.m., we'll tell one another about ourselves,' he said. 'Won't that be nice?'

'I've got a sort of committee meeting for my Battersea Settlement this evening,' I said. 'I go slumming, you see.'

'Don't call it that,' he said, putting his finger over my lips. 'Slum is an ugly word; you're helping people to help themselves, that's all.' He looked austere and rather shocked, as though I'd shouted a rude word in church.

'We have tea and biscuits,' I said, feeling guilty, 'and I usually drive my Aunty Roo home afterwards.' He smiled then, his whole face alight.

'In that case, I know what we'll do. I'll collect you from the Settlement. We drive your Aunty Roo home and then have supper at the Café Royal.' Of course, I agreed, but what on earth will Aunty Roo say? She adores Algy, then don't they all adore Algy?

3 Cheyne Square, Chelsea – 11th January 1933
Now I know where I've seen those eyes before. They belong to my poet, H. A. Elliott; it seems he's Barny's father!

'But I thought he was a pansy,' I said. 'He was,' he said,

'but he managed to father me. I've got the eyes to prove it.'

Let me go back to the beginning; there's not much time though. I'm taking Ann to a children's party at Richmond after lunch.

Well . . . he met me at the Settlement as we'd planned. Mrs Gladwyn: 'There's a gentleman to see you, Mrs Charterhouse. He says you'll know who he is.'

Everyone agog, of course; Aunty Roo put on her basilisk face and shut her spectacle case with a snap. 'Any relation to the Lincolnshire family, Mr Elliott? I used to stay with the Hornsby-Elliotts as a girl – mad on dogs and frightfully good at croquet.'

'No,' Barny said, smiling sweetly, 'but I wish I had been.'

Aunty Roo ignored this sally, although she looked as if she were trying not to giggle, and merely said, 'Put out the lights, dears and lock up. I'm for home and Bedfordshire.'

'But we're giving you a lift,' I said. 'You can't possibly walk all that way to the bus stop alone.' In the end she consented to come in the car, but she wasn't pleased and showed it.

'I wonder how dear Algy's getting on in Switzerland,' she said, as we drove over Battersea Bridge, breaking the somewhat charged silence. 'He's worked so hard lately, he needed a good rest. Such a pity, Char dear, you couldn't go with him.'

'He didn't ask me,' I said and we lapsed into silence again. Barny sat in the back smoking and winking at me whenever he caught my eye in the driving mirror.

It was noisy and hectic at the Café Royal, everyone talking at the tops of their voices. 'But at least no "Merry Widow" waltz,' Barny shouted above the din. We found a little table in an alcove where it was a bit quieter and ordered oysters, smoked salmon and champagne.

'Now,' he said, 'I want to know everything about you.'

So I told him and it didn't seem to amount to much, but he liked the bits about Old Bats and Hubert Stokes and laughed a lot over Pa and Babs Bellingham. 'And Algy the matador, what about him?'

'He was the handsome prince,' I said, 'who rescued the fair maiden from the tower; in my case, living with Ma in a sea of mud and broken-down machinery in the wilds of Dorset.'

'Do you love him?'

I had to think for a minute. 'Yes,' I said, 'I love him. Once I adored him, but now, when you're in the middle of things going wrong, it's hard to know.'

'I'd never marry you, you know,' he said, and it felt like a slap in the face, 'but I am in love with you. Does Algy still love you?'

'Of course.' I felt furious and wanted to hit him, but he smiled and put out his hand.

'Don't be angry, I'd make a rotten husband. I tried marriage once and it was a most grisly failure. Believe me, it would be again. I want us from the very beginning to know where we stand.'

'And if Algy finds out?'

'I'd run,' he said, 'to the ends of the earth.'

'You're a cad and a bounder,' I said.

'I am,' he said, 'but honest, you have to admit that.' He looked at me over the rim of his glass, his eyes laughing: his hair, as usual, needed a brush and his tie was just a little askew. Then, suddenly, I remembered. I saw again Bagland Common, the beautiful tramp throwing his hat for the monkey to fetch, laughing at its antics; heard the harsh, Cockney voice, 'Henry

Arthur Elliott, we are His Majesty's Officers of the Law . . .'

'Who are you?' I asked. 'Who was your father?' For the first time since I'd met him he looked nonplussed.

'I was about to give you my credentials, but—'

'Was he H. A. Elliott, the poet?'

'Someone's told you. They were bound to I suppose, London's so small—'

'No.'

'Then how—?'

'Because I met him. Because I was the little girl with him when he was shot by the police, and you see, I've always remembered his eyes.'

We just sat there then, with waiters and people milling about us.

'Sachie, darling, it's too sick-making. I've lost one of my gloves, do wait . . .' a pre-Raphaelite girl in green moaned past my chair.

At last Barny spoke. 'You must have known him better than I did,' he said. 'I only have two memories: one of him shaving under an apple tree with the shaving mirror hanging from a branch, his face all covered in lather, and the other, by the sea, taking me on his shoulders and running along the sands shouting and laughing. Are you an angel of death then, little Char; you brought it to him, will you bring it to me too?'

'Don't *say* such stupid things. He would have been caught anyway, the Common was crawling with police, Ma said—'

'I know,' he said. 'Don't worry, I'm only teasing. Shall we go, this place's too damned noisy.'

This time we walked along the Embankment, our arms round each other, and he told me about his life. How, after his father's arrest and his mother's death, he'd been taken to live with his paternal grandparents, who subsequently adopted him.

How he'd gone to public school, which he hated, to Oxford, where he'd been sent down and then, through a girlfriend, managed to get a job on a newspaper, since when he'd worked as a freelance journalist. 'Going anywhere and everywhere,' he said. 'It can be fun and keeps me off the drink.' His grandparents, old, doddery and saintly, had finally washed their hands of him.

'And your wife?' I asked.

'What was it Forster says in *Howards End*? "She was a rubbishy little thing and she knew it." A very fair description of Mollie. I ran away after six months; she married a pig farmer in Devon and is blissfully happy.'

We made love again; this time in the gardens along Cheyne Walk. My skirt was plastered in mud and Barny cut his hand on a stone.

'Must we?' I asked. 'Wouldn't it be better in a bed?'

'It might, I suppose,' he said. 'Let's have a try.' So we went back to Peter Steerforth's house and it was better – much, much better.

Algy home on Sat. Oh God.

3 Cheyne Square, Chelsea – 16th January 1933
Is it only sixteen days since I met Barny?

Algy home: sleek; brown from winter sun – and loving. 'Diana is a bit of a bore, darling,' he whispered into my hair. 'You were right; she never stopped moaning about her damned ankle and her nose turned bright red in the sun.'

'Oh, dear,' I said, 'how horrid for you.'

Perdita's right (she always is, except of course about her own life); having an affair helps one's marriage no end. Algy and I are getting on better than we have for years: he's even showing signs of interest in the bed department, so thank God for Diana. He and Barny are to meet! Dinner on Thursday: Barny to bring a woman, plus Per and Bunny.

'But who will you bring?' I asked Barny. 'She must be unattractive or I shall be jealous and give the game away.'

'Edwina Bolton,' he said promptly (too promptly?) 'She writes the Woman's Page on the *Echo*. She's a damned good sort: the matador'll love her, you see. She adores City gents, the more pucka the better – the matador is pucka, isn't he? She says they make a refreshing change from the rest of us.'

This afternoon he took me round the galleries in Bond Street: all snowy Dutch landscapes and bunches of flowers, and then to one in the Fulham Road presided over by a frowsty lady in purple with hairpins falling all over the place. It was freezing and badly lit, but had a picture by a man called Modigliani that would make a rat-infested cellar seem magical. A naked, elongated girl lying on a bed, her slanty eyes full of sadness. I wanted to bury my face in her lovely, soft, cool thighs and forget everything. 'You like it then?' Barny asked, sounding surprised.

'I do,' I said. 'It's the most beautiful thing I've ever seen.'

'Get Algy to buy it, then, to hang in his dining room.'

'He wouldn't,' I said. 'He only likes sporting prints.'

Ann said today, 'Mummy, when is the nice man going to read to us again?'

3 Cheyne Square, Chelsea – 20th January 1933

Algy likes the lady journalist! 'Such fun,' he says, 'and such a change from Diana. I always thought women journalists wore tweeds and trilbies and talked too much, but Edwina . . . You don't mind, darling, do you? She's taking me to Lord Cockermouth, the Press Baron's place, next weekend. You know you're always saying how boring my friends are, so here's my chance to meet some new ones. Edwina says the place will be simply crawling with artists and writer chappies.'

When I told Barny he looked pleased. 'Good old Edwina,' he said. 'Now I can take you to Jarrow and get on with your education.'

The dinner party was quite a success actually. Algy was a bit wary at first, but soon warmed to the sparkling Edwina. Bunny and Per in good form and my young man excelled himself. We laughed so much at his stories (none true, I'm sure), Algy did the nose trick and one of Per's false eyelashes fell into her crêpe Suzette. Later we danced at a new club Barny knows somewhere in Soho: stale sandwiches, bad champagne and a marvellous Negro band.

'But what on earth will we do in Jarrow?'

'You'll see,' he said, 'You'll see.'

Algy thinks I'm off to Ma's for the weekend: why do I have to lie and not him?

3 Cheyne Square, Chelsea – 31st January 1933
My back aches, my head aches, I've got curse pains but no curse and I'm bruised all over my backside. Last night on the way home, I lit a candle in Westminster Cathedral. I knelt in front of a rather sickly statue of the Virgin Mary. The chapel smelt of candle grease and unwashed bodies, and I damn near caught my sleeve alight in the candle flame. God, how alone one really is. It doesn't matter how many people love you, no one ever really reaches you. People like Barny get near, but they do more harm than good. They pry into your soul, batter you with ideas, force you to think about the world outside and then, when you're ready at last to take them in, turn round and blandly tell you it's not possible; they're not prepared to venture any further. And there you are, worse off than before,

because like Eve, turned out of the Garden of Eden, you can't go back. It's absurd, but I feel more alone than ever in my life before, and a little frightened too. I won't be for long; tomorrow, or perhaps the next day, I'll be strong again, but now . . .

Barny's going to China on Friday; sent by his agency. He knew he was going, he says, but didn't tell me until we were driving back from Jarrow because he didn't want to spoil it – CHRIST!

Algy and I had a ghastly row last night (hence the bruised backside). He said the beef at dinner was overcooked and threw his plate on the floor. I promptly hurled the salt cellar at him and Nanny had to separate us; she's the only one of the servants who'd dare, I suppose. I think I want to die, but am damned well going to join the Labour Party first. Barny's boat sails from Tilbury on Friday; he wants me to see him off, but can I bear to?

And the Jarrow weekend? It was sad, uncomfortable, lovely, funny, heartbreaking – oh, everything. If I never see Barny again I shall never, never forget it, even if I live to be a hundred. The reason for it was Barny had been commissioned to do a piece on the 'special areas', i.e. where unemployment is virtually out of control. He chose Jarrow because there it's reached sixty-seven per cent, and because a friend of his, one Reg Barstow, whom he met during the General Strike in '26, lives there. He's an ex-foreman in the shipyard, a senior official in the Union and a big wheel in the local Labour Party.

'He's always said, "Come and stay any time and bring a girl if you like, just so long as you tell them down South what's happening up here." So I'm taking him at his word. He's a darling man, you'll love him. When I asked what to bring in the way of a gift for the larder he said: "A ham from that fancy grocer's of yours in Piccadilly and enough whisky to keep my committee going for a couple of days." Knowing his committee, that means a crate.' In the end I bought the ham – the largest Fortnum's had – and Barny bought the whisky. We drove up there in an ancient Ford. 'The Hispano wouldn't go down too well,' Barny said. It was freezing and we broke down twice, but we sang Irish rebel songs, ate sticky buns and took a swig from B's silver flask when we felt the need for it.

We stayed the first night in a pub somewhere off the Great North Road on the edge of Yorkshire. They lit a fire in our bedroom and we went to sleep with the flames flickering on the ceiling. I woke cold and happy, to hear the sound of sheep under the window. Barny lay on his back, his black hair trailing on the pillow: I thought he was asleep, but he wasn't.

'What noisy sheep,' he said. 'It's time we were on our way.' It was only mid-afternoon when we reached Jarrow, but everywhere was dead. Our little car rattled through the empty streets, past boarded-up shops and empty offices and it started to snow gently.

We turned into a side street of respectable Victorian villas and stopped outside one with 'Glen Afton' in large, Gothic letters on the gate. Barny hooted and the noise echoed down the empty street. Then the front door to the house flew open and out came Reg, a tall, majestic-looking man in overalls, followed by Olive his wife, a tiny woman (smaller than me) in a pink flowered pinafore.

'Barny, it's been too bloody long – how are ye?' Reg said, embracing Barny. 'Who's the little lady?'

'This is Char and she's one of us,' Barny said, 'or will be by the time we've finished with her.' And by God I am. Whatever else the bastard's done, he's made a Socialist out of

me. After that I was embraced and we were swept into the house – oil cloth on the floor, aspidistra in the hall and a lovely, warm kitchen smelling of baking bread.

Our bedroom looked out on the sooty back alley behind the houses and was just big enough to take the huge brass bed in it. It was chillingly damp and cold, but in that room, in that bed, I found a happiness I thought impossible for one human being to experience. Perhaps it was the circumstances that made it so sweet and pure (silly words really but I can't think of any others). I don't know, but it was.

That night, after high tea, we met the committee and their wives. We drank B's whisky and they told us of Jarrow's shame and hopelessness. I couldn't help thinking, though, with men like them about, things couldn't be all that hopeless. Then back to 'Glen Afton', hot, strong tea and upstairs to our tiny bedroom. I undressed by the light of the gas lamp outside, and my feet congealed to ice on the freezing floor.

'You're beautiful,' Barny whispered. 'And somewhere locked inside you there's another Char, the real one. I was conceited enough to think I could free her, but now I know I can't, there just isn't time.'

'What do you mean by the real Char? It's not fair to start something and then not finish it.' But he put his finger over my lips as he had done that first evening and then we made love and forgot about everything.

Next morning the three of us – Reg, Barny and I – piled into the Ford and drove round Jarrow. Desolation beyond belief; at first I wanted to cry and then I just got angry.

'She's quite a militant, your Char,' Reg said as we drove away from a house in which a man, his wife plus four children, the youngest of which was suffering from croup, battled with, for me, quite unimaginable poverty, and I had tried to express

what I felt about a government who let such a wanton waste
of people's lives occur.

It was on our way back to London on Monday morning
that Barny told me about going to China. I couldn't speak at
first; just sat looking out of the car window, the muddy,
Midland fields and tawdry roadside cafes racing past me in a
blur of tears. He was going away for months, possibly years,
leaving me alone with nothing . . .

Cuckoo Farm, Dorset – 4th February 1933
Am down at Ma's. I fled from Tilbury yesterday; I simply
couldn't face going home. I rang Algy and told him Ma was
ill. 'You said she was so fit last weekend, what on earth's
gone wrong?' He sounded accusing and rather cross. 'We're
dining with the Maltravers on Saturday in case you've
forgotten. What the hell am I to say to them?'

'That Ma's ill, of course, what else? And why can't you
take Edwina?'

'Don't be childish,' he said, 'you know this dinner's
important . . .'

This afternoon I galloped Firefly over Digbery Down. The
wind was icy and my eyes watered from the cold. There was
just me, Firefly, and miles and miles of grass and I shouted
into the wind how I hated everything and everybody and no
one could be trusted any more. I felt a bit better after that and
rode home to tea.

Ma has a chef! He's a refugee from some Mid-European
country and is actually a professor of something or other. 'So
brilliant,' Ma says. 'A mind like that must not be wasted.' His
name's Paul and he is a good cook, actually, although his
cooking's wasted on Ma, who lives mainly on bread and
custard.

If I shut my eyes I can see the SS *Oriental Star* slowly moving away from the dockside. A band on the quay was playing 'Tipperary' and it was raining a bit. I could just see Barny high above me leaning over the rail waving, but there were so many heads it was difficult to see which one was his and I was crying anyway. I drove him down to Tilbury in the Hispano. He didn't seem to have much luggage, just a battered, leather suitcase covered in labels and a portable typewriter.

'Couldn't you have waited,' I said, 'just a little longer? We've only known each other a month and you're running away.'

'I'm not,' he said, 'running away. I want to go to China, I want to see for myself what's happening there; can't you understand?'

'But what about me? You said you were in love with me, you wanted to help.'

'I am in love with you,' he said, 'more than ever, but . . . but you must help yourself. Christ! Have you never thought how bloody lucky you are compared with ninety-nine per cent of the rest of the world?' I pulled the car into the side, switched off the engine and hit him in the face with all my might. He just rubbed his cheek and laughed. 'That's better, darling. I've never been able to stand self-pity.' I shut my eyes and tried to stop the tears.

After a bit I felt his arm go round me. 'There's a little time to spare,' he whispered. 'Shall we do it just once more? On board it won't be possible, I'm sharing a cabin with a man from the *News.*' And so we did, just once more, in a deserted warehouse somewhere in Wapping. When we got back to the car afterwards, a policeman was standing beside it.

'Is this your car, sir? I wouldn't leave it unattended again in an area like this, it's asking for trouble.'

'It's my wife, Officer. She's expecting a baby, you see, and I had to rush her round the corner to be sick.'

'I understand, sir, it takes them that way sometimes. I know, I've had seven myself.' After he'd gone we laughed so much I cried again, and then remembered.

'I'll write,' he said, 'I promise, and you'll be able to read my piece in the *Echo*.'

'Fuck the bloody *Echo*,' I shouted and he put his finger over my lips, but he was laughing.

And that was that, really.

Later, after he'd gone, I had a cup of revolting tea in some cafe near the docks, smoked two cigarettes and decided I couldn't go home, not for a day or two anyway. I rang Nanny and said I was off to Ma's and to ask Vera to pack a suitcase and I'd pick it up on the way, and here I am.

Ma was in bed when I arrived, Paul reading Browning's poems out loud to her. She knew at once that something was wrong. 'Make the child some of your lovely coffee with brandy in it, dear,' she ordered Paul, 'and leave us alone. We'll finish the poem another evening.' Of course, I told her everything. She listened without interruption; her knees under the bedclothes, drawn up to her chin, her eyes staring out into the dark garden – she never draws her bedroom curtains. When I'd finished, she put her hand on my head and ruffled my hair. 'My poor, poor, little girl,' she said. 'He sounds so amusing.'

It's odd how Ma can still surprise me, after all these years. 'It wasn't just he was amusing, Ma, it was—'

'I understand, dear. I'm not without experience of these things. Hubert and I, you know . . .' That was the nearest I've ever heard her come to admitting she had an affair with Hubert Stokes.

I must go back on Monday, I suppose, after all what else

can I do? I could run away, but where to? Ma says stick it out for the girls' sake; she's a fine one to talk.

I had such terrible dreams last night, all in brilliant, gorgeous colours. I swore, when I woke up, that I'd never forget them but I have already.

SS *Oriental Star*   10th February 1933

Char Darling –

Seven days out on this damned old crate and nothing to do but play poker, drink and argue with my fellow hacks.

How are you? Still cursing me for leaving you in the lurch? I hope so, it's better than crying. I think of you a lot and keep seeing your little figure in that absurd mink coat, waving from the quay. There was a fat lady leaning on the rail next to me who kept on obscuring my view. Eventually I had to ask her (politely of course) to get out of the bloody light, but by that time I'd lost you. The weather still cold, should be warmer when we reach Port Said, where I'll post this letter. Write to me via the Agency – if you feel like it, that is.

                                    Love, Barny

PS Someone gave me a copy of my father's collected poems for Christmas. I'd never read them before: they're truly marvellous – try them, but don't let the matador see. I'm sure he'd disapprove!

SS *Oriental Star* - Bombay   24th February 1933

Hope you got my letter posted in Port Said. Bombay hot but fun. Thought you'd like this picture – interesting positions, don't you agree? Don't let the matador see this either, it might give him ideas. Salt water seems to have got into my typewriter – was it sabotage or just fate?

Love, B

Cuckoo Farm, Dorset   24th April 1933

Dearest Char,

Home safely, but the train so hot and crowded. Arrived here to find Paul packed and waiting to leave – an offer of a job in America, he claims. I shan't be sorry to see him go, but one does expect a little gratitude.

Now dear: I had a long talk with Algy last night after you had gone to bed. He says that as far as he's concerned, the baby is his and will be brought up in exactly the same way as Ann and Evie. So there's no more need to worry, is there, on that score. People will talk, they always do, but if you and Algy maintain a united front no harm can come to the child, and it is his, or her, welfare that is of importance now. Algy understands this and I hope, my darling, that you do too. What you must now do is build up your strength, and no more visits to back street quacks or any tomfoolery of that sort. Dr Scott says he's very pleased with your progress, but you must rest and remember to take your iron tonic. Such a good idea to stay with Phyllis at Angmering. She's just the person you need: bracing and a good sort, but always so kind. Roo says Phyll and Ronnie's new house is quite lovely.

Pa writes 'why doesn't Char convalesce at Amberley – country air and peace is what she needs now.' Why he should be under the impression anyone would find Amberley peaceful I cannot imagine. The Russian woman, I understand, has a continual stream of indigent relations staying there. Bobby Prescott (you remember him, dear, you and he used to have lessons together. He's grown into such a nice young man) says he was woken up, when staying there the other day, by someone playing the balalaika under his bedroom window at four o'clock in the morning.

Give my love to dear Phyll when you see her.

All my fondest love,

Yr loving Ma

PS Paul has taken my Browning!

Temple Court, Angmering, Sussex – 15th May 1933
Dreamy, warm days of early summer. The shadows are spreading across the lawn and in a minute I must go in and change for dinner. Meanwhile, the woodpigeons coo in the shrubbery, Adam playing with a puppy, shouts with laughter from the rose garden and I just lie back and watch the smoke curling out of the chimneys and the swallows swooping and diving as they build their nests under the eaves.

It's months and months since I last wrote this diary; not since Barny went away. Next week I must go back to London and start life again. I feel so damned tired, though. I'm sure this baby will be a giant. It feels heavy already. Algy has a new girlfriend, Daphne Portman: dark, and rather clever, and mad on Algy (of course). He brought her down to meet me last weekend. 'And what about Edwina?' I asked.

'She is beginning to get a bit tiresome,' he said.

Since my illness he's been so polite. Will he be rude again once the baby's born? I hope so. Phyll said the other day, 'Oh Char, you are lucky to have such an attractive husband.' If she only knew . . .

From *The Times,* Monday, 2nd October 1933
CHARTERHOUSE: on 29th September, to Charlotte Mary
Charterhouse, wife of Algernon George Charterhouse of 3
Cheyne Square, Chelsea, London SW3 – a daughter.

Cuckoo Farm, Dorset – 14th October 1933
The baby turned out to be a girl after all – oh God! We've
called her Sophia; I don't know why, except Algy seems to
like the name. She's enormous, ginger haired and very quiet.
Yesterday, Nurse put her on my knee: she opened her eyes
and looked straight into mine and smiled. Only wind, of course,
and she was really looking at the brooch I was wearing, but
suddenly I saw Barny on New Year's Eve. 'That's a rather
childish game, isn't it, can anyone join in?'

I've no milk, thank God, so no ghastly feeding sessions.

'You must rest,' says Dr Scott, 'until you're really strong
again, and I would strongly recommend no more children.'
But I'm sick of resting, I want to live again. Ma drives Nurse
mad, me too, but the autumn trees are lovely and I'm getting
my figure back at last.

Mayfield Park, Morpeth, Northumberland

18th October 1933

Darling,

How are you both? You are resting I hope and eating properly.
I wonder how Nurse Gallop and your mother are hitting it off!
The weather up here has been marvellous and we've had several
good days. I bagged six brace yesterday – not bad! Per and Bunny
have now joined us, both in great form, and send you and Sophia
their love; the rest of the party rather mediocre.

By the way, I think it only right to tell you that a chap called Peter Steerforth appeared on Sunday with some girl in tow. He's rather thick with Per and told her that Barny Elliott is expected back at any moment. Apparently he sent this chap Steerforth a cable from Madrid threatening to park himself at his house in Flood Street again. Everyone here says he's the most frightful sponger.

Back Sunday and will be down the following weekend to bring you home.

All love,
Algy

Flood Street   6th November 1933

Char –

She's lovely . . . I saw her today in Chelsea Gardens. She was lying in her pram looking up at the trees and singing a little song to herself. She's mine, isn't she? She must be, she looks like my grandmother and anyway she's going to have those eyes.

'Good afternoon Mr Elliott,' says Nanny, looking up from her knitting. 'Back already?'

'Yes,' I say, raising my hat and sitting down beside her. 'I see there's been an addition to the family; how delightful.' Nanny purses her lips and goes on knitting.

'May I buy her a bunny rabbit?' I venture timidly.

'You must do what you think fit, sir,' says Nanny rising to her feet. 'We are going home for tea.'

Can I see you? What about dinner on Thursday? I've so much to tell. China was pretty hellish, but exhilarating all the same.

Barny

3 Cheyne Square, Chelsea – 10th November 1933
I won't see Barny, I won't. Why in God's name should I?
How *dare* he smarm round Nanny in the Park? He rang twice
yesterday, but Vera told him I was out. Algy, forgetting all
his promises, said last night at dinner, 'If that bastard comes
round here I'll break every bone in his body.' He couldn't, of
course, B's much stronger than he is, but how dare he when I
have to put up with all his ghastly girls.

Drove to Brooklands today with Tom Carstairs, a cousin
of A's. Such an amusing boy, with curly brown hair and bright,
blue eyes. He's just down from Oxford and he's absolutely
mad on cars. I think he might be falling for me . . .

3 Cheyne Square, Chelsea – 15th November 1933
I've seen Barny. He appeared, drunk, late last night. He must
have known somehow A was away. I was dead beat after hunting all day with the Surrey Union, and on my way up to bed,
when the front door bell rang. Vera, in her dressing gown, let
him in. He looked ghastly – unshaven, unwashed and ill. I told
Vera to bring black coffee and dragged him into the library.

'I want to see my daughter,' he kept on saying.

'You can't,' I said. 'She's asleep and she's not your
daughter anyway,' but he simply wasn't taking anything in.
Is this the man who took me to Jarrow? I sat him down on the
library sofa and when Vera brought the coffee, I whispered to
get a taxi from the rank outside. By this time B was shivering
and as he drank the coffee, some of it dribbled down his chin.

I felt sick and waited. By the time Vera put her head round
the door to say the taxi had arrived, he'd subsided into
incoherent muttering. Between us we managed to get him up
off the sofa and downstairs to the front door and the taxi driver
got him into the cab.

'You're a heartless, bloody bitch,' he shouted out of the window of the taxi, 'but I'll be back.'

Vera and I tottered into the house and Nanny appeared. 'Hot tea and brandy by the nursery fire, I think, Mrs Charterhouse.' How marvellous she is: thank God she refused the Pimlico greengrocer.

Flood Street   15th November 1933

Char,

I'm abject! Now you see what a hopeless contender for the marriage stakes I would have been. I really am most frightfully sorry. I have these bouts from time to time, you know, but swinish of me to have inflicted one on you. Will you ever forgive me? I suppose not.

I'll be out of town for a week or two; my grandmother has died at last – grandfather died in May – and I've to go to Oxford and sort things out. When I return *please* see me. I promise I'll be good. You're stronger than I am, darling, and thus you can afford to be magnanimous.

B

3 Cheyne Square, Chelsea – 4th December 1933

Algy and I have barely spoken for a fortnight. Then last night he came into my bedroom, took off his dressing gown and climbed into my bed. I told him to get out and go and find Daphne. I was sure she'd be only too glad for anything he had to offer. He took no notice and pulled my nightdress off my shoulders. 'You'll sleep with any man in London,' he said, 'so why not me?'

I managed to get hold of the carafe of water from my

bedside table and poured the contents over his head, then while he was spluttering and shouting imprecations, I dashed out of the room and upstairs to the nursery. In the end I spent the night in Nanny's bed.

To Harrods this afternoon Christmas shopping. Ann so funny talking to Father Christmas. Evie wouldn't. 'Take the horrid old man away,' she shrieked.

Per says Barny's back, but no word. She met him at the Café Royal looking rather subdued, she said. He told her he was on the wagon and she thinks this must be true; he's dining with them tomorrow night.

What is going to become of me? I feel like a mouse in a treadmill. 'You must eat,' says Pa at dinner last night. 'Your Great Aunt Connie was locked up because she wouldn't eat.' I said a lunatic asylum would be a rest compared to what I have to endure.

The Carlton Club   Monday, 11th December 1933

Dear Char,

I have decided to spend a few nights at my club. We simply cannot go on like this. I find I am no longer able to think properly and this is beginning to affect my work. Also these continual scenes cannot be good for the children. Will you please arrange for Vera to pack a bag for me – I shall need a white tie.

I will ring you in a day or two, when perhaps we can discuss our future in a more or less rational manner.

Yrs,
Algy

The Carlton Club   Friday, 15th December 1933

My dear Char,

I'm sure you will agree our dinner last night was an unmitigated disaster and should not be repeated. It only serves to prove my point: that until you consent to give up this rackety, futile life you've been leading these last months, there's no hope for our marriage. You're never at home and therefore unable to attend to the smooth running of the household, rarely bother to visit the children in the nursery and flatly refuse to conform to even the basic behaviour any normal man is entitled to expect from his wife. This latest nonsense of becoming a Socialist (presumably at the instigation of that slimy bounder, Elliott, in a ludicrous attempt to humiliate me) is simply the culmination of a series of self-centred, hysterical and hostile acts towards a husband who has always done his best for you and yours.

I'm sorry if this letter appears harsh; it's not intended to upset you, but to try and make you understand how impossible it is for us to continue in the way we have been. For the immediate future I suggest I take Ann and Evie to Father's for Christmas. It can't be good for them to witness the sort of scenes that have become a daily occurrence at home. Old Nanny Briggs will be there and Father and Anthea will, they say, be delighted to have us. I suggest you take the baby and Nanny to Amberley, unless you would prefer your mother's; we will then be able to shut up the house.

In the New Year we can decide what's best to do. As I told you last night, I consider the only answer is to get rid of the lease on 3 Cheyne Square and move to the country. You've always liked gardening and country life, and you would manage to get much more hunting in: such a move would, incidentally, benefit your health.

Let me have your view on the above as soon as possible. Meanwhile, I will confirm with Father that I am taking the girls there for Christmas.

Yours,
Algy

3 Cheyne Square, Chelsea – 19th December 1933
This afternoon I saw Barny. We met by chance in Royal Avenue in the pouring rain. I'd just come out of the dressmaker's and was looking for a cab; he was standing under the lamppost holding an umbrella and looking lost.

'Hullo,' I said.

'Hullo,' he said and then we were walking together through the rain. It was only three o'clock but it was so dark the lights were on in all the houses.

'I was thinking,' he said, 'of going to Battersea Dogs Home; would you like to come too?'

'Alright,' I said, and so we went.

Inside the Home it was warm and rather smelly and the noise was terrific. We hardly spoke, just wandered about looking in the cages. Then we stopped in front of one in which crouched a small, black collie. His head rested miserably on his paws, each one tipped with a minute dash of white as though they'd been dipped in a jug of cream; his eyes were the saddest I've ever seen. Above his door a notice read, 'Raffles, found on the canal bank with a stone tied round his neck'. We stood there for a minute or two just looking. Then Barny said, 'Shall I give him you for Christmas?' I thought of all the complications: of Algy sulking at his club; of the children; the servants; the mess I was in.

'Yes,' I said.

168

'He's about four months old by his teeth, and not house-trained of course,' the lady at the desk said, 'but a fine little fellow all the same.'

Outside on the pavement we stood together, jostled by people clutching their dripping umbrellas, Raffles jerking at the end of a piece of string, ecstatic at his sudden release.

'D'you want to come back to tea?' I asked.

'Yes, please,' he said, so we hailed a cab. Inside Raffles jumped on the seat between us, his soggy paws slithering on the upholstery. He lifted his face for a kiss, then jumped down and peed against Barny's leg.

'It's what I deserve,' Barny said. 'The animal shows discrimination.'

Vera opened the front door. 'Oh, Madam, what ever have you got there?' she said as Raffles dashed across the hall and into the library, leaving a trail of muddy footprints.

'Is she referring to me or the canine?' Barny whispered in my ear.

Later, Raffles ensconced in the servants' hall, a bone between his paws, surrounded by a sycophantic group which included Nanny and the girls, Barny said, 'Can I see her just this once: my daughter?'

'But why should you want to?' I said, 'Why?'

'I just do,' he said, 'that's all.' So we went upstairs to the night nursery, where Sophia lay on her back in her cot, blowing bubbles, her green-brown eyes squinting at the light, her long, thin, pink fingers clutching the enveloping blanket.

'What did the matador say?' Barny asked. 'Was he very, very angry?'

'He behaved like a gentleman,' I said, 'but I nearly died.' He reached into the cot and took Sophia's hand. She turned her head and gave him a long, unwinking stare.

'Will you tell her one day,' he said, 'who her father was?'

'No,' I said, 'why should I?' He didn't reply, but bent down and kissed Sophia on the forehead.

'We shan't know one another, then,' he said to her as though she were already adult. 'What a pity, we might have got on.'

She stared at him a little longer, then her lids began to droop and she slept. We crept out of the room and downstairs.

'I must go now,' he said. 'I'm dining with the Big White Chief and I leave for Mexico on Thursday. Thank you for letting me see her; may I send her a present?'

'If you like,' I said. 'If you really want to.'

Then he put his arms round me and kissed me long and hard. 'Goodbye then, little thing, look after Sophia and the dog, won't you? Don't fret too much for the matador, there are plenty more like him in the sea, and remember to keep the Red Flag flying.'

Then he ran downstairs and I heard him calling goodnight to Vera. The front door slammed; I heard Vera's footsteps going down the back stairs to the basement and after that – silence.

3 Cheyne Square, Chelsea – 21st December 1933
Another pompous, idiotic letter from Algy. Has Daphne finally driven him round the bend? The accusations pour from his pen daily now; it's not me who needs the doctor. He's found out about Raffles and says the animal must be instantly returned to Battersea Dogs Home; if not, he will be shot. Who, one wonders, will do the shooting? He doesn't specify – Daphne perhaps? Meanwhile, Raffles sleeps on my bed and has become the idol of the nursery.

This afternoon I and a tall, earnest, bespectacled youth, newly down from Cambridge, distributed Labour pamphlets in the World's End. During tea in a Lyons Tea Shop, he told me how he hoped one day to become Prime Minister! When we parted, he squeezed me on the shoulder and said, 'I can't tell you how much I admire your pluck Mrs C.' Silly, I suppose, but nice all the same.

To Amberley on Friday for Christmas; Sophia, Nanny and me plus Raffles. Pa says: 'The house is full of Ruskies, darling, but you won't mind that, will you?'

Ann and Evie don't want to go to Father's at Redhill. 'It's horrid there,' Ann says, 'and there's nothing to do except play boring word games with Aunt Anthea and listen to Grandpa Charterhouse snoring.'

Algy has been complaining about me to Ma. Dr S prescribes bromide; if that don't slow me down, nothing will, he says.

From the *Daily Echo,* Saturday, 23rd December 1933
Journalist and man-about-town, Barny Elliott, son of the poet, H. A. Elliott, is pictured here boarding the SS *California* at Tilbury yesterday en route for Mexico. Mr Elliott told our reporter he wished to study this fascinating country at first hand and hopes to gather enough material for a book on the subject.

Amberley – Boxing Day 1933
It's quiet by the library fire. Only the ticking of the grandfather clock nags at the silence. Natasha 'rests' upstairs, everyone else shooting, and here I sit with my bottle of bromide, 'poor little Char', who's fucked up her marriage. I can't go back to Algy now, it's too late and he doesn't want me anyway. Will he marry Daphne? Shall I run away to Mexico, or just go down to the river and jump in?

B's promised present to Sophia arrived. A box from

Hamleys, inside a lettuce and inside that a white, furry rabbit with pink eyes. 'What an extraordinary present,' says Pa, snorting into his champagne, but Sophia likes it: she laughs when the lettuce opens and pokes her long finger into the rabbit's eye.

The Russians wept on Christmas Day and all got very tight; I got tight too; but didn't weep. Natasha says I need to be fulfilled. 'Does Pa fulfil you?' I asked.

'Of course not,' she said, 'but I love him just the same.' I don't think I'll write this diary any more. In fact, on New Year's Eve I'll put it on Pa's bonfire. I wish I could do the same to the year 1933 . . .

11

Again, she didn't. The 1933 diary was not consigned to Pa's bonfire, but survived all the many moves of Char's later years. The story it had to tell was entirely new to me and to be truthful came as a considerable shock. It also begged a great many questions, not the least of which was did Sophia know Algy had not been her father? Had Char kept her promise never to tell her, and was Barny Elliott the love of her life or merely a catalyst?

I decided to ask Sophia to dinner, feeling oddly annoyed that after all these years it was me, of all people, who should be the one to tell her about her parentage. I never doubted, by the way, that I should. I prepared the meal with great care: beef bourguignon, followed by lemon sorbet, her favourites, I knew. When everything was ready, too tense to sit and wait for her arrival, I watched from the kitchen window for her blue Metro to appear in the car park below, my hands absurdly sticky with perspiration. In the event, she arrived twenty minutes late, on foot and in a temper, having had to wait half an hour for a bus at Hyde Park Corner. 'The bloody car's in dock,' she said as I followed her into the kitchen. 'Why do you have to live such miles from anywhere?'

During the meal, which she ate with relish, I found myself every now and again trying to trace those others, the poet and his son, in her features. She had their eyes, certainly: large, green, cat's eyes, flecked with brown. The white skin too, perhaps, and her hair, now streaked with grey, in youth had been black as a crow's feather. I remembered how years ago, when I first knew her, she'd frightened me a little: she'd seemed so powerful, forthright and uncompromising; one knew without a doubt she would never tell you what you'd like to hear, but only what she believed was the truth.

'Guy, poppet, aren't we a bit *distrait* this evening? For the last five minutes you haven't listened to a word I've said, and you've got that vacant look in the eye. What's up – Mum's past beginning to give you the gyp?'

I cut myself a small piece of Brie and placed it carefully on a Bath Oliver biscuit. 'There is something, actually, but let's wait till we've finished the meal, then we can go into the other room and have some of your brandy.' (She'd brought me back a bottle of Courvoisier from Brussels.) 'And I'll tell you.'

'I knew there was.' She sounded triumphant. 'From the moment I saw your face peering down at me from the kitchen window; you looked like an anxious school girl.'

Huffily I began to stack the plates and put out coffee cups; she could be damned annoying at times. She came up behind me and stuck her tongue in my ear; it was warm, wet and it tickled, it also excited me in a way that, at that moment, I had no wish to be excited. 'Come on, dish the dirt. What have you discovered about my Mum?' I turned to find the cat's eyes alight with laughter, and seemed to hear that other voice from long ago: 'That's a rather childish game, isn't it, can anyone join in?'

In silence we carried our coffee and the brandy into the sitting room. It was a warm evening, the big window open on to the slow-moving river, the scent of cherry blossom mixed with petrol and a dash of tar wafted up from the tidily 'landscaped' garden that surrounded the concrete garage boxes belonging to the flats. I poured two liberal brandies and we sat down side by side on the sofa. With hands that shook a little, I picked up Char's diary for 1933. 'Have you ever seen this before? It was in your mother's trunk.'

'I don't think so,' she said, snatching it from me and riffling through the pages. 'As a matter of fact, I didn't know Mum ever kept a proper diary after she'd grown up. What fun! It's the year of my birth too.' Brandy glass in her hand, she began to read avidly; a child immersed in its comic.

'Sophia,' I said desperately, 'have you ever considered the possibility that Algy might not be your father?' Her eyes were still travelling down the page, open, I noticed, for some time in January.

'I know he wasn't,' she said, and I was at once relieved and overcome with a ridiculous sense of anticlimax: I was not, after all, it seemed, to be the bearer of earth-shaking news.

'Do you,' I asked, 'know who he was?'

'Barny Elliott,' she said. 'I still have the white rabbit he gave me: it's lost its eyes and its lettuce is a bit moth-eaten, but otherwise —'

'Never mind all that,' I said crossly. 'Why didn't you tell me before, you must have known how important it was.'

'I don't see why it was important to you, you never—'

'Of course it was.'

'Anyway, if Mum had wanted you to know she'd have told you. You see, she was one of those women who seem to be rather like the female spider: they view all men as potential fathers to their children—'

'Oh, don't be silly.'

'It's perfectly true. It happened over and over again. Mum would fancy herself madly in love with some guy; would be,

I suppose, until that is, she produced their child; after that she had no further use for them. I realise I'm being much too simplistic, but that's roughly how it was.'

'Why d'you always have to be so damned cynical about your mother? Apart from all else, doesn't it mean anything to you that you're the granddaughter of one of the great English poets—'

'Oh, don't be so pompous.'

We were silent for a minute, then, 'How did you find out about your father?' I asked.

Sophia lit another cigarette and took a sip of brandy. 'By mistake, if you really want to know,' she said. 'I was fifteen at the time. It was when Mum and George were still living in Camberley and I was staying with them for part of my school holidays. I had a great friend then called Nina Barrington. Nina and I used to go out together, and one Saturday afternoon two guys picked us up in the local cinema. After the programme was over they asked us for a drink. We agreed, of course, and off we all went to the local hotel. However, after a couple of gin and oranges in the posh cocktail bar, Nina and I came to the conclusion that our escorts were a bit of a bore and no way did we want to spend the evening with them. We therefore put our normal escape plan into action – we were old hands at this lark, you see – which consisted of nipping off to the Ladies and simply not coming back.

'Unfortunately, just as we were on our way out of the bar, rather on the giggly side, both of us being unused to gin, who should we bump slap into, but bloody George; at that period very much into his role of heavy step-father. He immediately seized me by the arm and to my acute embarrassment more or less frogmarched me out to the car, shouting that I was behaving like a drunken tart and if he had his way he'd put me

over his knee and beat the living daylights out of me. Not
unnaturally, by this time I too was in a blazing temper. When
we got back to the house we found Mum stirring the soup, a
cigarette in her mouth and a glass of gin and French
conveniently placed on a table beside her. George pushed me
through the door. "This child will go the way of her wretched
father if something's not done about her pronto," he roared.
"She's drunk."

' "Don't bring Daddy into it," I shrieked. "And if you're
talking about bad examples, if anyone's to blame it's you and
Mum."

'In the ensuing scuffle, in which Mum hit me in the face, I
seized her by the hair and George had to separate us. I forgot
what he'd said about my father until much later. By the time I
did, Mum and I had made it up, and I asked her what George
had meant. At first she refused to come clean, but in the end
she told me, insisting I promise never to let on that I knew.'

'What a perfectly awful way to find out,' I said, genuinely
shocked. 'It must have been fearfully traumatic.'

'It was, I suppose,' she said. 'I seem to remember I even
cried.' She ran her long fingers through her hair and squinted
at me through a cloud of smoke. 'But later I began to get
interested. Then we did H. A. Elliott's poems for A-level Eng
Lit. Wasn't that funny?'

'I suppose so,' I said, not thinking so at all. 'But why, if it
was such a secret, did Char tell George? He'd be bound to
blab it all over the place.'

'He did,' she said, 'when I was younger. He used to shout
when goaded beyond endurance by Mum, that I had what he
referred to as "tainted blood".'

'The bastard,' I said, gripping my brandy glass, 'the old
bastard.'

'I'm the bastard, ducky, not poor old George,' she said. 'But I think in a way Mum was rather proud of her affair with Barny Elliott; somehow it became romanticised in her mind and ceased to be the rather squalid going-off-the-rails of a bored society bitch which in reality it must have been.'

'Sophia!' This time I really was shocked. 'How can you say such a thing? It wasn't like that at all.'

'Mum used to tell me I was conceived in a warehouse in Wapping; does it say that in there?' And she tapped the diary. 'A nice twist to an old theme, don't you agree? So amusing to fuck in a warehouse, darling —'

'IT WAS NOT LIKE THAT AT ALL,' I shouted, then realised suddenly she was on the verge of tears. 'Sophia, love, just read the diary, that's all, just read it.'

Later, when we'd made love and she lay beside me, her head resting on my shoulder, I asked her about Barny Elliott.

'I believe he saw me once when I was a baby. He was killed in a plane crash a couple of years after I was born. He worked for a news agency and was on his way to cover the war in Abyssinia. I've got his obituary from *The Times* somewhere: it says he was a "fine journalist and a fearless seeker after truth". Funny, I don't even know what he looked like.'

'Let's go to sleep,' I said. 'We have to be up early in the morning.'

A week or so later I paid another visit to Aunty Phyll; she greeted me with enthusiasm. 'Where ever have you been dear? I thought you'd deserted me. The home help gave me a pot of Gentleman's Relish last Christmas and I've made a few sandwiches. I do hope you like it.'

'My favourite,' I said. Actually I had never tasted the stuff before: there are, I'm afraid, an awful lot of gaps in my education, or so Char used to tell me. Something was different about the place. At first, I couldn't think what it was, then realised, no reggae music. Instead a frenzied commentator shouted above the roar of racing motor cars.

'New lodgers,' said Aunty Phyll, as she struggled up the stairs. 'They work at night and watch the box all day; I preferred the reggae.'

The Gentleman's Relish turned out to be delicious and so was the tea. I decided to broach the delicate subject of Sophia's birth. 'Barny Elliott,' said Aunty Phyll surprisingly, 'was a rather remarkable young man. Ronnie always said he was the right person for Char. He captured all of her, d'you see; her mind and her body. But he had a fatal weakness,' and she raised an imaginary tankard to her lips.

'You surprise me,' I said. 'Not about the fatal weakness, that I knew, but I thought he would have been looked on with disapproval by Char's family.'

'He was mostly. He came from a different world d'you see, and of course Algy loathed him.'

'You knew him, then. From Char's diary I thought—'

'He stayed with us at Angmering. He was desperately unhappy and very much in love with Char. I never told her I'd met him. He made me promise I wouldn't.'

'But I don't see —'

'Char convalesced with us in the May of the year Sophia was born – '33 it was, I think. I don't know if you're aware of the circumstances?'

'I can guess, but her diary's not specific.'

'I'm not surprised,' and Aunty Phyll's voice took on a slightly acid quality. 'Well, the truth was that when she discovered herself to be expecting Barny's child – she realised

Algy would know at once it wasn't his, she'd refused to sleep with him since the birth of Evelyn – she completely lost her head. Her only idea seems to have been to get rid of the baby. Instead, however, of telling someone like that frightful friend of hers, Perdita Grant, who would have been able to produce some expensive Harley Street abortionist, she dosed herself with every quack remedy from quinine to neat gin, and when that didn't work, got herself filthy drunk, climbed into a hot bath and started poking about with a knitting needle.'

'Oh my God,' I said.

'Oh God, it was. Luckily for her and Sophia, she left the bathroom door unlocked: that marvellous Nanny of theirs happened to be passing, heard rather odd noises, dashed in and saved the day. But of course Char was frightfully ill afterwards.'

'Do you think,' I said slowly, 'she didn't really want to get rid of the baby, but merely gain sympathy?'

'I think so,' said Aunty Phyll briskly, 'and of course she did.'

'But how did you come to meet Barny Elliott?'

Aunty Phyll poured us both another cup of tea, and lit a cigarette. 'It was after he got back from China. Some friend of his had told him about Sophia's birth. He never seems to have been in any doubt that the baby was his, and he tried to see Char, who of course would have nothing to do with him. Then Perdita Grant suggested he came to see me. She said I might be able to help.'

'And you liked him?'

'Yes,' she said simply, 'I liked him; we both did. I remember him coming so well. I was weeding the big border by the terrace; it was one of those lovely autumn afternoons one can get sometimes in November, and suddenly there was this tall, heavy-looking young man standing beside me. He was wearing one of those broad-brimmed felt hats men used to wear in those days, and he looked so pale and sad. "Are you by any chance Cousin Phyll?" he said. "I'm sorry to bother you, but I've been told you might help; it's about Char, you see." '

' "You're Barny Elliott," I said, "you've your daughter's eyes."

' "Have I really?" he said. "How nice."

'Well, in the end, he stayed three days. I was nervous about what Ronnie might say when he got back from the City and found the young man, but the dear simply took it in his stride. He was like that, my Ronnie. On the surface so conventional, but inside a romantic in the real sense. His advice to Barny was to run off with Char. "Abduct the girl," he said. "It's the only way with women like that. Then get her working; it doesn't matter what damn fool cause she takes up, but get her working; keep her busy in bed and out of it and she's yours." It was good advice up to a point, but we all knew really he'd lost Char by leaving her in that idiotic way so soon after they'd met.

' "Why did you do it?" I asked him.

' "Because I'm a self-destructive idiot," he said, "and needed the money. I was frightened, too, of marriage, I suppose." What could one say?

'The last evening he spent with us he cried with his head in my lap: it's a horrible thing to see a man cry. The next morning he caught the early train to town with Ronnie, and I never saw him again. He was killed a year or so later in an air crash, but I expect you know that.'

'Do you think if he hadn't bolted to China like that, he and Char might have made a go of it?'

'Yes,' said Aunty Phyll, firmly, 'I do. Of course, it would

have been a marriage full of fireworks, but it would have been a marriage. He was the man for her, no doubt of it, but she chose to play safe, d'you see. Barny would have treated her as a grown-up and she didn't want that, she felt safer as a child. And look where it got her; nearly forty years married to that bore George.'

We were silent, listening to the raucous, canned laughter emanating from the lodgers' TV. Suddenly the noise ceased, to be followed shortly by thunderous footsteps on the stairs, the slam of the front door, then blessed silence.

'You loved Char very much, didn't you?' Aunty Phyll said. 'In spite of everything.'

Carefully, I collected the tea things together and stacked them neatly on the tray, then swept the crumbs up with my handkerchief.

'Never mind that now, dear; you did, didn't you? Most men did, you know, it's nothing to be ashamed of.'

I nodded, 'Yes,' I said, 'I loved her.'

And that was that.

12

For several days after my visit to Aunty Phyll's I felt overcome with a sense of my own inadequacy. Was that really what people thought – Sophia too – that I was in love with the ghost of my mother-in-law? The last time I'd heard those words were from Beth, just before she walked out: 'You're in love with my bloody mother,' she'd said. 'You're just as mad as she is.'

I decided I was becoming morbidly obsessed with the past and needed a holiday. Sophia was in Geneva, involved in yet another conference, so as I had some leave due to me, I accepted a long-standing invitation from friends in New York. Returning ten days later having drunk more, talked more, met more people and visited more galleries and theatres than I had in years, I felt ready to tackle once again what seemed to be fast turning into some kind of personal odyssey; for I was slowly beginning to realise that whilst disinterring Char's past, I was also, albeit rather painfully, clearing some of the accumulated rubbish and clutter from my own.

While I'd been away Sophia had ferreted out the address of Natasha Marcolini, Pa's second wife; she who ran off with the Italian gardener. She was, apparently, still alive and living in Gloucestershire. 'Bed-ridden,' Sophia said, 'but on the ball. Her husband's fifteen years her junior and still runs the market garden.'

I told Sophia of Aunty Phyll's meeting with Barny Elliott, but she merely said, as she had done after reading her mother's diary, that she didn't as yet know what her reaction to the knowledge of the real relationship between her parents might be. She would, she said, let me know when she did. 'It was a long time ago and on the face of it, of little importance to anyone, but oddly enough I think it might have for me,' was the only comment she made on the subject.

Natasha Marcolini turned out to be a rather bacchanalian figure; a lady, perhaps, from a picture by Rubens. She greeted me from the depths of an enormous double bed covered in dogs. The famous hair, now dyed orange, was pinned into a sort of untidy cushion on top of her head, her body still voluptuous, beneath the slightly grubby flannelette nightdress and pink bed jacket she was wearing.

'So you are my little Char's son-in-law,' she said. Her voice, heavily accented in spite of a lifetime spent in England, was husky and seductive. 'Sit down and tell me what you want to know.' Then turning to the tall, gloomy young man who, having answered my rather timid summons at the front door, had silently conducted me upstairs to her bedroom, she shrieked: 'Take those damned dogs out of here, they smell, and bring Mr Horton some tea.' The young man's expression didn't change, but he suddenly let out a series of yodelling noises, in the manner of a huntsman calling in his hounds, to which the pack, much to my relief, instantly responded and surged, puffing, panting, tails wagging, off the bed and out of the room. The door closed behind them and Natasha smiled invitingly. One could see how gorgeous she must once have been. 'Now, tell me,' she said.

So I told her, as best I could, what it was I had been trying to do, also a little about Char's final years: the breakdowns;

the collapse of her marriage to George.

'He was no good for her, that George, not strong enough. I knew from the first, and told her so, but she wouldn't listen. Did you know I was with her when she met both her second and third husbands?'

I shook my head. 'George I know well, of course, but Char rarely spoke of Beth's father. She did keep some of his letters, though. He sounds rather fun.'

'He was beautiful,' Natasha said simply, 'but fun? No, I think not.' Outside the window someone was trying to start up a tractor; from another part of the house came the beat of rock music. There was a tap on the door and the young man reappeared carrying a tea tray. The tea pot was of heavily ornamented silver, the cracked sugar basin fine Chelsea, and instead of cups there were two mugs decorated with scenes from the life of Winnie the Pooh. The young man placed the tray on the rather spindly table by the bed, removing as he did so, several misty photographs in silver frames, which he carefully placed on the crowded dressing table. Natasha didn't thank him and waited until he had once again left the room before she spoke. Had they had a row, I wondered, and who was he, anyway?

'Now Guy – I can call you Guy, can't I? There's a bottle of vodka and two glasses in the jerry cupboard. It will help us to endure Igor Ivanovitch's tea.' I obediently poured us each a small vodka. She sipped hers and smiled. 'Aah, that is better. Now, where do you want me to begin?'

'Anywhere,' I said. 'Perhaps when you first met Char.'

'That is easy. I first met Char in the summer of 1926. She looked like a little brown bird, I remember. Her hair was short and fuzzy in those days and her figure like a boy. But then she would smile at you and throw back her head, so, and you could soon understand what the men saw in her. My Dick, her father, he had that smile too. It was formidable. Poor Algy, he adored her so it was quite ridiculous. We dined together, the four of us, at the Savoy, just after Dick and I were married. Dick was so nervous. He thought, you see, that Char and I would not get on. "To have a step-mother three years younger than herself, and she's always been difficult," he said. But it was like your Stanley and Livingstone; we looked at one another and clicked. "Ma's such a bore," Char would say. "Always going on about things; you're much better," and we would scream with laughter. The young can be very cruel.'

'What went wrong,' I asked, 'between her and Algy?'

'The sex ran out,' she said simply. 'Algy was a very attractive young man, but not so good as a lover. Once the babies started coming, he didn't understand that because she'd had such a bad time, Char needed gentleness, imagination, understanding.

' "It's just the same every night," she would say. "He cleans his teeth, brushes his hair, puts his loose change on the dressing table, then climbs into bed in his nice, clean, striped flannel pyjamas, blows his nose and starts. I can't stand it any more, and it hurts." I tried to get Dick to make Algy understand, but, of course, he couldn't; it was impossible for a man such as Dick to see such things. Well, naturally, soon Algy began to look elsewhere. He was never short of girlfriends, there were strings of them: his Dianas, and Daphnes, and Mollies. He would ask Char quite formally if she minded whether he took one away for the weekend. You know Char; she told him to do whatever he damned well liked, but the hurt was there all the same. But she simply could not understand that if she wanted to keep Algy, she must sleep with him, and gradually she lost him.'

'And Barny Elliott?'

'He was very important to her, I think. He woke her up, she said. But what was the good of that? The Prince rides up to the enchanted castle, wakes the Sleeping Beauty in her bower, and then rides off into the sunset without her. Dick and I were away for six months in '33, travelling around the world, so we never met him; we only got back in time to pick up the pieces.' She smiled suddenly and gulped her vodka. Fleetingly I wondered if it was doing her any harm, but at four p.m. on a warm afternoon, it had already succeeded in making me fairly light-headed, so I, too, took another sip myself.

'Little Sophia, such a funny, grown-up, guilty sort of child. Are you in touch with her? She never married I believe.'

'Actually, I see quite a lot of her,' I said. 'Did you know she's something pretty high up in NBZ?' Natasha shook her head not, it seemed, all that impressed with this piece of information.

'Ah,' and her leopard eyes searched my face, 'you sleep with her – no?'

I felt myself blush. 'As a matter of fact, I do, but it's in no way connected with—'

'Of course not.' Her voice was soothing; pandering to a child. 'She is beautiful?'

'Not beautiful exactly, but she has a quality, a sparkle; a sort of hint of wickedness mixed with goodness, hard to explain. We met at Char's funeral. I hadn't seen her in years. Perhaps it was me who had changed, but she seemed different to the way I remembered her.'

'Free from the guilt, perhaps. I wonder.' She took a gulp of vodka and looked at me with eyes half closed. 'No, you are not quite as I imagined, young man, not quite; there is something . . . something missing.' I looked at her blankly.

'But I wasn't aware. Sophia, has she—?'

Natasha shrieked with laughter and then started to cough. 'For many years after I left her father,' she said when she had recovered, 'Char and I would write each other a Christmas letter. We had no secrets, you know, she and I. We told each other everything. It was in her last letter, I think that she wrote of dear Guy, her oh-so-perfect son-in-law, and I thought, lucky Char to have such a one.'

'When did the letters stop?' I asked, hoping to get her off the subject.

'In the 1970s. I wrote as usual and she never replied. After that there seemed no point in going on. We hadn't seen each other for twenty years and probably never would again.'

For a moment we contemplated the inexorable passing of time. She gestured to me to refill our glasses. I obeyed, knowing I should have to spend the night in a local pub. I couldn't drive back to London in my present state.

'Did you know,' Natasha said once we had settled down again, 'Char became physically paralysed for a time, after the break-up of her marriage? We had her at Amberley and for weeks she lay in a darkened room. Of course, in those days there was little they could do for such cases but wait and hope things might get better. It was a trying time for all of us. Con insisted on coming to stay – Dick was always putty in that woman's hands – and drove away all the servants. And the specialists we had from town said that Char might never recover. But they were wrong and she came out of it at last. I remember the moment so well: I was sitting beside her one morning as she lay in bed, her eyes wide open, simply staring up at the ceiling, reading to her from the newspaper. I would do this each day for a little while; the specialist had said it might help her to return to life. On this particular morning I was reading about Barbara Hutton collapsing from starvation and being taken into a nursing home, when Char suddenly said in her normal voice: "Stop reading that balls, Nat, I think I can hear the cuckoo." We listened and so it was, a cuckoo, I mean; the first of summer, and the tears poured down my face.

'It was after that Dick and I took her to India with us. On the way home we stopped off at Colombo, and that's when she met her second husband.'

'He was an actor, wasn't he? My ex-wife, Beth, had an old photo of him as Sidney Carton, she—'

'We were dining out in Colombo,' Natasha, well into her story, ignored my interruption. 'Dick had many business acquaintances there – tea you know,' I nodded. 'Char was bored and sat smoking and twiddling her rings in the way she did when she was bored. Suddenly a little eternity ring she had, it was emerald and so pretty, shot off her finger and landed at the feet of a young man sitting two or three tables away from ours. He was with a party of noisy theatricals and was very handsome in an obvious sort of way: tall, good figure, black wavy hair, brown skin, you know the type, I'm sure.' I nodded sagely. 'Well, of course, he picked up the ring and brought it over to our table. He and Char looked at one another and pouf! That was it. He asked her to dance and off she went with him. Dick was furious and kept on about ill-mannered pansies, but there was nothing we could do. Later they disappeared to some nightclub or other and Dick and I went back to the ship without Char.

'Then about six o'clock the next morning there was a tap on my cabin door. I crept out of my bunk hoping not to wake Dick and there was Char looking quite radiant.

' "Nat, I'm in love. Dave and I have spent the night together."

' "Darling, how nice," I said. What else could one say, but my heart sank when she told me he was travelling back to England with us. The young man's name was David Brent and he was the juvenile lead in an English theatrical touring company called the Gemini Players. They'd been touring the Far East for the previous two years and Colombo was their final booking before going home. The man who ran the company had apparently let them down and all any of them had left was their fare back to England.

'I think Char must have lent the boy some money – she had a big allowance from Algy in those days. Anyway, he was able to transfer from second to first class on the boat, which annoyed the other Geminis who had to slum it somewhere down in the hold. Of course, Char insisted Dave sat at our table for meals, which we found a little tiresome. "If that young dago tells me how his Hamlet went down in Timbuktu, or paws my daughter over the soup just once more, I swear I'll wrap that damned silk scarf he wears round his neck and strangle him," Dick said. Luckily, we did not see much of them on the voyage apart from meals. They spent most of their time in Char's cabin, or playing ping pong; Dave was very good at that, I remember.

' "Nat, I feel cleansed," Char told me. "We fuck and fuck and it just gets better all the time."

'To everyone's relief, they left the boat at Marseilles; they were, they said, going to see the Russian ballet in Monte Carlo. "Dave needs educating," Char informed me. "He's never had a chance, you see."

'When I asked her what they would do when they got back to England, she looked quite surprised. "Get married, of course, what else? Dave doesn't mind being a co-respondent, and he adores children and animals." But what would they live on?

Money, I was told, wasn't important, and anyway, Dave was such a marvellous actor he would get a job in no time. If all else failed, she could always work in a bookshop.'

At this point in Natasha's narrative the bedroom door opened to reveal the taciturn young man, followed closely by two of the dogs.

'What to do about supper?' I realised suddenly it was dark outside and I must find a room for the night. 'May I come back tomorrow,' I asked, 'and hear some more?'

'Please come,' she said. 'The Spotted Calf will do you proud. Just mention my name to the landlord.'

Next morning Igor Ivanovitch had been replaced by a rather pretty blonde. She was, however, equally monosyllabic. 'She's waiting for you,' she said. 'D'you want coffee?'

'Thanks,' I said – when in Rome . . .

Natasha was sitting up in bed wearing a crochet shawl of many colours round her plump shoulders. She put out her hand and I kissed it. She beamed. 'Charming.' Then we got down to business.

'Was Dave Brent a good actor?' I asked, to start her off.

'He did a passable imitation of Noel Coward. He might, I think, have been not bad in films. Dick and I saw him once as the hero's best friend in some spy movie just before the war and he wasn't bad at all. He had a good voice; deep and a bit sexy.'

'And what about Algy and the children?'

'Algy bought a house in Suffolk, but never lived there. He got it for Char, you see; he couldn't bring himself to realise it was all over. He came to Amberley once when Char was ill, and sat beside her bed holding her hand. She didn't seem even to recognise him. "It wasn't my fault," he kept saying. "I always did my best for her," and there were tears in his eyes.

That was the last time, I think, I ever saw him.'

'Sophia told me the divorce was a messy business.'

Natasha nodded. 'Such things are usually messy, especially when the people involved had loved one another as Char and Algy.'

Suddenly I thought of Beth and me. 'It was a mistake, Guy, let's face it,' Beth's letter said, 'but no harm done and all the best for the future . . .' A few depressing, but fairly painless visits to the solicitor – 'The Petitioner therefore prays that the said marriage be dissolved . . .' Once again I felt a sense of inadequacy sweep over me; I hadn't even managed to have a full-scale hammer and tongs divorce.

'Char,' Natasha continued, 'expected to be allowed to keep the children. It didn't matter to her whether she was living in a caravan or a tumbledown cottage miles from anywhere with no drains; Ann, Evelyn and Sophia were part of her and that was that. She had no interest in caring for them in any practical sense; they just had to be there, making her laugh, learning about pictures, books, politics, all the things she was interested in and wanted them to be, too. Well, you can imagine what Algy and his smart-arse lawyers made of that. They insisted the children must be cared for properly, in a manner suited to their station in life, or some such nonsense, I forget their exact words but Char was caught in their net, and Algy was given the custody of the three girls, although they must spend a part of each holiday with their mother. Perhaps it was better so, though poor Char did not think so at the time, especially as Dave turned out not to be as fond of children or animals as Char had decided he should be. One cannot blame the young man; he was only twenty-four, ten years younger than Char; three noisy kids under nine was not quite what he'd bargained for, and then there was that frightful collie dog Char had from

the Battersea Home, too. She worshipped that little dog – now
what was his name . . . ?'

'Raffles?'

'Ah, Raffles, that was it. How clever of you to know.'

Natasha gave a throaty chuckle ending in a kind of a snort.
'We had to have him at Amberley when Char was sick, Raffles
I mean. He killed the chickens, bit the postman, frightened
the maids: we were at our wits' end to know what to do with
him. Then Dick discovered our butler, Tooley, was a dog man;
all he had to do was nod his head and dogs would do anything
he asked them, it was quite extraordinary, so after that, he
took care of Raffles.

'But that Raffles, he hated Dave Brent; jealous I suppose;
they were jealous of each other! Two angry young males
fighting over a woman! I remember one evening after we had
all gone to bed, there was a knock on my door; there was
Dave in his beautiful red silk pyjamas, simply trembling with
rage. "Nat, that bloody dog won't let me get into my own
bed! I'll have to get Tooley. Can you tell me where he sleeps
– Char's no use at all, just encourages the animal." Of course,
I couldn't stop laughing, which didn't help, but I obediently
put on my dressing gown and off we went in search of Tooley.
We found him in the pantry drinking Dick's best port. Then
the three of us traipsed back upstairs to Char and Dave's room,
and there she was, sitting up in bed stark naked, the dog in her
arms, screaming with laughter. She was a wicked little thing
at times.

'But those years just before the war were not plain sailing
for any of us. Algy and Char's divorce went through early in
1937 and she and Dave were married immediately after, in
the Register Office in Winchester. It was a quiet affair, just
Dick and I: Dave's parents had refused to come. They

considered Char to be a scarlet woman and ruining their precious boy's life. Mr Brent was such a rude little man. Dick and I met him and his wife to try and sort things out: I remember it was a pouring wet afternoon, and we had tea at some dreadful hotel in Virginia Water. "You must realise, Mrs Osborn, I've a position to keep up. I'm Secretary of the golf club; Chairmanship of the Rotary Club is on the cards for next year, and this divorce business just simply will not do."

' "But Mr Brent," I kept repeating, "it isn't you who are being divorced, it isn't even your son . . ." but he simply would not listen.'

'Were they happy, Char and Dave?' I asked.

There was a pause while Natasha considered the question. 'I think so. It couldn't have lasted, of course, but there was little chance of that: they'd barely been married two years when the War came and Dave joined the RAF. They had a little house on the river at Hammersmith: Con lent them the money for the lease. Char painted all the floors bright red, I remember, and they had a black bathroom. She learned to cook there. I can see her now, in that tiny kitchen they had, a cookery book open on the table, a cigarette in her mouth and a look of such concentration on her face. "Don't speak, Nat, I simply must get this right." But she would try such ambitious things, and if Dave even hinted they'd not turned out quite as they should, she'd throw the dish, contents and all, at him and storm upstairs! I remember once when we were in town for the Eton and Harrow match, they had asked us to dinner. Dave came downstairs to let us in. "I'm afraid my wife has thrown the dinner out of the window," he announced and you could see he was seething. "Would you mind awfully if we went out?" Dick laughed so much he cried.'

'She became a good cook, though, when she was in the

mood,' I said, and thought of the pile of hardbacked exercise books, each containing recipes carefully copied out in Char's bold hand. Some of the pages were blotched with antique gravy stains, others had odd little drawings in the margin, the work, no doubt, of one of her children, and I realised with a shock how much I still missed her.

'They can't have been very well off,' I said. 'How did they manage?'

'Once Dave got into films they didn't do too badly. Char had an allowance from Algy for the girls when they were with her. She had a nanny for Beth and a woman to scrub the floors; you could do a lot in those days with very little.

'Beth was born in the middle of the Munich Crisis in 1938, six weeks early. What a performance that was! London stifling hot, everyone talking about gas attacks and filling sandbags. I was staying the night with them and the pains began just as we were going to bed. We couldn't get hold of the doctor at first. He was out at some wretched official dinner. Dave was in tears, saying he knew Char would die and it was his fault, and Nanny was flapping about like a frightened sheep. "My mother was delivered of my brother in a cattle truck in the snow, while escaping the Bolsheviks," I told them. "I'm sure, if necessary, we can do the job ourselves."

'But we didn't have to; dear Dr Scott arrived, still wearing his dinner jacket, just in the nick of time. All Char could say when it was over was, "Christ, not another girl." She so much wanted a boy. I'm afraid it was a great disappointment.'

I knew this. It had been one of the things Beth had held against her mother.

Outside the window the sound of a car. The sulky girl poked her head round the door. 'Doctor's here, Mama. Is Mr Horton staying to lunch?'

I leaped to my feet. 'I must get back to London,' I said; the invitation to lunch had not been a warm one.

Natasha held out her hand to be kissed. 'I have enjoyed so much your visit and chatting about old times,' she said. 'No one here is interested, you see. It is sad you were not able to meet my Giovanni, but he is away – at a marketing conference, if you please. When I met him he was just a simple boy wheeling a garden barrow, now it is marketing conferences and TV commercials. Are you a gardener, Guy? Perhaps you would like to buy our seed catalogue, it is only 50p.'

'Thank you,' I said, 'it would be most useful, and thanks for all your help. May I write?'

'Of course,' she said. 'I like getting letters from nice young men.'

Her daughter accompanied me downstairs and out to my car. 'We have to ration her time with visitors. She's pretty frail, you know,' she said, and I thought she sounded rather apologetic. As I drove away, the tractor had started up again and someone had drawn the curtains in Natasha's room.

13

And then there were the War years. Letters from the children, letters from Ma, letters from Algy, letters from Dave (a few); yellowing cuttings from *The Times* on the progress of the War; hints from the Upper Blatchford Women's Institute on how to make sugarless jam and a meat loaf that contained no meat, and tiny wartime diaries written in tiny writing on utility paper, containing such cryptic announcements as: 'six eggs today', 'brown hen to sit', 'sowed B beans' and 'S to A's'. I ploughed on . . .

Cuckoo Farm   2nd January 1939

Dearest Char,

Snowed up yet again! We live like medieval peasants! However, the Jankowski children enjoy the snow and play all day, sliding down the hill on an old tin tray. Mrs J, I'm afraid, is beginning to be a little tiresome. She makes borsch all day and complains about no water. 'I am from the city, Madam O,' she says. 'I do not like this life.' These refugees are always so ungrateful. Never mind, one soldiers on as best as one can.

Now, dear, I must thank you for the really wonderful Christmas presents. So thoughtful and imaginative. Dear David, he's such a talented young man; you must cherish him.

Artists need cherishing; they are not like the rest of us. How exciting he has a small part in the new Korda film and how marvellous he will look in doublet and hose! Please give him my warmest congratulations.

Yes, dear, do bring the children for Easter. I think the Jankowskis will be gone by then so there will be a little more room.

Such a wonderful light over Digbery Hill today, I wish you were here to see it.

Your loving Ma

4 Rutland Mews, SW1   16th February 1939

My dear Char,

I agree to your having the girls for Easter. I suggest you get Nanny, or some equally responsible person, to collect them from here on the 5th April. They *must* be returned by the 15th, as we are going down to Wales for the last week of the holidays. Please don't send David. I've no wish for a repeat performance of what happened last time he came to fetch the girls and I would rather you didn't come yourself (I'm sure you will agree with this). Madeleine asks me to remind you not to let Sophia over-eat this time. She's much too fat and lethargic for her age. We are, in fact, taking her to see a specialist about this, but meanwhile, please bear it in mind. She also says please make sure they wear their old clothes when down at your mother's. Last time Ann's best dress was completely ruined; she had apparently slid down a haystack in it!

Maddy's divorce is finalised in April and we hope to be married in early May.

Yours,
Algy

PS In future, when writing over money matters, I would prefer you to correspond direct with my solicitors.

From the marriages' column of *The Times,* Saturday, 6th May 1939.
On 4th May at Kensington Register Office, Algernon George Charterhouse to Madeleine Veronica Scott (née Dudley).

The Hotel Crillon, Paris   10th May 1939

My dear Char,

Whilst appreciating your good wishes for my future happiness, I cannot but suspect your sincerity, especially as your congratulations on my marriage are closely followed by a complaint that I never congratulated you on yours. In answer to the charge, I can only say I saw no reason to do so, and indeed, felt that commiserations would be more in order. Your marriage to a common young man on the make, ten years your junior, remains and will always remain, a mystery to me.

I am sorry, my dear, unlike you I simply cannot shrug off the past, and cannot in my heart forgive you for the pain and suffering you caused me. Perhaps in the future – but now – no. Therefore, while accepting your good wishes for Madeleine and myself in the spirit in which (I hope) they are offered, I must ask you to write to me only when strictly necessary, on matters you are quite certain cannot be dealt with by my solicitors.

Yours,
Algy

54 Pine Tree Avenue, Westgate on Sea   5th October 1939

Dear Charlotte,

David writes us he has joined the RAF. His mother and I are, of course, proud that he has decided to give up a promising career in films in order to serve his King and country and would not have wished it otherwise. However, we are concerned about our little granddaughter. What arrangements (if any) have been made for you and the child to be evacuated from London? David is a caring boy, but too young, perhaps, to realise the full extent of the responsibilities he has chosen to take on. In his letter to us there is no mention of the safety of you and Beth.

Now, Charlotte, I realise that in the past we have not always seen eye to eye, but both Hilda and myself feel it's time to let bygones be bygones. I am sure you would agree that private differences must be set aside in our determination to get this War sewn up and Hitler put back in his box once and for all. Please let me know by return what arrangements are being made re you and the children.

With kindest regards,
Brian Brent

PS Can you send us David's new address as soon as you have it – Hilda is knitting him a pair of socks.

Cuckoo Farm   6th October 1939

Dearest Char,

How proud you must be of David – to give up so much – but so like him. He sent me such a killing postcard – of course, he could not say where from, just 'somewhere in England'.

How absurd these men are, playing their silly war games.

Now, dear, you simply must get the children out of London. It really is not safe, especially in that little house of yours on the river, a prime target for the German raiders when they come. Now David has been moved to Yorkshire for initial training – how handy for you all he did his first few weeks in London – there is no longer any point in your staying on to be near him. There is a perfectly good cottage in the village here, only £2 10s a week, which would suit you and little Beth admirably, and there is plenty of room for the girls when they visit in the holidays. I'm sure David would wish you to come.

Pa writes Amberley is being taken over by the army and they are to move into the chauffeur's cottage: one wonders how the Russian woman will take to that!

I must stop now. The vicar's evacuees are trying to steal the apples again. Such dreadful children; they killed poor Dr Speed's cat last week and literally run *rampant* through the village. The billeting officer is at her wits' end and says they may have to be sent back where they came from.

Hurry up and come, dear, you know it's the *right* thing to do.

Your loving Ma

ITW – Somewhere in England (in sight of the sea and B. cold)
30th November 1939

My Darling,

God, how I miss you. I keep going over in my mind that last weekend together in our little house: the empty rooms, the river, eating sausages by the fire, loving you – oh, everything. Then I compare it with ghastly now and it's more than I can take.

Mercifully, we're worked so hard and most of the time it's so damned cold, the mind becomes too numb to think.

Our Corporal calls me 'Nancy Boy' (naturally anyone on the stage is, *ipso facto*, a 'pansy' in the primitive life form of the RAF), which doesn't help, but as I'm not half bad at drill (which annoys him a bit, I think) and am the best polisher of kit in the Flight, though I say it myself, he mostly ignores me. I've applied to train as a pilot. Don't be cross darling, you know I've always wanted to fly and anyway, as things are in the services (I'm learning fast) I'll probably be posted somewhere as a cook!

Mother has sent enough 'woolly garments' to kit out an entire Flight, also one of those chewy cakes. Do you remember how we fed that one she made for my birthday to the swans and it even gave them indigestion? Was that only last summer – already it seems a million years ago.

Do you hate it very much at the cottage, darling? It won't be for long, I promise. It sounds pretty dreary, but honestly, it couldn't be as bad as here. When I get a commission (!) we'll find a house near the station, and then we can all be together again. I should get leave before posting at the end of my stint here, but not before, so won't get away for Christmas.

Oh, darling, you are glad you married me, aren't you? Sometimes I have such stupid doubts.

> All my love, my dearest,
> Dave

ITW – SIE   2nd December 1939

My darling,
    Your wonderful letters arrived last night. I'd just returned

from ghastly 'tea' (greasy bangers and cold chips) and was feeling absolutely wretched, when there was Cpl bloody Jones giving out the mail. 'One for you, flower,' he says in the special falsetto voice he uses when addressing me. 'That'll put a smile on your pretty face.' No matter. Who cares about morons like him when there's wonderful letters from you?

You write so vividly, darling. I wish I could. The row with Ma made me die; I can just see it – you dancing up and down spitting 'fire' and Ma all sugary calm, smiling gently. How I wish I had been there! I know she drives you nuts, but in a way you have to admit, she is rather marvellous. So you're learning First Aid: I hope it won't be like when you learned cooking (!) and pity the poor unfortunate who complains his bandages are too tight. And Nanny's in love with the air-raid warden – is it serious? Actually, their courtship in the warden's hut sounds rather romantic. You don't mention Beth in your letters; has she any new words yet?

Darling, it's no good your coming up here for Christmas, it really isn't. I'll be on duty all the time and there's nowhere you can stay. It's hell, I know, especially with Algy having the children, but it just can't be helped. HOWEVER, Dad has sent me quite a decent cheque for Christmas (good old Dad, he has his points), so I've an idea. What about when I finish in this morgue, we spend a couple of days' leave on our own in London – stay at some posh hotel and really do it in style? Wouldn't you love to dance at Quags again? I would, if I had you in my arms, of course! I can't give exact dates yet, but will let you know as soon as I can; probably around the end of Jan. Now, that will be something to look forward to, won't it?

Chin up, my love. (I'm one to talk!) Christmas at Amberley, even in the chauffeur's cottage, won't be too bad and Nat and your Pa are always good for a laugh.

Goodnight, my darling,
Dave
PS Is this War ever going to get cracking I wonder?

ITW - SIE   Boxing Night 1939

My Darling,
   I got drunk last night – did you? I stood on a table in the
canteen and gave them my Richard III, quite impressive by
candlelight with most of the audience squiffy. Then AC2
Bolton executed a quick clog dance, Cpl Jones, YES, Cpl Jones
in person, did his animal impressions (the mind boggles) and
we rounded the whole thing off with a few rousing choruses
of 'Roll out the Barrel' and 'Eskimo Nell' (unexpurgated
edition). Later, I was violently sick; it was so damned cold in
the latrines, my balls nearly dropped off. Is the RAF making
me vulgar, darling? You will tell me, won't you, if it is?
   How was your Christmas? Not too grim, I hope. I tried to
ring you last night, but it was impossible to get through. Had
a card from Sophia; a picture of a rather curiously shaped
plane with me, smiling madly, in it; or at least, I think it was
me. Now, all is OK for 25th Jan. Your Pa's a good old stick;
fancy booking us a room at the Savoy! Oh God, I can't *wait*.
   There's talk of what's euphemistically known as a
'toughening' course before EFTS (Elementary Flying Training
School). The thought of batting up and down some bloody
mountain in the pouring rain carrying all my kit doesn't fill
me with much enthusiasm, I have to admit: by the end of this
War I should be able to climb Everest using only one leg,
with one hand behind my back. Never mind, at least I've got
my exams (can't think how). So you see, darling, your husband

is not *just* a pretty face after all, and Biggles had better look to his laurels once Leading Aircraftsman Brent gets his Wings! Joking apart, though, the real reason I've got through is that The Powers that Be still think the War, when it really starts, will be in the air and they'll need all the pilots they can get, even if it does mean scraping the barrel.

Goodnight, my love – only four more weeks and then ...

Dave

I found the following, written on a sheet of Savoy Hotel note paper in Dave Brent's handwriting.

29th January 1940

Charlotte and David Brent lay in their warm, soft, CLEAN DOUBLE bed in the Savoy Hotel, London, drinking champagne and watching the snow whirling past their window. The bed had been paid for by Charlotte's father, the champagne by David's father (if he did but know it). No one had paid for the snow; it simply fell because it wanted to: great big, fluffy flakes floating down on the grey river, covering the barges and the trees in Temple Gardens, blanketing everywhere with silence. It was very, very, very quiet, only a melancholy hoot from a barge now and then breaking the silence.

'Is this the end of the world?' Charlotte said to David. 'I almost wish it were.'

'No,' said David to Charlotte. 'The end of the world is a long way off, but it's the end, perhaps, of something.'

'And the beginning of something else,' said Charlotte and bit David where it hurt.

After that, they didn't watch the snow falling any more, or drink their champagne or anything. Until ... the telephone rang; jarring, insistent, ripping into the spell that Charlotte and David had woven for each other.

'Hullo,' said David, 'room 402.'

'Your father-in-law, sir, downstairs waiting,' said the telephone. 'He thought perhaps you had forgotten – dinner at eight, he said.'

'Oh God,' said David and leaped from the bed, but Charlotte lay there still and cried.

Harold's Farm, Chipping Sodbury   15th July

Dear Guy,

Thank you so very much for your delightful letter and the gorgeous carnations. Such years since anyone has sent me flowers. Giovanni was quite suspicious, I can tell you! They are beside me now, reminding me of the old days and what fun it was to be young. Thank you, too, for the copy of the little thing written by Dave from the Savoy. It made me cry. Is it a poem, I wonder?

You ask me to write of those War years and Char. A tall order, but I will have a go. Be patient, though, I write with a little difficulty now because of my arthritis, and sometimes memory is slow in coming, but with all this, I will try. Here goes, then.

We did not see much of Char for the first months of the War. She took a cottage in the village near her mother while Dave was at his training camp. The phoney War was such a strange time for all of us; like waiting for a thunderstorm that did not come. Dick and I moved into a cottage when the Army took over our house. So sad; huts growing up like mushrooms everywhere, the gardens gone to ruin. Char came to us that Christmas: 'I can't stand to be alone with Ma; Dave drilling in Yorkshire; Algy has the children; can I come, Nat? At least together we might find something to laugh at.' And we did, but it was a sad time all the same.

Dave got his commission and learned to fly. It was a surprise how well he took to service life, almost as though that was the life he had been waiting for all along. And Char became a camp follower! She pitched her tent (Dick's words), anywhere Dave happened to be and where she was allowed to by the authorities. She would rent a cottage, a couple of rooms in a pub, or even a caravan. I visited her in the caravan – the discomfort, you could not believe! But she had to have her family with her, you see: Beth, Nanny, the dog Raffles and in the holidays the three girls.

Oh, the rows with Algy! Solicitors' clerks whizzing to and fro. 'The girls cannot spend their holidays parked in the middle of a turnip field and no proper sanitation.' You might have thought with Europe over-run by Germany and Hitler waiting to invade, they had something more important to do, but things were like that then. Algy wanted the girls sent to America, out of harm's way. Of course, Char said no, no and no.

'They're going,' Algy said. 'They're not,' she said, 'it's running away, and besides, their ship might be torpedoed.'

'Maddy says it's the best thing,' he said. 'All her friends are sending their children.'

'Bugger Maddy's friends,' said Char. 'They would.' Then she went to London to see Algy, right in the middle of the Blitz. She told me afterwards they had spent the time crouched under a table in total darkness. Well, I don't know what she said (or did) to Algy under that table, but that was the last we heard of the girls going to America. Dick said she'd probably blackmailed him; she was certainly capable of it.

Throughout this time Char and Dave kept on the lease of

the house in Hammersmith. It was empty most of the time, but I think they could not bear to part with it. And sometimes, when Dave had a forty-eight hour pass, they would leave the children and Nanny wherever they happened to be and spend it there, just the two of them. I saw Dave only once during that time. Dick and I had lunch with them one Sunday: Dave was at flying school near London and Char had rented a horrid little terrace house in Croydon. It was so hot, I remember, and we were all of us crammed into this tiny dining room; Beth whining and wasps flying everywhere. Dave was in uniform and looked dead beat, and he and Char spent the meal arguing about something ridiculous, like the mint sauce we had for lunch. Afterwards he slept and we didn't see him again before we left.

I must stop now, Guy, I cannot hold my pen any longer. Will try again tomorrow.

17th July

Two days' rest instead of one, how lazy I am! Where was I?

By 1941 Dave was flying on operations and was stationed at Coltishall in Norfolk. 'So cold,' Char wrote. 'Beth and Nanny are one huge chilblain.' But Dave managed to get home for a night now and then and she was busy sowing veg. Now, Guy, the hard part comes; even after so many years I hate to write of it.

It was early in May '41 when Char wrote Dave had some leave and as the raids on London had slackened off a bit, they'd decided to spend a couple of days at the house in Hammersmith. 'Mrs Maggs still looks in from time to time,' she wrote, 'and says water's coming in downstairs and several slates are off the roof; D says we must investigate. Why not bring Pa up and we'll all have a night out? D wants to hear

Carol Gibbons at the Savoy . . .' I wrote back yes, we would, and bugger the raids.

Such a jolly evening: the atmosphere then, you cannot imagine what it was like: the fizz, the excitement, everyone so gay, everyone in uniform. We danced and danced and Dick said, 'He's not half bad, that young man of Char's, after all.'

The next morning, which was a Saturday, Dick and I went home to Amberley, but Char and Dave stayed on. 'I'm busy plugging rat holes,' Dave told us. 'There'll be nothing left of the place by the time the War's over if I don't, and there's still another thirty years to go on the lease.'

It was on the Sunday morning, 11th May (I shall always remember the date) when the phone rang. I was upstairs in my bedroom doing my face and heard Dick answer it.

'Hullo, Brent,' and then, 'Oh, my God, Oh, God, I am so dreadfully sorry . . .' I knew at once what had happened; they'd said on the wireless another bad raid on London. Were they both dead? But it was only Dave: his HQ had rung Mr Brent as his next of kin. Char and Dave had been under the stairs when the house came down on top of them, and it was several hours before they could be dug out. Dave was dead when they found them, but Char was unhurt, apart from cuts and bruises and shock. Poor little Mr Brent was quite hysterical and went on about the disgrace that his son should have been killed as a civilian and not fighting the enemy and how they wouldn't even be able to put 'Died on active service' in the newspaper. 'And the boy was in the running for a gong after that last op,' he kept repeating to Dick. 'Now no one will ever know.'

Oh that dreadful Sunday, so long it seemed, so much to do. Char looked just angry when I saw her, a fiery red spot on either cheek and her eyes glittering. She was sitting up very straight in her bed at the far end of the casualty ward, the beds packed so tight together you could hardly squeeze between them. I put my arms round her, but she shook me off.

'Now I'm free,' she said, 'I'm going to join the WRNS. Can you take care of the children, Nat?' It was the most shocking thing to hear in all that shocking day.

'We must wire for Con to come at once,' said Dick. 'She'll know what to do with the child.' Con came next morning and Char, a little girl again, did what her mother told her: no more talk of the WRNS.

Mr Brent wanted poor Dave to be buried in the cemetery at his home at Westgate-on-Sea, but at that time the South coast was a forbidden area, even, it seemed, for the dead, so he is buried in the churchyard at Amberley. After the funeral was over, Char, to my knowledge, never again visited the grave. Dick used to pay someone to keep it tidy, but now I expect it's gone to rack and ruin.

For the rest of the War Char and Beth lived with Con at Cuckoo Farm. Char would come to us now and again, but she never mentioned Dave, or, as I have said, visited his grave. I found her attitude a little difficult to understand, but that is how she was; it was better to hold one's peace on such matters. For those years she kept men at arm's length (and there were plenty about), dug her garden, read her books, fought with her mother, visited the girls at school, and that was her life. Then came George. But I will write you of George another day, dear Guy. My daughter tells me it is time to sleep.

Natasha

I remembered Beth and I visiting Dave Brent's grave in the early sixties. To our surprise, the grass was neatly cut, a bunch of snowdrops placed at the foot of the granite headstone, which read simply: 'In memory of Flt Lt David Malcolm Brent, born

1912, killed 10th May 1941, a victim of enemy bombing. RIP.'
Someone still cared; we never found out who.

I thanked Natasha for her letter and received, almost by
return, another one from her.

Harold's Farm   30th July

My dear Guy,

Thank you so much for your letter. It is good to have news
of Amberley. I have not seen it for nearly forty years: I ask
myself, how can this be, but it is so. And you say it's still
beautiful and unspoiled and lived in by a 'pop star'! I like the
idea of a swimming pool in the shape of a penis; which is the
deep end, I wonder? And you say the churchyard, too, is neat
and tidy and a bunch of roses on Dave Brent's grave. To think
that the boy would be over seventy if he had lived! Perhaps he
was lucky, who knows, to go when he did.

Guy, I have little more to tell. By 1945 I had chosen to
break with Dick and start a new life with my dear Giovanni
(and never have I regretted that decision). Because of this, my
only contact with Char, after she had married George, was
our annual exchange of letters. It was I, nevertheless, who
introduced them to each other and it happened in this way.

Char was staying at Amberley the week the War in Europe
ended. 'If I don't get away from Ma for a bit, I swear I'll kill
her,' she said on the telephone, so of course I said come.

Giovanni and I had fallen in love by that time. What a
courtship! I could speak no Italian and he no English and
certainly no Russian. Char said it was like your Lady Chatterley
and her gamekeeper – for you see, Giovanni was an Italian
prisoner of war and worked in our garden – but it was not like

that at all. His parents were rich business people in Milan, not simple peasants as the gossips said. But never mind all that. There was Char at Amberley the last week of the War. Such lovely weather, do you remember? No, of course you don't, you are far too young to remember such things, I keep forgetting. And there was George, a young handsome captain in the Army, liaising with somebody or other, temporarily billeted up at the house.

The Army gave a cocktail party the day Char arrived. 'Nat, I've got nothing to wear, I can't possibly go,' she said, but I lent her a Paquin model from before the War, in sea-green chiffon. We had to pin it up, I remember. It was much too long, but she looked good in it all the same. Did you know her hair was already grey?

The band was playing 'In the Mood' on the lawn when we arrived, and Colonel Stevens said: 'May I introduce you to Captain Seymour? He's paying us a brief visit before dashing off to sunnier climes.' And there was George: tall, handsome, brown curls and bright blue eyes, all very correct in his uniform. There was something I didn't like about his mouth, though: the lips were full and red and pouting like a girl's, and he smiled too widely and too often. Anyway, he looked at Char, Char looked at him: oh, dear, I thought, not him surely, he's not her type at all, but of course I was wrong. He fell for her that very instant, I think; she took a little longer, but all too soon she did. All Dick could say was, 'Seems a reasonable sort of fella to me.'

'He's another Algy,' I said, 'but not as bright or as strong. We must stop it if we can.'

'Don't be an ass,' Dick said, 'we can't,' and, of course, he was right.

There was a record at that time you heard all over the place.

'Don't Fence me In', with Bing Crosby and the Andrews Sisters. They played it on the little radio I have by my bed not long ago, and I saw again Char and George dancing in the hall at Amberley: George so tall, bending his head to look into Char's face. Char, the top of her head no higher than his shoulder, smiling her secret smile, her hand resting on his arm, the long, red fingernails tapping to the beat of the music. She took him back to Cuckoo Farm with her. They looked so happy when I saw them off in the train at Basingstoke, and yet I cried, I remember, when I left the empty station after the train had gone.

I only saw Char once after that. The four of us – George and Char, Giovanni and myself – met in London a few months later, after Dick and I had parted. But our meeting was not a success: Giovanni and I were late and they were dining afterwards with George's parents. In the Ladies Char said, 'How can you – after Pa?'

'How can you, after Dave?' I said. And that was that. Later, we patched things up, but all the same that moment in the Ladies' room at the Berkeley was really the end of our friendship.

So Guy, I have, alas, no more to tell you. But now we've met, can we stay friends please? I would so like that. And will you one day bring Sophia to see me? I should like that, too.

Natasha

From the marriages column of *The Times,* 5th October 1945. Seymour-Brent. On 3rd October at Chelsea Register Office: George Frederick Seymour to Charlotte Mary Brent (née Osborn).

Attached to this yellowing newspaper cutting was a copy of

the wedding photograph that, framed, always stood on the mantelpiece in the sitting room at Maple and later in the dark house at Belton, the latter now replaced by one of the aged George, the same bright smile on his face, at his side the 'Welsh woman', her navy straw wedding hat tastefully decorated with a single, large, white rose.

From the births column of *The Times,* 26th February 1946.
On 24th February, to Charlotte Mary Seymour, the wife of Major George Frederick Seymour, a son.

Ripling Park, Stowmarket, Suffolk 28th February 1946

My dear Char,

Maddy and myself send our warmest congratulations on the birth of your son. What a cold, austere world to be born into: your Labour government hasn't done much for us yet, has it? Where's that 'Brave New World' they all used to talk about!

We moved in here just before Christmas, to be met with chaos complete and total. The army only left in September and the place is a shambles. Maddy is coping somehow, with the not very able assistance of a bevy of sullen young women of vague Middle European extraction. I'm not much use as I'm rushed off my feet at the office: only half of us have moved back to Basinghall Street, the other half remain in Gloucester until the spring, so chaos there as well.

I bumped into your Pa last week in the City Club. I hadn't seen him since before the War and he didn't look a day older. He told me your new husband has dashed off again to the Far East – not very good management on your part if I may say so! He also hinted at approaching nuptials for himself, but was a little evasive about the lady. Are you pleased?

It's quite a coincidence your living in Perdita Grant's flat in Charlotte Street while George is away: I'm living in Bunny's! He's still out in Germany and is letting me have his rooms in St James's as a pied à terre for the time being. How is Per? I haven't seen her for years. Bunny tells me that after they split up, practically the entire US army 'passed through her hands at one time or another', (his words). I'm afraid things must seem a little flat for her now; do give her my love.

As we're both in London, once you're out and about again, can we dine? One can still get a tolerable meal at Pruniers, no whale steaks or nonsense of that sort. I'll ring you, if I may, one day next week. There's a lot to discuss. Sophia writes she's joined the Debating Society and will I 'ante up' for a school trip to Hamburg. A rather odd place to want to go, on the face of it, but she claims it is to 'promote an awareness of the consequences of total war'. Oh my God, the young!

Maddy sends her regards,

Yours, Algy

With this letter from Algy is a note written on the back of one of his business cards; it appears to have accompanied a bouquet of flowers.

Wed

To Char

from

Algy

Dinner was such fun. I do hope you enjoyed it as much as I did. I'd forgotten how we could laugh together: next time we must remember to discuss the children!

A

Bombay   17th April 1946

My precious, precious Darling,

It looks as though by next week I'll be on my way home at
last. I seem to have been rushed off my feet for weeks now,
what with one thing and another, and to add to everything
else they've asked me to organise some wretched polo match!
Never mind, I've had time to buy you a marvellous length of
pink embroidered silk and a pair of red high-heeled sandals: I
hope the sandals fit. They are the right size, I think.

Your mother's idea of our buying a house near her is just
not on, I'm afraid, darling. We simply haven't the cash, and
even if we had, it would be much safer and simpler just to rent
a place. My parents would never lend me anything anyway,
and the last thing we want is to be in hock to your mother! No,
darling, now is *not* the time to buy property; everyone says
so: much best to wait and see what your precious Labour people
will do next. If we don't get them out pronto, no one will be
allowed to own anything anyway!

Sophia writes she's off to Hamburg with the school at
Easter: isn't that rather an odd place for them to go? Algy's
paying, I hope!

So longing to see you, my darling, and little Perry too. I'm
glad you're waiting until I get home for the christening. Only
one more letter before we sail.

All love,
Your Georgie

PS The house at Camberley you've found sounds promising.
It would probably be best to take it until September when I
should know where my next tour of duty will be: £4 a week
doesn't sound too bad – does that include electricity?

Cuckoo Farm   20th April 1946

Darling Mummy,

I hope you and Perry and Nanny are well. I am well and so
are Granny and the horses and the dogs. We have a postcard
from Sophia today from Hamburg, she says she is having a
luvly time but the food is not very nice and she has a runny
tummy.

I am glad I will be able to come and stay with you and
George and Perry at Camberley. I am practising for the
Gymkhana.

Lots of love from
Beth

14

Over a year had passed since Char's death and I was well down into the bowels of the green trunk. The stiff-backed notebooks, the fading photographs and letters, all were carefully annotated and put away in my filing cabinet for possible future reference. What were left were mostly letters and postcards from her children, odd diaries sketchily kept, programmes for long-forgotten gymkhanas, race meetings, hunt balls; boring stuff mostly, giving little away of the turbulent years they represented

The only items of any significance were the order of service for Dick Osborn's funeral at a church in Brighton in April 1955 and a cutting of the announcement of his death from *The Times*. The latter describes him as 'beloved husband of Mildred'. Was Char upset at being left out? There's nothing to say so. All I'd ever heard Char say on the subject of her father's third marriage was that he became 'quite impossible' in old age and was forced to marry his secretary in order to have someone to look after him. Be that as it may, the picture that emerged was slowly becoming a more familiar one for me. People as I remembered them began to appear; events I had heard mentioned, or in some cases taken part in; Maple, and of course Perry, the child of Char and George's first, fresh, newly discovered love: the last child, the child that helped turn their marriage from a moderately happy one into a desolate ruin.

'Isn't that putting it a bit strong?' Sophia asked. 'Don't blame poor Perry for George and Mum's hang-ups; they used him as some kind of emotional punchball.'

'I suppose they did, but all the same, you have to admit he helped destroy their marriage.'

'I don't admit anything of the sort.' She picked up a postcard of Caernarvon Castle from the scattered heap of letters and cards in front of her. It was a cold evening and we were sitting on the floor by the gas fire in my sitting room, the curtains drawn tightly against the autumn evening.

'Dear Old Mum,' Sophia read, 'I hope you are well. It has rained here every day but we have done a lot of climbing. Ponsonby has sprained his ankle and Devenish fell in the river. We have chips, sausages and peas every day. Love, Perry.'

Carefully she placed the card face downwards on the pile. I cleared my throat nervously; I knew how much she had loved Perry. Personally I had always found him rather obnoxious, and Beth and he had never got on. I picked up the programme for some village fête held to mark the coronation in 1953. On the back was an elongated drawing of the young Queen Elizabeth, sceptre in hand, seated on a chamber pot. Underneath was scrawled, 'Perry Seymour'. In silence I passed the thing to Sophia: she studied it carefully and smiled suddenly.

'He was such a happy little boy,' she said. 'When he was only three he could dance in time to music. There was a song then – "If I knew you were coming I'd have baked a cake" – we had it on an old seventy-eight record and I would play it over and over again for him. He used to dance round that horrid little sitting room at Foxglove Cottage clapping his hands and shouting, "baked a cake, Sophie, baked a cake".'

'That was the house near Camberley, wasn't it?'

'Yes. Mum moved there after Perry was born. They originally rented it for a few months, but stayed on until George came out of the Army in 1953. It wasn't very nice: it always looked as though it should have been a bungalow, but someone had built another floor on by mistake. When Mum first moved there, it stood in the middle of a scrubby field full of gorse bushes, but when they left it had been swallowed up in a huge housing estate.'

'I've seen photos,' I said. 'It doesn't look that special. Why on earth did they stay so long?'

'Because, as I'm sure you know only too well, George has always been a man of few ideas and even less initiative. Mum found the place while he was still out in India in 1946 and he was perfectly content to stay there until someone found him somewhere else to hang up his hat. His life has always been ordered by someone, as Mum's was: that's why they were so hopeless together.

'Did you know George was terrified of his father? If old Mr Seymour said jump, he damn well jumped. He sent George out to Shanghai after he left school to work in the family shipping office with his Uncle Horace, in spite of the fact George actually wanted to study to be a vet – he'd never have passed the exams, mind you, but that's by the way. He hated his Uncle Horace and the Chinese and was frightfully homesick, but there he stayed for five solid years, until he was ordered home again in 1936 because of the Japanese invasion of China. As far as I could make out, the only thing he learned during those five years was how to make love in a distinctly un-British way. Mum told me this, by the way, not George, who although he has been known to make the odd pass at one from time to time, never, ever discussed sex.' Had

George really made a pass at Sophia – I'd no idea. Wisely, I refrained from comment.

'When he got back,' Sophia continued, 'he lived in his parents' flat in the Bayswater Road until he was rescued by the outbreak of war and the Army. He'd been a territorial since 1938, so he went in as an officer. I'm sure he'd never have made one otherwise; of course, all that really happened was the War Office replaced his old Dad: the only independent thing he's ever done was to marry Mum. Even then, I think he assumed that as she was ten years older, it was she who would make the decisions, and up to a point, I suppose, she did, but she wasn't very good at it and relied heavily always on Gran. It wasn't until Gran became gaga and unable to cope, that Mum and George's marriage really went into a spin. Did you know not only did Gran get George his job with Drayton Motors, but she also found Maple and persuaded Mum and George to buy it?'

'No,' I said. This did surprise me: George's attitude towards his mother-in-law, in my presence anyway, had always been one of amused contempt.

'Gran sold Cuckoo Farm, the house she had near Sherborne, soon after the War. She moved to the Corsham area because that was where Aunty P's son Adam and his wife lived. I think she thought it would be useful to have a relative on hand in case she was ill – Mum, as no doubt you know, never having been too good in that department. You must have seen Cowleaze, Gran lived there until her death.' I nodded.

'Anyway,' Sophia continued, 'Adam, Aunty P's son, was a director of Drayton. So when George's mobile canteen lark failed – George went into this with some ex-army chum who, so he alleged, "let him down badly" – Gran persuaded Adam to take him on as personnel officer, and there he stayed, as

I'm sure you know, for the next twenty years. Well, Gran having found George a job, had to find him and Mum a house; hence Maple, semi-derelict in 1954 and going for a song. It had been uninhabited since the Army had it in 1945 and due for demolition when Gran discovered it. I can see her now: a witch wearing an orange pixy hood, striding through the house pursued by Mr Bone, the builder, clutching his clip board and pencil and whistling through his teeth every time Gran's ideas became too outrageous.' I remembered Mr Bone, a tiny, completely bald man, who rather resembled an aged jockey: in my time his son, Dolph, ran the business and was frequently invoked by George in moments of crisis.

'And your mother, didn't she have any say in the matter?' I asked.

'She drifted about saying she wanted a black bathroom and her bedroom floor painted white, and they must turn the lawn into a paddock for Perry's pony, you know how she went on.' I nodded crossly: the words had an unpalatable ring of truth. 'What about George, then. Didn't he object to his mother-in-law taking over?'

'George? Never! He simply accepted Gran's services and money and by the time they'd settled in at Maple and Mr Bone and his men departed, he'd persuaded himself he'd organised the whole thing single handed. That's how he is, you know that.' I nodded again: I knew that.

Sophia bent down and picked up a family wedding group *circa* 1954. Evie Charterhouse and David Holloway looking radiant, backed by a phalanx of (presumably) Charterhouse relations including Sophia herself, a bridesmaid encased in puppy fat, smiling apprehensively into the camera from beneath the brim of a large, pink, picture hat. 'Poor Evie,' she said, 'life is unfair. She and David were so happy together –

much happier than any of the rest of us. I remember staying with them in Melbourne – 1959 I think it was – and having such a marvellous time. Evie inherited my Pa's *joie de vivre*; everything you did with her somehow turned into a party. It's odd how often those sorts of people die young, and odder too that after she died David married Paula. Paula's somehow achieved the impossible and made a pompous bore out of David. They came back to the UK a couple of years after they were married, and I used to spend the odd weekend with them as David seemed to want to keep in touch. But I always dreaded going, especially as apart from everything else, Paula appeared to be quite pathologically jealous of all of us . . . Let's have another drink, Guy, I shall have to go in a minute.'

'But surely you're staying?' Even to me my voice sounded like a spoiled child's. Was I becoming too dependent on Sophia? 'I can't,' she said, 'I'm being collected at seven a.m., my flight's at eight fifteen.' She was off yet again, this time to Japan.

'Of course,' I said. 'I'd forgotten.'

'I suppose,' she said, still holding the wedding photo and peering into its depths as though from those bright, smiling faces in their smart, out-dated clothes she might somehow find a clue to life itself, 'it was after that, when Evie married and disappeared to Australia – Ann was already married and frightfully pucka living in the north of Scotland – that the way was clear for Mum to concentrate all her emotional energies on poor little Perry, with disastrous results. He wasn't a frightfully strong character, anyway, but until then he'd been used to battling away at the foot of the family, trying to get himself noticed. Then, suddenly, he was top of the heap and the competition had evaporated.'

'But surely it wasn't done consciously,' I asked, 'on Char's part? I mean, she didn't just say to herself one day, "Now that Ann and Evie have escaped my clutches, I'll turn my attention on Perry." '

My attempt at sarcasm was, however, wasted. Sophia took my remark at face value. 'I honestly don't know,' she said. 'Partly conscious, I should think. The trouble was she was that much older than when we were growing up and correspondingly had less to occupy her mind. Poor Perry, rising ten, a bit backward and lacking in confidence, simply hadn't a dog's chance. You see, if you found yourself the recipient of Mum's undivided love and attention you were in big trouble; like having a Star Wars ray-gun trained on you; more or less totally destructive. What's more,' she said, rising gracefully to her feet, 'you know I'm right; look what she did to you and Beth.'

For a moment I felt such a wave of absolute rage wash over me, I wanted to seize her by the hair, or bang her face against the wall. I didn't, of course. I just sat quite still, but I noticed the hand holding my drink shook a little, spilling a few drops of wine on to the carpet. There was silence while Sophia walked over to the mirror and started to fiddle with her hair. 'I must go. Goodnight, Guy dear, I'll send you a card from Tokyo.' She pecked me on the cheek and in silence I saw her downstairs to her car and in silence watched her fasten her seatbelt, start the engine and drive away. As the Metro turned into Vicarage Crescent, she let down the window and waved; I didn't wave back.

Later, I stood watching the lights across the river, thinking of what she had said about Beth's and my marriage, my anger slowly evaporating. The pain, however, stayed with me. She was right, damn her, as always. Was that, I wondered savagely, ashamed of the thought, the reason she had never married: to be right always is not a quality that endears one to others.

For a couple of weeks after Sophia's visit I was – fortuitously perhaps – too caught up in work to think of anything else. The overseas conference I had been arranging for months finally came to fruition, with all the attendant traumas that such an event usually brings in its wake. Once or twice, as I listened to an earnest young life manager from Ghana air his view on the latest software, or escorted a party of enthusiastic Malaysians round a seething Tower of London, Sophia's words returned, unbidden, to my mind, but I thrust them firmly back into my subconscious; they must wait, I told myself, until I had time to do them justice. All too soon, however, the conference was over and the smiling bespectacled delegates, in their neat lightweight suits, briefcases under their arms, had taken their last photocall for the house magazine, packed their holiday snaps and Marks & Spencer sweaters and melted away; it was time to return to Char. But now, I noted with some surprise and no little guilt, for it had never happened in all the years I had known her, I felt a reluctance to do so.

A few days after the conference had finished, for some reason or other I cannot now remember, I was seated on top of a number nineteen bus as it jerked ponderously along Theobalds Road in the midst of the rush-hour traffic. In front of me sat a girl wearing a camouflage jacket, her pale, blonde hair tied in a pony tail. I accidentally brushed against her as I sat down and she turned and smiled. Suddenly, I saw Beth as she had been when I first met her, and knew the time had come for me to face up to the implications of Sophia's comments on her mother's destructive powers and the doubts and uncertainties those comments had raised in me.

In a despairing effort to try and find the answer, I decided to go down to Maple for a couple of days; I might even drop in on old George, see how he was getting on. It helped, so people said, to revisit the scene of the crime. My love for Char hadn't been a crime, I knew that; it simply existed, neither right nor wrong, only there. But my marriage to Beth had, though, hadn't it: the ultimate treason indeed, the right thing, as Auden said, for the wrong reason. At least it was I who was paying for it now, not Beth. It was Beth, though, who'd paid for it throughout our marriage, there was no doubt of that.

Why was it only now I felt guilt, long after there was any need for it? Beth was happy now, happier than she'd ever been probably. I knew the answer to that one even before I asked the question. It was because, since her death, Char had deserted me; there simply seemed no way that I could reach her. I couldn't remember the sound of her voice, she wasn't even a ghost. And because she wasn't there to help me, I'd begun to doubt whether her love for me had ever existed, and even to half believe Sophia was right.

Suddenly, I felt such hatred for Sophia, for myself, even for Beth, that for a moment it seemed a waste of effort to continue the struggle at all. Why couldn't I just let go, take an overdose, slip away in a nice, clean, painless sleep? No more tears, just wipe the slate clean.

I didn't, though; that evening I rang the hotel in Corsham and booked a room for the following weekend.

15

'A man was shot dead outside a Post Office in West Belfast last night; two men are being detained for questioning . . .' I leaned forward and switched off the radio as I turned the car off the A4 into the once so familiar lane that leads up the hill to Maple. The oft-repeated announcement of sudden death in Ulster smacked too much of *déjà vu*; besides, I wanted to concentrate.

I had arrived in Corsham the night before, and after a tolerable dinner, gone to bed early. I'd toyed with the idea of ringing George; Belton was only eight miles away, but decided not. I'd call in, perhaps, on my way home on Sunday. He'd only get suspicious if he heard I was 'snooping' around Maple. Since his marriage to 'the Welsh woman' his paranoia, far from going away had, if anything, become more pronounced.

I had forgotten how narrow the lane was and how steep. There should be a patch of grass round the next bend, where for a few yards the ground levelled out before the lane began to climb once more for the last mile to the hamlet of Maple Ashley. Masses of primroses covered the patch of grass in the spring, and Beth and I would sometimes stop the car there and have a last cigarette before braving whatever perils awaited us on our arrival at Maple. I rounded the corner, and there it was, just as I'd remembered. I drove the car on to the grass and switched off the engine. The day was mild for early December; grey sky with now and again a hint of sun. The bare branches in the hedge bordering the lane rustled gently in the faint breeze, and in the distance an express roared out of the tunnel on its way to Bath.

I first met Beth in 1958, that period of Skiffle, early Elvis Presley and duffle coats, when coffee bars were all the rage and anyone you didn't agree with was 'a peasant'.

Having done two years' national service in the Army, followed by three years at university (red brick), where I achieved a modest 2(2) in History, I'd decided, mistakenly as it turned out, I had a vocation for teaching and just started as a junior master in a large South London secondary school. My home, a comfortable pre-War, three-bedroomed semi in Epping, I considered to be too far away to commute from. An only child, I accepted without question my role as the most important single thing in my parents' life, but after five years of freedom, I had no desire to return full-time to my mother's own particular brand of cherishing. I therefore decided to find digs where I could live during the week; returning home to number three Walnut Avenue at weekends, to sample the delights of my mother's incomparable Sunday dinners and, if pressed, allow her to do my weekly washing. A colleague had hinted that Chelsea was where it was all happening, so I took his advice and found myself a bed-sitter – cooker on the landing and bath two flights up – in a house in Oakley Street, at a rent of £2 10s a week.

Upon such trivia hangs one's destiny. My first evening I accidentally dropped a bottle of milk on the tile surround to my gas fire. Jug in hand, I tapped timidly on the door next to mine on the small landing: a girl with long, pale, blonde hair draped in a towel, and a shy, diffident smile, opened it. The girl turned out to be Beth.

For a time we maintained a rather loose relationship: the occasional visit to the cinema, the odd party on a Saturday night. All I knew of her family was that there were a lot of them and they all spoke with upper-crust accents. They would ring her, usually, it seemed, when she was out, and I frequently took the call. At that time I was having an affair with a married colleague called Sheila something-or-other – I've even forgotten her surname. Sheila's husband, a lecturer in English, was on sabbatical leave in the States: they were, I understood, having a trial separation. I took the affair very seriously, but she didn't and whenever she had let me down too badly, or my fear of her absent husband overcame me, I would turn to Beth, who always seemed to be around when I needed her.

She was, in those days, quite pretty, but rather too passive for my taste. The only time she exhibited any real animation was on the subject of her parents – I didn't then know that George was only her step-father. Then anger would flicker in her pale, blue eyes and her normally soft voice would take on a strident note. They were, she claimed, continually letting her down in some, never very clearly defined way. Her constant aim in life, it seemed, was to become entirely independent of them, but on her present meagre salary of nine pounds a week as junior secretary in an advertising agency, this was, for the moment, impossible. In my preoccupation with Sheila, I took little interest in this side of Beth's life, preferring to use her as a convenient sounding board for my opinions on the state of the film industry or the current political situation. I do remember, however, vaguely wondering why, if she disliked her parents as much as she claimed, did she so frequently return home and appear to be so very much involved with them.

Then early in 1959, Sheila's husband returned and she told me tearfully, but firmly, our affair must finish. Shortly afterwards, Beth and I slept together for the first time. Our friends began to regard us as a couple, and I took her down to Epping to meet my parents. The latter was, to my surprise, a great success. Why I should have been surprised, I don't know; Beth and my parents were made for each other. At their first meeting Dad unbent sufficiently to show Beth his stamp collection, an honour never normally bestowed upon strangers, and Mother got out the family photo album and offered to teach her crochet.

'Guy, you are lucky to have such lovely parents,' Beth said after that first meeting. I remember that quite clearly. We were seated on the front seat, upstairs, of an empty number eleven bus speeding through the City on our way from Liverpool Street to Chelsea. I also remember being surprised at her words: until that time I'd never thought about other people's parents: did I assume they were all like mine? I can't recall; too much has happened since and it was too long ago.

I did not, however, suggest we visit hers. Although I was fond of Beth and happy in her company, I was not in love with her and such a visit would, I felt, in some way commit me to our relationship. I soothed my slightly pricking conscience on the matter – by now I was sure that Beth was in love with me – by telling myself that in the light of her feelings of hostility towards her parents, the last thing she would wish to do would be to introduce us. I was wrong.

'It's my mother's birthday on the 23rd June,' she said one evening, as we sat in the bar of The Six Bells pub in the Kings Road, having our customary half pint of bitter. 'There's to be some sort of grisly celebration. Would you like to come?' I took a couple of sips of my beer: I had no option, really, had I?

232

'I'd love to,' I said. 'Ought I to buy her a present?'

George met us off the London train at Bath. A tall, shambling figure in baggy, grey flannels and a tweed jacket patched with leather at the elbows. His rather grubby cotton check shirt, I noticed, hadn't been properly tucked into his trousers, and a greyish stubble covered his chin. He was smoking.

'Hullo, hullo, how are you?' he shouted, as one bestowing some sort of benediction. He clearly didn't expect any answer, but strode ahead of us down the station steps and out to the waiting Cortina. As we drove through the city, he barked out two further questions – the nature of our train journey and whether it was hotter in London than in Bath – but again it appeared that these were of a purely rhetorical nature, no answer being expected. He didn't speak again until we had turned off the main road into the lane that led to Maple; the lane in which I now sat in my parked car remembering it all. Then, in a sort of hushed mumble very different to his previous booming tones, he said: 'Mama hasn't been feeling too good the last couple of days. Her back's playing her up again and she's got a bit of a tummy upset.'

'Oh God!' I jumped. Wasn't Beth over-reacting a bit? 'It's because I'm down, of course, or because I'm bringing Guy. Have you had the doctor?'

'He's given her some pills and told her to rest. Sophia's doing the cooking, she's got a few days holiday.'

'Poor old Sophie, she would be.'

No more was said until we turned into a short gravel drive bordered on either side with overgrown laurel bushes, and came to a halt at the front door of Maple. It was larger than I had expected, built of grey Cotswold stone with mullioned windows on the ground floor and three gables along the front.

233

The date above the porch read 1665. It was beautiful. Despite myself, I was impressed.

'Mama's upstairs, she says she's having her dinner in bed,' George shouted. 'See to Guy, will you? Mrs Bodkin's made up his bed in the railway room. I must get some more gin from the pub.' Pausing only to dump our luggage on the front doorstep, George climbed back into the car and drove rapidly away.

'You'd better see Mum first,' Beth said. 'She'll only go on if I don't take you to meet her.' Once inside the house we were greeted enthusiastically by a swarm of dogs. Beth kissed each one in turn – there were three – and her hitherto sulky expression faded a little.

'Come on,' she said, as one about to lead her men over the top, 'we'd better get it over with. Why they've put you in the railway room I can't imagine. It's miles from the loo and the bed's like cast iron.' Smiling bravely, I followed her up the beautiful Caroline staircase, wondering with some foreboding what was the significance of the word railway in connection with my proposed sleeping accommodation. Once upstairs, still pursued by assorted canines, we turned into a large bedroom on the right of the square landing. I blinked: the floor of the bedroom was painted a dazzling white, the evening sun streamed in through three long windows on to a small figure wearing large dark glasses, sitting propped up by pillows, in the middle of a huge, brass, double bed.

'Happy birthday, Mum.' Beth's voice was wary, as though the figure in the bed might bite. 'This is Guy.'

I stepped forward nervously and cleared my throat. 'Happy birthday, Mrs Seymour. I've brought you a small book on Wellington's peninsular campaigns; Beth tells me you're a fan of his and, as a matter of fact, so am I. I do hope you haven't got it.'

The small figure sat up briskly and removed the dark glasses. Char looked straight into my eyes and smiled her lovely smile. 'How terribly clever of you,' she said. 'You couldn't have given me anything that would have pleased me more. How clever, too, of Beth to find you; you're not a bit what I expected.' I found myself smiling idiotically, and then and there knew that I loved her and would do so always.

Later, as we sat round the big, scrubbed table in the stone-flagged kitchen having dinner, Char said to no one in particular – she had by this time miraculously recovered – she wondered whose idea it had been to banish 'Beth's young man' to the railway room. It was miles from the bathroom and what's more smelt of damp. 'Yours,' said George, with his mouth full of steak. 'You know it was, you said—'

'The girls will make up his bed in the yellow room and he can use my bathroom,' Char said. 'Cheese anybody?' She waved her arms in an imperious gesture, indicating that we should collect up the plates. The matter was closed; I slept in the yellow room.

I enjoyed that first weekend, I remember, very much. It was while the rather haphazard preparations for her birthday cocktail party were in progress that I had my first real tête-à-tête with Char.

It had been discovered that I was much better at the finicky job of rolling smoked salmon and cutting sandwiches into the tiny, useless triangles deemed necessary at these sort of affairs, than anyone else in the family. Sophia plainly regarded the whole business as a waste of time, and Beth preferred to wash up. The latter, shouting exaggerated endearments to the slobbering canines prancing round her feet, plunged each newly dirtied item noisily into the washing-up bowl as soon as it became available, with the air of aggressive disapproval that seemed a permanent adjunct to her normally passive personality whenever she was in the company of her mother or George. Meanwhile, George, smoking heavily, padded silently to and from making his 'punch'. Someone suddenly switched on the radio, and Char appeared at my elbow, secateurs in hand: she had, it seemed, been 'doing the flowers'.

'My dear, how clever you are,' she said. 'When I do that the bread always falls to pieces. Let's take this lot into the dining-room and I'll help you do the rest.' I agreed, albeit rather doubtfully: I was still a bit afraid of her.

Once in the dining-room, now full of sun and the scent of the evening stocks growing underneath the open windows, rather to my surprise, Char settled down to help with a will. We were silent for a moment or two while she battled, somewhat ineffectively with a recalcitrant piece of smoked salmon, a determined expression on her face. Then, aware of my eyes on her, she looked up suddenly and smiled her enchanting smile, a hint of self-mockery in her own.

'Such a waste of time, all this, isn't it? No one likes the stuff anyway. But Georgy says everyone else round here has it at parties, so we must. Making sandwiches for bores, what a way to spend one's birthday.' Horrified, I hastened to assure her that I could easily finish the job on my own. There were only the sticks to be put in the chipolata sausages and . . .

Suddenly I knew she was laughing at me, and at the same time became aware that somewhere, far down in me something was stirring and responding to her laughter. I stood quite still, Char's eyes upon me, my knife still in my hand, staring down at the chopping board. And it seemed to me that somehow my laughter met and united with hers and for one, brief, moment, in some magical way, she and I were joined together and had become one person.

We neither of us spoke for a moment, then: 'Mrs Seymour,' I asked, my voice neutral, my eyes on the rather hideous silver epergne (George's) that stood in the middle of the mahogany dining table, 'why was I put in the railway room, and why did you have me moved?'

'Damn! Now look what you've made me do.' Char held out her finger accusingly. A minute bead of blood trembled on its tip. 'Suck it,' I said boldly, 'it's only a scratch. And you haven't answered my question.' Obediently she stuck the offending finger in her mouth, then scrutinised it carefully. 'Because of the noise of the damned trains, of course,' she said, 'why else?'

I don't remember anything of the ensuing party; it's somehow merged into all the other cocktail parties I attended at Maple in those early years. They were surprisingly decorous affairs: the guests predominantly retired service people, with a dash of the Church thrown in for good measure. It was only later, when a grown-up Perry would appear at the last minute with a horde of 'undesirables'; when Char herself, having started on her journey into the shadows, could no longer be relied upon not to shout 'Balls!' at some elderly bore who'd buttonholed her to rail against the iniquities of Harold Wilson and the Labour Party, or even on one horrendous occasion, kick the secretary of the local Women's Institute on the shins, that Maple parties turned into the cliff-hanging nightmares they eventually became.

I do remember, however, that after it was over I borrowed George's Cortina and took Beth and Sophia into Bath on a pub crawl – no breathalyser in those days – and wondered why on earth Beth always became so het up about her mother. To me Char seemed an enchanting creature, only too anxious to accommodate her children's friends and not in the least possessive. And in the ensuing weeks, with the arrogance of youth, I chose to ignore the odd fact that while trying to explain the intricacies of the Reform Bill to thirty bored and lethargic fourteen-year-olds, or seated on top of a bus caught in the rush hour on Vauxhall Bridge, or even during Beth's and my somewhat tepid lovemaking – the latter not helped by the frequent complaints of the woman next door – Char, disturbing, secret and infinitely exciting, would without warning, suddenly come into my mind. People, I told myself, did not fall for their girlfriend's mother; at any rate intelligent grammar-school boys brought up in the healthy confines of number three Walnut Avenue, Epping, didn't, and that was that.

After that first weekend Beth and I would often visit Maple, driving down in the Morris Minor I had bought with the proceeds of a small but miraculous win on the football pools. I came to love the house and the garden with its tumbling, grey stone walls and rampant herbaceous borders. Through long, autumn afternoons Char and I would work together in the latter, vainly trying to create some kind of order. We wouldn't talk much during these sessions; except in the early days when Char would instruct me in the intricacies of dividing the tangled clumps of phlox and Michaelmas daisies, layering carnations, or taking cuttings.

'I see a mass of purple here,' she'd say grandly, a small figure in muddy corduroys and sensible boots, her hair blowing in the wind, 'backed, perhaps, by a clump or two of those big, yellow daisies.' I'd nod doubtfully, and get to work. Alas, most of our grand designs came to nothing, but we enjoyed executing them all the same, and because of, or in spite of, our efforts the garden at Maple, for me at any rate, would always remain an enchanted place. Beth, no gardener, would spend the time watching sport on television or doing our combined week's washing in the washing machine in the old scullery.

'Well, at least now Mum doesn't take to her bed as soon as I appear,' Beth said, as we drove back to London one Sunday evening. 'Last time Sophie was down she spent the whole weekend upstairs, and even hinted she hadn't long to live.' I shrugged: Sophia seemed to take a rather acid view of most things and was bossy to boot.

'D'you like my clever Sophie?' Char had asked. 'You know she got a first at Oxford? She's the one you should be after, not Beth.' I knew Sophia had got a first at Oxford; I only managed a second at Reading, and was painfully aware of this fact whenever we met.

Perry was just thirteen when I first encountered him. He was about to spend a year at a crammer's, as there were doubts as to whether without extra tuition, he would be able to pass the Common Entrance examination to Marlborough. George's parents, I understood, were paying for this.

'So nice,' Char said. 'Next time you come you'll be able to coach Perry in his cricket.' I tried, unsuccessfully, to look enthusiastic.

'You know damn well Perry hates cricket,' George said. 'I don't know why you will pretend he doesn't.'

But Char smiled and tapped her forehead with her finger. 'He's bonkers, you know,' she said. 'Don't listen to him.'

Gradually my role in the Maple hierarchy began to change from 'Beth's young man' to that of surrogate son. Even George started to communicate a little. 'Guy and I'll do that next time he's down,' he'd say, and took to inviting me to accompany him to the local pub for a 'quick pint before dinner'.

'Dear Guy, what should we do without you?' Char would

smile her secret smile and rub her face against my shoulder. Perry tolerated me, I suppose, but would brook no interference.

'It's none of your bloody business,' he shouted one Sunday afternoon, when I unwisely remonstrated with him for riding his bicycle over the herbaceous border. 'You're not our family.'

It was the summer of my twenty-sixth birthday that I took the decision to give up teaching and go into insurance. I was no use at teaching and knew it; somehow or other my heart wasn't in it and the sooner I embarked on another career the better. My present company, much smaller in those days, was advertising for young graduates to train for managerial positions. I applied, was accepted and have been there ever since. With a new job and better prospects I decided to move out of bed-sitter land and find myself a flat. Luckily for me my father approved of the scheme, and was prepared to loan me the down payment on a thirty-year lease of a maisonette on the South side of Clapham Common.

For Beth and myself my move to Clapham meant the end of an era, and we both knew that some decision would have to be made over our relationship; Beth wanted marriage, I knew, but did I? I tried pleading financial insecurity.

'Don't give me that,' Beth said. 'We're not living in the nineteenth century, and I earn nearly fourteen pounds a week.' In the end she issued an ultimatum: either we got married or stopped seeing one another altogether. The latter course made that much easier now we no longer lived next door to each other. I had a week to consider my options and at the end of it came down on the side of marriage. I was, I told myself, too fond of Beth and too used to having her around to let her go now. Besides, one should marry, it was good for one, and by this time most of my friends had already taken the plunge.

But now, as I sat in my car nearly a quarter of a century later, I knew my reasons for marrying had been quite different to the ones I gave myself at the time: it was not Beth I was afraid of losing but her mother. Even then life without Char was something I simply could not bear to contemplate.

George opened a bottle of champagne the day Beth and I announced our engagement. Was it then I saw for the first time that expression in Char's eyes, to become so familiar in later years? Hard to explain, but a kind of desperate brightness: as though she were willing you to see in her the image of a woman who has had everything life can offer, but underneath is crying out in bitterness and anguish that she has had nothing.

Beth's and my wedding the following summer was a pucka affair: a marquee on the lawn at Maple, morning suits and all that sort of thing. I rather enjoyed it actually and so, I think, did Char, who behaved with magnificent decorum: the bride's mother personified, except, unlike my mother, she flatly refused to wear purple. I have a picture of it all somewhere. I look insufferably smug, Beth very pretty and virginal, but rather sad, and Char in a toque with a feather in it, which didn't suit her, making her 'photograph' face.

Beth and I got drunk on our wedding night. We spent it in my flat; we were catching an early plane to Corfu the following morning, where we were to spend our honeymoon.

'You fancy my Mum, don't you?' I remember Beth saying at one point during the evening.

'She's still a very attractive woman,' I said warily, scenting even then a danger I didn't quite understand.

'I suppose she is, really,' Beth said. 'I've never seen it myself, but people seem to think she is, so I suppose she must be.' She took another gulp of champagne; we'd brought a couple of bottles back with us in the hope of prolonging the spirit of excited optimism that had prevailed at the wedding reception, but it had somehow evaporated on the journey up to London and the idea, although a good one, hadn't worked. 'But you have to admit,' Beth went on, 'Mum didn't look her best in that ghastly hat.'

I smiled, remembering how Char had stuck out her tongue at me, when earlier that day I had vouchsafed a slight criticism of the hat myself. 'No,' I said, delighted to be able to agree with my new wife about something, 'she didn't.' Then, idiotically, I had to add: 'I expect she wanted it to be your day—'

'Balls!' Suddenly Beth looked so like her mother I almost choked on my champagne. 'She couldn't care less about it being "my day". She probably bought that hat to bugger up the wedding photos.'

'Now you really are being stupid,' I said, wondering guiltily whether she was right, and that indeed was the reason. Then I discarded the thought: it was much more likely Char had just bought the hat without thinking, in a hurry to get the boring business over with. She was never very interested in clothes. In her rich years, Algy had insisted she patronised such fashionable couturiers of the period as Molyneux and Digby Moreton, but her succeeding husbands seem to have accepted her very much as she was: in any case, I doubt whether either of them would ever have dared to criticise her taste in dress.

Beth was staring at the floor, her mouth pursed in a certain way that in later years I was to become all too familiar with as marking the onset of a scene. Suddenly she looked up. 'She always hated me,' she said accusingly. 'You do know that, don't you? I've never been able to understand why. Sophie says it's because my father let her down by getting himself killed by that bomb—'

'If Sophia says that, she needs her head examined. How irresponsible can you get, she—'

'You don't deny it, then?'

'Of course I deny it, it's absolute rubbish.'

'Sophie's very bright, you know, and she understands Mum better than anyone. I know they have the most frightful rows – you've never been around to see them, but they do. Then, just as you think they're going to kill each other, you find them sitting happily discussing the Labour Party Conference, or something equally idiotic.'

'That's as may be,' I said, out of my depth: fatigue and too much champagne were making me feel muzzy. 'Sophie may have got a first, but from what I've seen, she's never been that hot on human relationships, and aren't we straying from the point? Of course your mother loves you. Look how pleased she was when we got engaged, and all the trouble she's gone to to make the wedding a success.'

For a moment it seemed I'd convinced her, then she shook her head angrily, causing a few, stray pieces of confetti that had somehow lodged in her elaborate wedding hair-do, to fall on the carpet. 'That wasn't for me,' she said almost inaudibly, 'you know it wasn't.'

I looked at her helplessly: what on earth was I supposed to do? You couldn't spend your wedding night arguing about whether your wife's mother loved her or not. In the end I did the only possible thing: I took her in my arms and told her I loved her and that was all that mattered anyway, wasn't it?

But later, when she was asleep, her fair hair straggled on the pillow, her thumb endearingly in her mouth, I rang Char just for a quick word; just to see how she was . . .

'I'm alright, you fool,' she said. 'Haven't you got something better to do?'

And after that? Those early years are somehow kaleidoscoped together; hard to recall now which event belongs to which year. I remember the shock of Evie's death in far-away Australia. Char had only seen her daughter once since Evie's marriage: Australia was a long way and, although she had often talked of visiting her in Melbourne, somehow she never had, and now it was too late. There was a memorial service in the village church at Maple to which old Mrs Osborn came – a mummified figure draped in shawls – probably her last public appearance. The church, I remember, was bright with summer flowers arranged by Char (with me a willing, but somewhat clumsy assistant) and a surprising number of people turned up. I remember too, Char's hand gripping mine so tightly as we went into the final hymn that afterwards my fingers were quite numb. Of course there was always the continuing saga of Perry.

Perry had somehow managed to scrape together several O-levels at Marlborough. 'I always knew he was clever,' Char said. 'He only needed the right school.' However, after this scholastic triumph, he flatly refused to stay on at school to do A-levels, and after a series of scenes, in the course of which he was alleged to have thrown a glass of wine at his father and knocked his mother down – I was not a witness – he was sent to France for six months to learn French. Peace reigned, but not for long, and only too soon he was back. He'd adored France, he said, but the language was quite incomprehensible. Briefly and disastrously, he lodged with us in Fulham. Some old flame of Char's, one Gilbert Parsloe, managed to get him a job in the City.

'Mum says I never think of anyone but myself, and if I had children of my own I'd understand,' Beth reported furiously, 'and if we don't have the little beast to live with us, she'll only sulk. Anyway, he'll soon get fed up.' He did. He drank like a fish from morning until night, had his driving licence taken away for driving the wrong way up a one-way street at forty m.p.h. at three in the morning, and was found by Beth making love to some girl in our bed one Saturday afternoon, when she'd brought my mother back for tea after a shopping expedition in Oxford Street. Then he got the sack. 'I simply cannot understand Gilbert,' Char said. 'Of course, I shall never speak to him again.'

We prospered, Beth and I, in those years, and moved from Clapham to a small house in Fulham, just then becoming fashionable. We went abroad for holidays, entertained our friends to dinner; I took up squash and Beth became personal assistant to the managing director of her advertising agency. There were no children. After three years of trying, Beth was told it was unlikely she would ever conceive.

'I'm barren, Guy,' she said after we'd had the specialist's report. 'I just bloody would be, wouldn't I?' and burst into tears.

'Don't be silly. It's not impossible, just unlikely,' I said, 'and even if there isn't a baby, we still have each other.'

'That's what I'm afraid of,' she said and turned her face to the wall.

It was cold now in the car and I shivered as I switched on the engine. I would drive up and have a look at the house, then perhaps go on to the Ashley Arms and get a bite to eat. I reached the top of the hill in third gear; in the old days there had always been a point where one was forced to change down. Cars, like so much else, had altered a great deal since the last time I had driven up the hill to Maple.

The old white gate had gone, replaced by wrought iron.

Instead of overgrown laurels, pinkish gravel and a scattering of those horrid little conifers so much beloved of garden centres. But the house looked much the same. I got out of the car and stood by the gate looking up at it, remembering.

Two cars were parked in the drive, and after a moment the front door opened and some people came out: a middle-aged couple and a young man. They stood talking and then the couple got into their car and drove away; the young man, seeing me standing by the gate, came over.

'Are you here to see the house?' Taken by surprise, I looked at him blankly. 'I've got to get back, but if you want to have a look round, by all means do; if you don't mind returning the key to our office in Bath.'

'Thanks very much,' I said. 'I didn't have time to make an appointment and just came on spec.'

'That's alright,' he said. 'Here's a copy of the particulars, in case you haven't got them. We close at one p.m. today, but you can always pop the key through the letter box and get in touch on Monday, if you're interested.' I thanked him again and he drove off at high speed in the direction of Bath, waving cheerily as he turned the car into the lane. Silence once more; only the sound of a branch rubbing against the gatepost and the distant hum of a tractor.

'Fine seventeenth-century farmhouse,' I read. 'Built by the Ashley family in the reign of Charles II. Spacious accommodation, gardens, garaging,' etc.

Stuffing the estate agent's particulars into my pocket, I wandered round the end of the house to the south side, the side that faced on to the lawn, the side dominated by the cedar tree. The lawn stretched smooth, bland, well cared-for to the ha-ha and the encircling fields beyond, but the cedar tree had gone, vanished utterly, not even its stump remained. I felt shocked, bereft, as though suddenly learning of an old friend's death long afterwards.

I turned and looked up at the house. Char's three bedroom windows gazed blindly down at me; my sense of desolation was complete. Slowly, I wandered back to the front door. Inside, the house smelt musty, unlived in; I wondered how long it had been up for sale.

There'd been a row at lunch that Saturday, I remember. The summer of 1968 was a rotten one, but there was one weekend in May when the temperature rocketed into the eighties. Beth and I were down for the local point-to-point. Or rather, Beth was down for it; I've always been bored stiff by such affairs. Perry and a horsy girlfriend, Petronella something-or-other, were also there, the former going through his brief legal phase; articled, I seem to remember, to a firm of solicitors in Bristol.

Char looked tired and strung-up. Old Mrs Osborn had died, aged ninety, in February of that same year, and despite frequent protestations to the effect she was delighted to have Ma off her back at last, and the fact Mrs Osborn had been intermittently senile for some years, the removal of so powerful and influential a figure from Char's life did appear to have taken its toll. Incidentally, in spite of overwhelming evidence to the contrary, Char never appeared to accept the fact of her mother's senility. I well remember the outrage in her voice when on her return from an audience with Ma – now devotedly cared for by a pair of long-suffering Pratt cousins – she told us: 'I absolutely refuse to visit her ever again. I picked those flowers *especially* and all she could say was, were they made of plastic! Of course, she knew perfectly well they weren't, she was just being foul.' And no amount of ribald comments from George, or soothing noises from me, could convince her that old Mrs Osborn had not been wilfully trying to upset her.

Be that as it may, whether or not it was reaction to her mother's death, I don't know, but certainly Char was drinking more than she should – to be fair, not as much as George, but still too much – and was more than usually aggressive with everyone, including me. She and Perry never stopping sniping at one another, and it was blatantly obvious that she had taken a strong dislike to Petronella. I couldn't help sneakingly agreeing with her over this, albeit, no doubt, for different reasons. By this time I was well aware that Char, no matter how hard she tried – and she did try, despite what people said, I know she did – could never bring herself to more than tolerate any of Perry's girlfriends.

Anyway, lunch that day was a grim affair. George, Perry and Petronella were late back from the pub. 'Lunch early,' Char had ordered before they left, 'if you all want to go to this bloody point-to-point.' And as a result of their lateness, the sausages were burned and one of the dogs stole the ham. Perry slammed out of the kitchen, having informed his mother she was a jealous, cantankerous bitch, dragging a subdued Petronella in his wake. Beth burst into tears and said she wished she'd never come, and why did everyone always have to behave like lunatics; George helped himself liberally to another whisky and gave his burned sausage to the dogs, and Char, her eyes meeting mine across the table, announced they could all go to hell. She intended, she said, to spend the afternoon resting in the garden, and if anyone thought that she was ever going to sweat her guts out preparing another meal for them again, they were grossly mistaken.

In the end, Beth drove George to the point-to-point in our car, Perry and Petronella having left in a cloud of smoke and a roar of exhaust sometime earlier. I pleaded a headache which, incidentally, was true – and retired upstairs for a kip, and Char settled down on a rug laid out under the cedar tree, an old straw hat tipped over her face, the dogs stretched out on the grass around her.

When I awoke a couple of hours later, the shadows had lengthened across the lawn and the dogs had disappeared, but Char was still lying there under the cedar tree, a splash of colour in the wide expanse of grass. The cuckoo was calling through the open bathroom window as I splashed my face with cold water, the first I'd heard that summer; somewhere up the lane a lawnmower hummed. I wandered downstairs and out into the stifling garden.

As I approached her Char didn't move. At first, I thought she was asleep. Then I realised that her eyes were open; they were staring up into the dark recesses of the cedar tree with such an expression of naked sadness in them, for a moment I was paralysed with shock. Then, as the shock waves receded, I became aware of such an overwhelming desire to remove that look on her face and take whatever burden she carried on myself, I almost cried out in echo of her pain.

I knelt down beside her: 'Char, darling, what is it, what on earth's the matter?'

She didn't answer, but slowly turned her head and looked at me, in her eyes a question. Then suddenly I was kissing her, the magic running through me. She spoke then: 'Fuck me, Guy, fuck me, please,' and, God help me, I did.

Afterwards, cedar needles in my hair, the sweetness of her still in my mouth, Char sat up and grinned at me, squinting a little at the sunlight glinting through the branches above us. 'What a waste,' she said, 'not to have done it before. So many years . . . and now . . .'

'And now?' I asked.

'And now,' she said briskly, combing her hair with a minute comb she'd extracted from the handbag she carried with her everywhere, 'I'll have to think what to give the bloody children for supper.'

A pair of blackbirds were hooking worms out of the lawn in the spot where the cedar tree had stood. The sun, for a moment, came out from behind the clouds and shone quite fiercely through the hall window: I blinked at the brightness. I'd go upstairs and have a quick look round, then drive to the pub for lunch; it was nearly one o'clock.

Char's white bedroom floor was covered now by an orange fitted carpet, the white walls by a matching wallpaper, tastefully patterned; there were net curtains at the windows. Had we really made love in this room, she and I, thirty years between us and whole worlds apart?

'Let's fight first,' she said. 'It's always better when you fight,' and mostly it was. Just sometimes in those first few months – later I learned to accept that it was too late to change her now – I longed for a more peaceful lovemaking. Then I would try to tell her how I felt; how I loved her so, that if it were possible I'd give my soul to somehow turn the clock back.

But she would get angry and tell me I was a romantic idiot, and she wasn't that old anyway, was she? I made her sound like the female equivalent of the Wandering Jew, or someone equally boring. Then we would fall about with childish laughter, and I'd forget my agony for a while. They had been agony, though, those first months of our affair, despite that, at the time, I idiotically refused to admit the fact. Were they for Char? Sometimes I thought they were. I would catch her looking at me across the room, her green eyes those of a wistful child. But then, becoming aware of my glance, she'd smile her secret smile and turn away to bury her face in one of the animals, or perhaps, if Perry were there, suddenly put her arms round his waist and tell him how perfect he was and wonder how George could ever have produced such a paragon.

And what did George think about it all? I never really knew, and I don't know now. Certainly after Char and I became lovers, his attitude to me remained exactly as it had always been. Perhaps he tended to shout a bit more, and when carrying on a conversation with him, his eyes appeared always to be looking at a spot somewhere over my left shoulder, but that was all. He came back once I remember, when Char and I were making love in her bedroom. We heard his footsteps on the stairs, but he never came in. Char said: 'Don't mind him, he doesn't care anyway': all the same I hid under the bed and Char, damn her, laughed until she cried.

It was not long after Char and I first made love that Beth started on about us buying a weekend cottage. All our friends were doing it, she said; now was the time to buy. I must know that as well as she did. And anyway it would do us good to get away from polluted old London – pollution was just coming in then – and unwind a bit.

'But what about Maple?' I asked, panic stricken, knowing she was right.

'What about Maple?' she said, crashing a pile of plates into the washing-up machine; we happened, at the time, to be clearing up after a dinner party. I carefully placed a tray of dirty glasses on the draining board. 'Well, the air's not polluted for a start, and we can always go there; not like some people—'

'You can bloody well say that again; we damned well aren't like other people!' Beth had drunk a bit more than usual that evening and it showed. 'How many other couples, after six years of marriage, spend every fucking weekend with their in-laws, may I ask?'

'Quite a few, I should think,' I said, trying to stay calm, but painfully aware that part of me, that newly awakened part of me, longed to seize my wife by her hair and throttle her with it. 'That is, if they had such a lovely spot as Maple to go to. Anyway, we can't afford a cottage at the moment. You've no idea how much money you can pour into places like that. And it's not as if you're ever prepared to pig it: you always have to have the latest gadget, stuff the place so full of mod cons there's no room to breathe, let alone unwind.'

'I've got to have something!' Beth banged open the pedal bin with her foot and tipped the remains of the lemon sorbet into it, then turned and looked at me, the cut-glass dish – a wedding present from Cousin Milly – still in her hand. For a moment I thought she was going to throw it, then I realised suddenly that the fight had gone out of her.

'OK, you win – as usual,' she said, and now her voice just sounded tired. 'Go to bloody Maple as much as you damn well like; go and live there if you want to, but don't expect me to accompany you, that's all.' I tried to put my arms round her then, and explained that soon, after next year's raise, after I'd got my promotion – the latter was in the pipeline I knew for a fact – we'd buy a cottage in the country, but not now, not just yet . . .

Of course, we never did, did we, but from then on Beth took to staying in London at weekends and leaving me to go to Maple on my own.

I trod carefully across the bright, new carpet, my shoes, wet from the garden, leaving their imprint on the pristine, orange coloured pile – solitary footmarks on a deserted beach

– and pulled aside a net curtain. A spider – one of those thin ones, all legs and no body – busied itself in the magnolia leaves beneath the window; above my head, last summer's flies hung ossified in last summer's web.

It changed, though, Char's and my relationship, once we became lovers. Paradoxically, a lot of the old, happy intimacy went. Was it guilt? I don't think so. Char didn't know the meaning of the word, and I think even then I knew Beth's and my marriage was doomed. No, it was something else. We became wary of each other. I, who had never criticised, began to criticise: to question her indulgence towards Perry, her intake of alcohol, even her treatment of George.

'Leave me alone, damn you,' I remember her shouting after one such session. 'You're not my bloody mother. If you want to bully someone, go and bully your wife.' Horrified, I pleaded I wasn't bullying her, I was simply trying to help. The three of them, she, George and Perry, would be so much happier, wouldn't they, if only they didn't always have to go to such extremes. Disconcertingly, she gave her snort of laughter – the laugh, so Sophia said, that came from Pa. 'And what the hell d'you think we're doing then,' she said, 'if not going to extremes?'

Sometimes, underneath all the nonsense, she had an uncanny knack of hitting the nail precisely on the head. It was, I think, one of the reasons that caused certain people to dislike her so intensely, especially certain women. And yet in some odd way Char appeared to expect, even want me to bully her. I had, it seemed, my allotted place in both sides of her nature: not only must I dominate, but I must also be dominated. It was a hellishly difficult path to travel, but the rewards, when they came, were sweet.

Strangely, or so it seems now – it didn't then – we seldom

felt the gap of years between us. Char never consciously aped the young or anything like that, she simply remained Char and it was enough. But sometimes she would talk of events that were to me part of history, as though they had happened the previous week: the summer manoeuvres of 1913, when she had played at pillow fights with the young subalterns encamped on Bagland Common; Pa masquerading as a porter on Euston Station during the General Strike in 1926; King Edward VII's little dog following the coffin at his master's funeral in 1910. Then I would look at her in amazement, and for a split second believe that I was living in a dream; a dream from which I would wake to find myself 'alone on the cold hillside'; another palely loitering knight, summarily released by his own *Belle Dame sans merci*. Fanciful stuff, I suppose, from a faceless insurance manager from Fulham, but there it is.

And so the years went on. By the early 1970s, Char's and my lovemaking had become more or less a routine. I don't mean the excitement had gone out of it, that never happened, but we had become used to the prevailing circumstances. I would even sometimes spend the odd weekend in London. I had begun to contribute fairly regularly to a history magazine and needed an occasional weekend to work on my articles. 'You slacker,' Char would say on the phone, when I rang to tell her I wouldn't be coming, 'think of poor me alone with Georgy.' But really I don't think she minded all that much.

Oddly enough I think it was George who minded more than Char. 'Pity you weren't here last weekend, Guy. I had to strip down the engine of Perry's Mini; could have done with some help,' he'd say fretfully, or: 'Those damned strawberries, it took me two hours last night to pick them and my back's giving me hell. You'd have thought Perry might lend a hand sometimes, but you know Perry . . .'

In the autumn of 1969, or was it 1970, I can't remember, Char and I went on holiday together. We hired a canal boat for a few days, the idea being we should visit some of the Civil War battlefields. I was doing a paper on General Fairfax at the time and wanted to get in a bit of local colour. The boat idea was Char's. Madness of course: I knew next to nothing about such things and she was no help at all, her only experience being weekends spent on Algy's father's yacht in the Solent when, as far as I could make out, all they'd ever done was eat bananas, drink black velvets and dance to the gramophone. 'We had a crew, you see,' she said, 'and they did all the work.' I bet they did.

But looking back, those few days were the best I ever spent with Char. The boat broke down; I nearly ruptured myself getting us through the locks; Lucas, her wretched West Highland terrier, fell overboard and she insisted I dive in and get him out – actually he could swim perfectly well – but somehow none of those things mattered, I don't know why, but they didn't. We stopped at a pub on the way home to Maple after it was over and Char said: 'There's only one other time when I've been as happy; but we'll pay for it, one always does.' I tried to make her tell me when that other time had been, and who else but me could make her happy, but she wouldn't tell me. And she was right about the paying for it.

By that time I was pretty sure Beth had a lover. She was taking much more care over her appearance and seemed less tense. She began staying late at the office a couple of nights a week, and quite often she'd be on the phone when I arrived home, but as soon as she heard my key in the lock, would hang up. Then, after a bout of bronchitis, when she claimed my coughing kept her awake, I started to sleep in the spare room and by tacit consent, my cough long gone, I didn't return to hers. From time to time we went on holiday together, usually to a fishing village on the coast of Spain, far away from the booming Costa del Sol. We'd discovered the place not long after we were married and it was still fairly unspoiled. God knows what it's like now. But we always went with another couple and so spent little time alone. And our lovemaking, when it did take place, was more often than not, a rather lifeless reproduction of the act of sex bearing little resemblance to the real thing.

It was late one January evening when I returned home from a four-day managerial conference in Scarborough. It had been a difficult few days, what with one thing and another, and I felt tired and rather dispirited as I let myself into the house. To my surprise, Beth was still up, lying on the sofa, a glass of whisky in her hand.

'Why didn't you tell me Mum was going round the bend? You must have known.' She sounded tense, not far from hysteria, edging towards a scene.

'What on earth do you mean; I would have told you, but she was perfectly alright when I saw her.' But I knew that was a lie, didn't I, and yet the words came out so glibly. I had, I suppose, become an expert.

'She can't have been; George says it's been going on for months.'

I poured myself a drink with hands that shook only slightly. 'George says what's been going on for months?' There was a pause. Beth sat up and held out her glass; in silence, I poured her another whisky.

'Sophie's back from the States for a few days,' she said. 'You were away, so she suggested we drove down to Maple for the night to see how things were.'

'And . . . ?'

'They were bloody awful. Perry's in trouble again; Fiona's chucked him because of his drinking and Mr Sloane says he never turns up at the office—'

'So, what's new? I thought you said it was your mother.' There was another pause. A taxi pulled up outside the house next door; the door slammed; footsteps going up to the front door; a key in the lock . . .

'George says . . . he says Mum's drinking far too much and when she's drunk, which is quite a lot of the time, she sleeps with anyone who offers.'

'Oh, don't be so absurd; who offers, for God's sake?' I felt like Judas.

'Lots of people, apparently: that frightful old Major Palmer for a start and—'

'George is making this up, can't you see?' This was, of course, a nightmare. I'd wake up in a minute.

'Not all of it,' Beth said, 'and anyway, Mum was boasting about it herself. She wanted to give Sophie the gory details, but Sophie wouldn't listen.'

I tried frantically to think, but somehow couldn't. All I felt was an insane and terrible jealousy. How could she? What had happened, for God's sake. Did George know about me? 'I wouldn't set too much store by what they say.' I hoped I sounded both sensible and objective, but doubted it. 'You know what George and your mother are like: they get drunk and start making up stories about one another; it's their way of amusing themselves. Anyway, they're worried sick about Perry.'

'You're talking rubbish and you know it,' Beth's voice sounded thin and harsh at the same time. 'Mum's not worried about Perry, she never has been; she doesn't even recognise there's a problem, and George doesn't care . . .'

Beth was right, of course. Something had been happening to Char in the last few months, I'd just refused to admit it. That look in her eyes I'd seen fleetingly years before at Beth's and my engagement was often there now. Only three weeks ago I'd walked into the library at Maple and found her standing in the middle of the room holding an empty vase, a mass of pink chrysanthemums scattered round her feet on the floor, a lost expression on her face. 'These are no good,' she said as though I wasn't there, 'thistles would be better . . .' and she slowly ground each flower head into the carpet with the heel of her slipper. Last time we'd made love she'd scratched and bitten me savagely, dragging her long nails down my back, biting into the flesh between my thighs until I screamed out in pain. Christ!

'If what you say is true, perhaps she should see a psychiatrist,' I said, hypocrite that I was.

Beth snorted. 'I'm going to bed,' she said. 'Sophie's coming to dinner tomorrow evening, we'll talk about it then. And I suppose we'll have to tell Ann.'

'No!' The word burst out before I could stop it. Beth got up from the sofa and walked slowly over to where I stood with my back to her, looking blindly out of the window. She turned my face towards hers, and very gently kissed me on the forehead; to my surprise, there was pity, not anger, in her eyes.

'Don't be too upset, darling,' she said, 'it's always been on the cards.'

I remember driving down to Maple that Friday evening, two days after Beth had dropped her bomb into the complacent citadel of my self-esteem, feeling such hatred for Char, I wanted to kill her. I'd joined the ranks, I told myself, of those other discarded lovers of hers. All she'd wanted from me was to prove she was still capable of attracting someone thirty years her junior; anyone, it didn't matter who, so long as the poor sod was fool enough to fall in love with her. I remember too the salt taste of tears in my mouth, mixing with the double brandy I bought myself in a pub on the way down, and the barmaid's face, puzzled and slightly apprehensive, as she took my money.

The previous two days had been an unremitting nightmare. Long, hysterical phone calls from George, rows with Beth, and a ghastly family lunch, consisting of Sophia, Andrew McFee, representing Ann, Beth and myself; Perry, for some reason, had not been asked. The lunch took place somewhere like Rules with Sophia being efficient and sensible, au fait already with all the current psychiatric jargon; Andrew looking out of his depth, announcing repeatedly that Ann had said she wanted her mother to have the best treatment money could buy and George mustn't be allowed to fob her off with the National Health Service, and Beth, my Beth, being emotional and useless, but somehow more endearing than either of the other two.

And myself? Just a dummy, eating his steak au poivre, listening to Char's children as they plotted her downfall: replying sensibly when referred to, but otherwise holding his peace, while all the time the real Guy Horton squirmed in hatred and loathing for the lot of them, and that included their hell-cat mother. Because he knew, didn't he, that they were wrong; Char was no more mad than they were themselves. She was just a lying, cheating, faithless bitch.

At the end of the meal, as Andrew was paying the bill, a pained expression on his face, Sophia looked across the table at me, her eyes challenging. 'Guy, you see more of Mum than any of us, what do you really think?' They all looked at me then: I felt naked, helpless, at bay, my mind a seething blank.

Suddenly, Beth, her face white as paper, beads of sweat on her forehead: 'I'm awfully sorry, but if we don't get out of here fast, I think I'm going to faint.'

'Oh, Lord,' Sophia again. 'Quick, she must have air. Take her out, Guy, Andrew and I'll follow in a moment . . .'

Saved by my wife! Had it been deliberate? I'll never know; suffice to say I shall always be grateful to her.

When I arrived at Maple that night it was raining and the back door was locked. The back doorbell had been broken years ago, and I remember hammering angrily on the glass panels with my bare knuckles. Then George's face, grey with worry, unshaven. 'Sorry, Guy, I had to lock it, or she might have got out, you see. I can't make her go to bed, she says she wants to go to a nightclub.'

I followed him down the dark passage that always smelled of dog and wet mackintoshes. At the end, the kitchen blazed with light. The dogs ran forward barking. Char was sitting on the edge of the big, scrubbed table, her legs dangling, a glass in her hand. She had put a red, plastic rose in her hair and her eyes, as they focused on me, held no hint of recognition. But she smiled her special smile and held out her arms.

'Hullo,' she said, 'have you come to take me to see the soldiers? We'd better hurry, or they'll all be dead.'

And I just stood there, holding on tightly to her hands. OK, OK, I admitted defeat: they'd been right and I'd been wrong. Char had, for the time being anyway, left us. Why she had I simply did not pretend to know. Her children hinted the seeds of madness had always been there; perhaps they were right. Somehow, it didn't matter whether they were or not. What did matter, and I remember feeling almost guilty at the wave of relief rolling over me, was that she had not betrayed me, at least not consciously, and with that to hang on to, I could cope with anything.

Gently I lifted her down from the table. 'It's a bit late to see the soldiers tonight, darling,' I said. 'Never mind, I'll take you in the morning . . .'

Char and I never made love again – physical love – after that. It wasn't that I didn't still love her, God knows I did, but in those weeks since I had seen her last, those weeks in which the illness that, unbeknown to me, had hovered over her for so long, finally won its battle against her, my role somehow became switched. I became, once more, Guy, the prop and mainstay, father, mother, brother, friend, but no longer Guy the lover. Like George, I was simply there, and always would be. Incidentally, I don't think Char ever completely accepted George's defection to Bronwen Mallory; for her such a thing was beyond the bounds of credibility. Until, that is, just before she died, and then I have a feeling she did. For my part, I was quite willing to accept my role. I don't think I would have wished it any other way. After all, I told myself, we'd loved one another, Char and I, long before we became lovers, and would do so long after we ceased to be. Besides, like a cat that bounds in each morning with the milk, wide-eyed and enigmatic, after a night spent on the tiles, who knew where she had been when the mood was on her? I, for one, didn't want to know.

The noise of my footsteps on the bare boards of the staircase sounded unnaturally loud. I crossed the hall and opened the front door; it had started to rain. I shut the door behind me and a sudden gust of wind blew a swirl of raindrops in my eyes.

16

They'd turned the old cartshed at the Ashley Arms into a restaurant: red plush seats, Victorian prints and tiny tables hopefully laid for a three-course meal. The place was empty and rather dark. A smartly dressed lady hovered in the passage that used to lead to the Gents.

'Can I eat in the bar?' I asked. 'I only want a sandwich.'

'Of course you can, my love,' she said. 'I'll find you a menu.' I wondered what had happened to old Sid Bean. The bar was not unpleasant; much larger than I remembered and much brighter. The rather inadequate Valor oil radiator had been replaced by a comforting woodburning stove, and instead of the brown and orange wallpaper, the walls were painted cream.

'What happened to Mr Bean?' I asked. 'I used to come here in the seventies. He was the landlord then.'

'Sid Bean? He died a while back now. Lived round here, did you?' The lady wore pink, plastic earrings and her brilliant, blonde hair had been newly lacquered. She removed an imaginary speck of dirt from the sleeve of her spotless, pink blouse.

I was the only customer. It must, I thought, be rather boring for her. 'I used to stay at the Court, my wife's parents – the Seymours?'

'Ah . . .' I tried to interpret the sound; was it nostalgia or disapproval? 'My husband sees the Major in Trowbridge sometimes. Getting on now, he must be.'

'Yes,' I said.

'He married that Mrs Mallory, then, after—?'

'Yes,' I said. 'He married again after my mother-in-law died.' I bit into a ham sandwich; the bread was good, but the ham was damp and tasteless.

'My Dad used to say the Court brought bad luck. He said there was a curse.'

'Really?' This was a new slant, or at least one I'd never heard before. 'No one ever stays long there, never have, not since old Lady Ashley died years and years ago: three owners it's had since the Major sold it, and all of them have had bad luck.' We were silent for a moment, thinking. 'I hope I don't speak out of turn, but the Major and Mrs Seymour had a few ups and downs – that poor boy of theirs – so young.' I nodded, my mouth full of sandwich. I couldn't think of anything to say anyway.

At that moment, however, the door of the bar obligingly opened to admit a large man wearing a donkey jacket, his hair plastered down by rain. 'Morning Vera, my love. Got any of that pie you had last time I came? And I'll have a pint of Best while I'm waiting.' In the ensuing bustle, I took my drink and the plate of sandwiches to a seat by the window. I was glad it was raining, it seemed fitting somehow.

I sipped my beer and listened to the rain drumming on the roof of Sid Bean's old greenhouse, and tried to will myself back to those years of the seventies; those years in which so much went wrong I'd wondered whether, for me, they would ever go right again; those years that I'd tried to forget.

Perversely, now I wanted to remember, only fragments

remained, vivid fragments, but nonetheless hard to place in the chronology of that time.

'We've got to get her into one of those places, Guy. I don't care what Dr Weil says, drugs just aren't enough. I know she can fool people that she's perfectly normal, but, by God, you should see her sometimes, and I can't take any more; sooner or later she's going to do me or herself an injury.' George's voice; desperate, drink-slurred. We had been sitting where I sat now, having one of our interminable discussions on Char's future. I remember the taste of the beer; warm and not very nice, and the sound of rock music. In those days a juke box stood in the corner of the bar, under the clock, next to the cigarette machine that seemed always out of cigarettes.

The phone ringing by my bed in the house in Fulham at three a.m. on a date I shall never forget – the 8th July. 'Guy? It's George. The police have just rung. They say Perry's dead. Fell into a swimming pool, or something, at some party; too drunk to swim, they all were. Can you go round? I've got the address, it's somewhere in Esher . . .'

'Char?'

'Dr Weil's coming in the morning; he'll have to cope, I can't . . .' I remember thinking should I wake Beth, then deciding I'd write a note. Earlier that evening she'd told me she was leaving me. We'd talked and talked, getting nowhere, then around midnight she'd taken a sleeping pill and gone to bed.

I remembered too, driving round Esher in the small hours, trying to find the house where the wretched party had taken place; the house, it seemed, though this was still impossible to believe, where Perry had died. Finding it at last, when I'd almost given up hope – mock Tudor, affluent, pretentious –

ringing the bell at the front door, one of those fancy, chiming affairs and no one answering for what seemed hours.

'The police have removed the body to the mortuary, I'm afraid. They couldn't wait, they said.' The party host at last; distraught, slightly dishevelled, wanting to appear in control of the situation, but manifestly not. My feelings of annoyance at a wasted journey; so typical of George to send me on a wildgoose chase.

'Have a chicken vol au vent, Mr Horton. I've just re-heated them.' The host's wife: she'd changed from party gear into business-like jeans and a shirt; she looked ghastly.

'No, thanks, I'd better go. Perry's mother, you see, she hasn't been told; I have to—'

'Such a tragedy,' the host's wife said. 'We can't take it in yet. Perry was such a splendid person.'

'I'll ring the police,' I said, 'in the morning. Goodbye.' The lights were still on as I drove past the pool; debris from the party lay scattered on the grass and a couple of empty bottles floated gently on the bright, blue water.

'You can't stop me seeing my son's body.'

The three of us, George, Dr Weil and myself, sitting round Char's bed at Maple. 'It would upset you too much, Mrs Seymour, believe me. Better, much better, to think of him as he was.'

Char looks at Dr Weil, her eyes glittering, desperate, savage with pain. 'I want to see my son's body.'

'Well, you can't.' George shouts. He always shouts at her now. 'You'll only make a scene, you know you will, and I simply won't take any more, I . . .'

Dr Weil allows his face briefly to register exasperation, and gently lays a warning hand on George's knee. 'I'm sure

you would not make a scene, Mrs Seymour, you are much too
brave for that, but all the same, it's better not; I do assure you,
it's better not.' With a sudden, quick movement, Char leans
forward and George, yelping with pain, snatches his hand from
where it rested on the side of the bed, blood oozing from the
bite marks on his thumb. He backs away.

'You're not safe, you bitch, they're going to lock you up at
last. It's your fault Perry's dead, he never had a chance, not
with your rotten family's blood in his veins, he hadn't.'

I'm shorter and lighter than George, but he is older and out
of condition. I stand up and clumsily lunging across Char's
bed, I manage to hit him quite hard in the face. Taken off
balance, he falls heavily against the dressing table, then slowly
slumps to the floor, bringing with him a cascade of lipsticks,
jars of cosmetics and a vase of dead flowers.

'It's about time you made yourself useful.' For the first
time Char looks at me. 'What a shame the vase is broken.'

'You rotten little Judas,' Char shouts at me just before they
slam the door of the ambulance on her. But that came after:
after, in strict adherence to the letter of the law, two doctors
and a social worker had put their signature to a paper declaring
Char Seymour to be a possible danger to herself or others,
and no longer responsible for her actions.

An ambulance had driven her away that first time. They'd
cornered her at last in her bedroom, where she crouched at
bay between the brass bed and the wardrobe.

'Come on, Mrs Seymour, give me your arm, there's a good
girl.' Dr Weil, coaxing, hypodermic at the ready, sweating
slightly.

'Leave me alone, you bloody moron. I'm going to my son's
funeral and you can't stop me . . .'

In the end it was one of the ambulance men who did the

trick. He noticed Char had a First World War Royal Artillery badge pinned upside down on the cardigan she was wearing.

'Look now, Ma'am, you've got your badge the wrong way up,' he said. 'We can't have that, can we? I was a gunner in the last lot.'

Char had briefly, miraculously, returned from whatever hell she'd been inhabiting and smiled up at him. 'Goodness, how stupid. Can you do it for me? My fingers don't seem to be working properly.'

Gently the ambulance man unpinned the brooch. 'I was in the Eighth Army myself,' he said. 'That was a caper and a half . . .' With ease, born of long practice, Dr Weil plunged the needle into Char's arm; then a quick dab with a piece of cotton wool and it was over. They'd got her. I remember feeling violently sick and overcome with relief at the same time.

I suppose Perry's funeral was the last time Beth and I appeared together in public as a couple. He was cremated: this against Char's express wish, but by then she had been officially designated a nonperson and her wishes had no bearing on the matter. The decision of how to dispose of their son's body was left to George.

So there we all sat – not Char, of course. She was safely put away by now – in a West London crematorium, glumly watching the bright, new coffin slide slowly forward towards the waiting flames beyond the screen.

'No point in moving the body down to Bath if it's going to be burned,' George had said with unanswerable logic. Did we have a 'bun fight' afterwards? I can't remember, but I do remember quite clearly the tears trickling down Sophia's face as she emerged from the crematorium chapel into the sunlight outside.

A week or so later Beth moved out. It was, as I may have

mentioned, a civilised parting. We were very business-like about everything. All passion, indeed, spent.

'You're welcome to most of the stuff,' Beth said. 'Ronald's got so much already, there won't be room anyway.' Ronald was the television producer she was moving in with and is now married to. They're very happy, and have a son, born just before Beth's fortieth birthday.

After Beth had gone, we sold the house in Fulham, dividing the proceeds, and I bought my present flat in Battersea. The block was brand new then: an affluent, middle-class ghetto, set in the midst of an area of tower blocks already in decline, boarded up warehouses and empty, terrace houses clinging precariously to small, mean streets that no longer led anywhere. I remember my first night in the place. I went out and got drunk in the pub – since demolished – next door. The Sailor's Haven was an extraordinary affair. A relic from the Festival of Britain, it appeared to be constructed entirely of weather boarding, and was designed to look like a ship, with portholes instead of windows and a gangplank in place of stairs. I don't think I ever went again, but somehow at the time its insane décor seemed eminently suited to the nightmare I seemed to be living through.

'Penny for them.' I jumped. The lady in the pink blouse stood beside me, keys in hand, smiling brightly. 'It's gone two o'clock, sir. I don't want to hurry you—'

'I'm sorry,' I said. 'I was miles away.'

'Thinking about old times?'

'You could say that.'

'Come again,' she said, 'next time you're passing.' I nodded, smiling, too. But I wouldn't be passing, though, would I, not again.

17

That evening, after a couple of Scotches and a fairly run-of-the-mill dinner, I felt too restless to stay in the hotel. Knowing I was taking a risk – insurance managers don't get nicked for drunken driving, not if they wish to remain insurance managers – I decided to take the car and visit one of our old haunts. There was a pub in a tiny hamlet, somewhere near where old Mrs Osborn had lived, that Char and I used to go to. I couldn't remember the name of the hamlet, but the pub was called The Rising Sun, and after the amount I'd had to drink, I thought I could, at a pinch, remember the way there. The Rising Sun was ours exclusively; no one else in the family went there, or even, I'm pretty sure, knew of its existence. Char had first come to use it years before; it was the nearest pub to her mother's house, and after a salutary hour or so spent in the company of Ma, all she wanted to do, she said, was make a bee-line for the nearest bar and there hope to recover her equilibrium.

It was what used to be known as a 'hedge tavern', its principal alcoholic beverage being a particularly lethal rough cider. It had khaki-coloured oilcloth on the floor and walls to match, the only concession to decoration being a bunch of plastic roses crammed tightly into a vase that looked as though it had been won at a fairground rifle range, and a large, yellowing, framed photograph of the Chippenham Rotary Club dinner, *circa* 1925. For light relief a flock of geese would peer balefully at you through the tiny, rather dirty, windows, and when you emerged, reeling slightly from the effects of the cider, not infrequently chase you to your car. Char and I loved the Rising Sun; it was one of our favourite places.

I was right, I did remember the way, and found the turning quite easily. It was a cold and windy night, the moon emerging now and again from behind the clouds racing across its surface to light up the surrounding fields. I drove slowly along the twisting lane, remembering, the past more alive to me now than the present.

The last time I had visited the place it had been high summer, and Char and I had made love in the long grass at the edge of a cornfield bright with poppies, a few hundred yards along the road from where I now was. At the climax of our lovemaking a hare had burst out of the bank behind us and fled away into the growing corn. And I remembered how I'd stood in the gateway watching Char as she picked her flowers – she loved wild flowers, and would always pick a bunch wherever we went, if she could – wishing that this moment might go on for ever, or that I might die there and then and never know what came afterwards . . .

'Don't ever hark back, darling; don't you *ever* hark back. If I've learned anything in my misspent life, it surely must be that.'

Suddenly, and for the first time since her death, I heard Char's voice, and so clearly she might have been sitting in the car beside me. I'd tried to remember the sound of her voice, Christ, how I'd tried, in all those weary months since her death, but the memory of it had gone as absolutely as she herself had gone. Now, suddenly I heard it again: loved, utterly familiar and – right.

I put my foot hard down on the brake, bringing the car to a slithering halt; I seemed to be shivering and sweating at the same time. I switched off the engine and opened the car window.

'Thank you, my love, I'll not forget again, and thank you for coming back to me.' It was my own voice I heard shouting into the icy wind. Then I switched on the engine, turned the car round and drove slowly back to Corsham. That night I slept as long and deeply as I can remember.

In the morning I rang George. 'Hullo, George, it's Guy. I'm in the vicinity. Had to visit our Bath office on Friday and thought I'd make a weekend of it.'

'Terrific.' He sounded like an excited schoolboy. 'Did you know we'd sold the house? Not quite the price I wanted, but bloody good all the same.'

'Oh,' I said, feeling deflated. 'I didn't even know you'd put it on the market.' Was everyone getting on with their lives but me – even old George?

'Months ago, I thought you knew. As a matter of fact, we're moving out next week. We've found our dream cottage in Wales. It's near Bronwen's sister, on the edge of the Brecon Beacons, a perfect spot . . .' He burbled on, superlatives spilling off his tongue at the rate of ten a minute.

I listened gloomily. 'I had thought of popping in for a couple of minutes on my way back to London,' I said, when he paused for breath.

'Frightfully sorry, old boy, no can do,' he shouted. 'We're out to lunch – so many goodbyes, you know how it is. Come and see us when we've had a chance to settle in. I'll send you a card with the new address. I can't give it you over the phone. It's one of those unpronounceable Welsh names,' and he roared with happy laughter.

'Great, I'll do that,' I said. I wouldn't, though, would I?

'I'll be in touch, then,' he said, and as an afterthought: 'Sophia OK?'

'As far as I know,' I said. 'She's in Tokyo.'

'Oh,' he said. 'Well, tell her our news, will you, when she gets back.'

'OK,' I said, 'goodbye,' but he had already gone. I replaced the receiver; somehow I felt cheated. It seemed almost obscene that old George should be so happy. But then he'd paid already, hadn't he? George was a fraud and a bit of a bully when he got the chance, but the old devil had suffered alright, no doubt of that; he'd paid his price. And now, there he was a schoolboy in the throes of first love; the nightmare years over, the wicked witch was dead, and what was wrong with that? Except that Char wasn't a witch, was she, she was Char.

I decided to drive back to London at once and eat when I got there. I couldn't face Sunday lunch in the hotel; besides, there was no point in staying any longer. I'd come to look for Char and I'd found her: I needn't worry any more, she'd always be with me now.

I remember dreading my first visit to Locksley Mental Hospital. I lost my way in the labyrinthine corridors of the place and was hot, flustered, and more nervous than ever by the time I arrived at Char's room and timidly put my head round the door. She was seated in an armchair by the window of the bright, cell-like bedroom, wearing a neat, blue dress, doing some tapestry. No longer the panting, blaspheming, hunted creature she had been when I last saw her, she looked completely sane and very pretty. I was so surprised, I could think of nothing to say, but stood in the doorway, a complete fool, with my mouth open. Then she looked up, suddenly aware

274

of my presence, and held out her arms. 'My Warrior,' she said. 'I've missed you so.'

'I've brought some flowers,' I said, 'and the new book on Charles II,' and burst into tears.

Char's first stay at Locksley lasted nine months. Every week I drove down from London to spend the day with her, until there was no corner of that damned place I didn't know. I would arrive each Saturday, laden like Father Christmas, with lengths of wool, matching cotton, drawing books, history books, notebooks, once even a pair of pants from Marks & Spencer's, all commissions from the week before.

'Georgy chooses to keep me a prisoner here,' she would say. 'It's the least you can do . . .' I would return to London equally burdened; this time with an assortment of raffia mats, pottery jugs and strange little pen and ink drawings, all bought at Char's instigation and at a prohibitive price, from the shop in the hospital therapy centre. As the months passed she became quite knowledgeable on the different forms of mental illness and would lecture me at length on such topics as drug therapy and the evils of the old closed ward system.

'Isn't it time she came out? She seems saner than most people,' I asked Dr Weil at one of our monthly interviews.

'It won't be long now, I think,' he said. 'But we have to be completely sure. You only see her at her best, Mr Horton, you must know that.'.

Meanwhile there was Bronwen . . .

It was during Char's first stay at Locksley that George sold Maple and bought the house in Belton, and on her first night home after nine months in hospital, told her that he wanted to leave her and marry Bronwen Mallory.

'He doesn't really,' Char told me, 'he's only saying it to upset me.'

A couple of months after that she was once again admitted to Locksley, this time on a twenty-eight day order. She'd started undressing in the local pub one Sunday morning and when the landlord objected, had thrown a glass at him.

From then on a pattern was set in our three lives, Char's, George's and mine, which would last more or less until Char's death. Gradually she came to spend longer and longer periods in Locksley and less and less time at home, eventually only returning to the latter for an occasional weekend 'treat'. On these occasions it was considered obligatory that I should be there, George claiming, rightly, that he could not possibly handle her on his own. Then she had a series of strokes, culminating in bronchial pneumonia from which, miraculously, she survived. Also miraculously this resulted in a return to partial normality as far as her mind was concerned, although her physical strength was greatly impaired, and from then on she could only get about with the help of a walking frame. Following her recovery from the stroke, Dr Weil decreed it was no longer necessary for her to occupy valuable bed space at Locksley. As it was considered out of the question for her to live at home with an alcoholic and unpredictable George, who was patently both unwilling and unable to cope, she was found a place in St Hilda's, the old people's home, so providentially situated in the village of Belton itself, where she remained until her death.

George, having abandoned the idea of escape into the arms of Bronwen – who nevertheless remained in the background patiently biding her time – spent those years in a more or less permanent alcoholic stupor. Char spent them carrying on intrigues with various elderly male inmates of St Hilda's, trying to teach herself Anglo-Saxon and complaining about George and her children.

And I? I spent those years looking after George and Char. I wrote to Char twice a week and visited her every other weekend. I endured interminable late-night telephone conversations with George, usually on the subject of his last visit to St Hilda's. 'She bit me, Guy. I tell you, she actually bit me: I nearly had to have stitches. That nice nurse, the one with the red hair and the teeth, you know – she said it wasn't right I should have to put up with it. I can't take much more, Guy, it just simply isn't on. But when I ask for a word with Dr Weil, they say he's on holiday. That damned man's always on holiday: I wouldn't mind his job . . .' And I would listen patiently; eternally trapped, it seemed, between their two conflicting egos: neither son nor lover, but a simple beast of burden condemned for ever to take their troubles on his unwilling back.

During that time my own mother died – my father had died some years before when Beth and I were still together – but her death, and I was fond of my mother, seemed to have little impact, for by this time my involvement with the Seymours was so complete, I had no emotion to spare for anything else.

Being a Sunday, there were no lorries on the M4 and very little of anything else; in fact for several miles at a stretch mine was the only vehicle travelling east: just a grey tin box under a grey sky, crawling through the featureless motorway landscape, a grey man inside. The last time I'd driven along this road on a Sunday had been the morning of Char's death.

Suddenly I began wondering if she'd been alone when she died, completely alone, I mean. I knew George was there, but had he managed, or indeed tried, to reach her? It seemed unlikely. Had she thought of those others, those other men who had loved her: Hubert, Algy, Barny, Dave? Most of all,

Barny? And had she thought of me? For the first time since her death I allowed my mind to go back, back to the last time I'd seen her. Until now I'd tried to avoid thinking of it; as a farewell scene it had not been the one I would have chosen, but then I hadn't known it was a farewell scene, had I, one seldom does, I suppose.

It had been a warm, thundery day with frequent, heavy showers. Char's bedroom in St Hilda's was thick with cigarette smoke and stiflingly hot: she had refused, maddeningly, to have the window open.

'Can't we sit out on the verandah, darling?' I said. 'It's so damned hot in here.'

'You can, if you like,' she said, 'but I see enough of those freaks at meals. The last thing I want to do is sit with them as well.' And she'd puffed away furiously at her cigarette, her eyes looking anywhere but at me, as I sat sweating on the plastic-seated chair in the corner of the room. Normally, I didn't get fed up when she was like this, but would try, usually successfully, to coax her out of her mood. Today, however, for some reason I just wasn't going to try. Instead, after about ten minutes, during which neither of us spoke, I got up from the chair, sweat by this time trickling uncomfortably down the back of my neck, and told her that if she wasn't going to speak, there was little point in my staying any longer.

'Do as you damn well like,' she said. 'You're not the most scintillating of companions anyway.'

'Thanks,' I said. I could have hit her. 'I'll remember that.' I bent down to kiss her goodbye.

'Don't bother,' she said and turned her face away. Without a backward glance, I walked out of the room. I never saw her alive again and it was the first time in all the years I'd known her that we'd parted in anger.

A too bright sun appeared from behind scurrying clouds, for a moment blinding my vision of the road ahead, then disappeared. There was more traffic now; London Airport loomed on my right.

Was that why Char gave up the fight those last few days before she died, because of our stupid quarrel? Was my walking out on her that stifling afternoon, simply the last straw; the rat leaving the sinking ship; the final defection? I faced the thought, cringing a little under the harshness of it. Then suddenly I knew with complete certainty that as a premise, it was false. Char was a fighter, she had been all her life. Wrong-headed, yes; an espouser of lost causes, of ideals long past their prime and therefore tarnished, yes. But more than any of those things, even taking into account that self-destructive streak in her – somehow the latter didn't count for much, though; she was self-destructive in doing rather than being – she was a fighter, and above all a survivor. No, she must have given up the fight, then, because she knew the time had come for her to do so. To linger on increasingly enfeebled in mind and body, she couldn't have borne that, so she just let go.

Perhaps that silly row we had was the only way she could bring herself to say goodbye . . .

I felt a sob rise in my throat, then remembered, and pressing my foot hard down on the accelerator, I moved into the fast lane to overtake a speeding lorry. As I raced past him, the driver leaned out of the cab window and made a two-fingered salute. I smiled: Char would have loved that. Never hark back . . .

18

So easy to tell a person 'write about your mother', but to do so quite another matter, especially as the more Guy, the conjurer, produces from his Pandora's Box, the less reality my mother seems to have for me.

I arranged the neatly typed pages on my blotter in front of me; they'd arrived by post at home that morning with a scrawled note from Sophia:

Guy, you wanted my view of Mum. Here it is; pretty inadequate stuff, I'm afraid, and totally subjective, but all I can produce at the moment.

See you soon?

Love
S

I looked at my watch. I had half an hour before Mrs Beaumont would be in with the mail. I started to read.

. . . the less reality my mother seems to have for me. The girl who sat by the roadside on a heap of stones and fell in love with the boy that was Algy Charterhouse and the woman who slept with my father in the freezing back bedroom of a house in Jarrow, are to me complete strangers; I simply cannot equate either of them with my mother.

And yet, whether I like it or no, a tenuous thread remains linking the two of us, my mother and I. Not just the tie of blood, but in the way we respond to, say, art, bad manners, ugliness, oh, lots of things: our desire to create (usually unsuccessfully) anything from a jersey to a garden, to a full-length novel, our sense of humour, of history. The list is endless. The people and events that influenced her, my father's Socialism, Dave Brent's death, George: because they affected her deeply they were, *ipso facto,* instrumental in helping shape the person I have become. (Though I like to think there is a little piece of just me in me.) For, paradoxically, despite the fact I had, in all, four fathers, in reality I had none; any influence there was came from my mother.

Mum was not, I think, a very affectionate woman. She never 'cuddled' her children. She would kiss us goodnight or goodbye, but it was a formal kiss, never one of exuberance or simple affection. Kissing and the like, for her, were confined to the act of sex or to her treatment of animals, especially dogs. Nevertheless, we, her children, were all important to her and we knew it. We were the human barrier she had created between herself and the rest of the world. She owed us nothing; we owed her everything. We were her playmates, her protectors, her toys. Later on, as we grew up, we girls became potential rivals and poor old Perry a potential lover, but through all the rows and pain we remained until her death her corporate *alter ego.*

My first memory of her is of her leaning over my cot – where this was I don't know, but probably the house in Hammersmith. She was wearing a pink evening dress of some sort of shiny material and her dark, curly hair just brushed my cheek as she bent over me. Someone was with her, but I don't know who, and she told me that if I wasn't careful I would receive a raspberry: I, in my innocence, took this to mean the promise of a treat.

My last memory of her was a week before she died. It was I who bent over her now and kissed her cold cheek, as she sat huddled in her blue tweed overcoat, waiting for a sulky George to drive her back to St Hilda's. Her walking frame stood beside her chair, its bag bursting with forgotten pieces of knitting, books, letters and packets of cigarettes. Her small hands, the fingers swollen with arthritis, played with the green chiffon scarf on her lap.

'Goodbye, Mum,' I said falsely cheerful. 'See you soon; I'll write.'

'I feel so tired,' she said, 'so terribly, terribly tired.'

'Guy, a quick word if you've a minute.' I jumped guiltily. My boss, his customary aura of efficient well-being and positive thinking so pronounced, one could practically touch it, poked his head round the castor oil plant that served to divide me from the remainder of my section. Hastily I pushed Sophia's notes under a pile of files.

'Certainly, Bernard. What's the problem?' The day's work had begun.

That evening I rang Sophia, but there was no reply, so I wrote her a note of thanks for her contribution instead. Oddly enough, I was rather relieved she wasn't at home. Since Char'd returned to me, my desire to delve into the past had, for the time being anyway, receded. And Char had returned all right, no doubt of that. Wherever I went, whatever I did, her presence was with me: her caustic, maddening, mocking self egging me on, making me say and do things with such an air of uncharacteristic self assertion, I found colleagues at work looking at me in surprise. My boss even commented that he was glad I'd decided at last to adopt a more positive attitude to my work, and perhaps I'd like to come over one weekend, it seemed ages since we'd had a game of golf.

By all this I don't mean that I'd become a sort of haunted Jamesian figure, peering over his shoulder all the time at the spectre of a lost love; far from it. It was simply that I had emerged from that ghastly state of limbo so many people who have loved long and deeply and are suddenly bereft are forced to endure. A state in which the beloved not only leaves you in body, but in mind as well and, like me, you can't even remember the sound of their voice. My particular torment was made much worse, I think – yet one more red hot cinder piled on the slow burning fire that is the agony of loss – because not only had I lost Char, but I no longer believed that she had ever loved me. The reasons seemed so cogent: I'd met her too late; there were too many years between us; she'd loved too many times before. In fact, the whole, damned, idiotic idyll without her presence to revitalise it, had begun to seem quite simply impossible: without credibility; a fantasy of my own making, and yet for it I had broken my marriage, and allowed my life to disintegrate into some kind of barren, wasted, shell.

Then the other night on my own, particular road to Damascus, Char had come back: her own, abrasive, heart-breaking self and called me to order. And I'd known again, without any doubt at all, she had indeed loved me, of course she had, and that was all that mattered.

But for all that, there was a long way to go yet. I was still one of the walking wounded; perhaps, I don't know, I always had been. Beth certainly thought so, although the wounds I was alleged to be suffering from varied with the mood she was in, or the latest book on the subject. Char, of course, refused to acknowledge the existence of such a condition. Be all that as it may, I did not yet feel ready to cope with Sophia's particular brand of robust honesty, and was glad of the breathing space her absence gave me.

Providentially, perhaps, from the point of view of my convalescence, Christmas was already looming and with it the usual round of office parties I couldn't get out of, late-night shopping and cards from people whose names weren't on my list. Amongst my cards were a rather alcoholic-looking robin from George and Bronwen, and a splendidly vulgar nude from Natasha, the latter sending me scurrying to the nearest florist to order, at vast expense, a dozen red roses.

A few days before Christmas, I paid a call on Aunty Phyll. The house in Peel Street seemed shabbier than ever and Aunty Phyll, herself, frail and rather querulous. Her eyes remained blank throughout my visit: shuttered windows in a house that patiently awaits the arrival of the demolition squad. Jolly Phyllis Pratt, it seemed, had already departed.

'Happy Christmas, Aunty Phyll.'

'Is it Christmas?' she said. 'Are you quite sure? No one's bothered to tell me . . .'

'She's not with us most of the time now, Mr Horton,' the home help said. 'She knows quite well it's Christmas.'

'I suppose,' I said, 'if you've lived through as many as she has, it doesn't matter much either way.'

My Christmas was spent in Brussels with business friends: alcoholic and, surprisingly, rather enjoyable. I even managed a brief fling with an attractive French girl half my age who, to my considerable surprise, evinced genuine interest.

'I come to London in July,' she said. 'A four-week course in business studies. I can stay with you in your flat – no?'

'I'm not sure,' I said. 'I may be away . . .'

All the same, it was good for the morale.

Two days before the end of the old year, I finally managed to bring myself to tackle, once again, the spare room, untouched since that last evening with Sophia. The room where year by year, in neat piles bound tidily together with pink tape from the office, Char's past awaited me. I had decided, after careful consideration, I would make one grand, symbolic gesture and destroy the lot: diaries, letters, photographs – everything. I would simply put all the stuff back in the green trunk, load the thing on to my car and sling it on some convenient rubbish tip. The trunk and its contents belonged to me, didn't they, to do what I liked with? Because now that Char had returned to me I had no wish, I told myself, to be reminded of that all too vivid past before I met her. I no longer wanted to know about Hubert Stokes and Piers Gurney and Algy; about that cold churchyard in the City where she and Barny Elliott had first made love amongst the crumbling gravestones; about those enchanted days in the middle of the War that she and Dave Brent, safely cocooned in their mutual passion, had spent in that opulent, over-heated, Savoy Hotel bedroom, whilst the snow fell gently on the freezing river outside; about George; about . . .

I only wanted to remember us, Char and me together: the way we'd made love that first time under the cedar tree at Maple, and all the other times that came afterwards, and how she'd come back to me.

The spare room smelt of damp and stale cigarettes. On the bedside table an unemptied ashtray bore witness to Sophia's last visit. I drew back the curtains and opened the window. The green trunk squatted in front of the fireplace, my notes stacked neatly on top. Something rustled amongst the papers and a black beetle crawled slowly across the lid of the trunk and disappeared over the edge. An old brown label, tied to the handle, fluttered in the faint breeze from the open window: 'Mrs D. Brent, 4 Riverside Road, Hammersmith, London.'

I decided I needed a drink before I could go any further. A few minutes later, suitably fortified, having carefully placed my glass on the dressing table, I opened the lid of the trunk, then picked up a pile of papers from the bed labelled '1925', took careful aim and flung it across the room into the open trunk.

After a bit I began to enjoy myself. Each bundle became a missile, thrown with such force the tape binding it burst open, scattering the contents in such a way that the years, once more, became inextricably mingled. Then in my mounting excitement, I missed my aim, and a bundle, instead of landing in the trunk, hit the outside with such impact that the contents were scattered all over the carpet. This stopped me in my tracks: suddenly I felt silly and rather childish. A photograph lay face-upwards at my feet, and I bent down and picked it up.

A girl stood in a doorway, grinning wickedly into the camera. She looked around ten years old. Her dark, curly hair was tied back with a large bow. She was dressed in a white blouse with a sailor collar, a full, tweed skirt and buttoned boots, and in her arms she held on firmly to a patently cheesed-off, patently wriggling, fox terrier. Underneath was written in Aunt Beth's bold, generous hand: 'Dear Char with "Rags", Christmas 1912.'

I stood quite still looking at the thing: it was so quiet I could hear my watch ticking. Then suddenly I knew I could never destroy those papers, never in a thousand years. They represented, however inadequately, all of Char. OK, she'd been mine for perhaps a third of her long life. No, that was an appalling conceit – Char could never have belonged to anybody

– I'll start again. I loved Char for perhaps a third of her long life, and just because I hadn't been around for the rest of it, it was patently absurd for me to claim like Henry Ford, that all history was bunk and I for one would have no part of it. Char *was* the sum total of her experience and there was no escaping the fact. I walked over to the window, for a moment flooded with bright, winter sunshine, and held the picture up to the light. The young face looking at me across a chasm of over seventy years, was recognisably the same face I'd turned my back on that summer afternoon at St Hilda's a few days before its owner's death.

Even at ten years old it had been an indomitable face: quirky, funny, alive, already compellingly attractive; full of life and curiosity, but above all there was an air of innocence about it; perhaps simplicity would be a better word. And it was this latter quality that had remained with Char throughout her life. She simply never grew up; never really grasped what people expected of her; never understood what they meant when they spoke glibly of such things as moral responsibilities and the like. An eternal Alice, she fought her way as best she could through what must have seemed to her an increasingly upside-down, looking-glass world, a world which, in her egotistical simplicity, she considered had turned its face against her.

It was only those people who recognised this quality in her – her mother, Sophia, possibly Barny Elliott and, I liked to think, myself – who were able to reach her. The rest spent their time imbuing her with motives she didn't even know existed, and in so doing accusing her of every crime in the book from sadism and moral exploitation to emotional blackmail. And in the end, she could take no more and escaped into madness. It was true she had made a hell of a lot of people unhappy, but she had also, simply by being in some extraordinary way, so utterly herself, given life, love and laughter to a great many others. She was not, no matter how hard you tried, a person you could forget, although during her life there were a thousand moments when you might have wished her dead.

I took one more look at the photograph, then carefully put it in my pocket. I would, I decided, get a frame for it. As for the rest, I'd think about what to do with that another day.

Two days later Sophia rang. 'Guy, Happy New Year; are you still sulking?'

'I never was,' I said, 'sulking, I mean. I just wanted to think things out, that's all. Anyway, you could have rung if you'd wanted to.'

'I suppose so,' she said. 'Did you see that Aunty Phyll died on New Year's Eve?'

'I'm glad,' I said. 'She was ready to go, I think.'

'Guy, actually I've got some news,' Sophia's voice sounded unusually diffident.

'Great. Let's hope it's good; I feel badly in need of some sort of uplift just now.'

'Well . . . it is for me, I think. I'm going to be married.'

'Congratulations,' I said, noticing suddenly that the telephone table was covered in dust and there was a stain on the carpet by the front door. 'That's marvellous news. Do I know him?'

'I doubt it,' she giggled, an uncharacteristically girlish sound. Sophia had never been girlish, she'd told me once rather sadly: adolescence and all that sort of thing had, it seemed, simply passed her by. 'Oddly enough,' she went on, 'he's a sort of cousin on my father's side.'

'A Charterhouse? That surely can't be bad; they're all

rolling, aren't they? I seem to remember Char always said—'

'An Elliott, actually.'

'Now, that really is a surprise. How on earth, I mean I thought they were all dead—'

'Oh, don't be silly, Guy, of course they aren't.' She sounded more like her old self again. 'Martin's father was Barny's first cousin, and his grandfather was a younger brother of the poet. He's the secretary of the H. A. Elliott Society and the custodian of the museum. The cottage in Gloucestershire where my grandparents lived has been turned into a little museum, you see. As a matter of fact, that's how I met Martin. I went to see it, and he was down for the day doing the garden. But Guy, it was so extraordinary: I felt, we both felt, we'd known each other our entire lives! Marriage seemed the only logical step only a day after our meeting. We just knew it was the only thing to do . . .'

I stood there, gazing down at the stain on the carpet, the receiver a foot or so away from my ear, experiencing a marked attack of *déjà vu*. It had been George last time, hadn't it, who'd burbled on about his new-found happiness. But marriage of two 'like-minded' Elliotts, my God! The truth, the unvarnished truth and nothing but the truth. What had Char said about Barny when she first met him? 'I felt as though he had opened a door into my soul and was briskly shining a torch round it to see what was wrong.' This certainly would be a marriage of pure minds. Char would have been pleased, though, but how she would have laughed.

'Guy, are you still there?'

'Of course I am. I was just thinking; that museum, isn't it the place where your grandfather bumped off your grandmother? Hardly the most suitable location for his museum, one would have thought—'

'If you're going to be facetious, there's no point in going on then—'

'Oh, darling. I'm not. I really am very pleased for you. You deserve all the happiness you can get. When's the wedding?'

'Quite soon, I hope. I'll let you know. And Guy . . . you will come, won't you?'

'Try and keep me away,' I said.

19

The wedding took place a couple of months later. The ceremony was private, attended only by Ann, Beth and Tristram, Martin Elliott's son by a former marriage. But the reception afterwards, in the banqueting room of some Bloomsbury hotel, was quite a large affair; the bridegroom, it appeared, had connections.

Among the crowd of Charterhouses, Osborns and Pratts – alas, of course, no Aunty Phyll – I noticed quite a few members of the current literati and even a well-known actor. The marriage of two Elliott grandchildren had, it seemed, caused quite a stir in media circles; that one of them had so recently emerged from the wrong side of the blanket, an added bonus. The current crop of Charterhouses seemed to take Sophia's translation from Charterhouse to Elliott, and then again to Elliott, in their collective stride. Indeed, they appeared quite proud of the connection and, so they said, found the whole thing 'frightfully interesting, and really rather splendid'.

Anyway, the food was good and the drink flowed, perhaps not quite as freely as one would have wished, but a wedding reception in London in the eighties must surely cost not far short of a king's ransom, so one couldn't complain. Martin, who seemed a decent chap, made an extremely witty speech – I noticed the media men smirking all over their shorthand pads – and I've never seen Sophia look so pretty or so alive. She was dressed in a suit the colour of Parma violets, and those eyes – Martin's are exactly the same, it's really quite extraordinary, even rather eerie – had a look in them I'd never seen before. Seeing her standing there so happy, suddenly brought home to me what a really very rough old life she'd had up to now. Perhaps, I told myself smugly, it was just as well Char never got round to burning that diary for 1933 and passed it on to me instead; at least I could claim I'd been partly responsible for the present happy state of affairs.

I was standing beside a rather decrepit-looking potted palm ruminating on all this, when someone gently twitched my sleeve. I jumped, spilling at least half a glass of champagne in the process, and turned to find Char, aged around twenty and looking agitated, standing behind me. She was entirely unsuitably dressed for the occasion, her outfit consisting of jeans, a long, bright orange sweater – rather grubby – and one of those padded jackets the young seem to live in. But her brown, curly hair shone with life and sprung away from her head free from any fashionable dye, and her skin – a sort of brown-peach colour – was flawless. From her ears dangled a pair of rather beautiful antique silver earrings.

For one, long, extraordinary moment I stood there paralysed. My heart was beating much too fast and my mouth was dry. I looked wildly round the room. Was this the beginning of a heart attack; didn't one sometimes have hallucinations, or was that with something else?

'You couldn't possibly lend me a couple of quid, could you? There's a taxi waiting outside and the driver's beginning to get a bit stroppy. I'm absolutely skint, you see.'

'Who the hell are you?' Even to me my voice sounded odd; sort of high pitched and squeaky.

'Char' raised her eyebrows haughtily. 'I'm perfectly

respectable, if that's what you're worried about.' She plainly assumed I was asking for references. 'I'm a niece of the bride, and if you can't lend me the money I'll have to find someone else. It was just I didn't want to bother Aunt Sophie, and I can't be too long; I've left Alexander in a sort of waiting room, and he'll wake up at any minute . . .'

Hastily I produced a fiver. 'Will this do to be going on with?' My heartbeat, I noted with relief, was slowing down, and my voice had dropped a couple of registers. 'And who is Alexander? If he's an animal, I have a feeling they're not allowed and—'

'Oh, thank you so much.' Her smile was all I knew it would be. 'Actually, Alexander's a baby, not an animal, so there's no problem there, except he'll be getting hungry at any minute, and then things may get a bit dicey.'

'Look,' I said, 'wouldn't it be simpler if I went down and paid off the taxi and you saw to Alexander? I mean, you don't want things to get dicey, do you?' She gave me another blinding smile.

'Christ, you're brilliant. Who are you, by the way? I'm Pip Holloway, my Mum was Evie Charterhouse.'

I took a deep breath. 'I'm your Aunt Beth's ex,' I said, as we hurried downstairs – she wasn't a girl to waste time – 'my name's Guy Horton.'

'Good heavens, are you really? I always imagined he'd look much older than that . . .'

I stumbled down a couple of stairs, this time spilling the rest of my champagne – for some reason I was still hanging on to my glass.

'You've heard of me, then?' I tried to sound casual.

'Daddy might have mentioned you once or twice.' She gave me a quick sideways glance. 'You know what families are.'

Providentially I was saved from replying, as she suddenly stopped dead in her tracks and raised an arm for silence: 'Christ, he's started.' From somewhere below us came an angry wail. Char's great-grandson wanted his tea.

We arrived breathless at the bottom of the stairs, to find the hotel porter crouching on the floor behind the reception desk; beside him the blue, plastic-covered box that contained Alexander. The porter was waving a rattle and making animal noises in an ineffectual attempt to calm down the yelling child.

'He seemed a bit fretful, Madam,' he told Pip, 'so I brought him in with me.' He sounded as if he thought the whole thing was his fault.

'How very kind of you. The thing is he's hungry, you see. It looks as if I'll have to feed the little wretch.' And Pip, rather to my surprise – I thought the young, liberated female immune from all that sort of thing – actually blushed.

The porter coughed discreetly. 'There's a comfortable Ladies Rest Room, Madam, just round to the left, with all the . . . er facilities.'

Pip smiled straight into the man's eyes. 'What a super idea. I was wondering where on earth I could go, and what an incredibly efficient porter you are.' This time it was the porter who blushed.

Briskly she turned to me. 'When you've paid the taxi, would you mind awfully nipping upstairs and telling Aunt Sophie I'm here and will be up myself in a minute or two, plus offspring. I promised Daddy I'd be at the wedding, you see, that's why he let me have the fare over from New York.'

'You've just arrived, then, from the States?' I had to shout, Alexander's screams were getting louder by the minute. 'Have you anywhere to stay?'

Ignoring my question, she gave her son's cot an angry

shake: 'Will you shut up, you little menace?' she ordered. 'And don't be so damned greedy, I'm coming as fast as I can.' And to both my own and the porter's surprise, Alexander obediently shut up. Once again she turned to me: 'Look, I'm not trying to hurry you, Uncle Guy,' I winced, 'but unless we want a case of assault on our hands, I do think you'd better go and pay the taxi.' I went.

Upstairs, I told Sophia, who was about to go and change. She laughed. 'Pip made it then, good for her. She's Evie's daughter, you know. She doesn't get on with David or her stepmother, and of course they're livid about the baby.'

'I would imagine they might be,' I said.

Sophia gave me a look. 'She's a chip off the old block, Guy ducky. You must have noticed that already, so be careful.'

Again I was saved from having to reply, this time by Martin, who appeared at her elbow. 'Look, darling, if we're going to catch that plane, I really think you should get a move on.'

'Goodbye, Guy darling,' Sophia gave me a long, and I thought rather sexy kiss. 'Tell Pip to come and help me change – Room 209. I want to see that baby. And Guy . . . remember what I said – watch it.'

After the happy pair had been given a suitable send-off, we took a taxi, Pip, Alexander and I, back to my flat. They appeared to have very little luggage, just a carrier bag containing a few basic necessities for Alexander – even then I had to dash out to the chemist before it closed and buy a box of disposable nappies – and a dilapidated hold-all minus its zip.

In the taxi, Pip, at my instigation, gave a brief outline of her present circumstances. She seemed unwilling to talk about herself: indeed, more inclined to discuss me and my 'relationship' with her grandmother. I managed, temporarily at least, to head her off this sensitive subject, by saying I thought our priorities lay – if I were to assist her – in my knowing her current situation, rather than wasting time discussing family gossip. To my surprise, this rather pompous speech appeared to impress her and she agreed to begin.

She had been too young to remember her mother, she told me, the latter having died when Pip was just over a year old. Indeed, she hadn't realised that Paula was not her real mother until she was eight – the knowledge when it came, came as a relief, she said darkly, but didn't explain why and I didn't like to ask. She did not, of course, remember Australia either, as they returned to England when she was around three years old. Reading between the lines, her childhood did not seem to have been a very happy one. Sent to boarding school at an early age, she had spent much of her holidays staying with relatives, especially Aunt Ann in Scotland, to whom she seemed devoted. Anyway, despite a few hiccups (her words) she left school with three A-levels under her belt, and the idea she should go on to university.

Then out of the blue, Daddy got promotion and was sent to New York to be in charge of his firm's US subsidiary. And – perhaps suffering a few tardy pangs of guilt at his obvious neglect of his daughter – despite protests from Paula, suggested Pip should join them. There was a Fine Arts course going in Manhattan that was just up her street, and she could always do university after that. Despite Paula, Pip said yes: 'I'd have been daft not to, wouldn't I,' and off to New York she went.

It had been a fantastic time, she said; opening her eyes to many things, not the least of which was Chinese porcelain. Unfortunately, most of her fellow students were weeds and she and Paula rowed more or less continuously.

'And Alexander?' I asked carefully.

'Alexander,' she said, looking dotingly down at the sleeping boy, 'comes from Scottish crofter stock.'

'Oh,' I said, feeling out of my depth. 'Does he? That's nice.'

'His father was the son of the janitor to the apartment block where Daddy and Paula live. Mr Milne went over from Scotland after the War; he's an ex-sergeant in the Argyll and Sutherland Highlanders.'

'I see,' I said. 'And his son?'

'Don drives a cab. I used to go round with him at night sometimes, it was fantastic.'

'And . . . and then you got yourself pregnant?'

Her green eyes looked at me coldly. 'You could put it that way if you like,' she said, 'but it was hardly an immaculate conception.'

'I'm sorry,' I said humbly, 'I didn't mean it like that. Do please go on.'

'Well, the trouble was, when I discovered I was pregnant, Don wanted to marry me. That was out, of course: I mean who wants to get married these days? Anyway, I should hate to live in New York. Daddy and Paula wanted me to get rid of the baby. Aren't people unethical, Uncle Guy? I mean really, it makes you wonder.' I nodded sagely.

'Anyway, even they couldn't force me to have an abortion, but Paula certainly didn't want me lurking round her tea parties getting bigger by the minute, with no husband to show for it, so I was sent away to some cousins of hers in Connecticut. Actually the Lyndons weren't bad. There were lots of animals there and it's lovely country. The only snag was I was expected to help with the housework, which I'm not too keen on – though I do like cooking – and Father Lyndon would insist on making love to me.'

'Good heavens.' Despite myself, I was shocked. 'Didn't you try to stop him?'

'It wasn't easy,' she said evasively. 'Anyway, that wasn't a problem for long, as by the time I was about seven months I went off sex completely.'

'I see,' I said again. Suddenly she bent down and tucked the blanket more tightly round the sleeping Alexander; all that was visible now was his nose and a tuft of reddish hair.

'When Alexander was born, no one knew what to do with me. I think Daddy hoped I'd agree to have him adopted, but, of course, I wouldn't. What on earth was the point of having him, just to give him away?'

There was silence for a moment, while she looked out of the cab window. Suddenly, underneath her enormous *savoir faire* – all Char's family have that, it's built in – I sensed a massive loneliness, desolation even: she and Alexander against the world? I put a tentative arm round her. 'So, what happened?'

'I have this friend Patsy, who was married last year. She has a baby a few months older than Alexander, and she wrote suggesting that we came over and stayed. She's married to a man in computers and they live in this huge flat in West Hampstead. She said there was plenty of space and I could rent a room there, and do a course at the university, or something. As there didn't seem that many options on offer, and Patsy and I get on quite well, I wrote and said yes, I'd come. Of course, I had to borrow the money for my fare over from Daddy. I had hell's own job to get it out of him, and he only let me have it on condition I represented him and Paula at Aunt Sophie's wedding. He thinks I'm going back in a fortnight, but I'm not. I'm staying here if it kills me – I hate America.'

'What went wrong, then, about Patsy and the flat?'

'Actually, it was rather traumatic. Alexander and I arrived there around lunchtime today in a taxi from London Airport. That cost a fortune, but I couldn't think how to get there otherwise, saddled with Alexander, and luckily I had some spending money from Daddy. Anyway, I kept on ringing and ringing and there was no reply. Then the lady in the flat next door appeared and said Patsy had left. She'd walked out a couple of days ago, taking the baby with her, and Peter – that's her husband – had gone to stay with his parents. That's why poor Alexander was so hungry when I met you. I just couldn't find anywhere to feed him.' Alexander stirred in his sleep.

'Christ, Uncle Guy, you live a long way out. Aren't we nearly there yet?'

'Only just over the river,' I said, 'not far now.' Pip leaned back and rested her head on my shoulder; a strand of her hair tickled my face. 'I'll cook supper tonight, if you like,' she said. 'I'm pretty good, you know, and I've got this marvellous recipe I want to try . . .'

And she could cook, too. The dinner was damned good. While she prepared it I was left to see to Alexander, coping as best I could with the help of her shouted instructions and a dog-eared manual on bringing up baby (American style) I found wrapped in a pair of knickers in the hold-all.

On our arrival earlier, her initial reaction to my flat had been damning. 'Christ, Uncle Guy, isn't this a little bit on the drab side?' was her comment after a lightning tour of the premises. 'All this porridge and beige? I mean, don't you ever long for a splodge of something else?'

'I'm an insurance man,' I said tartly. 'We're supposed to be colourless, didn't you know?' She gave me a long, appraising look through half-closed eyes; it was a look so familiar, I almost cried out. I didn't, of course. I propelled her firmly into the spare room – her grandmother's trunk and its contents were safely under lock and key; I didn't want her rummaging through that, not yet anyway – and told her to make a list of what she needed, and I'd nip out to the shops before they closed. I left her sitting on a chair by the window, the orange sweater on the floor at her feet, Alexander hanging greedily on to one perfect, pearl-coloured breast. The evening sun caught the lights in her hair: she was reading my copy of De Quincey's *Confessions of an Opium-eater.*

That night I was woken around two a.m. by the click of my bedroom door. We'd gone to bed early: Pip said she was beginning to suffer the effects of jet-lag, and I felt as though I'd been pulled through a mincer. I opened my eyes to find her naked, standing beside my bed.

'Uncle Guy, I'm frightened; my room's full of the wrong sort of vibes, and I can't get to sleep.'

'Well, I'm sorry about that, but there's absolutely nothing I can do about it. It happens to be the only spare room I've got,' I said crossly, 'unless you want a sleeping pill?'

'Of course I don't,' she said. 'Are you daft, or something? I want to come in with you.'

I was trying to keep calm, but it wasn't easy. 'Look, Pip, do I have to spell it out to you?' I said, sitting up. 'I may be your Uncle Guy and thirty years your senior, but if you get into my bed, I cannot possibly guarantee I won't make a pass at you. Anyway, what about Alexander?'

'Alexander's very good at night,' she said, climbing over me and squirming down between the sheets. 'I see you even go in for beige in bed.' She was looking disparagingly at my newly laundered sheets and matching duvet cover.

302

'Go to sleep,' I said stiffly, and leaned forward to switch off the bedside light.

'If you fuck me,' she whispered in my ear, 'I'll never, ever call you Uncle Guy again. I promise . . .'

20

'Look, if you're going to keep fussing, don't come; you can stay behind and look after Alexander. It's just it's such a worthwhile cause, that's all, and if everybody was put off by a spot of rain from making a stand for their principles, we'd all still be jellyfish.'

'I sometimes wish I were,' I said, and for a moment meant it.

Pip put on her cross face and started being efficient: cutting the crusts off our sandwiches, wiping over the worktops, organising Alexander: a sure sign she was angry. I decided to ignore the danger signs and wandered into the sitting room.

It was Sunday; chill, December rain poured down in torrents outside. I was dead beat after a heavy week at the office and evenings spent coping with a teething Alexander. The last thing I wanted to do was to go on some damned march.

'You'd have done it for Char, so why not me?' Suddenly, she was behind me, her arms round my waist, rubbing her face against my shoulder.

'I doubt it,' I said. 'Anyway, Char would never have wanted to do anything so dotty.'

'It's not dotty, you bloody well know it's not. You're just lazy, that's all, and frightened your stupid chairman might see you. Char would have done it. You've only got to read her diary to see that. It was just in those days things were more difficult for someone like her, she—'

'You don't have to defend Char to me,' I said stiffly. 'And incidentally, I'm not in the least afraid of being seen by the chairman. It's just I'm tired, and I'm not all that sure I agree with the issue anyway. It may well be that nuclear power is the best thing after all.'

'*Don't* be silly!' She spun me round so that I faced her; her green eyes looked into mine: angry, passionate and quite desperately sincere. 'You can't mean that. What about poor Alexander and all the others?'

I gave in; it had only been a token resistance, anyway. 'OK,' I said, 'you win, but I doubt whether I shall ever make it to Trafalgar Square.'

Later, as I drove through the wet streets to the pick-up point where we were to join the march, Pip and Alexander suitably enveloped in mackintoshes in the back, I found myself reviewing, as it were, the six months that had elapsed since Sophia's wedding. Officially, Pip was my lodger, but no one believed that. I'd had petulant phone calls from Paula Holloway: 'My dear Mr Horton, you surely must see how unsuitable the whole thing is. My husband and I . . .' and threatening ones from 'Daddy': 'Look here, Horton, haven't you caused enough trouble already? If you don't send my daughter and her son back to me forthwith, I'll have no alternative but to put the matter in the hands of my lawyers.'

After the first few weeks, the phone calls ceased, but were followed by a spate of pompous letters to Pip, the last of which had arrived only yesterday. The final paragraph read: 'You and my grandson, as I'm sure you know, will always be welcomed by both Paula and myself, but in saying this, I must make it quite clear your 'companion' will never, at any time, now or in the future, be welcome in any house of mine.' And that was that.

As for myself, I've lived from day to day, I think. To be with Pip is both exhausting and a bit of a trial, but always a joy and never, ever dull: she has so much of Char in her I don't know where one ends and the other begins. It's odd, but she scarcely knew her grandmother. All she can remember of her is a birthday party in the garden at Maple, when one of the dogs ate her slice of birthday cake. She'd cried a bit, and her grandmother had ordered her to stop: there were more important things to cry about in life, she'd said, than the loss of a piece of birthday cake. And she'd once overheard Char say to her father: 'That child's got my Pa's eyes, so watch out.' And she'd wondered who on earth Pa was and why he was so dangerous.

Pip appears to have no inhibitions about my love for her grandmother; indeed, seems fascinated by it, and has read her way steadily through the green trunk. Sometimes, when we're making love, she'll whisper: 'Did Char do that?' or 'Was this better with her?' but she never waits for an answer. How long she will stay, I don't know. I only know that her presence in my life seems, quite simply, right, and that's really all I can find to say about it.

'Here we are; there's Julian waving. Christ, we're going to get wet.' A tall, bearded, young man, encased in oilskins, was flagging us down. I parked the car, at his instructions, in the yard of a warehouse, and we hurried to the shelter of a nearby doorway to await the arrival of the procession.

'I think it's best if you have Alexander on your back and I carry the banner,' Pip said. I nodded miserably; rain was dripping down the neck of my anorak. I put the hood up and a shower of water sprayed into my eyes. Carefully, Alexander was fixed into a sort of cocoon thing on my back. I could hear him bubbling and crowing somewhere just below my left ear, a not unpleasant sound. Pip picked up the banner, and we waited. At last, after what seemed hours, but was in reality about five minutes, from somewhere up the street we heard the sound of beating drums.

'They're coming,' the young man in oilskins shouted excitedly. 'Ready everyone?'

Pip twitched my sleeve. 'Guy, I meant to tell you before, but you've been in such a mood this weekend, and I only heard on Friday; I'm going to have another baby. Now you see why this march is so important.'

But I was unable to answer her; at that moment the marchers burst upon us, and banner held high, Pip dived in amongst them. I hunched my shoulders, looked furtively round for any rogue TV cameras – in spite of my brave words, I'd no desire to be spotted by the chairman – took a deep breath, and with Char's great-grandson on my back, I followed her granddaughter out into the rain.

VIRGINIA BUDD

SUMMER'S SPRING

Bet Brandon, recently widowed, decides to start afresh.

With a peculiar assortment of relatives, and her troublesome dog, she leaves Hampstead to embark on a bizarre house-sharing enterprise in Suffolk. Domestic quarrels abound but her deliciously wicked sense of fun helps her to adjust to the dramas of her new life.

However Bet finds life in the country fiendishly quiet – until she meets the recklessly charming, would-be writer, Simon Morris. And soon she has an irresistible desire to throw caution to the wind and follow her heart.

HODDER AND STOUGHTON PAPERBACKS

SUSAN MOODY

HOUSE OF MOONS

Sometimes Tess Lovel dreamed of the house in Spain where she had been born.

Sun-bleached colours and the heavy stillness of noon. A hill town where memories of the Civil War, of blood and betrayal, lay dangerously close beneath the dusty surface of the present day.

In rain-grey England, Tess tried to deny the passion and mystery of her past. But from across the Atlantic, an older woman, revenge-obsessed, was reaching out to ensnare her.

'A complex and often compelling romantic thriller . . . *The* book to take on holiday'
Robert Goddard, *The Mail on Sunday*

'An assured well-plotted pageturner . . . But Susan Moody has also brought to her lush drama a quality of descriptive writing and an attention to characterisation which raises the novel to another level . . . *House of Moons* is a substantial achievement'
The Independent

'A big, enjoyable suspense novel'
The Sunday Telegraph

HODDER AND STOUGHTON PAPERBACKS

LYDIA BENNETT

DEEP WATERS

Anna Atwill is larger than life, a lusty redhead who's spent ten exhilarating years as a violinist and music student in Eastern Europe. Now, inexplicably, she's returned to sleepy Sedleigh on the Yorkshire coast to become the town's librarian. All that remains of her gypsy way of life is the fiddle she plays for wedding dances.

Until Dmitri Komarovsky, a big Russian bear of a man, strides into her library – seemingly from out of her past. Initial attraction turns to fear when he starts asking mysterious questions about her childhood. Suddenly the lovers' teasing cat-and-mouse game is in deadly earnest. Who is Komarovsky? What is his connection with her past?

Who, for that matter, is Anna?

HODDER AND STOUGHTON PAPERBACKS